DECADENT

THE DEVIL'S DUE (BOOK 4)

EVA CHARLES

QUARRY ROAD PUBLISHING

Copyright © 2020 by Eva Charles

All rights reserved.

No part of this book may be used or reproduced in any form whatsoever without express written permission from the author or publisher, except in the case of brief quotations embedded in critical articles and reviews.

This book is a work of fiction. Any references to historical events, real people, or real places are used fictitiously. All other names, characters, places, and incidents are products of the author's imagination. Any resemblance to actual events, places, organizations, or persons living or dead is entirely coincidental.

- Cover by Murphy Rae
- Dawn Alexander, Evident Ink, Content Editor
- Nancy Smay, Evident Ink, Copy and Line Editor
- Faith Williams, The Atwater Group, Proofreader
- Virginia Tesi Carey, Proofreader

For more information, contact eva@evacharles.com

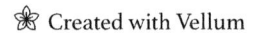

❧ Created with Vellum

To Chris, who makes my life easier, because she makes his easier. You have my eternal gratitude.

What is moral is what you feel good after, and what is immoral is what you feel bad after.

— Ernest Hemingway

1

DELILAH

When I'm outside the gates of the archbishop's lavish home, I pull off the mask and snake my way through a series of barren alleys to the rental car, careful to stay in the shadows. I've made this kind of getaway dozens of times, and used every precaution to ensure I wasn't followed tonight.

Then why does it feel like I'm being stalked?

I glance over my shoulder. Nothing—not a nocturnal hunter tracking a meal, or a leaf rustling in the distance. *Nothing.* Still, I can't shake the feeling.

I don't know what's spooking me. Probably that bastard priest who thought he was Jesus Christ.

This is the second time in a week that I've sensed someone close. The last time, Virginia Bennet's ankle was shattered by a bullet inside St. Maggie's Church. We still don't know who fired on her, only that the shot came from the balcony, near where I was positioned. Someone had gotten close to me that night. *Too close.*

As I reach for the car door handle, a large, gloved hand muzzles me, with a strong thumb positioned beneath my jaw in such a way that I'm unable to sink my teeth into the leather palm covering my mouth. A second hand captures my wrists, while powerful thighs cage my legs. Before my brain fully registers the danger, the muscular body has me pinned securely against the car door.

In mere seconds—that's all it takes—the attacker divests me of every tool I have to protect myself. He's a trained professional. *He has to be.*

I draw a deep breath, as reality sinks in. There's no escape.

No escape.

No escape.

No escape.

The warning blasts inside my head, activating the floodgates until the adrenaline rushes in, triggering every human survival instinct my body knows. Fortunately, years of CIA training fall front and center. Leaning on those lessons is my best chance for survival, but only if I keep my wits about me.

I curl my toes, digging them into the soles of my shoes, pressing hard enough that I can almost feel the hard ground beneath me. The connection is enough to shift my focus.

There's no *immediate* escape, but I need to let it play out a little. I need to wait for the opportunity to present itself. He wants something. Otherwise, he would have already slit my throat.

"Who are you?" I sputter through clenched teeth.

The man says nothing, letting my anxiety build.

Can he sense the growing fear? Smell terror seeping from my pores?

I regulate my breathing, and concentrate on detecting a scent or a tic, anything that might help me identify this stranger.

But there's nothing. Not a single thing to clue me in to his identity.

I'm at his mercy, and the longer this goes on, the more control he has over me. But there's not a damn thing I can do to help myself. *You can keep your head and find some patience.* Yes. That I can do.

While I wait for the stranger to reveal himself, I peer into the pitch-black night, at nothing.

The air around us is still, thick enough to choke a horse. And the only sound is the high-pitched call of the cicada, escalating the drama inside my head.

Will the assailant deliver his response with razor-sharp words or with a brutal physical act? I brace for the latter with the laser focus only adrenaline provides.

If he moves to strike me, I'll be able to free myself—as long as I don't hesitate. I can't squander the opportunity. It might be the only one I have.

Somewhere I find the discipline to remain quiet. It might be the most difficult thing I've ever done. But when I asked *who are you?*, the ball moved squarely into his court. Anything I say now will only be a show of weakness.

Finally, after what feels like hours, he lowers his head, his warm breath an inch from my temple, and the ridge of his steely cock pressing into my lower back. "More than just a pretty boy," he taunts.

2

DELILAH

*G*ray *Wilder*. Using my own words to mock me. I'd know his voice anywhere. It haunts my dreams. Day and night.

It's always Gray. *Always.*

His clever fingers teasing my needy flesh. His lazy drawl coaxing me to come again and again. *Demanding it.* And before the tremors subside, it's his spicy scent that lulls me into a restless sleep, stirring a primal need to submit that I haven't felt since Kyle died.

Gray Wilder is dangerous.

Never more so than now.

"Let go of me," I mumble into the supple leather stretched across his palm.

"In good time. I'm enjoying this too much. You, helpless. Mostly silenced. My hard cock near enough so you can think of nothing else, but not close enough to where you want it. It's like Christmas Eve at Wildflower, all over again." He lowers his head, until I feel his warm breath on my scalp. "I hope you've been a good girl. Otherwise Santa will leave you wet and wanting."

The memories come flooding back.

"Remember?" he murmurs, his lips grazing my hair.

When I don't make any effort to answer, he squeezes my thighs between his, tightening the vise little by little, until all I know is the ache in my core. "Remember?"

"Yes," I concede in a muddled response. It's enough to satisfy his arrogance, but not enough to bow fully to him.

"The opulent Sultan's Palace. You, bound to the bedposts with long silk cords. Open to me. A jewel in your navel and another in that pretty little ass. Do you remember how you whimpered when I tightened the jewels on your nipples? Do you remember how much you begged?"

I don't utter a sound.

"What were you beggin' for, Delilah?" His voice is low, wrapped in a luscious timbre as he cajoles an answer from me.

But tonight, unlike Christmas Eve, I don't acquiesce easily. If he wants something from me, he's going to have to take it.

As if he reads my mind, his teeth sink into my neck, into the very spot he knows will make my knees weak.

"*Ahhh.*" The lusty moan escapes into the humid night before I can stop it. *Damn you, Gray Wilder.*

"I can't hear you," he taunts, with the ring of victory in his voice. He loosens his hold on my jaw. *Why not? He knows he's won.* "What were you beggin' for that night?"

I'm not afraid of Gray. Not physically. But I do want him to let me go. *And I want to know how he managed to overpower me so easily.* He's a billionaire playboy, and I'm a trained agent—a lethal one. It's no contest.

Then why can't I move?

"Release," I hiss into his leather-clad fingers. The asshole loosens his grip so I can speak audibly, but not enough that I can weaponize my teeth. It's the only reason he still has all his fingers.

"You're going to have to do better than that, Delilah," he purrs. "What were you beggin' for?"

I'm going to knee the bastard in the balls the second I'm free. "An orgasm."

"Better. But not good enough." He sinks his teeth into me again. Biting and sucking the tendon in a way that's sure to leave a bruise—in a way that sends shivers skittering in every direction. *Dammit.* There's no way to hide my body's reaction from him.

The slow curl of his mouth singes my skin. *Bastard.* I squeeze my eyes shut.

There's no response too small for him to miss. I learned that lesson on Christmas. At the time, it felt like a gift. But now, I imagine a smug, self-satisfied smirk. The same look he had right before we left Wildflower late Christmas morning—when he told me I'd be thinking about his cock all day—every time I walked, or bent over, or sat down, or relieved myself. *The muscles will scream,* he murmured, while we waited for the elevator, his forehead resting against mine*, and every time they do, you'll remember how I owned your pussy. And you'll long for me to own it again.*

The bastard was right. The exquisite ache lingered for days. First as a stark reminder of the hedonistic pleasure, then as a craving, eating at me until I fed it. But no matter how much I gorged, neither my fingers nor my favorite toy ever satisfied the urge completely. And no matter how hard I tried to forget, I saw him everywhere, in everything. It scared me to death. Sometimes it still scares me.

Pull up your big-girl panties and swallow your pride, Delilah. He owns you right now. You can still get your licks in, but not until you're free. I never swallow my pride easily. I'm not that kind of woman, but there's no damn choice.

"I begged for your cock." *Something I'll never do again, asshole.*

"*Mmhm.* That's how I remember it too. You writhing, back arched off the mattress, your juices soaking the silk sheets. The musky scent saturating every molecule of air I breathed." He licks the bruised tendon, before blowing on it gently. I shiver at the sensation. "But your helpless screams thrumming in my veins—that's what made my cock weep."

I wish I could say his filthy talk isn't affecting me. That my breasts aren't growing heavy, that my nipples aren't tightening and tingling, sending steamy messages directly to my throbbing pussy. I wish I could say that I don't want his cock. That I don't want him. But I can't say any of it.

"Do you know how many times I've thought about that night? How many women I've fucked in that room, trying to replace the memory of your tight little pussy? How many times I've pushed away images of your submissive body, spread in glorious offering under the sheer canopy that enclosed us in our own dirty little world? Do you know how many times I've come thinking about that night? Do you?"

I can't let him pull me back into the fantasy. Not here. Not now. *Not ever.* I draw a long breath in an effort to slow my pounding heart.

My muscles are beginning to cramp from being immobilized, but I don't ask him to release me. He won't until he's good and ready, and I refuse to give him the satisfaction of telling me *no*.

What does he want? *I don't have a damn clue.* But I do know *all* about the Sultan's Palace on Christmas Eve. I knew then he would destroy me if I allowed it.

Without a word, Gray removes his hand from my mouth, freeing it completely. I open and close my jaw a few times, wiggling it from side to side before speaking. "How did you—"

The hand that had been over my mouth is now tangled in the hair at the base of my neck, pulling on the long strands hard enough to tip my head back. "*Shhh!*" he hisses. "You're going to listen, not talk, for a change. This is the address where I'm staying tonight." He slips something deep into my front pocket. His long fingers linger at the edge of my mound while he speaks. "I have a job for you. Go directly to that address when you leave here and we'll talk."

What? "You have a job for me?" *What the hell is wrong with this man?* "Most people just text or email when they want something." I feel his cock twitch against me. "I'm not having sex with you. If that's the kind of job you're talkin' about, you can forget it."

He tugs my hair harder. "You are *done* giving orders."

"That remains to be seen. But regardless, I'm still not having sex with you."

"I advise you to do as I say. Otherwise, this goes to the authorities." He holds his phone up so I can see the screen. It's a photo of me hovering over the archbishop's lifeless body.

My pulse hammers as I struggle to breathe. "You—you wouldn't do that—to me."

"Try me," he threatens in a tone that bears the shrill ring of finality. With nothing more, Gray releases me and walks away.

When it seems safe, I turn my head cautiously, catching his long familiar stride in the distance. He's so certain I pose no danger, he doesn't spare me even a fleeting glance over his shoulder. It's arrogant and foolish, but the confidence it exudes is heart-stopping.

For several seconds, I watch him, taking note of the sharp lines and creases. His proud gait. His hair, which he's let grow, secured in a knot at the nape of his neck. His broad back tapering gently as it approaches narrow hips. His dark shirt stretched across his shoulders, yielding to the muscle. The same muscle I clutched and buried my fingers in as he carried me to the steamy shower and took me hard against the imported stone.

It was early Christmas morning. We hadn't yet slept. His

unshaven face was covered in translucent droplets. A mixture of condensation and sweat shimmered under the soft light. I craned my neck and lapped the salty beads from his skin like a thirsty whore, while he rutted deeply. He had already used me well, but still, he showed no mercy.

Stop it, Delilah! Pull yourself together, woman.

I force myself into the car and lock the doors. But when I close my eyes to clear the cobwebs, all I see is the force of his release. His slack jaw. His shuttered eyelids. His face contorted as though the surrender cost him deeply. As though pain had clawed its way into the bliss, until it pried a strangled roar from somewhere deep within.

I bang my forehead on the steering wheel, cursing softly.

When I open my eyes, Gray has disappeared into the moonless night, like an apparition that visits while we sleep. But he exists. Everything about those fevered hours we spent together was real. And late at night, alone in my bed, I still hear the echoes of his pleasure off the Italian marble.

My fingertips find the place on my neck where he marked me. Despite his little show of strength tonight, I'm still not afraid of him. Not in the traditional sense of the word. But I am terrified of my feelings. Feelings I developed while working at Wildflower. Feelings that found me submitting to his every whim, after too much brandy milk punch and too many warm and fuzzy emotions. The magic of Christmas can lure a woman astray. Even a woman like me.

But not tonight, Satan.

I lift my chin. I'm not going to his damn hotel room. No matter how curious I am about the job, and about how he subdued me so easily. No matter how much I want...*no, Delilah.* Just no.

Was it Gray in the church? Did he fire on Virginia? I grip the wheel tighter. It doesn't matter. I'm not going to that hotel.

He went to a lot of trouble to take that picture of me with

the archbishop, but he's not sending it to anyone, because once he does, it's of no value to him. And he wants something. It might not be help with a job, but he wants something from me.

I turn on the radio, and before I know it, I'm at the rental car lot.

After dropping the keys into the after-hours depository, I walk over to the coffee shop across from the station, where I wait for the bus that will take me back to Charleston.

I sip a Dr. Pepper in a booth at the back of the shop, where I can watch the street for any sign of trouble. By now, Gray knows I'm not meeting him.

Did he follow me here? It's possible. After all, he found me at the archbishop's summer home outside Charleston. *How could that be?*

As I board the bus thirty minutes later, I glance over my shoulder, taking one last look around the deserted road. Not for the authorities, but for the man who already overpowered me once tonight without breaking a sweat.

3

DELILAH

The alarm blares, startling me from a deep sleep. I set it every night, but I'm always awake before it goes off. *Not today.* Hopefully it's not an omen of things to come. It's been awhile since I've had an uneventful day, and I can sure use one.

Once the alarm is silenced, I scroll through the messages, half-expecting to find a threatening one from Gray, but there's nothing.

A small pang of regret shifts inside my chest. It's short-lived, but annoying. I should be focused on the damning photo he has of me with the archbishop—not that the holy bastard didn't get everything he deserved. But instead, here I am, hoping the hot guy texted while I was asleep, like I'm some stupid high school girl crushing on the bad boy. The one draped in fire engine-red flags that nobody with a lick of common sense would go anywhere near.

But Gray Wilder messes with my head in a way that no one has ever managed to do. *Not even Kyle, and he was an expert at messing with my head.*

It's precisely why he's so dangerous.

After brushing my teeth, I throw on running clothes, and

head to the Battery section of Charleston while most of the city is still asleep. Rain or shine, I never miss a morning run. No matter how much upheaval there's been in my life, it's been the one constant. A comforting ritual that rarely disappoints. My version of afternoon tea.

I give my mind a wide berth while running, let it wander freely until the thoughts venture into forbidden territory. When that happens, I push my body harder and harder, allowing the pain to reel me back into the moment and ground me. *The way Kyle's belt did.*

The Battery is a far cry from the dirt-poor corner of Mississippi where my mama raised me. Never knew my daddy. There were times when I wasn't sure Mama knew him either—or at least knew who had actually planted the seed.

Mama had one ambition in life that she never strayed from: to be a wealthy man's queen. Despite her gorgeous veneer, it never worked out for her, of course, because rich men marry rich women, or women who bring something more than beauty to the table. Beauty is a depreciating asset. Nobody understands that better than a powerful man who regularly dips his dick into a pretty face.

My looks might have made me prom queen and a Magnolia Princess. *Imagine that.* But unlike Mama, my dreams have *never* included marrying a rich man.

As I round the corner onto Water Street, I nearly collide with the junior senator from South Carolina. He stops, continuing to jog in place. "You all right, miss?"

I nod. "Thank you." He's on his way before I have the chance to ask if he's all right. Even in skimpy shorts, with a thick sweat covering his red face, I recognize him. He's a regular at Wildflower, Gray Wilder's *social* club.

While there's plenty of socializing at Wildflower, the most interesting *socializing* happens deep in the bowels of the club, in rooms with names like the Dungeon, the Stable, and the Sultan's Palace.

When I came to Charleston to work for Smith Sinclair, Gray's father was running for president. Smith is in charge of security for the Wilders and their businesses. He stationed me undercover, as a hostess, at the club. Even shrouded in the kind of secrecy money and power can buy, Wildflower was an obvious liability for a presidential candidate. Smith expected trouble and he didn't trust Gray to see it coming.

No one knew I worked for Smith. Not even Gray. To him, I was just the accommodating hostess, happy to help out wherever needed.

That's when the attraction between us blossomed. It started out innocent, as these things often do, but there was an undeniable pull from the beginning. Gray looked for excuses to have me work longer hours, and I looked for every excuse to be there too.

Although I was never allowed downstairs, I was privy to all the comings and goings at the club. I didn't need to see Gray in action to know he was an experienced Dominant. His demeanor, the subtle shift in tone, broadcasts that vibe to anyone familiar with the lifestyle.

On the surface, Gray is a charming playboy. That's what he wants people to believe. Although most everyone he's rubbed elbows with knows he's not to be crossed. That becomes abundantly clear the very second someone gets too close to the line he's drawn carefully in the sand. It's all fun and games—until it isn't. And even in the best of times, all the fun and all the games are controlled by him.

Gray doesn't use a big stick to grab control—not normally. There's no need. His employees and the club members are more than happy to hand over their power to him. In exchange, he makes sure all their needs are met.

He pulls off the ruse with a winsome smile that rarely reaches his eyes, and an innate understanding of the human condition. I've watched him draw out even the most reticent, enticing them to do whatever he requires in the moment. They don't see it coming until it's too late. Most people are so captivated by his bank account and good looks that they never see it at all. But I saw it.

I recognized his thirst for control right away. It beckoned, pulling me toward him like he was the center of gravity and I would be forever adrift without him. The attraction was potent, and late at night after the club closed, when we were alone in the office, sipping expensive whiskey, it became a demonic temptation.

On those nights, I wanted nothing more than to hand him control *over me*. And there were many times, when he tracked me with the dark gaze of a predator, that I was sure he wanted it too.

But I was there to do a job, not to play sexy games. It didn't matter how much I wanted or *needed* those games. And it didn't matter how much he wanted or needed them either.

We fought the attraction. Gray with any number of beautiful women who sailed in and out of his aura, and by training submissives. The part of his job, I once overheard him say, that he enjoyed most.

I resisted too. I threw myself into the work, put miles on my running shoes, and reached for a sleek vibrator when I craved release. I never strayed from my mission, and kept far, far away from the powerful men who frequented the club. That would have been my mother's game. But I believe queens are most powerful when they ascend the throne by their own devices, not when they stand on a man's shoulders to reach the vaunted seat. Besides, there was only one king who interested me.

Then *the* kiss happened. It changed everything. There was no going back after that. For either of us. I have only myself to blame.

Gray Wilder is many things, not all of them honorable, but he isn't the kind of man who would *touch* an employee—and he didn't—until I touched first.

When I didn't have anywhere to go on Christmas Eve, he invited me to Sweetgrass, his brother JD's home. The starry night, coupled with the free-flowing booze, made us both stupid. When the pull became too much to resist, when I couldn't deny myself any longer, I kissed him. And he kissed me back. It was *everything* my mind had conjured, and *so* much more.

Although I might have acted first, from the moment my lips grazed his, he had complete control. Looking back, I often wonder if the kiss was actually my idea or something he orchestrated.

I went directly to Smith the day after Christmas. The day after Gray *thoroughly* fucked me—body, mind, and soul. There was no heart in anything he did—in anything I let him do. It was safer that way.

While I didn't share the sordid details with Smith, I confessed my attraction to Gray was getting in the way of the job. Smith knows the pitfalls in this line of work too well, and didn't bother to tell me to suck it up. He moved me from the club immediately.

That's when Gray learned that Mae, the accommodating hostess, the woman who begged shamelessly for his cock, was Delilah Mae Porter, outed CIA agent who testified before Congress wearing a disguise, so she could go on to live some semblance of a normal life. He didn't take the news well.

The contents of my desk and locker were left at the curb, and I wasn't permitted back into the club to explain. Gray never spoke to me after he learned I was a plant. It was for the best, I assured myself then, but the attraction never waned. Not for me.

Now I satisfy my longing with a sneak peek at him from

across the room when he isn't looking, or with the heat that filters through me when I feel the sear of his gaze on my skin.

But the man who cornered me last night—I'd never seen that side of him before. And I'm not sure what his game is, but I'm not playing. I can't afford it.

4

DELILAH

When I get to the office, I pour myself a coffee and glance at the top news of the day for anything that might impact our ongoing cases.

That's when I see it.

Archbishop Darden's death is front and center. Although it's jarring, I expected nothing less. But there's something else. A plea from the local authorities for help in identifying a photo *of me*. The image is grainy and distorted, and it's impossible to tell if it's a man or a woman hovering over the archbishop.

That sonofabitch. How could he compromise me that way? *How?*

Before I lose it completely, I shut the office door quietly, so as not to alarm anyone, and call Gray's cell phone. My blood pressure climbs while I wait for the call to connect. It goes straight to voicemail. There are so many things I want to shriek into the phone, but I hang up without leaving a message and call Wildflower.

Gray's assistant answers on the second ring.

"Hello, Miss Fox, this is Delilah Porter."

"How are you, dear?"

"Very well, thank you." The last thing I want to do is chitchat, but the road to Gray is through Miss Fox, or Foxy, as she's better known. While she comes off as a nice middle-aged lady, she's as sly and mean as any mama fox when it comes to protecting him. "How have you been, ma'am?" I inquire with all the politeness I can muster.

After she tells me *all* about her son's family in California, she's ready to get down to business. It's a good thing too, because my patience with Girl Scout cookies and T-ball practice is limited on the best of days, but at this moment, it takes everything I have not to reach through the phone and shake her. "I'm sure you didn't call to get an update on my grandchildren. What can I do for you, Delilah?"

I unclench my teeth and take a deep breath. "I need to speak to Mr. Wilder, please. I believe he's expecting my call."

"Let me see if he's free to talk." She puts me on hold and when the annoying music begins to play, I want to scream. The longer it plays, the louder I want to scream.

When the acoustic torture finally stops, Foxy is back on the line. "Delilah, I'm sorry. Mr. Wilder isn't available right now."

What an asshole. I break the point off the pencil clenched in my fist. "Did he say when he'd be available?"

"I'm afraid not. Why don't I take your number? I'm sure he'll call you when he's free."

Really? Because I'm sure he's free right now, probably sitting back with his feet up on his desk, laughing at me. But there's not a damn thing I can do, so I give her my number and wish her a good day.

I glance at the image of the dead archbishop on the screen. *Fuck.* What now? Smith's parents are visiting, and he's got his hands full with Kate. Besides, I can't share this with him. Once he knows, he'll be implicated in the cover-up, or worse. I can't have that. There's no other choice but to wait for Gray to contact me.

What if he doesn't? He will. He wants something. *Patience, Delilah. Patience.*

I study the image carefully. It's been heavily edited. There's no way to identify me from what they have now.

But what if it can be enhanced? *What then?*

I won't survive prison.

Thanks to that scum Congressman Marino, my personal life was broadcast all over cable news. After I refused to be his plaything, he retaliated, outing me as a covert agent and ruining my career. The worst part of the entire episode was being dragged before committees by congressmen and senators who wanted to pick a political fight with the other party.

Under oath, there was nothing I could do but answer their probing questions truthfully, some of which were designed to tease out the most salacious details of my sex life—the one I'd shared with Kyle. At the end of each day, staffers leaked the most tawdry bits and pieces to the press. One side made it seem like the congressman had a right to expect that I'd play kinky games with him, and the other side made it seem as though he was a miscreant because he wanted a filthy whore like me.

Somehow the fact that he was a traitor got lost in the scandal. Little by little, they tore at my soul, and I was alone to pick up the shreds when they were done.

I take another peek at the screen.

Prison isn't a walk in the park for anyone, but it would be a special kind of hell for me. I was a covert agent. *A spy.* In some quarters, that's a notch or two below a snitch. Sure, they'll promise to protect me, but I know *all* about that kind of protection. Men's prisons are unsafe, but women's prisons are far, far worse.

My stomach turns somersaults just thinking about it. Every guard will feel as though it's their right to dominate me, to beat and rape me on a whim. The prisoners too.

I'm prepared to die before I allow that to be my fate. But it's too soon to think about swallowing the barrel of a gun. Gray laid down a threat. He doesn't want me in prison. Not yet, anyway.

I need to marshal my resources and create a plan while I wait for him to show his hand. I'm not running. It's not in my nature, and besides, I have family here. They're not blood kin, but I wouldn't love them any more if we shared DNA.

Why would Gray do this? What could possibly make him behave this vindictively? Is this his way of exacting revenge because I spied on him and reported back to Smith? *No.* It's something else. It has to be. *But what?*

5

DELILAH

After spending the rest of the day hunting through Gray Wilder's personal information—the files Sinclair Industries has access to—I go home and splash some bourbon over a big ice cube.

When the glass is empty, I head for the shower, leaving a trail of clothing in my wake. I'll pick it up later or tomorrow. It's one of the benefits of living alone.

I take my time under the spray, letting the sweet combination of hot water and whiskey work out the knots. When I'm done, I slather some fancy lotion over my damp skin. The lotion was a birthday present from Gabby, my best friend and Gray's sister-in-law, who uses every opportunity to spoil me.

When I inhale the rich scent, it reminds me to count my blessings. Even if Gray is hell-bent on destroying my life, I'm loved, and not alone in this world. *Not like last time.*

After hanging the towel, I crack the bathroom door to let the steam escape. That's when something catches my eye. By something, I mean Gray Wilder sprawled in the chair a few feet from my bed, with the clothing I shed earlier folded neatly on the corner of the mattress.

It takes several long seconds for my brain to process the handsome intruder lounging in the rocking chair, one leg crossed over the other, an ankle resting on a knee, nimble fingers tapping a denim-clad thigh. The soft, faded fabric conceals the smooth muscle. But it's there. I've seen it. I've felt the power of those legs, run my hands over the thick cords, clenched them tightly while his cock was in my throat.

I blink away the memory when Gray whistles, long and low. "*Delilah,*" he murmurs. "How can such a beautiful woman be such a slob?"

My arms fly to shield my girlie parts. "Fuck you," I hiss, but the bravado quickly evaporates when I realize how silly and vulnerable I must look with my hands, fig leaves, covering my breasts and pussy like a nymph in a Renaissance painting.

Screw him. This is my house. I ignore the prickle of gooseflesh and drop my arms to the side, before marching into the bedroom, *my* bedroom, to grab a robe from the closet.

His eyes rove shamelessly while I slip the thin robe over my shoulders and belt it snugly. "How could you have sent that image to the authorities? I hurt your little boy feelings because I didn't show up at the hotel, so you throw a fucking grenade." I unleash all the negative energy that's been building all day. Apparently, it didn't drain away with the soapy water. "Why are you doing this to me? And who are you to be breaking into my house and stalking me without—without me knowing? I mean —who are you, *really*?"

Gray cocks his head and takes a good long look at me. When his eyes linger on my breasts, I feel a flush bloom, as though the robe wrapped around me is made of saran, allowing him to see everything.

"I'm the man who requested your presence last night," he says, his hard gaze finding mine. "The one who was crystal-clear about the consequences if you didn't obey. Smith might allow you to do whatever the hell you want, but I won't put up with it."

He gets up and strides over, our eyes still engaged in a knife fight, and splays his hand on my throat. When I attempt to pull away, he applies some pressure, drawing me to him with my back against his front. "I have time for a little breath play. Would you like that?"

I will myself to stay calm and let my training take over.

"Use your words, *De-li-lah.*" He emphasizes each syllable, drawing it out with a mocking twang.

It's not easy, but I force my body to relax against his, brushing my backside casually against his cock to lure him into complacency. When his mouth grazes my outer ear, I catch the low rumble in his throat, and lift my leg, building momentum to slam a heel into the top of his foot. I want him to recoil from the unexpected pain and drop his hold, but Gray senses the attack and twists me around, still holding my neck firmly.

"If you ever try something like that again," he murmurs, lowering his forehead to mine, "you'll be a snot-covered mess before I show you an ounce of mercy."

The combination of the harsh words and the low, silky baritone he uses to deliver the threat takes my breath away. Only a man in complete control lowers his voice like that. Scores of women are attracted to Gray's gorgeous face and fat wallet, but it's his unrepentant brashness and cool demeanor that's always called to me.

"You need to learn to behave," he chides, "and I'm going to teach you." His eyes fall to my nipples poking through the thin fabric. He cups my breast lightly and skims his thumb over a tight furl with the patience of a man who has nothing better to tend to and nowhere else to be.

When I'm lulled by the gentle sensation, he adds some light pressure to my throat, his fingertips on the carotid artery. It's just a few seconds, but enough to cloud my vision with black spots dotting the edges. "I can make the lessons as difficult or as easy as you wish. That part is completely in your control."

"Why do you want to hurt me?" My voice is shaky, laying bare my fears. While I'm cursing myself for the weakness, I see a glimmer of compassion in his striking blue eyes. But like a sleight of hand, it's fleeting and I can't be sure my eyes aren't playing tricks. I can't be sure of anything when it comes to him.

"I have no reason to hurt you. None."

He drops his hand, although I wasn't talking about his hold on my throat. It's the bullying that I hate.

"But don't give me one," he adds, "because I won't hesitate to destroy you if necessary. The photo was a warning. The image is formatted in a way they'll never be able to enhance. You're safe. *This* time. But don't push me, Delilah."

My heart is pounding, and even though he's taken his thumb off my airway, I'm still using my breath judiciously.

"Get dressed. As much as I enjoy watching your nipples respond to my voice, we have business to discuss, and you're too much of a distraction in that flimsy robe."

He glides two long fingers down my throat, over the hollow, and between my breasts, sliding deep into the vee of the robe that has fallen open. "Are you wet for me?"

My brain is in a fog, and I couldn't answer him if I wanted to.

"Put some clothes on," he demands softly, although his eyes are smoldering and he doesn't look at all like he wants me dressed. And right now, I'm not entirely sure I want to be dressed.

"Be quick about it," he warns, before pulling his hand away and striding out of the bedroom, leaving me standing there with my mouth agape and my flesh tingling.

6

DELILAH

Despite Gray's warning, I take a few extra minutes to dress, trying to right my head before dealing with him. My body and brain are sparring, and any survival skills I might have possessed are a bloody casualty of the battle.

When I get to the kitchen, Gray's leaning against the counter, eating the last slice of blueberry pie like he owns the damn place. His eyes rake over my body deliberately as he takes the final bite. It's bold and arousing. But unlike the satin robe, the baggy sweatpants and oversized hoodie that belonged to Kyle hide all my interested parts—the ones that haven't gotten the message that sex with Gray Wilder is a *very* bad idea.

His gaze pauses on the FBI logo on the sweatshirt, regarding it carefully, but he says nothing.

"Surprised you didn't help yourself to some ice cream to go along with that pie."

"Not a fan of ice cream with pie. Makes the crust soggy."

"I'm not interested in your food eccentricities. But I'm *very* interested in knowing how you followed me the other night without being detected, and then restrained me so effectively—in the way only a trained professional could do." I square my shoulders, holding my head high and my gaze steady. "I'm not discussing anything else with you until I have answers to those questions." I plant my feet firmly, bracing for an attack that doesn't come.

"I'm better trained than you are, bigger and stronger." His cunning eyes drill into me while he speaks, telling me nothing. "It's that simple."

"No. You are—"

"A pretty-boy billionaire who runs a sex club?"

Yes. "Clearly there's more to you than that."

"Clearly." His mouth quirks at the edges, and I'd like to slap the smirk off his pretty-boy face. "Where do you keep the whiskey?"

"This isn't a social call. I didn't invite you here, and you already ate my pie. You're not drinkin' my whiskey too."

"The whiskey is for you. You need to settle your nerves."

"My nerves don't need settling." I search his face, hoping to find a clue about what he's up to, but there's nothing to see. Nothing but a day's worth of stubble and a tiny cleft in his strong chin. "What do you want from me?"

"I'm in need of some arm candy. It would be a huge plus if that arm candy was multilingual and knew how to use a weapon."

What the hell? I release the breath I've been holding. "I'm in need of a new pair of shit-kickers, but I don't go around stalking people who might have a pair I like, and breaking into their homes to harass them into giving them up."

There's a twinkle in his eyes. *Bastard.*

"I'm glad you find me so amusing. But ain't no arm candy here. Sorry for your trouble." I take the empty dessert plate out of his hand, rinse the crumbs, and place it in the dishwasher.

When he steps closer, I pull out a scouring pad from a box under the sink and begin to scrub the stainless-steel basin like my life depends on it, ignoring the singe of his glare.

"Perhaps I wasn't plainspoken enough for a simple girl from Mississippi. You *will* join me for an upcoming mission. And it *will* require you to terminate your employment with Smith."

I've officially entered the twilight zone. My hands are shaking, and I suspect there are at least a half dozen other tells that I don't want him to see. "You've lost your damn mind." I toss the scouring pad in the trash and wipe my hands. "I hear there are doctors who can help with that sort of thing." My back is toward him as I head out of the kitchen. "Lock the door and turn on the alarm on your way out so no more assholes break in tonight. My quota for the day has been met." I pause for a second before reaching the doorway, but I don't turn to face him. "If that's not *plainspoken* enough for a spoiled rich boy from Charleston, let me put it another way. Fuck you. And get out of my house."

In one move, he grabs my arm and spins me around until I'm between him and the kitchen counter. "Don't you dare turn your back and walk away until I'm finished."

He's in a mood, and I'm about to bear the brunt of it—maybe that's apt since I believe I'm responsible for the crankiness.

"These are your choices," he says, as though he might actually give me a choice. "One, you continue to behave like a brat. I walk out that door and send every image I have to the local authorities and to the Bureau. You go to prison." He tugs on my arm. "How much fun do you think the guards will have with your pretty little covert ass? Within a day, you'll be everybody's favorite cum bucket." I cringe because it's true. "And Smith's business will be ruined by his close association with the woman who murdered Archbishop Darden in cold blood. Everybody will think he put you up to it, to avenge Kate. That's what they'll all believe, and you know it."

He doesn't miss a beat. "Or two, you learn your place, and do as I say. This is an important mission. One that will allow you not only to do good, but to get your hands good and dirty in the process. To use all the tools in your arsenal, just as you were trained to do."

Important mission. Allow you to do good. Use all the tools in your arsenal, just as you were trained to do. His words spin round and round in my head. I'm intrigued, but I'm also out of sorts and not thinking straight. "What's behind door number three?"

I should have asked about door number two, but I lashed out impulsively, because I'm a fighter. I don't run. Never have. I punch back, hard. It's my default setting when I'm cornered. "Is that where the shiny new car and the beach vacation is hiding? There's always a car." As soon as the words come out of my mouth, I regret them.

The fury in his eyes is stunning, but I don't blink.

"Number three," he says, in a tone that raises the hair on the back of my neck, "is I bend you over this," his knuckles rap against the countertop, "pull down those ratty sweatpants, and fuck you until you can't walk for a month. Then you'll do what I want, because you know I'm not playing about those photos."

I lift my chin defiantly.

He shakes his head. "You might be able to handle being the prison whore, but I don't think you're prepared to see Smith ruined."

Of all the things Gray has ever said, that holds the most truth. I will slit my wrists before becoming the prison whore, but I will not allow Smith to go down in ashes because of me. He is the most important member of the little family I've cobbled together. He's the man who took me in and gave me a job after I'd become a pariah. He held out his hand, when everyone else was still kicking me. No, I will not let anyone destroy him. And Gray damn well knows it.

"Smith is part of your family, as much as he's part of mine." I'm surprised my voice doesn't echo how powerless I feel right now. "You would hurt him to punish me?"

Gray steps back, and I can breathe again.

"Smith lost his big-brother status when he planted you in my club without a word about it."

"He did it to protect your family. To protect you."

"I have no desire to see Smith burn. But if he becomes collateral damage, so be it. His fortune is in your hands."

Bullshit. I don't believe it. "What would your brother say about this? Smith is JD's best friend. And Gabby. What would she say?"

His teeth slide over his bottom lip, with a nasty snarl. "The more people you involve, the more people get hurt. But the bottom line is still the same. The stakes are high. Bigger than any one person—any one family. Even my own."

His words are sobering, and I don't know what to make of them. While I can't say for sure how he feels about Smith, I am absolutely certain he loves his brothers. And Gabby. And his baby niece. You can't hide those kinds of feelings, and they're plain as day when he's with them.

"What am I to tell Smith?"

"Whatever you want. You might start with the truth. How dissatisfied you've become, because you miss the field work. He'll understand that. He just went through something similar himself. Then tell him you need him to trust you. Bat those long eyelashes at him when you talk."

Fucker. "Bat my eyelashes? That's not what my relationship with Smith is about. He respects me and the work I do."

"He does. And he should. But you need more than someone who respects you. You need someone to capture your attention and keep you in line so you don't run around killing off the local clergy." He takes a fistful of my hair. "Have I captured your attention, *De-li-lah*?"

"You're a vile excuse for a human being. I hate you."

"That matters not at all in this equation. Although the

prospect of a little demon fighting back does make my dick hard."

I look away, focusing on a tiny gash at the bottom right corner of the refrigerator. I never noticed it before, but I'm desperate to find a distraction. Because I'm ashamed. Ashamed that I would like nothing more than for this despicable asshole to shove his hard cock into me. I've wanted him so bad for so long that I don't know how not to want him—even when he's behaving like a world-class prick.

"Why did you do it?" he asks, letting go of my hair.

I'm still thinking about his cock and not at all sure what he's asking.

"Kill Archbishop Darden."

We're back to that. "He was the one who put that devil Creighton at St. Maggie's."

"So?"

"So, do you know how many women Creighton tortured and killed? In my book, Darden was just as responsible." *And that's not even the half of it. That sonofabitch has been spreading evil for decades.* "I spent hours with Kate at the hospital. I held her hand while she was being examined. Stood there and listened to the things he did to her. I listened to the fear in her voice and to the shame she's going to carry for a long time—maybe forever. Shame that should *not* be her burden."

Gray eyes me suspiciously. *I need to stop talking.*

"Let's see if I've got this straight. You're such a big fan of Kate McKenna that you decided to seek vengeance in her name. You murdered a man of God while he slept, because of loyalty to the sisterhood. Did I get that right?"

I don't bother responding because he knows I'm not being entirely truthful, and it can only get worse from here. "It's none of your damn business, asshole."

He wedges his thumb under my chin, forcing me to look into the depths of those ice-cold blue eyes. "Pick number three," he goads, snapping the waistband of my sweatpants. "Go ahead. Do it. I'm begging you."

"I could kill you in your sleep, too," I assure him sweetly, without a thimbleful of self-preservation. It's not that I'm so brave—or foolish, for that matter. It's that I'm confident he won't hurt me.

"You could try." He takes his hands off me and moves a few feet away, leaning back against the counter with his arms crossed. "But you won't. Because I'm promising you things you haven't had in a long time. Things you enjoy."

God, he's insufferable. "And exactly what are those things?"

"Excitement. Fun. A chance to use your skills—all of them—for the benefit of humanity." He watches me carefully as he continues ticking off the perks. "An opportunity for submission—an outlet for your deepest desires. That's the icing on top."

"In your dreams." The words come out rough and low, and reticent, because for the last few years, that's been *my* dream. But there's no way I'm telling him that. It will just become one more thing to use against me. "Submission isn't demanded—through extortion, no less. It's given freely to those who earn it. You haven't earned a fucking thing."

"I'm well aware." He captures my gaze and doesn't let go. "But this is a mission we're discussing. Not a relationship."

I swallow the retort on the tip of my tongue. I'm tired and it's not worth the energy. We both know I'm going to pick door number two. Maybe we've known it since the beginning. "I need more information before agreeing to anything."

"I'll read you in as much as I can when the time is right. First, you need to cut professional ties with Smith."

Read me in? It's a classified mission. *A black op? Can't be.* "Who exactly do you work for?"

"The good guys," he answers, without hesitation.

"That's it? I'm supposed to quit my job and go on some half-cocked mission with you? I don't even know who you are anymore." His Adam's apple bobs, but he doesn't say anything.

"Quit my job—hell. Are you even planning on paying me?"

"In cash?"

I roll my eyes. "Yes, in cash. A woman's got to pay her rent and eat. If you can't promise—"

"You'll be paid. In all sorts of ways, including cash."

"I'm only interested in the cash. The rest I can take care of myself."

Gray studies me with a wicked gleam in his eyes, as though he's imagining me on my back, naked, feet sole to sole, strumming my clit for his pleasure. After several long seconds, his mouth twists into the mocking sneer of a predator who has cornered his prey and wants to spend some time toying with it before he eats. "You wound me, Delilah."

"Your cock is nowhere near as magical as you seem to think it is. Doesn't even warrant an honorable mention. But maybe they have a participation trophy for you." I meet his eyes with a self-satisfied sneer of my own. "Someone had to tell you."

He doesn't say anything. But if that smug look on his face could talk, it would say, *we'll see how magical my cock is when you're begging for it.*

I need him to leave. It's not that I want the damn thing pressing against his zipper. *Not right now, anyway.* It's that I could be persuaded. And men with erections are not to be trusted. *Ever.*

"It's late," I say, turning off the light over the sink. "Are we done?"

"For tonight. Get in touch with me after you talk to Smith."

"I haven't agreed to anything."

"Yes, you have." He pulls a phone from his pocket. "Use this to contact me. Only this. My number is already programmed. The password is Sultan's Palace. All one word." He tips his head to the side. "Just like that night, you have the ultimate control. You just have to be prepared to live with the consequences."

He opens the back door and steps out into the night. Seconds after the screen door bangs behind him, my new phone vibrates. When I turn it over, there's a message with a series of images. They're all of me with the archbishop.

I want to chase him into the darkness, all the way to the gates of Hell, and use the damn phone to beat some decency into him, but I don't. Not tonight. But the moment will come. I can be cold and calculating too.

7
GRAY

Before my feet hit the pavement, I send Delilah a reminder of the consequences if she goes rogue. Then I send another message.

GW: She's in.
Unknown: How did you get her on board?
GW: Between me and her. Not your concern.
Unknown: If you ruin her, I'll kill you myself.
GW: Fuck you, Smith.

8
GRAY
TWO WEEKS EARLIER

It's hot as hell, and sticky from all the rain last night. There's not a soul back here, nor will there be, until the sun burns away the remnants of the storm. Wet brush overhead, pesky critters swarming, and no Wi-Fi makes Jessamine Café the perfect place for a clandestine meeting.

I'm here to drop a bomb. The mother of all bombs. Not an actual explosive, but it will cause plenty of damage, just the same.

I hope like hell that I haven't misjudged the players I'm assembling. While there's no shortage of talent and character among them, the yarn that holds us together is a complicated weave, with a number of weak spots that could unravel the entire mission. Those weak spots are emotions, and that mission is the culmination of my life's work.

The frosted glass door swings open and Smith steps onto the deserted patio, coffee in hand, startled look on his face. *And it's just the beginning.* His composure returns before he reaches the table where I'm seated. "Didn't expect to find you out here in the swamp. Aren't you worried about melting all over your custom-made shirt?"

I snicker and take a gulp of coffee before peering into his eyes. "That's interesting, because you're exactly the man I expected to see here."

Smith stiffens, every inch of muscle tense, but the wheels turning madly.

While he searches his internal drive, his eyes narrow, with the surrounding skin drawn into tight creases. "You were expecting *me*?"

I nod.

I've known Smith since I was sixteen, and I've never seen him quite so off his game. He can be deadly serious, but he's never at a loss for words. He's the guy who always has a quick comeback at the ready. Something clever and cutting. But right now, he's got nothing.

"I'm Lone Wolf," I say, divulging my covert identity. He's been told his meeting is with Lone Wolf, but this is more than he bargained for—much more.

Smith continues to eye me cautiously. "You're Lone Wolf?" he repeats, testing the words as they roll off his tongue, much the way one does when speaking a foreign language.

"It's a bit pretentious, even for my tastes, but Gray Wolf would have been too obvious." I motion toward an empty seat. "Take a load off."

Smith pulls out the chair across from me and plops his ass down. "I—I—*fuck me*." He leans back and rubs his palm over an unshaven jaw. "You better start talking, princess."

Princess. The nickname my brother JD tagged me with when we were kids. It stuck because he's always thought I was soft and liked to be comfortable. And because it's what brothers do. Taunt each other and wheedle themselves under each other's skin. I call him asshole every chance I get. It's one of the many dysfunctional ways we say I love you in my family.

"What the hell is going on, Gray?" The color is gone from Smith's face, and the alarm in his voice is palpable.

My gut burns like a sonofabitch. Smith's not blood family, but he's damn close.

I mulled over the words I would use with him today. Sifting carefully until they were milled into a fine grain that could be swallowed easily. My focus had been on making it palatable for him, without divulging too much. What I never considered were my own feelings and the emotion that would bubble up as I prepared to tell him that everything he knew about me up until this point was a lie. Maybe not everything, but enough to unsettle anyone, even a tough sonofabitch like Smith.

I had imagined there would be some measure of relief in confessing. Some lightness from the unburdening. But reality feels more like the heavy ache of grief.

As I wrestle with my emotions, I draw a breath and blow it out slowly. Even after my lungs are empty, the weight in my chest is still there. But I don't hide. I look Smith right in the eye, because I'm not a coward and he deserves the respect.

"I'm running a black op that's going down sometime in the next month—six weeks at the outside. I need to borrow a couple operatives for the duration, and I might need your team to provide cover if the mission comes to Charleston—although I don't expect that to happen."

Smith's brow is furrowed tight. "I already know all that from my meeting at the Pentagon. I want to know how *you're* involved. I do want the details, but first—what the hell are you doing running a black op? And who the fuck do you work for?"

"I can't talk about who I work for, not specifically. But from your meeting, you know the government is involved—the US and the Amidane governments. That's all I can say about it. You know the drill as well as I do."

"No." He pounds a fist on the wrought-iron table, causing it to wobble.

I grab my coffee so it doesn't become a casualty of the outburst.

"That's not good enough. How did you become involved in paramilitary activities? And when?" he barks.

"Not paramilitary. Covert."

"The CIA?"

I shake my head.

"The Bureau." It's not really a question, and I'm not a fan of guessing games, so I don't respond. "Did they reach out to you while your father was running for president, or after he was elected?"

I take another drink of coffee, letting the bitter roast saturate my tongue. "I was recruited in college."

Smith gapes at me like I have two heads. "College?"

I nod.

"*Christ.* How have you kept it a secret for so long?"

"It really wasn't that hard to pull off." Sad, but true. "My mother was dead. My father focused most of his energy on criminal activity, and on keeping JD in line. As it turns out, he spent some of that energy molesting little girls too." The thought of it makes me want to dig up the bastard and kill him again. *This time with my bare hands.*

I glance at Smith's stony face. He isn't a babe in the woods, but he doesn't have an inkling about how my father got his just deserts. This isn't the time to savor my father's death.

"JD was preoccupied with everyone's safety," I continue, "especially Gabby's, taking care of Zack, and plotting his revenge against *Dad*. Chase was young. By the time you came into the picture and began poking around in my business, it had become a way of life. And I had gotten good at it."

He opens his mouth to say something, but I raise a hand to stop him. "We can discuss the particulars of my life at another time, if it's really necessary, but right now we have more important things to talk about."

Smith rolls the coffee cup between his hands, seemingly

transfixed by the motion. "Puts me in a difficult position," he says quietly. "JD is my business partner, not to mention—"

"JD is an interested investor in Sinclair Industries. He's not an active partner. In any case, he doesn't have the clearance necessary to be read in on any aspect of this mission. Wouldn't matter if it were me or someone else running the show."

Smith nods. He knows it's true, and I know he would never disclose classified information to anyone—not even JD. "What do you want from me?"

If something happens to me during the mission, I want you to protect Delilah with your life. I want you to get her out and ensure her safety. That's why I selected his company over the other two I was offered. I know he'll do everything in his power to save Delilah, if it should come to that.

"I need you to lend me an operative who can provide security and act as my driver. It has to be someone known to you. They need strong skills, and must be entirely trustworthy. Some familiarity with Amadi culture is a huge plus, but not a deal breaker. It will require at least one trip abroad. I'll expedite the necessary clearance and paperwork."

"What about Trippi? I'm sure he's involved in this somehow."

Trippi is my driver and provides security. He's not here now, but he's close. Smith is right. Trippi is involved and has been for a long time. "He'll be providing security for someone else." I look Smith squarely in the face. "I want Delilah too."

"What?" he roars.

"The mission requires a woman. One who's multilingual, won't crumple in the face of danger, and who looks like someone I might fuck. Delilah fits that to a T."

His fists are clenched on the table. "It makes me sick to hear you talk about her like she's a whore. If I didn't know how you really feel about her, I would grind your pretty face into the cobblestones."

This is the part—one of them—where emotions weaken the fabric. But rightfully so. His reaction tells me that my instincts are right. He will do everything in his power to protect her if things take a bad turn.

He contemplates me carefully, trying to put the pieces together. "You need a driver and security because you're assigning Trippi, your trusted sidekick, to Delilah?"

"I'm assigning him to Delilah for a whole host of reasons that I'm not getting into with you."

"The Bureau is bringing her in?"

"I'm bringing her in. I can use whatever assets I feel are necessary to complete this mission successfully. As you are fully aware, that's how these things always work."

"No one knows about her?" Smith cocks his head, gauging my reaction.

"Everyone who needs to know, knows. I don't take any unnecessary risks with my team, and I won't take any unnecessary risks with yours." *And I sure as hell am not taking any risks with Delilah.*

Smith is fuming, but he knows that even the best-run ops are messy. It's the nature of the beast. From his meeting at the Pentagon, he also knows this is a vital mission for the country. Words like duty and honor mean everything to him. Plus, he hasn't told me to go fuck myself yet. That's encouraging.

"Delilah came to me after Christmas. Said she couldn't work at Wildflower anymore because her feelings for you were getting in the way of the job."

"Did she?" I knew Delilah had run to Smith after the night we spent together. It had pissed me off that she went to him without talking to me first. I'm still pissed about it. But I never knew what she told him. "What else did she say?"

"None of your goddamn business." Smith empties his coffee cup and places it carefully on the table. "She agreed to this?"

The skepticism in his voice is scathing. But if I were in his place, I'd be skeptical too.

"She will." I respond with more confidence than I'm feeling. I'm still not entirely sure how I'm going to convince her, but it's going to be ugly. That part I am sure about. "It will be easier on her if you let her go without a fuss when she asks. I don't want her to know you're involved with this yet."

"Why not?" Smith challenges. "Why can't I loan her to you the way I'm loaning my other guy? Why do I have to let her go?"

"Because she'll begin overthinking everything if she believes she's serving two masters. If she isn't focused, she'll put the mission at risk and it will become dangerous for everyone, especially for her. It's not a big secret that Delilah worships you."

Smith swats a swarm of gnats away from his face. "You're going to use her feelings for you, and your feelings for her, to make whatever story you're concocting believable. That's not going to interfere with her focus?"

"Don't be ridiculous. I don't have *feelings* for her." The only person I'm kidding here is myself, but I force a jeer to make a more persuasive argument. "But I must be on top of my game, if I've convinced even you of that."

"You're a sonofabitch, and a goddamn liar." The tips of his ears are flaming and his words are caustic, but his tone is measured. "I don't care who you work for or how long you've been running ops. You're playing a fool's game if you involve a woman you can barely keep your hands off in a covert mission."

"Why don't we let Delilah make the decision? I'm just asking you not make it difficult for her to leave when she comes to you. This is a matter of national security," I add for good measure. "You know this from your meeting at the Pentagon."

Smith's lips are pursed, and the smoke is bellowing from his ears.

"She's perfect for this assignment—and it's perfect for her," I say quietly. "She needs this." The last part is the nail in the coffin. It's manipulative, but it's true. And Smith knows it.

He fills his cheeks with air and when it escapes, it's like a deflating balloon. "How is someone who was in the limelight like she was going to be able to fool a big fish with airtight security in place?"

"She can't. We're going to do it in plain sight. She's the flavor of the month—actually, she'll have to be more than that to be convincing."

Smith glowers and curses softly.

"Delilah's gorgeous. There isn't a man alive who wouldn't want to trade places with me. She's been publicly shunned by her government, and she's found a nice little landing place in my lap. It won't be difficult to sell that story to the people I'm dealing with."

"*Pfft*. Delilah will never agree to what you're proposing."

"We'll see."

"So this is why you're so damn protective of Wildflower. It's your cover. I can't believe I've been so stupid."

It is a cover, and a vehicle for me to spy on political and industry leaders from around the globe. My father opened Wildflower to gather dirt on his detractors so he could blackmail them when it became expedient. I harvest member information and feed it to the government. Their motivations aren't always any more noble than my father's were. Perhaps mine aren't either.

"It's more than just my cover. Maybe it started that way, but it's become an important part of who I am." It's true. Wildflower has allowed me to indulge and perfect my Dominant ways to my heart's desire.

Smith looks beaten. He might feel stupid, but I suspect he mostly feels betrayed.

My gut twists, and the coffee sloshes against my stomach

wall, the acid burning the lining. Smith's feelings are nothing compared to the pain my brothers would feel if I told them I'd been lying to them for nearly fifteen years—especially JD. The betrayal would be devastating. Unforgiveable. I push the thought away.

"You're not stupid. I was always JD's little brother," I say gently. "There was never a reason to look any further." I don't apologize. Smith isn't a naïve civilian. He was a member of the elite Delta Force, and has plenty of his own dark secrets. Although none of this makes me feel any better as I watch him battle with his emotions.

When I've had enough of sitting with the guilt, I stand to leave. "I'll take care of your team. Get them back to you in one piece. You have my word." Smith doesn't look up. "I'll be in touch," I add, before walking away.

"Gray?"

I stop and turn.

"She's good people. The best. She's tough and prickly and she can slit a man's throat in the blink of an eye, but inside, her heart bleeds like any other woman's. Don't add to the heap of misery she's already faced in her life."

My hope is to lighten her burden, not add to the pain. But I don't share that with him. "Understood."

"You better do more than understand."

"We worked up close for the better part of two years. You don't have to tell me about her vulnerability." *It keeps me awake at night. It has for years. Long before she ever set foot into Wildflower.*

9

DELILAH
PRESENT DAY

When I arrive at the security office, Smith is already here. I was hoping to have a few minutes to myself, but maybe it's better if I don't have any more time to think. I spent most of last night tossing and turning, worrying about telling him that I'm leaving.

As I approach Smith's doorway, he's on the phone, looking out the window. All I see is the back of his sandy head above the chair.

If I go sit at my desk until he's finished, I might not find the courage to come back. So I stand outside his office quietly, trying not to eavesdrop. It's not hard, because my mind is elsewhere, bogged down by my own problems.

What am I doing? Leaving a job that I love—well, maybe not love, but I like it a lot. It gives me security and stability. And I love my teammates—all of them—and Smith. He trusts me implicitly, and leans on me more than anyone else. This feels like the most selfish thing I've ever done. *Damn you, Gray Wilder.*

"Delilah. You need something?"

I blink a few times. I didn't hear Smith end the call.

"Um." I nod. *It's only a temporary leave, Delilah. Like a vacation. You've earned a few weeks off.* "Got a minute?"

He motions for me to come inside. I shut the door behind me, my fingers white-knuckling the cold knob. My mind is racing, but my body is moving in slow motion, weighed down by a sense of dread.

"You okay?" he asks.

"I'm fine," I assure him, taking a seat across the desk.

He leans back in the chair, bouncing a pencil eraser on the desk top. I don't know where to begin. Smith watches me patiently, waiting for me to speak, but my well-rehearsed bullshit is stuck in my throat.

"How's Kate?" I ask, in a grand show of cowardice.

"She's tough. The road's rocky, littered with landmines, but we'll get through it."

"It'll take her some time. It's amazing what the human spirit can withstand. If she needs anything—if you need anything—" *I can't do this.* I can't leave him now. Not until things are better with Kate. It's not right. "I should get back to work." I stand and rub my sweaty palms on my pants, pretending to smooth the wrinkles.

"Sit," he says gently, but firmly.

I'm not sure what to do, so I sit my backside on the edge of the chair.

"Do you need me to do something?" I ask, hoping he'll give me an assignment that requires all my attention so I don't spend the day thinking about what I'm going to tell Gray.

Smith chuckles. "Yeah. I need you to tell me what's on your mind."

Of course you do. "Not a lot. You know me." *Sweet Jesus, that sounded stupid.*

"I do know you. You're not an airhead. And you don't beat around the bush. You plow straight through it. So cut the bullshit and tell me what's going on."

I'm fresh out of pep talks for myself. Exhausted from weighing the pros and cons about working with Gray again, albeit in a different capacity. And I'm bone-tired of justifying to myself why I deserve a chance to do work that I love, even if it's temporary. I have to do this. Not because of some picture that I'm afraid of, but because I will regret it if I don't. My life is already too full of regret.

When I glance at Smith, my left eye twitches, but I press on. "I need some time off. Like a leave of absence—or something."

He doesn't say anything right away, and the silence is so heavy it's suffocating.

"I'll be gone a month, maybe a bit longer."

"You sick?"

I shake my head. "No. It's nothing like that. I—I've been offered an opportunity—that I'd like to accept. It's not something I'm free to talk about." There. I said it. But I don't feel any better.

Smith eyes me suspiciously while I try not to squirm. "The agency call you to come back?"

Even as he asks, I hear the disbelief in his voice. He knows the agency would *never* call me back. The director himself made it clear they were done with me. *You're no good to us as a covert operative now, Special Agent Porter. I could put you behind a desk, but you won't be happy. I'm sorry this happened to you.*

I blink away the memory. "No. It's something different." I take a long breath. "It's all legal—as legal as this shit can be—but I'm not at liberty to say anything more." I don't actually know anything more. Not really.

Smith is quiet.

As well as I know him, I can't read him right now. This was a mistake. That I do know. "I realize this is bad timing—I had actually changed my mind about asking you because I know this isn't a great time to be asking for time off."

"It's actually not a bad time at all. We're in a transition

period. That's not what concerns me." He captures my gaze and holds it steady. "Are you sure about this? Are you certain it's something you want to get involved with?"

No. I'm not at all sure. I'm not nervous about the work. I would love the opportunity to be part of a covert operation again. *Love it.* I live for the opportunity. But I am terrified of the man running the op. There's no denying it. Not to Smith, and not to myself. "Before I answer, can I ask you a question?"

He sits back in the chair. "I'm listening."

"As you branch out and Sinclair Industries takes on more covert operations—will there ever be an opportunity for me to work in the field?" I know the answer. I just need to hear him say it.

"You work in the field now."

"Not like that. Undercover. The way I did at Wildflower. The way I was trained."

He shifts in his chair. "Delilah. You're damn good at what you do, and you are, hands down, the most important and trusted member of my team." His brow is drawn tight, and even though he knows I won't be surprised, it pains him to deliver the news. "But I won't lie to you. I don't see how I can put you undercover again. You were outed publicly. Your face—your story—it doesn't take much digging to put it together. We were confident that no one at Wildflower would look hard at you. That's why I put you there. It would have to be something like that—something unique—I can't even think of what it might be."

I nod, staring at my hands, squeezing the fingers I've laced together until they ache. "I don't know the full extent of the operation. But it seems like it would challenge me and—and that it might be one of those unique opportunities where my past won't be an issue."

I glance up at him. I need to see what's in his eyes. In his soul. I need the connection—and in a way I don't really understand, I need his blessing. "It's hard," I continue, "so hard to say this. It feels like such an enormous betrayal, but yes, I'd like to do it. I might never get another chance."

It's true. Every word. Even if Gray weren't involved—if the CIA or the FBI or the NSA or any of them, came to me with the proposition that Gray laid at my feet, I would do it in a heartbeat. At least, I would want to. "I don't want to leave you in the lurch. That's my only hesitation." There's Gray too, of course, but I don't tell Smith that.

"It would require you to start right away?"

I nod.

He drums his fingers on the desk. "If you want to do it—if you feel it's important, I won't stand in your way."

It's not exactly a blessing, but close enough. "This should make me happy, but I feel bad."

"I'm the one who feels bad," Smith says softly. "You've brought so much to my team, but I haven't given enough thought to what the work has given you."

"It's given me plenty—so much."

"Maybe. But not enough. For people like us, the challenge is what fuels us. It wears you down if you feel like your skills aren't being fully utilized. I know that feeling well."

"Smith—"

"Go. Do what you need to do, then come back—if that's what you want. There will always be a place for you here. But if you don't do it, if you stay, you'll get fat and sloppy from being insufficiently challenged. It'll wear on your soul and you'll be a risk to yourself and to the team."

Anger, or maybe pride, is bubbling up and it tastes rancid. "I would never—"

"Not intentionally, but it would happen, eventually. Now that it's out in the open, I can't afford the risk. Neither can you."

"So I can come back when the mission is over?" He's already said as much, but I need to hear it again.

"I hope you do come back. But that's up to you. You need to feed your soul, Delilah, and as much as I'll miss your sassy mouth, I want that for you."

Smith gets up, and I stand too. "Thank you. I'll never forget everything you've done for me."

He comes around the desk and wraps me in his arms. We're close, but he's never hugged me before. I press my eyelids together firmly, until the sting of tears dissipates.

Smith releases me, but keeps a heavy hand on my shoulder. "If at any point the operation goes south—at *any* point—or if you just want out, you call me."

I don't dare look at him, because the dam will open, releasing a flood the likes of which we've never seen.

He squeezes my shoulder. "Promise me, Delilah."

My chest aches. There haven't been many people in my life who have given a damn about my well-being.

Smith squeezes, again. "Promise me."

I cover his loyal hand with mine, and clutch it tightly. "I promise."

10

GRAY

"Come in." I glance up from the screen as Foxy marches into my office, like the taskmaster she is, carrying a tray that she sets down on my desk.

"I had the kitchen send over breakfast."

"I already had breakfast."

"Yes. I know. A protein shake." She rolls her eyes, not bothering to hide her disapproval. Something most people who want to continue to work for me wouldn't dare do. But Maggie Fox isn't most people. She's been with me since long before I took over at Wildflower. Saved my ass more times than I can count. That's not hyperbole.

"Eggs and an English muffin isn't going to ruin your girlish figure," she snaps, lifting the silver dome off an omelet.

"Keep it covered. I'll have it later." Foxy knows it's a lie, but she reads my mood, and holds her tongue.

I take another glance at the tray. "No coffee?"

"You've had enough."

I don't utter a word, but I glare at her until she understands that I've about had my fill of insolence.

I'm edgy, but it has nothing to do with coffee and everything to do with a smart-mouthed blonde who should be terminating her employment with Smith about now. But with Delilah, who knows what she's actually doing? The woman makes me crazy.

After Foxy collects the contents of my outbox, she turns to leave, and I go back to studying a spreadsheet with the monthly expenses. "When you get back to your office, have them send over a fresh carafe. *Please.*" I add the nicety, because she means well, and I'm not a total dick.

"You've been jittery and irritable from the moment you arrived. It's a bad look. You need some food to counteract the effects of the five cups of coffee you've already enjoyed this morning, not more of the same."

It's six, but who's counting. "Is there something else you need before you go back to your desk and kindly order me some coffee?"

"Eat," she mutters, shutting the door behind her.

"Coffee," I bark before the door latches.

No matter how many times I review this motherfucking spreadsheet, I can't make sense of it today. And the stench of eggs isn't helping. *Damn Foxy.* I get up and dump the tray on the credenza across the room.

Delilah will contact me. Any minute now. I'm confident about that. The truth is she wants what I'm offering—all of it. She needs it too. Although I'm not convinced she understands that part yet.

I sink back into my chair and glance at the phone. Thirty-seven emails in the last forty-five minutes. Not one worthy of my time. The phone lights up, but it's not her, so the call goes to voicemail, where I'll deal with it later, or Foxy will.

Time is a bitch for those who wait. Shakespeare was right, and nothing's changed since then.

I push aside the spreadsheet, and check my phone again. Hopefully I haven't made a mistake dragging Delilah into something without giving her ample time to prepare. This mission is tailor-made for her. *If only there was more time.*

I slam my fist on the desktop. I'm not impulsive, but I don't second-guess myself *ever*—it's too dangerous in my line of work. But everything with Delilah pushes me in directions I rarely go. *Damn woman.*

The timing on this isn't perfect—it never is—but she's beginning to take risks that will only get her into trouble...or worse. Mission or no mission, I'd have to intervene now, anyway.

This opportunity will be good for her. I've watched her closely for nearly three years, and even before that, when she was married to that stupid fucker Kyle, I knew her secrets.

Kyle had no honor and a big mouth that he ran all the damn time. He was a piss-poor excuse for a Dominant, and I was a piss-poor excuse for a man, so I let him be an abusive asshole and did nothing to intervene. But I have a chance to make it right. Something we don't always get in life. At least that's been my experience.

Delilah needs new coping mechanisms. She needs to be reined in, and allowed to live her dream—even for a short while. And she needs a safe place to submit, a way to quiet her anxiety, and a Dominant who will help her find peace without gaslighting and manipulating her for his own needs and wants. I'll begin the process with her, and when the mission is over—*I can't entertain it.* I'm not into long-term relationships, contractual or otherwise. Period.

The phone rings while I'm still trying to convince myself that when the mission is complete, I'll move on.

I don't need to look at the screen. It's her. I feel it in my bones. I should be pleased she obeyed, but I'm torn up inside. Delilah is a wild card who's wedged her way under my skin. Smith is right. I'm playing a fool's game.

I take a deep breath before answering. "Good morning."

"It's done. Like you asked." She fires out the words with a good dose of resentment.

But I hear the sorrow, and it lands on my conscience with the sting of rubber pellets.

What many people don't understand about Dominants is that we have hearts. That it's often easier to wrap a submissive into a warm embrace than to show her the steel spine that the moment requires—and that she needs.

Delilah isn't my submissive, and aside from the game we're going to play for the benefit of the mission, she never will be. But my heart aches for her. That doesn't mean I'll give in to the soft feelings. It won't further the mission, and it won't help her at all.

"Where are you now?" I ask calmly.

"In my car, outside Sweetgrass, wondering what the hell I just did. Why I left a good job with security and health insurance. And I'm wondering how the hell I'm going to pay my mortgage when it comes due next month."

The money itself is a small factor. It's the security it gives her that she's already mourning. I've never gone without—at least not when it comes to the things money can buy—so I don't pretend to know what it's like for someone like Delilah. All I can do is provide assurances and follow through. "You don't need to worry about any of it. You'll earn good pay, and you'll have everything you need if you get sick."

"I better."

I ignore the implied threat—for now. It's something we'll work on in the next couple of weeks. "Enough about your needs for now. What I need, is you, at Wildflower. Trippi will meet you in the parking lot. Give him your car keys, and he'll take you upstairs. Stay out of my bedroom and my office. Otherwise the apartment is yours to do as you please."

"Where will you be?" she demands.

I rub my forehead in an effort to remain calm. "I'll be downstairs at the club until lunchtime, and then I'll be up."

"What am I supposed to do until then, bake cookies?"

The thought of Delilah in my pristine kitchen creating a disaster that would rival the destruction of a tornado makes me cringe. "You'll have plenty to do. A personal shopper, Jessica, and a seamstress whose name I don't know, will meet you there in about an hour. They'll bring fabric and some samples with them. Don't worry about the cost of anything. Just try to have fun with it."

"I don't need a personal shopper," she replies, indignantly, "or a seamstress. And shopping is not my idea of fun."

There's not a single woman I've been with—*ever*—who wouldn't just say *thank you*. But I expected this from her. "You need both if you're going to be spending time with me."

She's breathing heavily, and I brace myself for the fury about to be unleashed.

"If my clothing choices aren't up to your standards, then maybe you need to find someone else for the job."

Not a chance.

"You're not dressing me like a Barbie doll," she adds, in case I didn't get the message.

I adjust my hardening cock roughly. "Oh, but I am dressing you. All the way down to the color of your silk thong. You can be Covert Agent Barbie. Or maybe I'll call you Charleston Barbie. I'll even buy you a sparkly pink convertible to drive around town in."

"Fuck you, Gray Wilder."

"Listen carefully, because this is the last time I'm going to say this. I don't care if you run around in rags from the thrift store or bare-ass, but there's no way you can accompany me to some of the places where the mission will take us if you aren't expensively and exquisitely dressed. It's part of your cover, so get over it."

It's not entirely true. While I don't care what she wears, I like the idea of her being dressed in ways that seem as though she has no financial worries. I don't care if she shops at Goodwill, as long as she knows she doesn't have to.

"I—"

"You will do as your told or suffer the consequences. You can meet with the shopper and have input into your wardrobe, or I'll meet with her and choose your clothing for you. Your choice." I sit back and wait for her to come to terms with the shopper. There's no way in hell Delilah would let me choose her clothes.

She stews for several seconds. "Fine. But at other times, I wear my own clothes, not the costumes you pay for. I'm not your whore."

Oh, Delilah. My gut churns. That's what this is about. "First, we both have a clothing allowance to purchase the things we need to make it believable. I have everything I need, so you can use my allowance and yours." I'll personally cover any overrun—happily. But I don't say that. No reason to throw gasoline on a raging fire.

"And second, you're not a whore." I say it with the utmost respect and sincerity. It's not a judgment I make about anyone when it comes to their sexual needs and desires—and I sure as hell would never judge her in that way. "You'll never hear me call you that unless it makes you wet. Then I'll say it all the time."

Delilah doesn't utter a peep. She likes dirty talk. I remember how aroused she was when I whispered filthy things to her. How she moaned and whimpered, and how willing she was to repeat my words back to me when I demanded it.

"In the future, things will go a lot easier if you just tell me what's bothering you, rather than have me guess. I'm not a mind reader."

"I don't know what you're talkin' about."

This is bullshit. She let me see a small piece of what's inside and now she's playing dumb.

"You could have said, *I feel cheap when you make decisions about my clothing or pay for it.* And I would have explained that it was necessary for the mission."

"Isn't that the conversation we just had?"

The woman is going to kill me before this is over, or I'm going to kill myself. One way or the other, I'm not going to survive her. "We have a lot to accomplish today. Come directly here, so we can get started."

11

GRAY

It's nearly two o'clock before I finally break away from the club. When I get to the apartment, Delilah is in the living room, scrolling through her phone.

"How did it go?" I ask, although I already know how it went. Jessica called me as soon as she left the apartment. Delilah was pleasant and polite, but preoccupied with how much things cost. So much so that she only purchased a small fraction of the clothing she needs for the trip. I instructed Jessica to send over everything that she liked but didn't purchase. I'll deal with the fallout when it happens.

"I hope that allowance is mighty big, because the clothing I bought today was mighty expensive. Are we going to visit the royal family as part of the mission?"

Yes. But not the harmless crew you're thinking about. "Something like that."

"When exactly will I be learning what's expected of me?"

"Today." I drop my keys and wallet on the console table in the foyer. "I'm going to change. I'll be out in a few minutes."

Delilah jumps off the sofa and follows me down the hall into my bedroom. She's not going to give me a moment's peace.

"Are you expecting me to live here?"

"What part of *I'm going to change and I'll be out in a few minutes* did you not understand?"

"Don't tell me you're shy all of a sudden. I've already seen your droopy white ass. Answer my question."

I unbuckle my belt and drop my pants in front of her. Despite her bluster, Delilah takes great pains not to look anywhere below my chest. "What question is that?" I hang my trousers, and go into the bathroom to wash my hands and splash some water on my face, mostly ignoring her.

"Are. You. Expecting. Me. To. Live. Here?"

"Temporarily. And it's not an expectation. It's a requirement. You need to be mission ready in two weeks. That's not a lot of time for training." *Even if you're completely sold on the op, and we won't know that for a few hours.*

When I come out of the bathroom, she's chewing on the edge of her bottom lip, looking completely fuckable, but there's no time for that right now. And it isn't part of the plan—not yet.

"What kind of training are we talking about?"

"Well, you know how to use a weapon, and you seem to have no trouble killing a man with your bare hands, so that leaves training your sassy mouth." I pretend not to see the exaggerated eye roll. "We need to learn to live together comfortably, so that it appears natural even under close scrutiny. You also need to learn all the moving pieces. That part is complicated." *Hopefully not too complicated.*

"Complicated how?"

"It's a chess board. My expectation is that you'll rise as the queen, not wither as one of the pawns."

She's perched on the arm of a chair, listening intently.

"Things never end well for the pawns. This operation won't be an exception." *And I'll be damned if you become a casualty. I simply won't allow it to happen.*

"You seem to keep forgetting that I worked for the CIA as a covert agent."

"Watch your tone with me," I warn with a pointed look. "I haven't forgotten. That's why you're here. There are a lot of pretty faces with nice asses in the world. Most of them are more charming, too, might I add."

Delilah gives me another eye roll that I'm not prepared to let go this time. She's begging for a good tug of the leash and I won't deny her.

I stride over to where she's sitting and grab her chin between my fingers, forcing her to look at me. "From the way you're acting, it seems you got your training in the playground of a trailer park or a middle school. Are you up for this, or are you more interested in a schoolyard fight? Because I can arrange that right after I wash my hands of you and find a real agent with some heart and balls. This is too important for bullshit."

"I am a real agent," she replies softly, with just a trace of indignation. The woman doesn't back down easily, but she responds some to my pushback.

"Then start acting like one." As soon as I move away, her hand flies to her chin, rubbing, as if trying to banish the sensation of my fingers from her skin. "You're highly skilled in some areas, and you've been trained in deceptive tactics, but you never had a chance to test those skills—not in the way that this op expects of you. You need to be immersed, so that when we get the go signal—you're ready. My job is to get you ready, so you don't endanger the mission, the team, or yourself." *Especially yourself. Fuck that.* It's *all* important. It's also my job to see that it's a success and that *everyone* comes through safely on the other side. Not just her. This is another weak spot in the weave.

Delilah swallows hard, digesting every word. She knows it's all true. "If I'm going to live here, I need to get some things from my house."

"You need nothing from your house, or from your life as Delilah Mae Porter. Not a single thing."

"I need—"

"Did you get to take all your mementos and personal belongings along when you were training with the CIA?"

Her chest rises and falls erratically, but she doesn't respond because the answer is *no*. When an agent goes undercover, they leave the clothes on their back and their wallet in a locker, and walk away from their old life. That's how it is. You shed your identity completely to make it easier to take on a new one. That's not exactly what's happening here, but it's the best way to get her to accommodate to her new role quickly.

I grab a long-sleeve T-shirt and a pair of jeans from the closet, and glance across the room at her. She's wearing a pair of black pants that are molded around her gorgeous ass and closed-toe shoes. Not perfect for a bike trip, but it'll do. "Did Jessica leave a jacket for you?"

"Yes. Why?"

"You'll need it for where we're going."

She cocks her head. "Where are we going?"

"To the beach. We'll spend a couple days there getting you up to speed on the mission. You'll gain an understanding of the players, the operation, and your role in it. When we come back, you'll be immersed in training. We don't have a lot of time, but we can make it work if you don't fight me every step of the way."

Not that there's a prayer in hell of that happening.

"What about a bathing suit and a toothbrush?"

"Everything we need is there." She's watching me finish dressing, but her mind is somewhere else. Nowhere good, I'm sure.

"You're taking a good long look for someone who thinks my cock isn't magical and my ass is droopy."

Delilah blinks several times. She squares her shoulders, but she's worried—her face betrays her. Her facial expressions, as much as I love them, are something we need to work on. They could unknowingly give her away.

"Gray—is this some kind of huge mindfuck? You pretend there's a mission to reel me in, but it's all about you humiliating me because you're still angry that I was undercover at Wildflower?"

There's uncertainty in her voice, and it doesn't matter what I say—she doesn't trust me. And she's right not to, because I haven't earned it. "I knew who you were the moment you stepped through the door."

She opens her mouth, and closes it. The realization has to be a bitter pill to swallow. "You didn't answer my question. Is there a mission, or are you planning to humiliate me and use me for sex?"

"Would that be so bad?"

I don't know why I ask. Except the woman is wedged so deep under my skin it's impossible for me to be around her for long without my mind drifting back to Christmas. There was no humiliation, but I used her well, and in truth, she used me well, too. The sex was—epic. *Yeah.* That's the right word.

Her eyes are narrowed, the irises the color of a washed-out sky rather than the crystal-clear blue I'm used to. "I need to know," she says firmly.

"While I'm all for an angry fuck, I don't use sex for revenge. Not my style." *Unlike your asshole dead husband.* "There's a mission. You'll be an important member of the team. Maybe the most important."

"The most important? I don't believe—"

I nod, and hold a finger to her lips to silence her. "I realize it's a lot to ask, but I need you to trust me. I might not answer all your questions the moment you want the answers, but I won't lie to you."

She pulls away and steps back. "But you have."

"As have you."

She winces at the words, perhaps from the realization that we're not all that different. Our paths started out differently—mine paved in gold and hers in base gravel—but somewhere along the line, they converged.

"We can't change the past, Delilah, only the future."

"I want you to understand something." She moves closer, until she's almost near enough to touch. "I'm choosing to work with you as part of the team, but I reserve the right to back out if when we get to the beach, I learn it's some harebrained scheme that's not sanctioned through the proper channels."

I'm not at all worried about her backing out once she learns more. Infiltrating a foreign power is a once-in-a-lifetime gig for most operatives. She's not going to love every aspect of the preparation, but she's going to relish the mission itself. "You'll find—"

She holds up her hand to stop me. "Let me finish."

I pause to give her my full attention, and to admire her pluck. She stands tall, head high and proud, like a fucking queen who isn't going to bow to me under any circumstances. This is not an attitude I normally enjoy or tolerate, but right now, I'm enjoying the hell out of her.

"If, after hearing the details," she explains, "I still choose to work with you, it won't be because of those photos you took. I know you won't really send them to the authorities. It will be because—"

"Because you miss the work," I say quietly. "Because it was your dream." I step closer. "Because you never had a real chance to experience it, before it was stolen away."

She nods. It's barely a perceptible movement, and I wonder if she's even aware she's doing it. It's the truth, *her* truth, laid bare, without the usual masks and disguises she uses to protect herself. It's far more intimate than any sexual act could ever aspire to be.

We're both taking heavy, shallow breaths—her, grappling with the intimacy, and me, waiting for her retreat.

After several seconds, she blinks away the fog. "I thought we were going to the beach. What are we waiting for?" she asks in a sassy tone.

I'm not surprised she reached for that mask. It's her favorite.

"Well?" she asks again, this time with her chin tipped up.

Her resilience is something to see. I both respect and loathe it at the same time. It's the protective shell of a survivor, a retreat buttressed with pride. It appears strong and tough, and it is, but it's built on a foundation of neglect and abandonment, the sides erected from bits of shoe leather left after she was kicked and stepped on.

It enrages me to think about all the ways she's been hurt. Her scars gnaw at my soul, and have for some time. I could have made life easier for her—not all of it, of course, but some of it.

But I didn't.

I gaze into her eyes. They've lost the gray clouds from earlier, but the sparkle that touches my soul is gone. I motion for her to lead. "After you, baby girl."

She glares at me over her shoulder, with fire in her eyes. "You better find something else, *boy*, because mission or no mission, I'll whoop your butt good if you even think about calling me that again."

I smile and follow her out of the room, my eyes locked on her tight little ass. The next two days shouldn't be too bad. The real challenge begins when we get back.

12

DELILAH

"Have you ever been on the back of a bike?" Gray asks, as the elevator doors close.

"A motorcycle?"

"No, a Schwinn Sting-Ray with a banana seat." He peers at me, his eyes as sharp as his tongue, burrowing deeply, searching for answers that have nothing to do with bikes.

There's nothing worse than someone trying to get inside your head—especially someone who's good at it.

The elevator seems too small right now. We're standing too close. Even as I fill my lungs with the stale air, I'm suffocating. I start to look away, but one edge of his mouth twitches, and I feel the nervous tug of my lips too. Nobody on this earth wears a playful smirk better than Gray. *Nobody.*

"Yes, a motorcycle," he adds, when I take too long to respond.

"Many times. I've driven one, too. When Kyle and I were first married, it was our only mode of transportation." I don't know why I mention my marriage. I rarely bring it up. There's something about being a widow—a young widow—that makes people uncomfortable. It always results in long, awkward pauses, so I've learned to avoid the subject. But today I needed something substantial to wedge between me and the man with the scruffy chiseled jaw and the panty-melting smirk.

Awkward did the trick, because after I mention Kyle, Gray says nothing more, even when the elevator pings and the doors open.

I follow him to the corner of the pristine garage, to where a Ducati and a Harley are parked. Who has a Harley *and* a Ducati? Not to mention three cars and a truck, that I know of. People with too much money on their hands, that's who. This is just another reminder that Gray and I come from different worlds.

"Nice bikes," I say, admiring the sleeker one. I've never seen a Ducati up close. "How about if you take the Harley and I'll take this baby for a ride." I'm only half-joking. I'd love to get it on the open road and see what it can do.

His mouth curls gently, and for a few seconds I forget I'm here to work, not to play.

"How about if you put on that jacket and try these gloves on for size." He hands me a couple pairs of vented gloves from a drawer tucked under what looks to be a fiberglass shelf where several helmets are lined up in a neat row. Everything about Gray is clean and orderly—except for the way he fucks. Nothing clean about that.

"The helmets are equipped with Bluetooth," he explains, "but occasionally it fails. If you talk to me and I don't respond right away, it's because I can't hear you. If that happens and you need me to pull over, tap my left shoulder, twice. If it's an emergency, grab my right shoulder. Understand?"

I nod as he lowers a helmet onto my head, adjusting the chin strap snugly. He's careful with my hair, but focused on getting the fit right. Once he's tugged at the rear of the helmet, and is satisfied with the fit, he puts on his own helmet.

The care he takes to make sure that I have protective gear

and a secure helmet is touching—and seductive. I'll admit it. This kind of behavior is difficult to reconcile with the man who pinned me against the car door and threatened to send me to prison for the rest of my life.

While I worked at the club, I occasionally caught a glimpse of callous ruthlessness, and when I left, it was ugly. But otherwise, I never saw the cruel side of him, and I'm struggling to understand it.

After stowing a small backpack in the side compartment, he climbs onto the Harley and I climb on behind him. The backseat is elevated and I can see over his shoulder. "Ready?" he asks, as the garage door opens.

"Yes." I say it with confidence, but I'm not sure I am ready. Not about the ride—that's the easy part—but about spending a night alone with him. A night with unspoken expectations, in a place far removed from real-world ramifications. Like Christmas at Wildflower. *How did that work out for you, Delilah? You want another chance to wreck your life? It's not too late to back out. Not yet.*

I was born with the common sense and practicality of a Depression-era mamaw. And I listen to my gut all the time. Always have. But that Spidey sense is different from the little nagging voice. The one that whispers *you shouldn't have that fourth margarita*, or *you shouldn't kick the asshole harassing you in the nuts*. I've always found that voice to be a whiny little bitch and I rarely pay it any mind. Today is no different.

When we're out of traffic, Gray lets the bike go. I hold on tighter, my fingertips acutely aware of his skin, even though there are layers of fabric between us.

It's been almost six years since I've been on the back of a bike. *Right before Kyle died.* It's as exhilarating and as thrilling as I remember. But I don't recall it ever being as freeing and calming as it is today. I cling to Gray's waist, enjoying the ride while the powerful machine hums between my legs.

The temperature has dropped a few degrees by the time we pull into the driveway of a two-story shingled house, with sprays of bright-pink beach roses climbing a wooden fence. The house sits all alone at the end of the point, practically on the sand. There's a widow's watch with an enclosed cupola were a copper rooster sits at the highest point, basking in the afternoon sun. The house seems like an integral part of the natural habitat. Everything about it exudes peace and serenity.

"Is this your place?" I ask, removing the helmet, and running my fingers through my hair.

"You ask like you're surprised."

Shocked would be more apt. "I thought your tastes were more hoity-toity—like the club and your apartment. Never figured you for a white picket fence kind of guy."

"Why don't you tell me what you really think." Gray chuckles, fixing his gaze on the rose-covered fence. "I'm not. The fence was here when I bought the place, and when the house was renovated, the architect insisted we keep it. It's grown on me." He takes my helmet. "Let's go inside."

After unlocking the door, he steps aside so I can go in first.

"Wow. Gray." I walk straight to the back of the house, barely noticing the professional kitchen on my way to the wall of glass, where I gaze out over the ocean. It's breathtaking. "The view is incredible. I'd never leave this place. Do you get out here often?"

"Not often enough," he says, from another room.

While I'm still gawking, I feel him approach. He hands me a water bottle, but I'm too mesmerized by the waves breaking against the shore to take a drink.

Since moving to Charleston, I've been in some swanky places. Sweetgrass, where Gray's brother and Gabby live, is show-stopping, and then there's Wildflower and the apartments upstairs. Much of historic Charleston is monied. It was a lot to take in for a girl who grew up in a single-wide trailer.

Normally, I pretend to take it in stride so that I don't seem too much like a hick, but this blows me away. "I can't believe this place."

"You haven't even left the window. Although the view is the best part of the place. Come on. Let me show you the rest."

I reluctantly leave the window and follow him for a tour.

Downstairs is an open floor plan, with a sleeping porch. At least that's what we call them where I'm from. The ceilings are high, but the house doesn't have a lot of heavy furniture or dark colors like Wildflower. Everything is light and airy, pale grays and tans, and an array of blues and greens—all the colors of nature. The woodwork is painted a soft white, which gives the house a warm, cozy feel.

Gray points to a door on the opposite side of the kitchen. "My office is through there—it's my private space, same as at the apartment—don't go in unless you're invited."

Something about the way he says it annoys me. As though I might go poking around in his personal business. Okay, I might want to, but I would never—not unless I had good cause.

I follow him quietly up the stairs.

"Not a lot to see up here," he says, "although the view's better."

That's hard to believe.

The entire top floor is a single bedroom with hardwood floors and a soaring ceiling. A crystal chandelier hangs from an exposed beam that runs the width of the room. There's a wall of windows, and a window seat—*a window seat*—that I can't stop smiling at, and some furniture around the fireplace.

But the star of the room is an elaborately carved Tantra chair. Although the name is deceiving. Except for the characteristic dips and curves, Tantra chairs are actually more like Victorian fainting sofas or chaise lounges than chairs. Gray has one in the apartment too, but it isn't as beautiful. This one's a sturdy antique.

His eyes twinkle when he catches me admiring the chair. "It's a beauty, isn't it?"

It's hard to see the chair without imagining him enjoying it with *some* woman. Someone leggy and glamorous, who was born knowing the difference between a wine glass and a water goblet. All of a sudden, I'm feeling peevish. "It looks like a museum piece. Not something you'd use." This is wishful thinking.

"It's never been used."

"Never?" I challenge, even though I don't really want him to say otherwise. "It's hard to believe you haven't at least christened it."

"Never." He pivots to the corner of the room. "The bathroom is through that doorway. There are towels and extra toiletries in the cupboards. Trippi picked up some things from your house that you might want. They're in that closet." Gray points to a door on the far wall. "Some of it's hanging, and the rest is in the bank of drawers on the left side."

I still for a moment. Even the serenity of the room isn't enough to temper the anger simmering inside. "You went to *my* house, riffled through *my* belongings, and violated *my* privacy, Mister Stay-out-of-my-office-it's-my-private-space?"

"*Pfft*. Not me. That would have about given me a heart attack. I saw your closet when I was at your house. Once was enough."

I'm going to wring his neck. "Gray—"

"Let it go, Delilah. Let's just try to make some peace while we're here. We can fight about it when we get back to the city."

He doesn't wait for me to respond before continuing the tour, but I won't be brushed aside that easily. Although the prospect of peace is inviting.

I glance at Gray, and then out the bay window—the one with the padded cushion on the seat, where I imagine nothing better in life than curling up with a cup of hot tea to watch a storm roll in. I glance back at him, and sigh. We'll have the discussion, but maybe it can wait a few days.

"There's only one full bath in the house. I'll need to use this bathroom to shower, and my things are in that closet too. Otherwise, this space is yours while we're here."

It occurs to me, for the first time, that there's also only one bedroom in the house, and I don't remember seeing anything that looked like a pull-out sofa. Maybe in his office. Although I'm not even sure rich people have such things in their homes. I catch myself chewing on the corner of my thumb, a habit I thought I broke years ago. *One bed.* "Where are you sleeping?"

"Downstairs."

Downstairs. I feel a twinge of disappointment. *Why? So you could argue with him when he said he was sharing the bed with you?* I don't know what I expected. Or what I want, for that matter.

"You can work here, or you're welcome to use the kitchen table."

I'm not interested in the kitchen. But the window seat or the porch? That's a big *yes*. "I'd like to work on the porch, if that's not a problem."

"There's no table or desk in there."

"I don't need one. It's such a treat to be at the beach—in this house." *With you.* I don't say the last part, because even if I was sure of those feelings, which I'm not, I would never take the risk. A heart is a fragile thing. It can only withstand a certain amount of punishment before it stops working altogether. Mine doesn't have much life left in it. I need to be careful.

"I'd love to hear the surf while I work," I admit. "I'm perfectly comfortable on the floor."

"Whatever you want." He pauses at the staircase, and when he looks at me, it seems like there's something more he wants to say. I feel it. But then he blinks a few times, and we're back to the mundane. "I have a secure laptop for you to use, and a few other things I want to give you. We're here to work," he grumbles under his breath. "Don't forget that."

I nod, but I'm not sure if he was talking to me, or to himself.

When we get downstairs, Gray's all business. He goes into the office and returns with a laptop, a fat binder, and some office supplies. "Here's the briefing book. It will fill in a lot of holes. By the time you're finished, we'll be ready for supper, and I'll answer the hundreds of questions you'll have while we eat." He hands me a manila envelope. "Fill this out, too."

"What is it?"

"It's the form we use at the club to match people who have similar interests."

I pull out the paperwork. I've never seen this particular form, but I've seen one like it. Kinksters fill them out at sex clubs before they play. It can also be used as the basis for a contract in a power exchange dynamic. Kyle and I never had a contract, but I've learned a lot about them since he died.

"Are you familiar with this type of questionnaire?"

I glance at the first page, not really seeing any of the individual words, and nod.

"What I want you to do is use the red, yellow, green system. Mark the color next to each one and then tell me if you've done it with a yes or no. Then tell me why you've marked it red or yellow—don't bother about green. I don't need a treatise. A few words should suffice. Ordinarily we'd create our own negotiated terms, but this isn't…fun and games," he says, haltingly. "It's a job for both of us."

Gray hesitates for a few seconds and his brow furrows before he speaks again. "I can't promise that I'll be able to respect all your terms," he pauses, to run his tongue over his bottom lip, "but I'll make every effort. You have my word."

I take a deep breath to right myself. This goes against everything I now know about power exchanges and consensual play

—but this isn't play. *Still.* "If you can't agree to respect my limits, then why am I bothering to fill this out?"

"Because I don't want this to be more difficult on you than it needs to be. I'll do my damnedest to stay within the boundaries you set." His voice is raw, and his eyes ripe with concern. "And if it can't be helped, I'll attempt to mitigate where I can."

He's lost some of the color in his cheeks. *What have I gotten myself into?* "Gray, what's this about? What *exactly* is expected of me?"

"It will all make more sense after you read the briefing book. When you're through, we'll talk."

I hold up the questionnaire, and wave it in the air. "Will I be getting one of these from you?"

"If you'd like." He turns toward the doorway.

"I'd like. I want to have some understanding of your boundaries, too." At least I think I do.

He nods. "I'll be in my office if you need anything."

I need a lot of things. *So many things.* Answers, chief among them. *I guess that's where you come in,* I say to the briefing book. *Just don't tell me a bunch of shit that's going to give me heartburn—or nightmares.*

13

GRAY

I find Delilah out on the porch, sitting cross-legged on the sisal rug, her back against a chair. "Crown Prince Ahmad bin Khalid," she says soberly. "What a monster."

I nod, and sit on the chair across from her. "Throughout history, the Amadis have proven themselves time and time again to be a brutal regime. But the crown prince makes his ancestors look like saints."

"Whoever prepared the briefing book did a great job. But I still have a ton of questions." She points to a yellow legal pad. "I made a list."

I expected nothing less. "Shoot."

"This doesn't seem like a CIA operation—not exactly. It feels more like something the CIA's Special Activities Center would be involved in."

Delilah's smart, and she understands the big players in the world of espionage. There's no sense in hiding my association from her. I had already decided that it would be a futile exercise. But let's see where she goes with this. "CIA's not involved at all."

"The Bureau," she says, keen eyes on me, watching for a tell. "The EAD."

Bingo. That was quicker than I expected. The Elite Activities Division is the FBI's equivalent of the CIA's Special Activities Center. Since the terrorist attacks of September 11, they mirror one another. While the CIA still operates only on foreign soil, *theoretically*, the FBI operates at home and abroad.

Both organizations have an elite paramilitary unit, and a covert political action unit. Delilah had her sights on the CIA's political action unit, and I'm a member of the FBI's political action unit. They are the government's two most secretive weapons to protect national security.

"I'm with the EAD, although no one at the Bureau would ever confirm that." It's a big admission, at least to me, but she takes it in stride.

"You're with the FBI," she says, carefully. "Kyle was with the Bureau. Did you know him?"

She chews on her bottom lip, maybe hoping I'll tell her something. It's only natural that she'd want more information about Kyle's work—about his death. I wish there was something to tell her. Something good, like he was a hero or a stand-up guy. But I've got nothing like that. The truth would only cause her pain, and I'm not going there.

"It's a big agency. I don't know everyone." It's not technically a lie, more of a duck and cover. But I promised her I wouldn't lie, and my conscience is twitching. "I just told you I was with the EAD and that's all you've got to say?"

"I'm still coming to terms with it. But since the night you followed me, I've known you were some sort of agent. It couldn't have gone down like it did otherwise." Delilah studies me for a few seconds. "You shot Virginia Bennett?" she asks, her eyes trained on me.

I have nothing to lose at this point from admitting to a fact that's on record—buried to the hilt, but still on record somewhere. "I did."

"Why?"

"Because Smith was being a stupid bastard, taking risks he shouldn't have been taking, and if I hadn't, you were going to take the shot."

"So you took it for me?"

She's fuming.

"I wanted you for this mission. That would have put an unnecessary spotlight on you." *And I wanted to protect you from any more scandal.* I leave that part out. "Let's forget about the clusterfuck at the church, and focus on this one. I need your head here."

"Why did you follow me? And threaten me? Instead of just straight up asking if I wanted to be part of this? You knew all along I would say yes." She shakes her head. "I don't get it."

"I believed you were perfect for this from the beginning. But I wanted some assurances." *I needed to prove to myself that you were up to the job and that it wasn't just my dick making decisions.*

"I needed to see how you'd react under pressure, when cornered without any moves. That's the real crux of this work, right?" She nods, but I'm not sure I've convinced her. "Anybody can pretend anything when the stakes are low and the wolves are at bay. What matters is how you react when your life's on the line and the bastards are nipping at your ankles. That's what separates the boys from the men. Or in your case, the girls from the women."

She gathers her hair and pulls it back into a ponytail, taking a purple band off her wrist to secure it. She's buying time, wondering if she should let it go and move on, or if she needs more from me. "You've been on this case for more than a decade?" she asks, still playing with her hair.

"It hasn't been the only thing I've worked on, but yes. I infiltrated the Amadi royal family while I was in college."

"So I'm going to be your—woman."

"You make it sound so distasteful."

She tips her head to the side, and there's a small pull at the corners of her mouth, but it never becomes a real smile. "And my job is to get a message to the crown prince's sister, Princess Saher bint Khalid, without tipping anyone off. The message is to beg her father, again, to let her go to London with her son to visit her dying aunt. She's to insist on taking her son."

"In a nutshell. But getting her alone to pass the message is going to be difficult. There is surveillance everywhere in the palace. She's closely watched, and you will be too. If you're caught, it will mean prison for you—for all of us, probably—and death for her." The ramifications are sobering as I lay them out.

Delilah nods, appropriately pensive. The stakes are enormous. "I know what I read, but what I still don't understand is, if her father's the king, why can't he orchestrate this himself? Why does he need the United States government to intervene?"

She looks young and innocent with her hair pulled off her face. And beautiful—no hairstyle can change that about her, but she's also savvy. "It's complicated, and so far out of our realm that you'll probably never understand it. You just need to trust the intelligence. He can't have the discussion with her without causing turmoil in the country. Maybe a civil war."

"A civil war?" She wrinkles her nose. "Now I'm more confused."

I've been immersed in this for so many years that the peculiarities of the relationships are second nature to me. But I need to distill this into something she can wrap her head around. "The king is old and ill. The crown prince has taken over most of his father's royal duties. He essentially oversees the day-to-day operations of the country. Many of the people who were once loyal to the king are now loyal to the crown prince. Everybody understands the king's days are numbered, and they know where their bread is buttered. It's unclear who the king can trust."

"This still doesn't make sense to me." She hugs her knees to her chest and rests her chin between the peaks. "We're talking about the US government getting involved in a scheme to move an Amadi princess and her son to London as a favor to a king who has one foot in the grave? There's got to be more to it than that."

That's for damn sure. "There is. But your level of clearance doesn't allow for you to know any more than what I've already told you."

She stares at her wiggling toes, weighing the risks. It's dicey to get involved in a mission you don't fully understand. But that's the way it is when you work for the government. Only the president and a few top aides have the whole picture. Delilah knows this, but I'm sure she hates that I know more than she does.

"If it makes you feel any better," I assure her, "I don't know everything either. But you're on the right track. The government wouldn't get involved unless it was beneficial to our own national security interests."

She nods, and I see the wheels turning. "If this is classified information that requires a clearance, why are we discussing it here?"

"I'm glad you asked. This place has been cleared." While Delilah skims the list of questions she prepared, I get up. "I'll be back in a minute."

I retrieve a deck of cards from my office that I use to keep my focus laser sharp, even when I don't know all the answers. When I get back to the porch, I move the coffee table out of the way, and lay out the cards carefully on the rug. One at a time.

Making the same promise to each individual face: *The bastard will pay.*

"What's all this?" she asks.

I don't answer until I'm finished. When the last card is faceup, I pull Delilah to her feet.

"One hundred and eighty-one American passengers from the crash outside of Houston. Two *New York Times* journalists dismembered. Seventeen teenage girls, three of whom were from right here in South Carolina. These are just the Americans. There are countless others, faceless and nameless.

"All dead. The innocent victims of Crown Prince Ahmad bin Khalid."

Delilah's mouth is open. A hand clutches her chest. She's speechless. This information was in the briefing book, but once you put a face to a number, everything changes.

"I try not to let myself get caught up in the bigger picture," I explain quietly. "In the things I don't know. This mission is for them."

After giving her a few minutes to meet each face, I pick up the cards reverently, one at a time, and hand them to her. We don't talk until I'm seated again.

"Do you have any pressing concerns before we break for supper?" I ask, hoping to pull her outside of her head.

She lowers herself onto the rug, avoiding the area where the cards had been, as though not to desecrate a holy burial ground. "This," Delilah says, lifting the deck of cards, "gives me everything I need. But there is one thing I'm worried about."

"Just one?"

She taps an index finger against her lips nervously. "If you recall, I was dragged into a public scandal while at the agency. The reason I left covert work was because my face is recognizable—maybe not to the average person, but to anyone who knows, or bothers to look. All you need to do is a simple Google search."

I nod. "That's why we're doing this out in the open. We're not giving you an alias or pretending you're someone other than who you are."

"And you think that's going to fly?" She eyes me skeptically.

"I do." I lean back in the chair. "There are things about you that will make it easy to believe we're involved. Even to someone like the crown prince, who has spent a lot of time with me over the years."

She swallows hard. "What things?"

"Your face. Your history with kink. And you're sexy as fuck."

"Well, my brain and my winning personality have never been my best assets." Her forehead puckers, as the insecurity rises to the surface.

"They are to me," I say decisively.

She glances up, a bit startled, as though she didn't mean to say it out loud, or maybe she's surprised by my response.

"I need your brain and your professional skills for this mission. The pretty face and luscious curves are a distraction to keep *others* off guard." *I just can't allow them to become a distraction to me.* "As for the winning personality, I don't know a thing about that."

She reaches over and swats me with the questionnaire, before tossing it in my lap. "If I had filled it out prior to reading the briefing, it would have looked different. But this is clearly a matter of national security, and I'm willing to push myself beyond my ordinary boundaries."

I feel her stare while I study the form.

"There are things I would have never green-lighted under any other circumstances," she adds.

I skim the rest, before glancing at her. "You like pain." I know she does, but I want to hear it from her mouth.

She draws a breath, and nods.

"Do you need it?"

"Is that somehow germane to the mission?"

"Not really." I read through her responses again, and stop at a question she red-lighted. My stomach twists as I prepare to break the bad news.

"I can't promise that you won't be used by more than one man at a time." She lowers her eyes, so that I can't see the result of the blow I just delivered. "I *can* promise that I will do everything in my power to prevent that from happening." *To save you from that. To save myself from that.* "But these are bad men. And we both know that even the best-laid plans can go awry."

"You don't need to coddle me," she says indignantly. "I understand the perils."

That might be true, but understanding is different than experiencing. I don't say it, because I don't want to make her any more anxious than necessary.

"The one thing I am sure about is that you'll be watched constantly. We'll be watched. Nothing we say or do will be private. *Nothing.* I can't protect you from that."

Delilah red-lighted exhibitionism on the questionnaire. She's okay with voyeurism, but she doesn't want to be watched having sex. I don't want anyone watching me fuck her either, but there's no goddamn choice.

She pulls her knees back into her chest, hugging them tight. "I can put up with anything for the sake of a mission. I might not be the most experienced operative, but I'm not a coward. And I'm a good team member—I'll more than pull my weight. I understand there will be things that I don't like."

My insides burn with regret. *She needs this*, I remind myself. *Regardless of how uncomfortable it makes you,* she *needs it.* "I need you to do more than understand. I need you to come to terms with it."

"I'm a professional," she snaps, glaring at me, but I see the concern in her face.

Society shames women into using their bodies sparingly—and only—for love. It's such a crock of shit. But regardless of how modern a woman is, how comfortable she is with her sexuality, or in this case, how professional she might be, asking any woman to use sex as a prop is a big ask. It is for some men, too.

"You're a highly skilled professional. That's why I chose you to be part of the team. But you've never done anything like this before. You'll be on display, like an animal at the zoo. It can be unnerving, even for an experienced operative."

"Nice analogy." She squints at me. "I thought I was getting your form?"

I watch her for several seconds. She's avoiding the discussion because she knows the complete lack of privacy is going to be hard. I hand her my form, but we will revisit this.

"It's blank." She looks up at me. "Really? You made me write down all my stuff, but you didn't want to share yours?"

"It's not blank—it's all green—read the sentence before my signature."

She scans the form, fixated on the last few sentences. "You're open to anything?"

I nod. "I make mistakes and I'm not a mind reader. But I understand how to train a submissive, and what it means to be a Dominant. A submissive's needs come first—*always*. Not her wants, but her needs. I'm willing to set aside my own needs and wants to fulfill that promise." *Especially for you.*

She's quiet, wetting her lips, while she wraps her head around what I just said. It's unclear how much experience she's had with power exchange relationships since Kyle. But Kyle was an abusive asshole who groomed her for pain to fulfill his own sadistic needs. Then bragged about it. He met her when she was seventeen and vulnerable. He was patient, gaslighting and manipulating her up until he took his last breath. He ruined her. I'm not a saint, but I'm not the devil either.

She still hasn't said a word, but she's guarded, looking at me like I have two heads.

"Why don't you go up and shower? I'll throw a couple steaks on the grill."

Delilah gets up, still without saying anything. She makes it as far as the doorway. "Yes."

Yes, what? I don't have a damn clue.

"I need pain." She hesitates. "It grounds me. And I almost always need it—you know—for sex to be satisfying." She hasn't turned to look at me. I might not be able to read her expression, but her body is rigid.

"Almost?" I ask softly. "Tell me what you mean."

She clutches the doorframe as if to steady herself. "The night we were together—I don't know. There was some pain, but not as much as I normally need to find release. Maybe it's because it had been so long since—since I had that kind of sex. You know—with another person. It was intense enough for me to—I need pain. Physical pain. Not emotional pain. I don't need, or like, humiliation—but I'll put up with it for the mission, if I need to. Just don't expect me to like it."

She just gave me a lot. My jaw is on the ground. I want to say something to acknowledge her courage and forthrightness, but I don't have the words. "We'll talk more over supper."

When she starts to walk away, it hits me that her honesty is a double-edged sword. As much as I crave her openness, I can't let the waters get too muddy. Not for either of us.

"Delilah."

She turns from the landing, and her slumped shoulders almost prevent me from saying what I need to say. But I can't be swayed by soft feelings or we'll all end up dead. "I appreciate your candor. More than I can express. Thank you for trusting me." I pause, to let her absorb the praise, because I mean it. I'm grateful and humbled by her honesty. But it's not that simple. "The paperwork you filled out is a guide. You're not my submissive. This is a mission. It's going to be hard at times, but you've got to keep the roles straight." My voice is sterner than I mean it to be, but she doesn't flinch.

"I'm a big girl. Don't you worry about me."

I watch her jog up the stairs until she disappears.

Now, if *I* can just keep the roles straight, we'll be good. Although it's starting to feel like it's going to take a goddamn miracle to keep things separated.

She's tempting. And everything about her calls to my worst impulses.

14

GRAY

While Delilah's showering, I pull the steaks out of the refrigerator and light the grill. Once the charcoal catches, I call Mel. Master Sergeant Melvin Walker, the man who taught me how to be a man.

The lessons weren't always easy to learn, and I'm sure they weren't easy to teach, either. I was hard-headed back then, in the way that boys are when they lack confidence down deep. Mel had little patience for it. He put me through basic and advanced training—the EAD's version, which is even more challenging than the military's—and kicked my ass until I had every lesson down pat.

He answers on the third ring. "Walker here."

"Hey, Sarge."

"Hay is for horses, didn't your mama teach you that?"

"I was probably napping during the lesson."

He chuckles. "What's good, boy?"

I check the coals and walk off the patio, onto the sand. "Same shit, different day. No complaints. How about you?"

"Can't complain, either. I've got food in the pantry, a roof over my head, and a beautiful woman who warms my bed every night and tolerates most of my nonsense with good humor. Can't ask for more than that. What can I do for you, son?"

"I have a favor to ask."

"Ask away. My supper's gettin' cold."

I reach down to turn over a shell. It's empty. "I need a yoga instructor."

After he left the military, I convinced Mel to move to Charleston and helped him start a fitness business. He's raking in the money hand over fist now. I might have given him a leg up in the beginning, but his success belongs all to him and his no-nonsense approach to life.

"Is this someone for your personal enjoyment, or you looking for a good stretch and to get your mind right? Because I don't run a dating service."

I smile. He's just what Delilah needs. "It's not for me," I say with some hesitation. "There's a woman—"

Mel groans. "Nothin' good ever started with *there's a woman*."

"Before you say anything, it's not what you think."

"'Course not," he mutters.

"She's a former CIA agent. Kyle Reade's widow. Did you know him?"

"Knew of him, but I can't say that I ever had the pleasure."

"You didn't miss anything. Although he could have used your foot up his ass. Anyway, she's smart, tough as nails, and wields a weapon like nobody's business. Physically, she's strong, lots of lean muscle, and limber—although not as flexible as she thinks she is. But she needs some grounding. A place to turn when the boogieman comes knocking. Right now, she runs, longer and harder than she should. But it doesn't seem to be working anymore, and she's spinning out of control."

"And you're thinking she can find that place inside of

herself." He says it more as an observation than a question, but I answer anyway.

"I'm not sure. That's what we're going to figure out."

"I'm guessing you've already tried a different kind of pain."

"No," I say defensively, grinding my heel into the sand. "She needs to move away from pain as her sole source of comfort."

"Did she say that, or is that your opinion?"

"She has an intimate relationship with pain, Mel. She was groomed to need it."

Mel is a Dominant. A real Dominant, not some bullshit poser who takes advantage of vulnerable women to get laid.

"I don't think she knows how to find comfort elsewhere."

"I see. Like someone else I used to know."

He's referring to me. When I met Mel, I acted out solely for the punishment it would get me. The more it hurt, the better it made me feel, and the more I grew to like it. It's a circular pattern, not uncommon. But I wasn't groomed for it, like Delilah. I just needed guidance. "Not exactly. Although there might be similarities."

"You want—"

"To expand her horizons."

"Okay," he says matter-of-factly. "I assume the yoga instruction will take place in the studio at the club? We are still talking about yoga here, right?"

"My apartment at Wildflower to start." We'd have to drag her kicking and screaming to the studio. I keep that tidbit to myself. "Day after tomorrow, at 5:30 a.m. And yes, yoga."

"That's awfully early. Let me see who I can find."

"No, Mel. She needs you." *Like I needed you.*

"You expect me to leave my lady before the light peeks through the blinds to teach yoga to some woman you've decided needs to be gentler with herself?" He didn't say, *you're crazy, boy*. But it was implied.

"I wouldn't ask if it wasn't important."

"I know you wouldn't," he says, low and gruff. "I don't like how you're thinking about this, Gray. You can lead a horse to water, but you can't make them drink. Ever hear that before?"

"I'm familiar with the sentiment. Look, she's working with me on an important op, and needs to be mission ready in two weeks. A lot's riding on it. And I don't trust anyone else but you to handle her. You'll know what she needs."

"Son?"

"Sergeant?"

"You're asking for trouble. You stay clear of subs who crave pain for a reason. The urge to cross that line and give her what you know she's hankering for is too tempting. It's a fine line, easy to cross, but it won't serve either of you well if you do."

"I never said she was a submissive," I say with a defensive tone that even I don't miss.

Mel clears his throat. I suspect his patience with me is getting thin. "I've been holding the leash for a long time. I don't require your input in identifying a submissive."

"You meet her first, before you draw any conclusions. But regardless, it's not important. I'm not training a sub, Mel. And I'm well aware of the perils." *Only half of which you know.* "It's all under control."

"Sounds like bullshit to me, but if you say so. This woman got a name?"

"Delilah."

"*Delilah.* I suggest you dust off your Bible, and become acquainted with a different man who got involved with a woman named Delilah. You might learn a thing or two from his mishap."

"It's more likely she'd take my balls than my hair."

He snorts. "Sounds to me like she's already done that."

I go back toward the house to see if the grill's hot enough. "Speaking of which. Send my love to Violet. Tell her there's always a spare room at my place when she gets tired of your shit."

I end the call, and slide my phone into my back pocket as Delilah steps onto the patio. She's barefoot, golden hair fanning her slender shoulders, wearing a sundress that skims her thighs with straps so thin that a bra is out of the question. *Damn Trippi.* What the hell was he thinking, packing that little number? He either wanted to kill me or make my night special. Either way, I'd like to beat his ass.

It's all under control. What a crock of shit.

"That shower is something else," she says with a relaxed smile. "I felt like I was in a cave or a lagoon—showering in nature. I was half-expecting a squirrel or some other woodland creature to scurry across the stone."

I smile now, too. "It's a grotto shower. That's how it's supposed to make you feel. It's got a lot of bells and whistles. I should have shown you how it works."

"Was it here when you bought the house?"

"No." I shake my head. "Gil and Jolie planned it. They're the same people who designed the playrooms at Wildflower."

"Explains the fantasy element," she says, approaching the grill.

Delilah must have found the toiletries. There's a faint smell of orange surrounding her, not a cloying scent, but something very grown-up.

"Need me to do something?" she asks, catching my eye.

You have no idea. If you did, you wouldn't ask.

15

DELILAH

While we ate, the sun set over the ocean, painting the sky in swirls of oranges and reds that melted into darkness. Unlike in the city, millions of stars keep the moon company here.

Gray and I talked over supper like we sometimes did at the club after closing, when everyone else had gone home. We brainstormed about the mission a bit, but mostly we chatted about movies and music and food. Topics that are easy on the heart.

We've about finished a second bottle of wine, and I'm in the languid mood of a lazy house cat after a good meal. Gray is relaxed too. I've seen his smile more than a few times tonight. The *real* smile that makes his eyes twinkle, not that phony thing he pastes on for the world.

"Your brothers must love this place. Gabby too."

He scratches the back of his head. "My brothers came out after I first bought it, but they haven't been back since. Gabby's never been here."

"Really?"

"No one—besides you—has been out here since the renovation."

"Really?" I ask again, because I'm flabbergasted, and don't know what else to say. Gray is close to his brothers. He might keep his association with the EAD a secret from them, but that's a non-negotiable aspect of the job.

"It's a gorgeous spot, but I keep it to myself. It's selfish, I suppose." He leans back in the chair and stretches out his legs. His ankle brushes mine. He doesn't seem to notice, but I can't stop thinking about it. "I come out when I need a break from my life. It's uncomplicated here, and being by the ocean soothes me."

But you brought me here. You welcomed me into your oasis. I sit quietly with the knowledge, even though it's heavy. Although I have no idea what it means. *If anything.*

"I brought you here to regroup," he explains, as though he needs to. Sometimes I think the man reads my mind. "We both needed the break. A fresh start with a new focus." He pulls his legs back, and I immediately miss the warmth of his skin. "You up for dessert?"

I guess that's the end of that discussion. Just as well. I'm not in the mood for anything too serious. "What do you have?"

"Peach cobbler. The kitchen at Wildflower brought it over before we got here. There's cinnamon ice cream to go with it," Gray adds, as though I might need convincing.

I feel a grin spread across my face. The kind that makes your cheeks ache. It's my favorite summer dessert, and when it was on the menu, it was my go-to dinner at the club. Gray knows it, too. He gave me endless grief about it. "I wish I could, but I'm too stuffed to eat another bite. I'll have some for breakfast."

"Breakfast?" He raises his brow. "You might as well dip a spoon into the sugar bowl. What kind of breakfast is that?"

"A tasty one." I get up to clear the plates, and before I can blink, he's on his feet too, holding my wrists with a gentle, but firm grasp. There's a gleam in his eyes, and I feel a tug of desire that's not in line with a fresh start and a new focus. *Isn't that what he said earlier?*

"I'll take the dishes," he says. "I need to grab a couple of things from inside. Where's the hairband you had earlier?"

"On the nightstand in the bedroom. Why do—"

He interrupts before I finish. "While I'm gone, why don't you use the bathroom?"

"Gray." I say his name because I'm not sure what else to say —or even what he means. The wine and the emotion have hit at once and I'm a little lost.

He places a fingertip on my lips to shush me. "It's not what you think. I planned to start when we were back in the city, but the wait is too much. You're too tempting." He cups my cheek, weaving his strong fingers into my hair. "I need to touch you."

I need it too. More than I'll ever admit, even to myself.

His thumb grazes my bottom lip. I wait for him to lower his mouth to mine, but instead, he pulls away abruptly and begins to collect utensils from the table.

Unsettled, and more than just a tad confused, I wrap my arms around myself to ward off the uneasiness. "I don't need you, or anyone else to tell me when it's time to use the bathroom. I'm not a four-year-old."

"When I suggest you relieve yourself, it's not for my comfort." His glare is piercing. "Do it, or don't. I won't be standing outside the door listening for the tinkle. I also won't be the one living with the consequences of a full bladder."

I can't remember the last time I had a discussion that was so infuriating—*and embarrassing*. "Your seduction game needs work."

I see the corner of his mouth twitch when he turns to go inside. "I already told you it's not what you think."

After I regain my composure, I go inside, trying not to overthink *everything* while I use the bathroom. *It's not what you think.* Then what the hell is it?

I dawdle in the bathroom, because even though I'm aggravated with him, I want him to touch me, and I want to touch him too. After primping my hair in the mirror, I brush my teeth with my finger because my toothbrush is upstairs, but mostly I spend the time hoping that his plans are exactly what I'm thinking.

When I get back outside, Gray has changed into a pair of light sweatpants. Shirtless, he's covering the table where we had supper with fuzzy blankets, folded in half, and layered atop one another. I'm riveted by the muscles in his broad back, the way they contract, as he lays a snow-white sheet on top of the blankets, letting it drape over the sides of the table.

"What's all this?" I ask, still riveted by his hard body.

Gray smooths the sheet and rests his backside against the padded edge of the table, his hands on either side for support. He catches me steal a glance at the outline of his cock through the thin, stretchy fabric. He's not wearing underwear.

He doesn't say anything snarky. Instead, his eyes wander over me from head to toe without a single word. I tuck some hair behind my ear while he appraises me, like chattel he's interested in bidding on.

When he's through with my body, he finds my eyes. "Take off your clothes for me, Delilah."

His voice is cloaked in the warm, deliberate cadence of seduction. *Maybe his game doesn't need work.* It's so mesmerizing, I begin to reach for the bottom of my dress to pull it over my head. But common sense kicks in before my hands get anywhere near the hem. "You expect me to take off my clothes—out here?"

He tips his head to the side. "It's exactly what I expect."

"You said it's not what I think."

He shakes his head. "It's not."

"Then why do my clothes need to be off?"

"Because I asked you to undress, and you've agreed to trust me—even when it's hard." He's got a take-no-prisoners kind of attitude going on, and I brace myself for an earful. "You're not comfortable being naked in front of me, in a secluded area without another soul in sight, but you're prepared to have sex while who knows how many men are watching?"

The bastard is actually calling my bluff.

"If you can't do something this simple, then I don't see how you'll ever be mission ready in two weeks."

He aimed well, and struck a nerve. "This is manipulative bullshit."

"If that's what you think, go pack your things and I'll drop you off at your house tonight."

I don't move. Our eyes are locked in a pissing match that I'm clearly going to lose. I don't want to go home. *And it's not just about the op.*

While I'm trying to come up with a way to take my clothes off without seeming like I've given in to his whims, he gets up and cradles my face in his hands. His eyes never stray from mine. The heat between us is suffocating.

I can barely breathe, but I don't look away. Not when his fingertips glide down my cheeks, over my jaw, and past my throat. Not when they reach the neckline of my dress and rest impatiently at the top of my breasts. Not even when he tears the sundress down the middle, and the decorative buttons scatter as they bounce off the flagstone floor.

"I asked you to get undressed. But it was too hard for you." He pauses, his teeth scraping his bottom lip. "I'm here to help you when life's decisions become too hard." He's holding the tattered fabric in his clenched fists. "If you're partial to those panties, you'll have them off before I'm finished preparing the table." He opens his hands, letting the torn dress pool at my feet.

His show of strength leaves me breathless, and the tug of desire is powerful, and building as I remove my panties. I want him, but I'm not prepared to blindly hand over control. I will never again give my submission to a man who hasn't earned it. I made that mistake with Kyle. I won't make it with Gray. "What, exactly, is the plan?"

"Right now, I'm going to tie back your hair so that it stays out of the oil."

Oil. He didn't say lube. He said oil. Before I can question him, he takes my hair, handling it like this isn't the first time he's braided a woman's hair. The jealousy creeps up, but before it causes injury, Gray intervenes.

"On the table. This side up," he murmurs, squeezing my ass lightly.

"What's this about?"

"Pleasure," he says, and the word, with all its promise, vibrates between us. "You're going to do nothing but lie quietly while my hands work out some of the knots in your beautiful body."

"You're going to give me a massage?" *A massage? Now?* It's not at all what I expected and I'm off-kilter. But I suppose that was his intention.

"Lie down, Blue Eyes. I'm getting impatient."

I climb on the table and stretch out on the soft, cool sheet, resting my head in my folded arms. There's a light breeze over the ocean, and the surf has picked up, the white froth striking the shore before retreating. It's a good night to sleep with the windows open. It's all true and total nonsense, but it's what I think about to distract me from my nakedness.

"Close your eyes," he whispers, before bringing an unfamiliar scent to my nose. Something spicy, but subtle. "You okay with the smell of amber?"

I nod, opening my eyes slightly.

"It's just lightly scented oil. There's nothing in it that will hurt you."

I nod again, letting my eyelids flutter shut. I do trust him—at least with this.

"Clear your head," he commands in *that* bossy tone, "and just feel."

With long strokes, he glides his hands up and down my back, before settling into my shoulders. My body yields without struggle as he prods the tight muscles to relax. The surrender is sweet, with soft moans escaping from my lips as he works.

"Where did you learn how to give a massage? And how am I just finding out about it now?"

"I learned a long time ago. It's a nice way to reward good girls. You've had a rough few days. I thought you could use a little pampering."

I gasp when he starts on my lower back.

An electric current races through me as his fingers coax the muscles into submission. It feels amazing, but I still can't understand why there had to be so much secrecy about him giving me a massage. Had I known what he was planning, I would have gladly taken off my clothes.

"Why couldn't you just tell me, up front, that you wanted to rub my back? It would have saved us both some grief."

He applies more pressure, his fingers digging deeper into the flesh. "I lead the team. You need to follow my instructions, without hesitating, and without asking me to justify every order. This isn't a foreign concept. It's how every mission works. Right?"

I push the errant thoughts away. The ones that push and pull, messing with my brain and my body. And yes, my soul too. "Right," I somehow manage, as his hands knead with unremitting focus.

Once my mind begins to clear, my breathing slides into a

comfortable rhythm. I hear the waves crest and hit the shore, but they're starting to sound far, far away. I've drifted somewhere heavenly when Gray's hands move to my buttocks, manipulating the large muscles.

His touch is intimate, and I try to remain relaxed. But when the warm oil drips onto my lower back and slides between the cheeks, I shudder, squirming against the tabletop.

"You're tense again. Let go," he encourages, his fingers deft and skilled. "This isn't about sex. This is about you getting comfortable with my hands on your body. Instinctively knowing that they will only bring you pleasure—even in pain."

I sigh wistfully. There is nothing I crave more desperately than the delicious pain that brings pleasure. When he nudges my legs apart, there is no resistance. Lavishing one leg with attention, and then the other, he works the warm oil into my skin, his knuckles occasionally grazing my pussy. I wait in anticipation, longing for more of that kind of touch.

I'm no longer relaxed. All I can think about is my arousal, growing and growing, until it's bigger than I am. Until it's bigger than both of us. It's then, when I'm about to beg him to fuck me, that he slides two fingers into my aching pussy. A gasp twined with a grateful groan twists its way out into the salty air. Somewhere in my head, somewhere faraway, a little voice reminds me that this is a mission. But the surf and the unremitting bliss drown out the good counsel.

"Squeeze," he demands, and I do, eagerly obeying. I clench my walls around his fingers, hugging tight. "Release, and relax."

He keeps his fingers inside me, while the other hand massages the back of my neck. "Squeeze those walls around me," he instructs, again. "That's it. Feels good, doesn't it?"

"*Mmhm*," I whisper. It's as though his careful ministrations have zapped so much of my strength that even my voice is barely audible.

Without any warning, he pulls his fingers away. I whimper at the loss.

"Turn over," he says simply.

I roll onto my side, and then to my back without giving it any thought. It's as though, in my listless state, I've been programmed to follow his commands. In a sense, that's what all this is about—but right now, I don't care.

I lie quietly, looking up at him. His features are relaxed, and even in my dreaminess, I admire his maleness—maybe even more so in my fog.

He brushes a few strands of hair off my forehead with the back of his hand. It's a gentle caress. "Your skin is so soft, I can't get enough of it. But you are still much too tense. Let's see if I can fix it."

He begins with my feet, and when I'm purring, he moves to my calves and then higher and higher until my back arches off the table. "Keep still." He splays a hand on my belly, his thumb skirting my mound, and presses until my back is flat. "Close your eyes. This is about what you hear and smell, and above all, what you feel."

Gray slides his hands up my body, avoiding my breasts in a cruel tease. He rolls my arms and shoulders, finding the pressure points and excising the negative energy.

Ahhh! His warm mouth covers my nipple, sucking it into a hard, tight tip. When I whimper, he rests a heavy hand on my belly, holding me firmly in place while his mouth and tongue massage my breasts. My nipples ache from pleasure, but it's nothing compared to the throb between my legs. A throb I can easily remedy.

I let my hand find its way to my pussy. But in seconds, he snatches my wrist, wrenching it away from the hot, slick flesh. My desperate groan echoes.

"As tempting as it would be to watch you play with your

pussy until you come," he says in a lazy drawl, "that's not happening right now. Squeeze those inner muscles," he murmurs, "just like you did around my fingers." He lays his hand low on my belly, where he can feel the muscles quiver as they tense. "That's it. Do it again."

I'm so worked up. My nerve endings are screeching like banshees, and my core is wet and needy, wild with want, but the rest of my body is heavy and limp from the massage.

He stands over me, and brushes my cheek. "Let's get you up."

I don't want to get up. I want more. But I'm slightly woozy from the massage, and let him help me.

"Just sit for a minute. Let your legs dangle." He hands me some water. "Take it slow."

As I sip the water, I notice the tent in his pants. I reach for it—for him.

He grabs my wrist, before I hit my target. "Not tonight. I told you this wasn't about sex."

Even in my fog, I'm embarrassed for begging.

"Go up and take a quick shower," he says in a gruff, thick voice. "You'll sleep well tonight. Good night."

I pick up my torn dress and panties, balling them under my arm. "Good night." I turn in the doorway, glancing at the outline of his cock. The thin fabric is no match for what's awakened inside. He's as ready as I am. Why is he doing this? "I would sleep better if—you're clearly interested too."

"Not tonight, Delilah." His tone is final. I might get off, but he's not going to participate. "Don't make me say it again."

I take my clothes inside with as much dignity as I can muster. There's nothing that can cut a woman to the quick faster than being turned down after she asks for sex. At least I didn't beg. *Did I? Oh, God.* This is going to be one big mindfuck, as training for a covert mission always is. Only this will be worse. It already is.

After a long shower, I fall into bed. I think about giving myself the release I desperately want, but I'm not sure if there are cameras. I'm also not sure why I even care, although I don't want him to see me give myself an orgasm, after begging him for it. I do have some pride.

16

DELILAH

The burble of running water wakes me from a sound sleep. It's pitch-black in the room. I fumble for my phone—one thirty.

It takes me a minute to orient myself. *The beach.* I'm at the beach, in Gray Wilder's bed. I glance at the undisturbed side of the mattress. *Alone.*

Once my eyes adjust to the dark, I throw off the quilt, and follow the sound of water into the bathroom. I don't know why I go—*yes you do*. We have unfinished *business* from the patio—*business* that he started. Even after a nap, I still want the grand finale.

The light's dim, but the glow of the chandelier casts shadows on the ceiling. There's something enchanting about it, and I take a few seconds to admire how the light and the prisms play off one another.

When the splash of water beckons, I creep to the edge of the room and peek into the cave-like entrance to the shower.

I freeze there, with a silent gasp, my toes curling into the cold floor.

Gray is under a cascading waterfall. His legs apart, one

hand gripping a smooth stone jutting from the wall, the other gripping the rock-hard cock jutting from his body.

There's no door into the natural setting of the grotto shower. Nothing separating us.

He's at an angle, and I can't see him full on from here, but I can see plenty.

My eyes dart between his handsome face with its taut jaw, and the fist pumping his swollen cock. The breath gets caught in my chest as I watch his sculpted muscles clench—beauty and violence intertwined in each rough pull.

While he doesn't stop, his movements slow as though he senses someone watching. I continue to stand perfectly still, breathless. Only when his head pivots in my direction does my pulse take off. But even after he catches me, I don't shy away.

His eyes are ablaze when they meet mine, his hand still on his thick angry cock. I'm mesmerized by his stark arousal. His primitive need.

I don't want him to finish without me.

The possibility consumes me as I yank the nightshirt over my head like a madwoman, and step into the shower. The drive of arousal propels me forward, and I don't stop until I'm under the spray, inches from him.

His sure hands slide into my hair, splaying flat against my scalp while his mouth ravages mine, until we're both gasping for air. "You were spying on me. In my own house."

"I'm sorry."

"I don't think you are," he drawls.

It's a warning, and anyone with good sense would run.

I tip my head back and stare into his hooded eyes. "Punish me." It's a simple, yet potent invitation, each syllable enunciated carefully. Not a dare or a challenge, but a plea, and it's rewarded with a low growl.

"You'd like that, wouldn't you?" he demands, the words

raspy through the rushing water. "If I grabbed my belt and welted your ass?"

"Yes," I say without a moment's hesitation, or a drop of shame.

His cock jumps against my belly, prodding for an entry point. "You do need to learn a lesson."

"I do."

He steps away and presses some buttons inside an enclosed case. A glass door descends from the ceiling and seals the shower entrance. The main waterfall stops, and jets emerge from the stone, filling the cave with warm steam and a woodsy scent, like a lush forest after a good rain.

Gray stalks toward me, backing me into the wall. His eyes are wild, and I'm exhilarated by the primal energy filling the enclosure. *I want him.* I want the rough edges, and all the unyielding demands he'll make on my body. I want it all.

"Keep your hands on the stone," he commands, lifting my arms over my head and guiding them to the spot where he wants them to remain.

Before I can form a coherent thought, his mouth is on mine. He's ruthless and unapologetic as his tongue explores freely, leaving lingering traces of costly bourbon behind.

Every nerve ending is dancing on the surface, and even the warm droplets of water prickle when they land on my sensitive skin.

Gray palms my breasts without a whiff of gentleness. And his impatient cock nudges my flesh, as though it's already waited much too long. There's no pretense between us, only unfiltered lust.

I'm on overload. The steam has taken over the cave, with gurgling bursts fanning the stone. It's as though we've ventured into the canopy of an Amazon jungle, deep in the rain forest, enveloped by dense fog.

I *need* to touch him. But when I lower my arms, he captures them in one swoop and pins them securely above my head. "Please," I beg. I don't know what I want, or what I need. My senses are intoxicated and there's no clarity to be found.

I feel the brush of his fingers against my pussy, confirming what he already knows. "You're soaked, Delilah. You need it bad, don't you?" I nod, and he slides his cock across my wet flesh, again and again, rubbing the thick crown over the swollen nub. My legs quiver with each swipe. It's merciless—too much, yet not enough.

"You want me to fuck you?" he murmurs near my ear.

"Yes." I whimper.

"That's why you came into the shower, isn't it? Even after I told you no."

"Yes."

He turns me around, and pulls my hips well away from the stone. "Keep your hands flat on the wall to buttress yourself. This is going to be hard. Harder than you can imagine," he adds in a whisper, running his tongue along my spine. "I don't want your beautiful body scraped by the stone. Although a scrape or two might teach you a lasting lesson."

I want that lesson. God forgive me, but I want it.

He holds me steady, and notches at the opening of my cunt, pausing briefly before pushing inside. It's a long, brutal slide, and I groan at the invasion, but he doesn't stop. Instead, he ruts harder, and deeper, biting my neck and shoulders. *He's marking you*, a voice inside me cautions. But I'm so close, I don't give a damn.

Gray's panting, and bucking erratically. He's close too, with his cock hot and hard inside me, nudging me closer to the edge, then wrenching me back.

I'm struggling to keep my face away from the stone, while I chase my own orgasm. It coils tighter and tighter with each thrust. Just as I give in to a few scratches for the pleasure, I hear the roar of his release.

His body trembles against mine as he ruthlessly pounds out every drop of seed. It takes all my energy to brace myself so that I'm not ground into the unforgiving stone.

After a final brutal thrust, he pulls out and lets go of my hips. I reach to drag him back as the semen runs down my inner thigh. For a split-second I panic. *I'm on birth control. I decided no condoms. I put it on the form.*

I'm so unsteady without him, that I almost collapse, limp on the floor.

"You still need to come, Delilah, don't you?" He's towering over me. His upper lip curls cruelly. "How bad do you need it?"

Enough to beg as much as necessary. "Please," I plead, not grasping that his words are merely a taunt. But when he walks away, it hits me. "That's it?" I pant. "It was just for you?"

He presses a few buttons and the steam begins to dissipate before the door slowly rises. His back is to me. He doesn't have the courage, or even the minimal respect, to face me. "You can use your fingers to get off, or hump anything in the room that suits you. Next time when I say no sex, you'll listen. Consider it merciful that I'm not binding you to the bed with your legs spread so that you'll have nothing but an ache to keep you company tonight. When I say *no*, that's what I mean."

Some people are fueled by anger. It ignites a fuse that launches them into action. I'm one of those people. But here and now, naked and spurned, that fury has a heightened dimension. And I wouldn't be at all surprised to see fire coming out of my mouth as I fight to breathe.

I pull myself up straight, with my back supported by the wall. My insides are shaking, but I will not be silenced by this arrogant sonofabitch. "I might be forced to my knees before this is all over," I shout from the safety of the shower wall, "but I will *never* kneel for you. I will *never* go to that calm head space that kneeling provides. I will *never* get on my knees as a sign of respect for you. Yes, I might kneel, but it will be *nothing* more than a charade." My heart is beating so hard, I'm certain he would see it if he bothered to turn around. But he's done with me.

The door continues its maddeningly slow ascension. It's such a contrast from the energy ricocheting inside me.

"If you think the voices inside your head are important to me, then you're a foolish little girl," he says over one shoulder, without turning his head enough to glance at me. "I don't care about your intent. And I don't give a damn if you respect me, as long as your throat can handle my cock."

He ducks under the door, and I pause to catch my breath. By the time I get to the bedroom, he's gone.

17
GRAY

Damn woman. We haven't even officially started preparing for the mission, and I'm already regretting reading her in. I knew the risk, but I was confident I could put firm boundaries in place.

So much for that.

The sun's peeking over the horizon, as I grind fresh coffee beans, trying not to make too much noise. Just because I can't sleep doesn't mean she shouldn't. Although, after the meltdown last night, I doubt she slept much either.

Sex wasn't supposed to be on the table—not yet. I took it off so it wouldn't weigh on her—so that she could relax for a couple of days without the elephant in the room. The problem is, whenever we're together, the goddamn elephant's always in the room, trumpeting loudly in shiny, bright colors neither of us can ignore.

No more excuses. I fucked up last night. *Big time.* Plain and simple.

I hear her on the stairs, and before I can figure out what to say to her, she's in the kitchen, dressed for a run. "Good morning," I say cautiously. It seems like a reasonable place to start.

"Mornin'. I thought you'd be out by now—jumpin' in the waves or whatever it is you like to do."

"I decided to run this morning. I waited for you."

"I run alone," she tosses over her shoulder on the way out the door.

"Not today." I'm not giving her a chance to work this out alone with a punishing run. She can pound the ground, but I'll be alongside her.

"Don't expect chitchat," she huffs.

It's impossible to explain the effect her spurious contempt and sass have on me. It's not how I normally interact with women. I don't even like it—unless it's from her. Unless it's her smart mouth telling me to go fuck myself, in that Mississippi drawl that I feel deep in my balls every time I hear it.

We hit the sand at the same time. "You didn't expect there to be consequences when you interrupted my shower? Even after I had made it clear there would be no sex."

"I expected—"

"Me to slap your ass and give you a nice big orgasm. Is that how it worked in your relationship with Kyle?" Douchebag move. The very second I say it, I regret it.

"The relationship I had with my husband is out of bounds. It's a hard limit. So if you need me to stroke your ego and tell you how much better you are than any other lover I've ever had, or that your dick is bigger, then you'll be disappointed. Because it would be a lie—and even if it weren't, I would never sully any past relationship with the likes of you."

Just because I deserve being notched a few pegs below an abusive asshole doesn't make it sting less.

Delilah lengthens her stride and takes off ahead of me. I let her go, staying just a few steps behind. She pushes harder and harder as we run up the beach. I'm in excellent shape, but I'm struggling to keep pace. This needs to end. *Now.*

I pick up my stride and grab her arm, forcing her to stop.

"Let go of me," she cries, trying to shake her arm free.

But I don't let go. "If you want to finish the run, you need to talk to me first. Say what's on your mind. Go ahead."

"You're an asshole."

"That's a start. Now tell me why."

"There aren't enough hours left in my lifetime for me to fully answer that."

I squeeze her arm tighter. "You have a voice. You'll always have a voice with me."

"Like last night, you mean? Or this morning when I told you I run alone?"

"I said you have a voice. I didn't say you'll always get what you want. I need to hear your words," I say softly. "I care about how you feel. And if you don't talk to me, it will be hard to meet your needs."

She lowers her eyes, and some of the pent-up energy dissipates. I drop her arm, but not before rubbing the spot where I clutched it.

"I'm confused, Gray. I like the waters clear. It's how I work best. This—between us—it's murky. I don't navigate murky very well."

"I can navigate for both of us, but you need to let me."

She doesn't say anything.

"I fucked up last night. I should have sent you back to bed when you came into the shower. That's what you needed—what the moment required—consistent, firm boundaries that we could both respect." She gazes up at me. The anger is mostly gone but the pain from last night is all over her face. "But I wanted you. More than I've ever wanted anything. And I acted without self-control or discipline."

As much as I want to look away, I force myself to stare into her sad face. To memorize every furrow and line. To commit the lifeless color in her eyes to memory. I want the vulnerability that's surrounding her to be tattooed on my brain. All of it. So that the next time I'm tempted to be reckless, it'll all come flooding back. "I should have never let it happen."

She regards me quietly, her chest rising and falling. I expect her to say something. I *want* her to say something. But instead, she reaches for my hand, squeezes my fingers in a quick, easy move, and takes off running down the beach.

"I suppose that's how rich boys from Charleston apologize," she calls over her shoulder. "Apology accepted." The last part is carried by the wind, but it reaches me. Her grace is not lost on me either.

She's much too quick to forgive an asshole. But I'll take the peace...*while it lasts.*

WHEN WE GET BACK to the house, I hand Delilah a water and pour some coffee. I keep half an eye on her while I scroll through a barrage of messages.

While these moments seem insignificant, the routine interactions are vitally important. It's the way a trained eye will assess our relationship. Even strangers can play kissy games. It's the other stuff, the small stuff, that's the real test of whether a relationship is authentic or bullshit. That's why we're spending the next two weeks together, day and night. It should be enough time for us to fall into a comfortable rhythm.

After Delilah finishes her water, she goes to the refrigerator and pulls out the cobbler we didn't eat last night. "I'm going to warm this. Do you want some?"

I shake my head. "I'm all set." She spoons a generous portion into a glass bowl and shoves it into the microwave. Chef Renaud at Wildflower would have a heart attack if he knew she was microwaving his precious cobbler. "You're really going to have that for breakfast? There's yogurt, eggs, and some fresh fruit."

"I like something sweet in the morning. I usually have a Pop-Tart."

"A Pop-Tart?"

"Yeah. You know, the toaster pastries."

"The breakfast of champions."

She whacks me on the arm playfully. "Don't be a snob. We can't all enjoy foie gras on toast points. Not enough ducks and geese in the world for that." She grimaces, sticking out her tongue. "I like strawberry Pop-Tarts with icing and rainbow sugar crystals. If I'm going to stay at your place, you better put it on the shopping list."

Delilah takes the ice cream out of the freezer and puts a scoop on the warm cobbler. She glances my way and catches me watching her.

"You want a taste, don't you?" she teases, taking a bite. "Oh. My. God. This is *so* good."

I'm sure it's tasty, but mainly she's putting on a show for my benefit. "You have the eating habits of a teenage boy."

"I get a ton of exercise. Besides, if I would rather eat cobbler and tacos than have a flat stomach, that's none of your damn business. I didn't hear you complaining about my body when you were using it last night." She turns toward the stairs.

"Where are you going?"

"To take a shower."

"No food upstairs."

"What?"

"No food upstairs, here, or in the bedroom at Wildflower. It's a non-negotiable rule. Finish your dessert. I'll shower first and leave you to enjoy some quiet time, unless you want to join me."

She stares at me, not as though she's contemplating the shower, but like she wants to smash the cobbler in my face but doesn't want to waste any of it. "I'm good. But you go, and take care of yourself, darlin'." Her voice has more sugar in it than her breakfast. She flashes me a sweet little smile before taking another bite.

I should just go upstairs, but she needs to hear this before we get back to the city. "That voice I said that you have, it's to be used privately. Say what you want when we're alone, but if you question me publicly, especially while we're in Amidane, or undermine me with your sarcasm, or in any other way, you won't like the consequences."

Her eyes are wide, but she doesn't say anything. Although it's apparent from her expression that the small truce we forged on the beach is on shaky ground. It was fragile, anyway.

"There's one more briefing book for you to study before we leave. I'll leave it on the porch." I know she's pissed, but my job isn't to make her happy. My job is to get her mission ready. To give her the tools she needs to be successful. Happiness will follow.

18

DELILAH

When we arrived at the apartment, Gray went directly downstairs to the club after instructing me to order dinner and make myself at home.

He sent me up a slice of cheesecake, but once it was gone, I was still alone.

It's after midnight when he comes upstairs. I'm already in my pajamas, rereading the section of the briefing book on Princess Saher, and wondering how I'm going to make nice with her.

I'm well-trained, but I've had little practice with this kind of mission. Sure, I can subdue a suspect and force them to talk. I have all sorts of tried-and-true methods for that. And I'm not afraid to maim or kill. Archbishop Darden can attest to that from the fires of Hell. But I left the CIA with little field experience in high-stakes spy games. Maybe because I'm exhausted, but right now the possibility of an Amadi princess befriending me seems highly unlikely.

"Sorry," Gray says somewhat sheepishly, when he comes into the living room. "I hadn't planned on being so late tonight. Did you eat?"

"I did. And I would be asleep right now, but I wasn't sure if it was okay to get comfy in the room at the end of the hall. I didn't want to break any *non-negotiable* rules."

"You'll sleep in my bed—our bed, for now. We need to get comfortable with the sleeping arrangements." He glances at me from the corner of his eye. "But we can start tomorrow if that suits you better."

Honestly, I'm not sure anymore what suits me. Sleeping in the same bed with Gray, especially if touching is off the table, is likely to be as comfortable as sleeping at the edge of the swamp after a rainstorm. But he has a point about getting accustomed to one another.

It's not like he's asking you to storm the beaches of Normandy. That's Smith's favorite saying to silence a whiner. *I wonder how he's doing? I miss him. Miss the whole team, but especially Smith. I was on top of my game with them, rarely second-guessed myself. Not like this. But that's precisely why I'm here—to stretch and challenge myself in new ways.*

"We'll likely be assigned separate bedrooms in the palace," Gray adds, "but there will be an expectation that we'll share a bed, at least for some portion of the night. They'll make it easy for us, but we need to be discreet."

"*Discreet.* What you're describing is nothing more than us sneaking around while they look the other way. But I get it. We'll all pretend that I'm virtuous and that you're a gentleman."

He smiles, but it takes some effort. "I think the expectation is that you're virtuous. No one expects me to be a gentleman. But a lot of pretending goes on in the Amadi royal family. It gets old after a while, but you'll have to remain respectful and play along the entire time."

I'm not worried about that. The one thing I can do is pretend.

I watch while he goes behind the bar and fixes himself a drink. He's dragging. It's not like him. "Did you eat?" I ask.

He hesitates for a few seconds, and nods.

"Sending me cheesecake isn't going to make up for leaving me alone every night," I tell him, pointedly. "There are things I can do downstairs. The mission is gearing up, and Wildflower is a full-time gig—you could use the help. I worked at the club, remember?"

Gray takes a long swig of bourbon, then rubs the heel of his palm over his jaw. "Beginning tomorrow you'll have plenty on your plate." He disappears into the foyer and comes back with a sheet of paper, hands it to me, and walks away.

"What's this?"

"It's your schedule for the next few days. I emailed you a copy too. I didn't know which calendar program you prefer."

Calendar program? That would be the one hanging in my kitchen, inside the pantry door. I read through the schedule, becoming more and more agitated. "Yoga with Mel at five thirty a.m.? You're fucking kidding me. That's when I run."

"It'll be good for you. And more challenging than you think. Mel's a hard-ass."

I have to calm down and try to reason with him. If we get into an argument, chances are I'm going to lose. "I *need* that run, Gray. Especially now. Need it more than my next breath." What I don't need is yoga. I leave that part out because it doesn't help my case at all.

"What you need is to broaden your horizons."

"I'll agree to the rest of the schedule, but I need the run." My voice is shaky. "You've turned my world upside down in the matter of a week. Don't make me give up that too."

"I'll take responsibility for part of it, but you agreed to have your world turned upside down."

I don't respond. A part of me is shaken by how important the run has become. No, not important—necessary. The thought of not running is painful. It's become an addiction. A *healthy* addiction, I remind myself.

"What happens if you're injured or stuck someplace where there's no place to run," he asks calmly, "like on a boat, or on a plane, or in a palace where women aren't free to do as they please? You'll need another outlet. Otherwise you'll be no good to yourself or to the mission."

I'm conflicted. I know he's right, but I also know that I'll be a mess without the outlet and the grounding that the early morning run provides.

"I'll help you find other ways to get to the same place," he continues. "This is going to be a challenge. For both of us. We talked about it at the beach. Nothing's changed now that we're back in the city. If anything, it's going to be harder while we prepare." My phone slides off the edge of the sofa, and he picks it up and places it near me, giving my hand a quick squeeze. "Normally I would tell you to enjoy the ride, but in this case, I think you need to keep your focus on the endgame."

"I'm a simple girl from Mississippi," I admit candidly. It's been eating at me all evening. "You said so yourself. I'm never going to be royalty or a high-society type. It's not baked in. What if the princess doesn't want to have anything to do with me? What happens then?"

Gray swoops me off the sofa, and deposits me on the bar in the corner of the room. It happens so fast I barely have time to protest.

"Listen to me. You're a smart, well-educated, beautiful woman." We're eye to eye and he doesn't let me look away. "You're not a princess. You're a damn queen. A badass queen. Don't ever let anyone make you feel less than that."

I don't know where to look, so I glance down at my toes. There's a pedicure on my schedule for tomorrow. Good thing, too.

"What is it?" he asks, lifting my chin.

I push his hand away. "Nothing,"

"I've told you, I'm not a mind reader." He nudges my thighs

apart and steps between them, his hands resting low on my hips. "I want to know what you're thinking."

"I need some fresh polish on my toes."

His eyes are steady and probing. He's not buying any of it. I don't know where to begin—or even if I want to talk about it at all. But I force myself, because of all those faces on the cards. Because we have to work through our challenges if we're going to be successful—for them.

"You—make me feel less than that." The words come slowly. It takes some doing to pry them loose, but I'm determined. "Not when I worked for you—but—when you talk about me being a simple girl from Mississippi, or learning how to fight in a trailer park. Those comments cut to the quick. Not because they're a lie, or even because I'm ashamed of my roots, but because you use them as a weapon to hurt me."

He blinks a few times, his long, dark lashes casting spiky shadows on his cheeks. There's sorrow in his face. It's what I've always adored about him, even from the beginning. He feels empathy. He knows compassion. When I reach out to smooth a worry line with my fingertips, Gray takes my hand and brings it to his lips.

"Say the rest. I need to hear it. All of it." His voice is low and rough, like it gets when there's too much emotion stirring inside him.

I'm not sure I want to say the rest. I don't know how to share it with him in a way that he'll understand. The feelings are right there, on the surface. I can touch them. But the words—searching for the right words is like playing a matching game. At the beginning, there are so many cards and it's only sheer luck when you turn over a match. That's how this seems. I'm holding the feeling card, but I can't find the word to match.

"Hey," he says softly.

His gaze is alert and steady, and I know he's not going to let me off the hook. *And maybe I don't want to be let off the hook.* I sigh, and somehow find the words to pair with my fears and insecurities.

"I've worked hard to trim the scraggly edges and shed the outer layers, because it makes people more accepting—more comfortable around me. But it's who I am inside. A simple girl from the poorest corner of the South." The facts aren't new to either of us, but saying the words out loud is freeing, and the more matches I make, the easier it gets. I don't stop.

"Nobody pulls themselves up without help. I had some, too. But I paid my dues," I say proudly. "I never took anything that didn't belong to me, and I never cheated. That simple girl is proud and loyal, and she might not be for everyone, but she informs the woman I am—every single day. I don't want that to change. But it doesn't mean that in some situations I don't feel small and like less."

After I stop talking, it's quiet. Not just silent, but still. My soul feels like it's been wrenched open, exposing all the oddities, the nicks and bruises. He doesn't say anything for what feels like forever, but it isn't awkward. The silence is productive and healing. At least for me.

"I'm sorry." His voice is tight, but he has the courage to look right at me when he speaks. "So sorry." It's earnest and sincere. Gray smooths my hair in a way that I suspect soothes him. In a small way, it soothes me too.

"I don't mean to make you feel that way," he continues, rubbing his thumb along the curve of my ear. "Although I suppose I did at the time. I wanted to get under your skin. But I don't feel that you're any less." He lifts his heavy shoulders. "I've never felt that way. I've always felt that you're more."

I press my cheek into his hand.

"I don't want you to change. I admire that girl. She's infuriating at times, and I'm quite sure she's going to be the death of me." He pauses for a beat. "But she's perfect. As is the woman she's become. I'm the one who can do better."

My eyes sting. But my heart is full. Not because the road is going to be smooth from now on—it isn't—but because I didn't make a mistake this time. I didn't misjudge Gray. *Although the fat lady hasn't sung yet.* Unlike with Kyle, I used my voice when it mattered, and this time, I hold all the power—even when it doesn't appear that way.

"I'll follow your lead," I say softly. It's not acquiescence. It's a decision. *My* decision. It's what I want. What I need. *What we both need.* And most importantly, what the mission requires. "I'll reserve my input for the times when we're alone. But you best bring your A game, because I'm not an easy woman."

The grin spreads slowly across his beautiful face, before he throws his head back and laughs. The sound of his happiness makes me smile. Maybe it shouldn't, but it does.

"Not easy?" he teases. "I've tangled with crocodiles less troublesome than you."

I smile to myself. Adding a wrinkle to his carefully ordered life pleases me. But I'm sure it makes it difficult for him. Although maybe that's not all there is to it. Maybe, *just maybe,* he's attracted to me in a way that complicates the mission for him as much as it does for me. *If by attracted you mean he wants to have dirty sex with your pretty face.*

"I need a shower and you need to get some sleep," he says, helping me off the bar. "You have yoga at five thirty, and a run late afternoon, if you're not too tired by then."

Well, what do you know? Rich boys from Charleston not only know how to apologize, they know how to compromise, too. I stop to appreciate his lean, muscular frame while he checks the locks and turns out the lights.

"Hopefully Mel is worth my time. I don't want to waste my morning with some New Age Karen who mainlines oat milk and gluten-free crackers when I could be exercising. What's that sly smile about?"

"Nothing," he says, heading toward the shower.

Nothing, my ass.

19

DELILAH

The next morning, I wake up cranky and frustrated that there is no run happening until later today, if at all. After I do my business and throw on some sweatpants and a baggy T-shirt, I follow the voices into the kitchen. One is Gray's deep timbre, and the other, which I don't recognize, is even deeper.

"Good morning," Gray says with a mischievous twinkle in his eyes. "This is Mel, your yoga instructor. Mel, meet Delilah."

Mel isn't the bony-ass woman I was expecting. *He* must be six feet four, with wide shoulders, dark-brown skin, and close-cropped black hair. I can't see his backside, but I assure you it's not scrawny. He looks to be well into his forties, but you'd never know it from the muscle rippling in his arms. Mel nods, and holds out an enormous hand. "Nice to meet you, Delilah."

For a half-second, just a half-second, I hesitate.

"Do we have a problem?" he asks when I don't immediately jump to take his hand.

"No—no problem," I stammer, reaching for his hand. His grip is firm and no-nonsense, like him. "It's just that—"

"Just what?" he challenges. "You got a problem with black men?"

"Of course not," I say indignantly. "I was expecting someone with perky tits and a high ponytail, that's all." *Oh my God*. I can't believe I just said that out loud.

"Me too," Mel replies, while I'm in the throes of a heart attack. "And I expected her to be dressed appropriately for yoga too. I guess we'll both have to get over our disappointment."

I look from one man to the other. Gray is doing a poor job of hiding a grin. "I apologize, Mel. I didn't mean to be rude. Gray led me to believe the yoga instructor was a skinny white girl." I glare at Gray. "Do you two know each other from yoga?" It sounds preposterous, but whatever it takes to steer the subject away from me works.

Mel hooks his thumb toward Gray. "He was my bitch, here and there, years ago."

When I pick up my jaw off the floor, I glance at Gray, hoping he'll shed some light on that last comment.

"I did basic and advanced training with the master sergeant," he says with a gleam of pride.

Master Sergeant Mel sounds so much better than *New Age Karen*. "So he's a ballbuster?"

"He's a ballbuster," Gray repeats, his eyes sparkling. "You won't find a bigger one. I don't know anything about oat milk, but I assure you, he won't waste your time."

"Oh, that's a guarantee," Mel chimes in. "And I hope you're not planning on wasting mine," he says, emphatically. "You ever practiced yoga?"

I shake my head. "I'm more of a runner and a pull-up kind of woman."

"I'll leave you two," Gray says, with the smirk not far from his lips. "I'll be up to shower after my run."

After my run? I'm going to kill him. I shoot daggers at the back of his head as he leaves.

"I'm not exactly sure what Gray told you he wants from me," I say to ease the silence, "but—"

"This isn't about what he wants *from* you," Mel says, as though chiding a bratty middle-school girl. "It's what he wants *for* you. Gray's a giver, not a taker—right down to the marrow. If you see something else in him, it's because you're only seeing what you want to see. Or maybe you're the kind of woman who uses every opportunity as an excuse."

He pauses, his eyes burrowing through the layers of carefully constructed façade that I reserve for strangers. It's not going to work with him. He sees too much.

"This here," he raises the rolled mat he's holding, "this is about what you want for yourself. Let's get started. We'll see if you have the courage to look inward."

Ninety minutes later, I'm in the shower, aware of muscles that I never knew existed. It wasn't stretching and chanting like I expected, but controlled breathing, taxing poses, and mindfulness—Mel said it was a basic lesson for a beginner, although it was challenging enough to give me my comeuppance. It wasn't anywhere near the same as a run, but he did give me a decent workout.

By the time I get out to the kitchen, Gray is there, freshly showered, and looking divine in a dark bespoke suit with stripes so subtle they wouldn't be noticeable unless you were gawking at him like I am. "Hey," I say casually, like we bump into each other in the kitchen every morning.

"Hey. What did you think of Mel?" he asks, holding what looks to be a protein shake.

My empty stomach quivers at the murky green drink. It's probably spinach or kale or something equally dreadful. It's not that I don't enjoy leafy greens. I'll eat almost anything. But not for breakfast.

"He kicked my ass. I'm sure you already heard the ugly

details." I approach the coffee service that must have been sent up from the Wildflower kitchen while I was showering, and pour myself a cup. "You want some?"

He shakes his head. "Actually, Mel said you're strong, and that you held your own pretty well for a beginner."

Mel doesn't strike me as the kind of guy who hands out praise like chocolate bars on Halloween, so it's nice to hear.

"I've committed to yoga," I say, splashing some milk into my coffee, "and you've committed to adding a daily run to the schedule." He didn't actually commit to it, but I want to see if I can wheedle it out of him now. "I also have a workout plan that includes weight lifting and resistance training, plus I'm at the range twice a week. It's all part of what I do to stay sharp for the job." Gray's leaning with his back against the counter, listening attentively. His expression isn't giving anything away, but I'm quite sure he's thinking something. "If my skills get rusty, they'll be hard to sharpen."

"So we're clear, I never *promised* a daily run. I recall saying there was room in the calendar for a run this afternoon." He takes the last gulp of swamp juice, and rinses the glass. "I expect you to keep your skills sharp, and maybe even pick up one or two new ones while you're working with me. You can use the gym downstairs any time you'd like. It's less crowded mid-afternoon and after eight in the evening. I'm at the range a couple times a week too. We'll go together."

I expect you to keep your skills sharp, and maybe even pick up one or two new ones while you're working with me. That's what a strong leader would expect—that those under his, or her, command would grow and develop from the association. It's why Smith was upset when he realized he wasn't giving me enough. I let Gray's words marinate a bit while I scan the kitchen counter for any sign of food.

"I don't suppose you had a chance to pick up Pop-Tarts?"

He chuckles. "There's a yogurt parfait with fresh berries

and some granola in the refrigerator. The granola is made in house. It's sweet, but the kitchen sent up some honey in case you prefer it sweeter."

I open the sparkling-clean refrigerator with its blindingly white interior and spotless glass shelves. Aside from the parfait, there's nothing in there but water and a jar of brandied cherries. Luxardo cherries, but not a single egg or a bottle of ketchup. I've opened empty refrigerators before, plenty of times, but it's not like Gray can't afford to keep his stocked.

I shake my head and take out the tall, stemmed parfait glass. While it's not exactly the kind of sweet I like with my morning coffee, it does look good. I refuse to admit that to Gray, though.

"There's no food in the refrigerator." I snatch a long-handled spoon from the coffee cart. "Does the kitchen prepare all your meals?"

"Pretty much. Unless I'm meeting someone at a restaurant, I normally eat in my office or at the bar downstairs."

I take a bite of the yogurt concoction, while Gray watches. "I'd like to have supper in the apartment," I tell him. *Like a normal person.* "If you don't want to join me, that's fine. But what's the sense of having a nice kitchen if you never use it?"

"We'll be eating out a lot. But you can talk to Renaud and plan menus for the evenings we're in."

"I don't need to discuss menus with the chef," I say emphatically. "I'm talking about simple meals that I can prepare from staples most people keep in the house."

Gray looks like that swamp juice is repeating on him.

"Your schedule is busy—the last thing you need to think about is cooking. I don't normally eat fancy. Renaud doesn't like it, but he's capable of having one of his minions make a burger or roast a chicken. Work it out with him. And count on me joining you," he adds. "It's a good time to catch up from the day and spend a little time together. I don't want to short-change that part of the preparation."

"Preparation? That's so disappointing. I thought you were talking about playing house."

He ignores the cheeky comment. "Most nights, I'll have to go back to the club when we're done."

Maybe I can go with you and help out. This isn't the time to bring it up—maybe tonight over supper. "Besides swamp grass, what do you like to eat?"

"I have a protein shake in the morning," Gray says a tad too defensively, "but I'll eat anything after that. Not big on toaster pastries or foie gras, though." He squeezes my arm as I reach around him for the honey.

I'm sure he intended it to be just a playful squeeze, but it becomes another one of those intimate moments that we can't seem to avoid. The ones that pulsate with live sparks and electricity.

Gray's eyes darken and for several seconds I'm convinced he won't be wearing that suit for much longer, and I'm more than ready for whatever he's thinking. But something shifts before we've taken off a single article of clothing, before our lips even meet. He pulls away, physically and emotionally. It's a small physical movement, with a powerful message that's enough to send us both spiraling into retreat.

The hot and cold with him makes me crazy. There are so many mixed signals, half the time my head is spinning.

I drizzle honey on my yogurt like I'm conducting brain surgery, and he pours hot coffee into an insulated travel mug. We don't talk.

That's when it hits me. This is what I'll be eating for breakfast in Amidane. Yogurt and fruit with honey, and maybe, because there's probably a pastry chef at the palace, a croissant or other delicate pastry. *Gray Wilder, you need to stop being so damn obtuse.*

In college, with my heart set on the CIA, I learned to speak several languages, and studied numerous cultures from around the globe. I studied the Saudi and Iranian cultures, but I don't know much about the Amadis. I glance at Gray. He wants me to get accustomed to the food I'll be served so that the change isn't too disruptive. The less disruption, the easier it is to maintain a high level of focus.

Would it be too much to expect you to just read me in, instead of manipulating and controlling everything like a sneaky bastard?

"I'll speak to Renaud," I say, between bites. "Maybe he can prepare a few typical Amadi dishes for us. That way our palates will begin to adjust."

There's a ghost of a smile on Gray's lips, and he visibly relaxes. *I'm right.* "Did you see what I just did?" I ask.

He glances at me with a blank look on his face.

"I didn't plan exotic meals behind your back. I was up front about it. I clearly stated, I'm going to do *this*, so that we get *that* result. It's not rocket science. You could have done that with the yogurt instead of making me feel that my food choices were not worthy of your fancy apartment."

His jaw is clenched. And it's not clear that he's taking my little lesson to heart. "It's not just about the food," he explains in his *I'm the boss* voice. "It's about you doing what I ask, without questioning me. It's about learning to trust that I'll make good decisions for you, and for the entire team."

Nice try, Captain America. "Your best chance of winning my trust quickly is by including me in the decision-making process. I might look like Covert Agent Barbie, but I have a brain and I understand how to get from point A to point C without a map. You can be in charge. I don't need to be the boss. It's not how I'm built. But you might be surprised at how amenable I can be when I'm included in the planning."

I pour another coffee, letting him think about what I've said —what I've offered.

"I'm accustomed to working alone," he says without any real emotion. "And your clearance is limited. But your concerns are duly noted."

"Duly noted?" Someone needs to put him on his ass. "The correct response was, *I'll work on it.*"

Gray pulls out a card from his wallet, and hands it to me. "It's a last-minute change to the schedule that we haven't discussed. Mira will be coming by at ten. She's a professor of Amadi studies at the University of South Carolina and speaks the language fluently. She's not read in at all. As far as she knows, this is a business—mostly pleasure—trip we're taking."

"I understand. I won't divulge anything."

"I'm not worried," he says, without hesitating. It's a huge boost of confidence. "You can practice your conversational skills with her," he continues, "and she can also answer any questions regarding the culture. She has some limited knowledge of the royal family, but I'm probably a better resource in that regard. Mira is at your disposal for the next two weeks—or until we leave. She's an invaluable resource, and I would schedule her every day."

I haven't met Mira, so I shouldn't start celebrating yet, but this feels like an enormous gift. It's how any operative would be briefed before a mission, if time provided, but I didn't expect to have an Amadi expert at my disposal. I thought my knowledge would be limited to the briefing books and to information Gray shares with me. "This is great. Thank you."

He nods. "She can accompany us on the trip if it would make you feel more comfortable. It wouldn't be unusual, at all, for a woman of your stature to bring along an assistant."

Of my stature. That's pretty damn funny.

"But there are pros and cons to bringing a companion."

"Like?"

"The most obvious benefit is that it will be easier for you with an ally who is a font of knowledge. On the other hand, there would be some danger to her. It's small. I don't expect things to go bad, but if they do," he sighs, "it will be the shitstorm of all shitstorms."

Gray pauses for a few seconds before continuing. "And if you bring along someone to keep you company, the crown prince will be less motivated to introduce you to Saher. He's going to want to have a little fun with me, and if you're alone, I won't be as free to play."

I don't need to think about it. I have enough concerns about connecting with the princess without adding additional obstacles. "Let's leave Mira in Charleston. I want this to be a success as much as you do."

He gazes at me, and I'm certain that's pride shining in his eyes. "You're a tough cookie, Blue Eyes. Still floors me. It shouldn't, but it still does."

Although I don't need constant reassurance, his approval matters to me. I look down, concentrating on fishing the last fat blueberry from the bottom of the stemmed glass, and contemplating exactly what *I won't be as free to play* means. The prince is married, but I doubt a little thing like that keeps his dick in his pants. But what about Gray? Will our relationship mean anything when he's presented with a willing partner?

"We're having dinner at the club tonight," Gray says, jolting me out of my head. "Think of it like a coming-out party for us. A lot of eyes will be on you."

Sweet Jesus. The thought of being on display isn't at all appealing. But that's what the assignment requires of me. *Suck it up, Delilah.* "Good thing you hooked me up with a mani and a pedi." I'm only being half-sarcastic. The other half is relieved for a little polish before encountering the vultures.

"I need to go," he says, from the doorway. "You know where to find me if there are any problems."

"Gray."

He turns. The dark circles that were under his eyes last

night are gone, and from this angle, the navy swirls in his tie play off his eyes, making them seem brighter and bluer.

"Thank you."

"For what?"

"For engaging me in a discussion about whether Mira should accompany us. And for not telling me to dress appropriately tonight, like I might not be able to figure out what to wear on my own."

He raps his knuckles against the elaborate doorframe, and nods. "Call if you need anything."

For the first time since he dragged me into this, I feel like it's going to be okay. *Maybe better than okay.*

20

GRAY

Delilah is adjusting an earring when I get to the apartment. I can't take my eyes off her reflection in the mirror. She's stunning, with just enough makeup to let her natural beauty shine through.

Neither of us says a word while we gaze at each other in the glass. There's a glimmer of apprehension in her eyes that I hate. It's that little girl she described last night—the one who never feels she's enough. My gut twists when I think about it.

"Turn around," I say gently, drinking in every inch of her. She smooths the dress, nervously, as she swivels to face me. The silky fabric falls gracefully over her curves, hugging, but not clinging to her luscious tits. She chose a sophisticated dress that's modest enough for dinner at the club, but dips low enough in the front to keep my attention all evening. It's the perfect tease. "You're gorgeous."

The color in her cheeks deepens, but she waves off the compliment. "Anyone can look good with a couple hours in the salon, and a closet filled with beautifully made clothing."

"Good? That's an understatement. Good enough to eat, maybe." I pick up the jeweled necklace off the console, and move her hair aside before I clasp it at the back of her long, graceful neck. Her skin is warm against my fingers, and my cock immediately takes notice.

"You smell delicious," I murmur, my lips grazing her earlobe. She shivers, and if I don't stop now, *right now*, dinner isn't happening. Tonight's too important to blow off to make my dick happy. I force myself to step back.

"What time is it?" she asks, slipping on a pair of heels that make my mouth water.

Nice pivot.

"We have a few minutes. I have something for you before we go." She follows my hand, as it retrieves the pouch from my pocket. I hold the small velvet bag out to her. "It's just a little something."

She's apprehensive, but she takes it. "I hope this isn't some fancy piece of jewelry that cost enough to feed a family of four for a year."

"It's an accessory, but not jewelry." She glances up at me through long, thick lashes. "It doesn't bite. Open it," I coax, when she continues to hesitate.

While Delilah loosens the strings on the pouch and peeks inside, I use the app on my watch to activate the small bullet vibrator. It rattles, startling her—at least momentarily. I laugh at her reaction like I'm a stupid teenager who just got a rise out of the pretty girl.

"I can control it with a remote, or from my watch, or my phone, or from all the way across the world from my laptop."

Delilah flinches, backing away. "There's no way I'm wearing that thing out in public." She shoves the bag at me, but I don't take it.

"We're not going to a sex party," she adds, aggrieved. "We're having dinner in the most exclusive restaurant in Charleston—*that you own*. We'll be out together for the first time. The busybodies will be falling all over each other while they crane their necks to get a good look. Are you crazy?"

I'm beginning to think so. I have two weeks, give or take a few days, to make it believable that kink is a part of our relationship. There is no way Ahmad buys it otherwise. He's known me for way too long. "Put your hands on the console, and bend over."

"Gray—I'm not—"

"You are, and you will. The vibrator will remind you to behave. It's the newest Lush prototype, not even on the market yet," I explain, hoping to garner some interest in the toy, but that little fact doesn't seem to impress her.

"To behave?" she spits back at me. "You'll zap me when I get too close to the property boundary, like I'm a dog?"

Jesus Christ. I don't know if I'm more annoyed at her, or at myself for using the analogy. "You're not a dog. And you're also not a naïve girl. You're a grown woman who consented to this relationship, and who agreed to let me lead. Implicit in that agreement was that you would follow. Now turn around and place your hands on the table. Don't make me say it again."

Delilah lifts her chin, but to my surprise she does as instructed. "Do it," she grumbles, with resignation. "Just get it the hell over with."

Fuck. I don't want her to simply tolerate the vibrator. I want her to enjoy it, physically and emotionally. I want her to willingly *and happily* relinquish control. That's why this whole thing is so fucked up. I wouldn't care so much if she was just another operative. But she's not. And I'm on shaky, unfamiliar ground. *You're playing a fool's game if you involve a woman you can barely keep your hands off in a covert mission.* Fuck you, Smith.

After a few seconds pass, I stand directly behind her and gently tug at the ends of her hair, until her reflection meets mine in the mirror. "Tonight's important. There won't be photographs, because the paparazzi aren't allowed anywhere near the club, but as you surmised, there will be a lot of tongue wagging. I need you to trust that I've thought through every detail carefully. That includes your feelings." I run my hand down her back, and her lips part as she draws a large breath.

Above all else, the one thing that will make the mission successful is our insatiable desire for each other. It's also what makes it soul-wrenching.

"The only thing I hadn't anticipated is how gorgeous you'd be all dressed up, and how much I'd want to fuck you. But that's my problem, not yours. And I won't allow it to interfere with the plan." I pause, allowing her to digest all of it.

I have responsibilities to Delilah that I intend on fulfilling at some point. But I also have a mission to think about, and while I'm not prepared to scrap her role in it, I need to know if she's still on board. Better now than in a week.

"We're going to be late for our reservation," she says softly, gazing at me in the mirror.

I search her face, hoping for something more than resignation. As if she knows what I need, she nods. And I can breathe again.

"Think of tonight like one long scene." I let my hand slide across her ass and down her shapely legs. "Do you trust me not to wrinkle your dress, or would you like to pull it up?"

She reaches down, and carefully lifts the bottom of her dress, until her ass is bared to me. I resist the urge to sink my teeth into the firm muscle.

I want her aroused. It will give her the flushed look of a woman in love—a new love. If she pulls it off, I have a reward for her, and if she doesn't, she won't get to ease the ache I'm going to make sure she has all night.

I rub my palm over her round little ass, and when I feel her relax, I bring my hand down hard on her tight cheek. She gasps at the bite of the blow. I'm going to give her the pain she craves, just enough to take the edge off and settle her.

Spanking her eats at me. It's not what I want for her future —at least not all the time. But emotionally she needs the pain, and I haven't had enough time to guide her elsewhere.

I might be conflicted, but I'm also aroused.

I slap her ass several more times, letting my fingers dip into her pussy between the sharp strikes, but never for long enough to give her the orgasm that she deserves. That's for later.

When her skin is reddened, and her pussy primed, I nudge her thong aside and slip the pink vibrator into her, carefully adjusting the thin curve over her clit and the antenna on her almost bare mound. "Panties are optional," I murmur, kissing the top of her head. "What do you think? Want to leave them here?"

"I think I would quit while I was ahead if I were you."

I laugh softly. "You okay?"

"Other than my tender backside?"

"It sounds like you're complaining." Our eyes meet in the mirror. There's no uncertainty now. Her eyes are bright and clear.

Delilah shakes her head. "No," she says so softly I can barely hear it. "No complaints."

Her calm demeanor should make me feel better, but it doesn't. Inflicting pain is easy. It takes no skill and little effort. She deserves better.

After running a damp washcloth between her legs, I adjust her thong, smooth her dress over her hips, and help her upright. "Showtime."

The walk to the elevator is quiet, with each of us embroiled in our own thoughts. While we wait for the doors to open, she peeks at me from the corner of her eye. The evening, and all it holds, is weighing on her again. She needs another distraction, and I reach for my phone, but change my mind. Not yet.

When we get into the private elevator, I cage her in the corner, with one hand on the side of her head and the other on my phone. I stop the elevator. "You're beautiful, Delilah. No one will be able to keep their eyes off you. But you're mine." I kiss her roughly. "Say it."

"I'm yours for the mission," she says with a spark of defiance that makes my cock harder.

We'll see. I shrug off the idea of keeping her when we're done. That's *not* the plan.

"If you behave yourself tonight, I have something special planned for you. Something you'll really enjoy."

"Maybe my reward can be that you'll stay on your side of the bed and leave me the hell alone." There's a glimmer of challenge in her eyes.

Challenge accepted. I activate the vibrator and it jumps to life. There's not the faintest buzz, but her mouth falls open and she sucks in a breath. I'm so close to her, I can feel the heat off her body. "Feels good, doesn't it, darlin'?"

When she holds onto the elevator wall to steady herself, my mouth crashes into hers. It's only the small moans in her throat that pull me back to reality. *What the hell, Gray? What are you doing? It can't be like this. You need to be in control. Otherwise the entire mission and everything you hope to accomplish is going to blow up in your face.*

I turn off the vibrator, and restart the elevator.

Delilah pulls out a small compact and begins repairing her lipstick. The phallic tube against her lips sends a signal straight to my dick. I look away, trying to right myself before the damn doors open.

You're fucking with my head, woman. And it's my own goddamn fault.

21

DELILAH

When we get off the elevator, Gray's hand is on my back guiding me toward the hostess station—to the very spot where I stood, night after night.

As we walk through the restaurant, I smile and say hello to at least a half dozen staff who I know. It's uncomfortable—I don't know why exactly, maybe because I'm more at home being a staff member than a guest in a place like Wildflower.

Gray whispers something to the hostess, Laurel, who was hired right before I left. She nods and smiles, but I'm not sure she recognizes me. When they're finished, he leads me into the dining room, to a table in the center of the room where everyone can see us.

The familiar way he touches my back and waits for me to be seated suggests this isn't a business meeting. I'm sure the nosey-noses trying not to gawk think we're a couple—or at the very least, on a third or fourth date.

The waiter and sommelier come over together to greet us, and though normally they would introduce themselves, no introductions are necessary.

"You can leave the menus, but we'd like a few minutes to enjoy a drink before we order."

"Of course," the waiter says, respectfully, turning his attention to me. But before I can order a drink, Gray takes the reins.

"Miss Porter will have a champagne cocktail, and I'll have Blanton's. A generous pour, please."

My expression must betray my distaste for the words *champagne cocktail*, because the vibrator jumps to life for a second, zapping me like I'm a dog with an electric collar. I don't care what Gray says about it. That's what it feels like to me.

When the waiter walks away, I smile adoringly at Gray. "I know a champagne cocktail is dainty and ladylike, but the next time you order me an aperitif, remember how much I like Blanton's too, darlin'."

The vibrator springs to life, this time for longer than the last. One more time, and I'm going to pull it out, right here in the fancy-ass dining room, and drop it in his *Blanton's*.

"I appreciate you speaking so lovingly. But I'm in a wolfish mood tonight, Delilah. It's best you keep your wits about you."

I make every effort not to roll my eyes. The pretending to be something I'm not is so much more difficult than I imagined. If Gray and I were at Tallulah's Bar, or even in the apartment, sharing a meal would feel more natural, the way it did at the beach. But a dinner with pressed linen and more forks than I own makes it awkward, even in a familiar place.

Fortunately, Gray is a master at small talk. And I dust off my Southern manners and partake of the bullshit until the white-gloved waiter returns. He places small bowls of warm nuts, olives, and cheddar crackers on the table, along with our drinks. Gray's bourbon is over a large ice cube with a strip of orange peel lying on the surface. It makes my mouth water. I glance at my drink. In comparison, it looks—better than nothing.

When the waiter walks away, Gray lifts his glass toward me.

"Have a sip." I'm surprised he's sharing. But I suppose that's what couples do. "Go on. See if it's as good as you remember."

I lift the tumbler while he watches attentively, a small sparkle in his eyes. "Better than I remember," I reply in a low, husky voice, as though the whiskey primed my throat for sex.

"Take another sip, just to be sure."

"*Mmmm*. It smells like vanilla caramels," I say, bringing the tumbler to my nose, before taking another sip.

"There's nothing I'd like more than to indulge you, Blue Eyes. Let me."

The flush creeps up my neck, and I search for a distraction. "I love these little crackers. The chef puts cayenne in them."

Gray takes a long drink of bourbon, but doesn't take his eyes off me. The growing flush moves from pleasantly warm to toasty. If he hasn't already noticed the pink stain on my skin, he'll surely see it now.

"Tell me about your day," he says, popping an olive into his mouth.

"My day." Such a perfectly civilized question, but wrought with so much angst and turmoil. "Aside from Gabby when we meet for supper or a drink, I don't think anyone's ever asked about my day."

"*Hmmm*." He scoops up another olive. "Never?"

I shake my head. "I've never thought about it before, but I don't think so."

"Well, I'm asking, and I'm going to keep asking, at least for the next few weeks."

The next few weeks—then it's over. *Then you'll be free of him, Delilah.* It doesn't give me the jolt of happiness I would expect. "Busy. The day was busy, although I accomplished *nothing*." It's true. I've never had such a busy but unproductive day. "The yoga was challenging. But you already know that. Have I thanked you yet for leading me to believe Mel was a white girl with a scrawny ass?"

Gray laughs.

"I don't think Mel is that impressed with me, but he's going to let me incorporate martial arts and kickboxing into our routine."

Gray raises his brow, offering me a cheddar cracker. "Really?"

"If he's satisfied that I'm committing to my yoga practice, on my own time. Don't worry, he's not letting me off easily."

"How did it feel to run on a treadmill in the afternoon?"

"Not anywhere near as satisfying, if you want to know the truth. But better than nothing. Kind of like my champagne cocktail."

The edge of his mouth quirks, and I flash him a small, feigned smile, which he ignores.

"How did it go with Mira?"

"I liked her. A lot. You were right. She's a font of information. Apparently, women don't run outside in Amadi. Not on the public streets anyway."

"Is that right?" He brings the amber liquid to his lips and empties the tumbler.

"That's what the yoga is about. You're preparing me."

He scoffs, but the gleam in his eyes betrays him. "Pity. I'm disappointed you didn't continue to believe I'm a monster in that regard for a bit longer."

Before I can respond, there's a loud thud at the entrance to the restaurant, like something heavy fell over, and staff are scurrying out front.

"Excuse me," Gray says, getting up.

I follow him out, and close the French doors behind me so that guests can continue to enjoy dinner.

Laurel is on the floor with the hostess stand on top of her.

Gray shoos everyone away, and with little effort he pulls the stand upright, then lowers himself to his haunches, beside her. "Are you okay?"

"Yes," she gasps. "I'm so sorry." She starts to sit up, and then lies back down again. "Mr. Wilder, I'm so nauseous, I'm afraid if I lift my head, I'll be sick."

Poor woman. She sounds mortified.

"Get a bag, or something, in case she vomits," Gray tells the busboy loitering a few feet away. Laurel drapes an arm over her eyes. "What happened?" Gray asks. His voice is gentle and filled with concern.

When I worked at Wildflower, Gray was always fair-minded. Not just toward me, but toward others who worked here too. He was demanding and exacting about *everything* at the club, but he was also generous and kind, especially with the long-term employees who had demonstrated their loyalty over the years. Laurel hasn't been here a year, but he's clearly fond of her.

"I got dizzy and held onto the stand. When I fell, it came with me. I'll be fine as soon as my head stops spinning. It's just the heat."

The heat? It's pretty cool in here.

"Does it hurt anywhere?"

"Only my pride," she says with her arm still shielding her eyes.

The busboy returns back with a large disposable container.

"You hold this," Gray instructs, wrapping Laurel's fingers around the container. "Don't be afraid to use it if you need to. I'm going to carry you to my office and we'll call your husband and an ambulance. Hold on." He lifts her off the floor, and I follow behind, through the kitchen, to the rear of the building.

Trippi appears out of nowhere and stops me at the entrance to Gray's office. "She needs a little privacy," he explains, in his own terse way. That's how it always is with him. Short and never sweet. No one ever accused the man of talking their ear off. That's for sure. "This is a personnel matter," he adds, when I don't immediately back off.

I'm not prepared to make a stink, and I'm certainly not going to bother Gray. Plus, Laurel is entitled to some privacy. "Of course. Let me know if I can help in any way."

He nods and shuts the door in my face.

What do I do now? Go back to the table, I guess, and wait. I don't relish the idea of sitting alone, with dozens of eyes watching and wondering if Gray is ever coming back.

When I get to the front, a waitress and a waiter, who know the floor well, are discussing who should take over for Laurel. Gray prefers the term *hostess*, but the hostess at the club is actually the maître d' with the *de facto* job of restaurant manager for the evening. With Laurel and Gray both out of commission, and Foxy gone for the day, no one's in charge.

This was my old job. I can welcome guests and keep the floor running smoothly in my sleep. I did it for two years.

"I'll be the hostess for the rest of the evening," I advise the much relieved, albeit cautious, waitstaff. "Let's all go back to our stations."

About fifteen minutes later, Trippi approaches me outside the dining room after I've seated a small party. "Mr. Wilder is wondering if you know the name of the doctor who delivered Gabby Wilder's baby?"

Laurel must be pregnant. Hopefully the fall is nothing serious. I don't bother asking, because Trippi isn't going to divulge a thing. "Dr. Williams. With Angel Oak Obstetrics and Gynecology." Dr. Williams is my doctor too, but I keep that to myself.

"He also wanted me to tell you to go up to the apartment, and he'll meet you when he can. He said to order dinner for yourself and the kitchen will bring it up."

Did he? Well, I'm going to go into the bathroom and take out his little toy, and he'll have to come tell me himself, with words, if that's what he expects.

"Tell Mr. Wilder that he should take as long as he needs. I can amuse myself until he's free."

Trippi, who is a former SEAL and the size of a Mack truck, glances between me and the menus in my hand.

"If you tell him I'm working the floor, I'll help myself to your balls when you least expect it. It won't be a good time for you."

He's twice my size, but has the good graces not to laugh in my face. "Yes, ma'am," he says deferentially before walking away.

I'd say there's a less than fifty-fifty chance he'll keep his mouth shut.

22

DELILAH

I've changed into a pair of shorts and a tank top by the time the lock clicks, and Gray drops his keys into a small glass tray in the foyer.

"Hey," he says from the living room doorway. "I didn't expect you to still be up." He's carrying his jacket, his tie is off, and his sleeves are rolled to the elbow. He looks beat.

"Is that why you stayed away so long?" I tease. "Hoped I'd fall asleep before you got home? How's Laurel?"

"She's fine. I'm sorry about the way things turned out tonight." He walks to the bar in the corner of the room and pours a bourbon. One glass.

"No thanks, I don't care for any."

His hand freezes mid-pour, his lips pulled into a tight line. "Do you want a drink, or are you just busting my balls?"

"I'm all set for now." I sit up and lay my iPad on the sofa beside me, and watch while he drains his glass and pours himself another. He's broody tonight, with a darkness surrounding him that's not normally there. At least not one this gloomy.

"I'm going to shower."

"I'll put out supper while you're showering. Don't deep-condition your hair and shave your legs, and all that other stuff that takes time. I'm starving."

He stops, and turns to me. "You haven't eaten?"

"I waited for my date. It seemed ladylike and proper, like a champagne cocktail."

When he shakes his head, I spy a whisper of a smile, but not enough to lift the gloom. "I'll be out in ten minutes."

While he's showering, I reheat the crab dip and pull the chicken salad from the refrigerator. I wonder if something happened with Laurel. Maybe that's what's put him in a mood. It was hot as hell outside and soupy, but the club was cool and dry. I doubt it was the heat that made her go down, even if she is pregnant. It's not as though pregnant women turn into hothouse flowers.

While I'm still figuring things out, Gray comes out onto the balcony where I've set out the food and lit a few candles I found decorating the inside of the fireplace. His hair is damp, and he's wearing a pair of sweatpants and a T-shirt with the sleeves cut off. I'd bet my last dollar there's no underwear under those thin gray sweatpants. Just like at the beach.

"This is nice," he says, almost surprised.

"I thought we'd eat out here. It's cooled off and the fresh air feels good. I hope you don't mind that I borrowed the candles from the fireplace. I'll put them back just like they were when we're finished." *Wouldn't want you to have a heart attack because something was out of place.*

"Don't worry about it," he says, stretching out on a chaise lounge. "What did you order?"

I lift the lids off the platters. "Chicken salad on soft white bread, with sweet potato fries and some crab dip."

He's sitting back, with his eyes closed, but he's not asleep.

I slather some crab dip on a piece of baguette and bring it to him.

"Chef Renaud must have loved filling your order."

"He's lucky I don't trust him to make a decent taco, because that's what I really had a hankering for. But not to be outmaneuvered, he chose a *crisp chardonnay that would pair well with my choices.*" I purse my lips. "I never cared for that guy. Too snooty for my tastes. But he can cook. Got to give him that."

Gray gets up and opens the glass door to the living room. "I'm not a fan of chardonnay, crisp or otherwise. Do you want a beer?"

"Love one."

The balcony overlooks the city, with the harbor in the distance. It's a nice view, but nothing like the beach house.

I make us each a plate with some of everything while he's inside, and take the seat closest to him.

He hands me a beer. "I didn't realize how hungry I was. This is perfect. Thanks for—"

"Ordering? It didn't take much effort." I pick at my food, unsure about whether it's okay to ask what happened with Laurel. I don't want to violate her privacy. I suppose Gray will let me know if I overstep. "I heard you went to the hospital with Laurel."

"Where did you hear that?" he asks, taking a bite of the sandwich.

"Chatter among the waitstaff. You know how it is in the restaurant—no secrets, even if the ambulance pulls up around back. Plus, they like her, and they were worried."

He shrugs. "She'd never been in an ambulance before. She started to cry when the EMTs hooked her up to an IV and said she needed to go to the emergency room. She was shaking, and I couldn't see sending her alone. Trippi followed in the car. We stayed until her husband could find someone to take care of their kid."

Empathy and compassion—there it is again. "That was nice of you."

"It's not like I had a choice."

"We always have a choice. But you have a soft spot for vulnerable women. I've seen it before."

"Don't ever ask Trippi to lie to me. He won't, but it puts him in a bad spot. Especially since he's fond of his balls." He reaches over and tugs on my hair, stealing a fry off my plate, while he's at it.

I swat his hand away from my food. "The last thing I want are his balls." But my instincts are right not to trust him to keep his mouth shut.

Gray gets up to grab another sandwich. "I asked you to come upstairs and wait for me."

"Actually, you *told* me to go upstairs and wait. It might be just semantics, but there was no asking and a lot of telling. Trippi might have gotten the gist of it wrong, but I doubt it."

He deposits a handful of fries on my plate before sitting down. "You were my guest. When I—"

"It was the right thing to do," I interrupt, before he goes any further down that road and I end up wanting to smack him. "You own the place, yet when something needs to get done, regardless of what it is, you pitch in. Your woman would do that too. Besides, I can run that dining room in my sleep."

"My woman, huh?" There's a small smile playing on his lips.

"Isn't that what we want the world to believe?"

He doesn't respond, and all of a sudden, he seems faraway and broody again.

I rest my plate on the small table between us, and close my eyes, enjoying the breeze. It's been a long day, filled with new experiences and bits and pieces of information that I need to hold onto. No wonder I'm tired.

"Am I a monster?"

What? My eyes shoot open, and I turn my head toward him. I need him to repeat the question, before I go anywhere near it. What if I nodded off and completely misunderstood? "I'm sorry. I missed part of that."

"No, you didn't. You're just not sure how to answer." He snickers. It has a ring of sadness to it. "You're probably the wrong person to ask."

Monster? Where did this come from?

"I'm exactly the right person." I respond too quickly and reflexively, almost as though I'm gearing up to defend him—but against what? Himself?

"I've seen a lot of sides to you, Gray. And I'm the right person to ask because I'll tell you the truth." I shrug. "When I worked at the club, I saw mostly good in you—toward everyone. But once I left, you were ugly to me. And now?" I gaze up at him. "Some of your behavior has been downright deplorable, and confusing, to be honest. But no, I don't think you're a monster. Far from it. That's why I agreed to join you in a mission."

"You agreed?" The cords in his neck are so tight, I can see them under the dim light. This is the broodiest he's ever been around me. "Is that what we're calling coercion now?"

"Yes. I agreed. I've been clear about that. Your threats got my attention, but they didn't play *any* role in the final decision. I'm not afraid of you. I never have been." I get up and reach for my plate, but Gray grabs hold of my arm, and pulls me into his lap. There's something about his mood that guts me.

"Sit here with me for a minute. Let me enjoy the way your hair and skin smell. The way you feel. All soft, and at the same time strong. You're such a contradiction. It's beguiling."

I curl into him, laying my cheek against his hammering heart, and close my eyes. He's a contradiction too. *Maybe we're made for each other.*

His heart eventually slows to a beat that feels familiar. "What did you get for dessert?" he asks after several minutes of just quietly being together.

"You want dessert?"

"I thought you might."

"It was pecan pie. And it was delicious." I feel his shoulders shake before I hear the laughter. A great relief washes through me. This is the man I know—the version of him that I like best. "It was getting late, and it's not like you keep any food in the house. I didn't want to pick at the chicken salad. I was saving it until you got home." *Home. Why did I say that? This isn't my home.*

"I don't want dessert." He holds me tight, so I can't move, and kisses my head. "Make a list of things you think we should have in the apartment. Next time someone goes to the market, they'll pick it up."

A list of things we should have in the apartment. Not *I should have*, but *we should have*.

It's pretend, Delilah. All pretend. You'd do well to remember that.

I should probably leave it alone, but his heart was heavy when he came in tonight. I can't believe whatever was on his mind is gone completely. "What made you ask if you were a monster?" I ask, rubbing his chest lightly.

He doesn't respond immediately, and after a couple minutes I'm convinced he isn't going to respond at all. But sometimes it takes a little extra time to collect the courage to bare your soul.

"Laurel didn't want to tell me she was pregnant. She needs the health insurance and thought if I knew, I'd find a reason to fire her." Gray lifts my chin until our eyes meet. "Am I so shallow that someone who works for me would think I'd fire her because she's pregnant?"

There's something about him that looks vulnerable. I'm sure he wants my reassurance, but the truth is, in her shoes, I would have been concerned too.

"Pregnant women have a whole host of hormonal things going on that neither you nor I can appreciate. Hell, Gabby once cried at a commercial for a feminine hygiene product. But I can understand why Laurel was worried," I say gently.

He stiffens under me, and I feel terrible about hurting him, but I'm not going to lie. That serves no purpose. "It's not you, Gray. Wildflower is a carefully crafted fantasy. Everything about it is beautiful and decadent—even the part that's above ground. You sell sex. A big belly and swollen ankles are a repellent to the kind of sin you peddle. They're the result of sin, a warning of what's to come when you partake in the fun, not an enticement."

"I'm a perfectionist and I demand loyalty. But I was always under the impression that my employees understood that their loyalty would be returned. I've always tried to do right by them. It's important to me."

"While I worked at Wildflower," I say, sincerely, "I always had the impression that everyone adored you, despite your exacting ways. You're good to people who work there. You do it quietly—like going in the ambulance with Laurel without making a big deal."

I pull his face toward mine, until my lips reach his. It's not the kind of kiss that's big and sexy—it's the kind that says *I'm on your side*.

"You're a good soul, Delilah."

His mouth meets mine, with a raw energy that stokes the sleeping fire. He sinks his teeth into my bottom lip, sending jolts of pleasure through me. When I begin to pant, he slides a hand under my shirt, caressing one breast, then the other. Not sweet, gentle caresses, but firm, skilled strokes that demand my nipples furl in appreciation.

"What are we going to do about the little lapse tonight?" he murmurs.

My brain is in a fog. Between his sexy mouth and those hands—I'm a muddled mess. "What little lapse?"

"The one where I told you to go upstairs and you defied

me." His tone has a roguish edge that makes my heart skip a beat.

"I guess you'll have to punish me."

Gray wraps my hair around his hand, tipping my head back and leaving my neck exposed. "I don't punish grown women unless it's part of a scene." He runs his tongue along my throat until he reaches my ear. His teeth sink into the lobe, making me shudder. "I dole out consequences for behavior, good and bad. Everything we do, or fail to do, has a consequence. Human behavior is shaped by our willingness to bear the consequences."

"It sounds complicated. Maybe you can show me what you mean."

The edge of his mouth curls. "You just bought yourself another consequence, Blue Eyes. Let's go inside."

23

DELILAH

Gray opens the door and steps aside so I can go in first. I stop just inside the living room because I'm not sure where to go. I'm not even sure what we're doing. Not exactly. But I'm all in. That, I am sure about.

He cradles my face in his hands. "This is going to be a short, uncomplicated scene. But intense. Will you follow where I lead?"

I've come to understand that this is Gray's way of asking for my consent. "Yes." I emphasize my assent with a slight nod.

"Yes, what? What are you agreeing to?" He stills, waiting for my response.

"You lead, and I'll follow. Wherever it takes me."

I feel his hands tense around my face. He places his warm lips on my forehead, where it meets the hairline. "Green, yellow, or red when I check in with you during the scene. Red anytime you want to stop. It's your safe word. Don't be afraid to use it."

"Of course." I can handle whatever he has in store for me—physically, anyway. I don't plan on using the safe word. Although I don't suppose anyone ever does.

I follow Gray to the bedroom, past the enormous bed we'll be sharing tonight, into his closet.

I've never been inside before. It's not that different from the one where my new clothing hangs, although this closet is decidedly more masculine. It's the size of a large dressing room, outfitted along two walls with rods and racks. A bank of drawers covers the far wall, and there are two built-in dressers flanking a wide, floor-to-ceiling gold-framed mirror. The woodwork is dark, and the walls and ceiling are lined with cedar panels.

Gray locks the door from the inside, making sure I see him slip the key into his pocket. I'm his captive. His *willing* captive.

He leaves me standing in the center of the dimly lit room, while he climbs into an elaborately carved chair. It appears to be some sort of a throne, resting on a dais off the floor. But as I examine it more closely, I realize it's a vintage shoeshine chair that men once sat in to have their shoes polished to a mirrored finish.

Even in sweatpants and a T-shirt cut at the sleeves, Gray looks like he belongs in that leather chair with its gilded frame. Rich, powerful men don't relinquish their birthright when they shed their fine clothing. By the same token, you can't put couture on a girl from Mississippi and expect her to be a queen.

"Is this my consequence?" I ask tentatively.

He peers down at me from his antique perch, like a king on a peasant. "No. This is play time. We'll discuss the consequences later. Or tomorrow. I don't think you'll be up to discussing anything when we're done."

The buzz of anxiety is well-entrenched inside me, humming along nicely. Just like he wants.

"But for now," Gray continues, "unless I ask you a question, or you need to use your safe word, I want you quiet. No words. But not silent. I want to hear those whimpers of pleasure and the groans of frustration. I want your screams to thrum in my veins." I shudder in response, and he smiles devilishly. "What's your safe word?"

"Red." I don't need to think about it.

Gray nods. "Take off your clothes, Delilah. *For me.*" He leans back with his forearms propped on the chair. "Every. Last. Stitch."

I lift my head and pull my shoulders back, not in a balk, but resolute and determined. I intend to do this not only for his pleasure, but for mine.

Although it's not my intention to put on a show, I feel myself disrobing with moony, graceful movements, my gaze drawn to his. I'm already aroused and Gray is too. The evidence is not just his hard cock probing the thin fabric, but in his dark eyes, with their heavy lids.

"You're beautiful, darlin'. I don't tell you that often enough." His voice is the soothing stroke of a master caressing a pet. "Look into the mirror."

I swivel, following his command without wavering.

"On your knees," he instructs with that same inviting tone.

Only this time, I don't rush to obey. Instead, I meet his eyes in the mirror. Pleading silently. I'm not ready to kneel for him.

"I'm not requiring you to get into a submissive pose. That's entirely up to you. But I do want you on your knees. *Now.*"

I'm not sure if it's a concession, or if he never expected me to kneel for him. Getting on my knees is different from *kneeling*. It's not just semantics. I wouldn't expect just anyone to understand the distinction, but Gray does.

I lower my knees to the well-padded silk rug, with my body long and proud, and my arms dangling at my side. It's not a submissive posture. It's nothing like it. Although it doesn't take long before I realize the humble position might be more comfortable. But I don't move.

Gray watches me in the mirror with a keen eye. "Quiet your mind," he demands. The soothing tenor is gone, replaced by the commanding Dominant. The shift is subtle, but unmistakable.

I lower my head to save myself from his probing stare. But I'm not spared. The sear sizzles on my exposed skin, and I struggle not to squirm.

His patience will surely outlast mine, especially with the heady scent of cedar whirling with his spicy cologne. When I first entered the closet, the dance was subtle and oddly comforting, but now, it's loud, permeating my senses, and it's all I smell.

After what seems like an eternity, there's a rustling behind me. I glance into the mirror as he approaches with a swath of fabric in one hand and what appears to be a crop in the other.

My skin is already singing for the crop.

"Spread your thighs wide," he instructs. "That's it. A little more."

I'm unsteady with my knees so far apart, and even though my legs are strong, I don't know how long I'll be able to hold this position without toppling over.

Gray places a hand on my shoulder, squeezing gently. "I'm going to blindfold you," he explains, before tying the soft fabric around my eyes and robbing me of all sight. "I prefer not to tie your hands. But I want you to keep them behind your back with your fingers laced. Can you do that of your own accord, or do you need the assistance of the binding?"

Anyone can be kept immobile when bound. But it takes a strong will and great fortitude to keep still and embrace the sting of the crop. He's challenging me.

I choose my words cautiously. "I don't need to be bound to submit to the crop." I'm careful not to say a word about submitting to him from my knees.

Gray slides his hands over my shoulders and neck, with firm but gentle strokes that make it difficult not to sway. It would be easier if I were in a submissive pose—and I consider it briefly. *No*, I decide. He hasn't earned it, and if I give it up too easily, it will be an empty offering that means nothing.

I lace my fingers against my lower back.

His lips carefully graze the hair at my crown, as the crop slithers between my thighs, inching up slowly, in a satanic tease.

The striking part of the crop, the keeper, is a pliable, unforgiving leather tongue that will sting sweetly when wielded by a skilled hand. The darkness heightens my anticipation, and every nerve ending is on high alert, waiting for the first scrumptious bite of the crop.

Gray slides the keeper across my mound, taking great pains to avoid the sensitive pink flesh begging for a taste.

He lays a steady hand on my shoulder, and strikes my ass. The *swoosh* of the crop cuts through the air almost as the sting lands. "*Ahhh!*" I gasp. Before I have time to collect myself, he strikes the other cheek.

Just one wallop on each side, before he begins the excruciating slide up the other thigh. Stopping at my pussy, he rests the leather tongue against the wet skin and holds it there.

Focused on self-preservation, I draw a breath and brace myself for what is sure to come next.

Gray hovers over me, and I feel his hand between my legs. But it's much too brief. "Such a needy girl," he murmurs, bringing his fingers to my lips.

I suck them clean. I don't need to be told.

"You're so good, darlin'. When you lave my fingers with your hot little mouth, I feel it in my cock."

I begin to sway, and he brings a hand to my breast, fingering the nipple roughly while the crop snaps and licks my pussy with rhythmic beats against the slick flesh. Gray wields it expertly, varying gentle caresses with delicious bites.

He holds me steady, by my breasts, kneading one and then

the other. When my legs begin to quiver, the crop disappears. I groan at the loss, squeezing my interlocked fingers in agony.

My pulse slows, and Gray begins again. The soft blows build, the cadence sure as I climb. But this time I know. It doesn't matter how desperate I am to come, he won't allow it. My cunt is aching. I need the release. I concentrate on keeping my legs still so he doesn't know how close I am, but it's all for nothing. He pulls the damn thing away when I'm *right there*.

The pressure behind my eyes is growing. The tears threaten. Not from the sting of the crop, but from the frustration.

I feel Gray move. He's in front of me, with his cock on my lips. My tongue darts out eagerly to taste the smooth, stretched skin, and I'm rewarded with a milky bead.

"Just like my fingers, Delilah. Suck it good."

He feeds me his thick cock little by little. I want to use my hands to pull him closer, to dig into the cords of muscle on his thighs, to grip the silky shaft and fondle the tightening sack, but I don't dare. Instead I lick the taut skin, running my teeth gently over the crown.

He hisses, pushing deeper. "Relax and breathe," he demands, in a raspy voice. "Take it all."

Count on it. I tip my head back to lengthen my throat, and swallow as he pushes deeper. The saliva pools and dribbles. But I don't gag.

I hear the rumble of release, and feel his seed on my skin before my mouth registers the loss of his cock. The spray goes on and on. I ache to dip my fingers into it and taste the salty brine.

His hands are in my hair, petting me, with the tender touch of a man who has just had his cock sucked. "Give me a color," he says, in a voice that still sounds like fine gravel.

"Green. Green," I repeat louder, so he understands I'm not anywhere near ready to stop.

He's behind me again, untying the blindfold, and binding my hands with the silky fabric.

"I want you to see what I see. A smart, strong woman, on her knees, marked, swept up not by unrelenting pain, but by intense pleasure."

My eyes adjust to the low light quickly. The woman in the mirror is uninhibited, covered in a wanton flush, with heavy breasts and swollen lips, her hooded eyes filled with lust.

She reeks of sin.

Gray picks up the crop off the floor and brandishes it mercilessly, harder this time and faster than before. The intensity overshadows the smarting sensation. My hips buck wildly and my legs won't hold me up any longer. I begin to topple, but he catches me with a free hand, using my breasts to steady me, tweaking one nipple, then the other, until pleading moans are all I hear.

I lean back against his legs for support, and pull at the bindings as my orgasm rushes through me in an almost painful explosion. I don't see myself in the glass as I fly. I see him. Only him. His soft eyes riveted on me, his strong frame ready to absorb everything I can't handle, ready to catch me before I fall.

Gray lowers himself behind me, freeing my hands as I tremble. And with the utmost care, he carries me to the bed and lays me on the quilt.

I'm exhausted and sated—physically and emotionally spent. But my body doesn't ache like a woman who's been beaten.

He brings a bowl of warm water and a soft cloth, and gently washes away the evidence of our play. His touch is tender and kind, and contented mewls slip from my lips as he dries me with a heated towel.

When my teeth chatter, Gray rubs a firm hand over my skin before pulling down the quilt and layering me with luxurious blankets, delicate and weightless. "I'll be right back," he murmurs, smoothing my hair.

I'm not sure how long he's gone, but he brings apple juice back with him. I shake my head. I'm too cold to drink anything.

"Just a few sips," he insists, bringing the straw to my mouth.

When he's satisfied I've had enough to drink, he lies down beside me, enveloping my body in his warmth.

"You're safe," he promises. "I'll keep watch while you sleep. Just rest. Let me take care of you."

"We're partners," I mumble, already half asleep.

"We are," he agrees, wrapping me tighter against him. "In all things."

As I drift off, it occurs to me that there was no pain. No real pain. No belts. No beatings until I screamed. No welts that needed immediate attention so they wouldn't scar.

I fall into a fitful sleep. Because even Gray's careful vigilance can't keep my inner demons at bay.

24

DELILAH

There's a big pot of oil heating on the stove, slaw in the refrigerator, and biscuits almost ready for the oven. Plus, the corn pudding I made earlier smells divine. I'm just waiting on Gray. He's supposed to text about thirty minutes before he comes upstairs.

We've been out most evenings, and I thought it might be nice to make him supper for a change. Something decidedly Southern and homey that he can't get in a five-star restaurant or in Amadi.

The more I study with Mira, the more I realize how much effort Gray has put into preparation for the mission. To prepare *me* for the mission.

Pass along a message. Child's play—unless you're a spy in a foreign country who's under constant surveillance. Then words like treason and espionage get thrown around.

Gray and I have been making it work. Relationship building —in and out of bed. Most days the lines seem only slightly blurred, and on others, I'm convinced there's more to what's going on between us than just the mission.

He has the last word on anything mission-related, but with

the day-to-day stuff there's negotiation and real compromise. In the bedroom, he's always in control of the play, whether it's vanilla-ish or kink, and I always have the power to end it with a safe word. I've never once worried that he might not stop if I used it.

Although the sex is mostly kink and always intense, it's without the kind of torment masochists and sadists normally revel in. Gray stays clear of the bruising physical pain. He prefers to raise the intensity by toying with my mind.

Once or twice, there have been moments of internal panic when I've been sure that I'm being groomed again. But they turned out to be just remnants of my relationship with Kyle—it had nothing to do with Gray.

The man is a beast. But not the kind of monster Kyle turned out to be.

Kyle was an abuser and a cheat. Although I don't have any solid evidence of the last part, just innuendo and speculation from the congressional hearings. But I don't doubt it's true. I could investigate his past, and I have thought about it over the years. But why bother? I've already given my relationship with Kyle too much time and effort.

I was young and naïve when we first met, living off ramen noodles and boxed mac and cheese, but mostly I was alone. My mother had taken up with yet another *man of her dreams*, and they went off together the summer before I started college. She didn't bother to tell me that she'd sold the place until two men in a pickup truck showed up one morning to clean out the trailer a week before I left for school. When I finally reached my mother, she swore up and down she had told me about the sale, and chastised me for being an airhead. I'm quite sure I would have remembered her telling me a small thing like *I sold the house and you'll need to find somewhere else to live.*

The Marshalls, who lived across the street, let me stay with them until I left for college. They gave me a wonderful send-off with a hummingbird cake and a silver charm in the shape of a key. *It's to remind you that you, and nobody else, hold the key to your future.*

It was the nicest thing anyone had ever done for me, and the Marshalls had done plenty. Even then, the small charm seemed weighty.

Richie Marshall gave me a teddy bear that he'd picked out himself so I wouldn't be too lonely at school. *We're so proud of you, Lilah*, they gushed, when they hugged me at the bus station. *Don't forget us.*

I never have.

The hole in my heart hasn't gotten any smaller. Even stealing the archbishop's last breath didn't help close that gap. But their deaths have been avenged. Although it turned out to be small comfort.

I check the temperature on the oil, and turn it up a drop. I expect to hear from Gray any minute. He's good about following through—if he's says he'll call or text, he will. *Unlike Kyle.*

Kyle and I met at a symposium on careers with the government. He gave the presentation on the FBI. He approached me while I was waiting in line to talk to the CIA recruiter, and teased me endlessly about choosing the CIA over the FBI. Kyle was handsome and charming, and I was a not-quite-eighteen-year-old freshman. It didn't take much effort to convince me to have supper so he could change my mind about joining the Bureau.

He never did change my mind. My heart was long-set on being a spy. But he did convince me to go out with him again, and again. He eventually confessed he was a Dominant, and introduced me to the BDSM lifestyle.

It wasn't until after he died, when I screwed up the courage to dip my toes into the local BDSM community, that I learned Kyle was a poser. There are a lot of them out there. Men who pretend to be Dominants to get sex, or to abuse in a socially acceptable way. Kyle was good-looking, and he had no trouble finding sex, but a willing partner to play his sadistic games was harder to come by. No family, new to the area, and broken inside, I was perfect.

At a community get-together, I met Tony, who was significantly older than me, and an experienced Dom. *A real Dom.* We spent at least forty-five minutes talking, and I agreed to meet him for coffee the next day.

Over a frothy beverage, he gave me an education. He asked me questions and patiently explained the exchange of power, and so many other things I didn't know about the lifestyle. He recommended books, websites, and informative articles to read. He would have answered my questions too, but I was too overwhelmed to come up with any.

There was no sex, and there would be no sex with Tony, ever. Dominants like Tony don't play with big messes like me. He never said that, and honestly, sex was the last thing on my mind once he started talking. Tony was a good guy, who did me a huge service without making me feel any stupider than I already felt.

I never showed my face at another community gathering, and I never saw Tony again either. But I read and researched everything he recommended, and the more I learned, the more I realized my relationship with Kyle was fucked up.

Kyle gaslighted me into believing I was a pain slut—created just for him. It didn't happen overnight. He was patient, carefully grooming me, step by step, until in the end, I couldn't have an orgasm even with a Hitachi held to my clit, unless he'd beaten the shit out of me first.

I should have talked to a therapist, but I spoke to no one about that part of my life. I was too ashamed of having allowed the abuse. As it turns out, being abused is a lot like being widowed at a young age. It has no place in polite conversation

—it makes people too uncomfortable. That's fine. The victim tag isn't one I've ever been willing to wear anyway.

My phone buzzes, but it's Gabby returning a text from earlier. *I should set the table.* I don't need to even think about which glasses to take out. Gray likes water without ice, and he drinks red wine, never white, but prefers a beer or bourbon. We're comfortable, not the married-twenty-years-with-four-kids kind of comfortable, but the crown prince won't expect that level of familiarity from us.

Sometimes, I worry I'm getting too comfortable. Fancy clothes. A driver. I look around the well-appointed kitchen. They're all empty trappings, I remind myself. Nothing more than window dressing. Things my mother would have longed for. Not me.

I set out small dishes of baking soda and sliced lemons to absorb the odors. As I dredge the catfish, I can't help but think about Mrs. Marshall. It's her recipe. Her lemon and baking soda trick. "I hope I do you proud," I whisper out loud, just in case she's near. "I miss you. Send my love to Mr. Marshall, and give Richie a big hug for me."

The phone vibrates again.

GRAY: 30 minutes.

I put the biscuits in the oven and add the catfish to the hot oil. It splatters, and I jump back to avoid a nasty burn. After a few minutes, I turn the sizzling fillet over. It's brown and gorgeous when I pull it out of the oil bath and lay it on a rack in the warming tray under the stove. I repeat the entire process, until—*the smell. Fuck.* It's so pungent it's starting to overwhelm the kitchen.

Gray's going to kill me. *Oh my God.*

I run around like a crazy woman, shutting all the doors in the apartment to contain the odor while I call Lally. She was the cook at the Wilder house while Gray was growing up, and now she works for Gabby and JD. She's also a good soul and my friend. If anyone has a solution to this, it's her.

I open the balcony door and turn the fan on full speed, while I wait for Lally to answer. I don't even pause for her to say hello. "I ain't got no time for pleasantries. I'm in trouble."

"What's wrong?"

"I fried catfish and even though I set out lemon slices and small bowls of baking soda, Gray's apartment stinks to high heaven."

It's quiet for a second, before her voice booms through the phone. "You fried catfish in Gray's apartment? The same Gray Wilder who doesn't put on a piece of clothing that hasn't just returned from a visit to the laundry? The same man who has floors you can eat off?"

Yes. Yes. Yes. "Are you going to bust my balls or help me? He's on his way up. How can I make the stench go away?"

"You can't," she answers decisively. "It's stubborn. Goes away in its own time. That's why most people fry fish on the back porch or out in the yard. Even then it can stink up the house if you're not careful. That baking soda and lemon thing is just an old wives' tale. It doesn't really help much."

Oh my God. "He's almost here! What am I going to do?"

"First, calm down. Put a lid on the pot with the oil and open all the windows. Then get some grime-cutting cleaner, and wash off any splatters on the stove and around the countertop."

I race around the apartment, following her instructions, but there's not enough time.

"When you're done, take out the trash. And don't burn yourself—oil stays hot for a long time."

"I've gotta go. He's here. Thanks." *He's here. I can't tell if the smell has dissipated or if I've just gotten used to it. I am so screwed.*

"Jesus, it stinks in here," he says, before the door clicks shut. "What the hell is going on?"

My stomach turns somersaults at the sound of his voice, but I'm fresh out of time.

Before I can come up with a decent apology, Gray's in the doorway, eyes wide and alert as they scan the kitchen. He looks like he belongs on a magazine cover, while I smell like a grease pit and probably look like one too.

"I wanted to surprise you—"

"I'm surprised," he says, before I finish. "Maybe in the future, you could limit the surprises to exotic-smelling body lotions and lacy lingerie. Let—"

"With supper," I say softly. "I felt like I wasn't earning my keep, and I wanted to do something special for you."

He doesn't utter a word for several long seconds, and I'm dying inside, like someone who hands over a gift they spent hours selecting, and as the present is unwrapped they grow more and more uncertain about the choice.

"So what did you make?" he asks almost nonchalantly, his initial irritation replaced by genuine curiosity.

"Catfish, slaw, corn pudding, and biscuits. Tartar sauce, too." I spit it all out in a single breath. The menu sounds ridiculous as I look at Gray in his designer suit. It's as though I let the little girl inside out to play, and she made mud pies and expected the grownups to eat them for supper.

His features soften while I talk. "I'm starving and it sounds delicious. I love catfish."

I'm so focused on his facial expression, I don't really hear the words. But some part of me understands that it's okay, and the stress rolls off my shoulders.

"Let me get out of these clothes. I'll only be a minute. Why don't we eat on the balcony?" he calls over his shoulder, as he strides down the hall.

He's gone, but I nod anyway. When I turn around, I get a fresh look at the kitchen as he just saw it. *What a mess.* A stinky mess. I'll clean it later, after we're done eating.

By the time I get my bearings and put the food out, Gray's back in shorts and a Gamecock T-shirt. I hand him a plate. "Help yourself. The fish is keeping warm in the tray."

"This is delicious," he says, breaking off a piece of crispy fish and popping it in his mouth.

"You're not mad about the way it stinks in here?"

He shrugs, taking an extra spoonful of corn pudding. "It's not often that someone I'm not paying makes me supper." He runs his thumb over my cheek. "Thank you," he murmurs, placing a small kiss on my nose. "As for the smell, we can call one of those industrial restoration companies that people hire to clean up after a fire or flood to get the smoke and mildew out. If that doesn't work, we'll have a big bonfire, invite the neighbors, and toast some marshmallows for s'mores."

My face-splitting grin turns into a laugh.

"Come here." He uses his free hand to pull me into him.

I don't complain because I like it here. I like the smell of him, the way his skin feels, and the sound his heart makes while he holds me against his chest. I like all of it. And if that makes me a weak woman, so be it. Life's too short not to treat yourself now and again.

"The clearance came through today, on both ends," he says, his chin resting on my head. "We leave in four days." When I don't answer, he pulls away. "What are you thinking?"

"I'm thinking I'm ready." No one is ever fully prepared, but I feel good about my chances. "What are you thinking?"

"I'm thinking that this is a pretty good way to end a long day. A good start, anyway." His thumb caresses my breast, and I feel the low pull of desire. "But after we eat, I have something to show you. Downstairs."

My emotions twist into a wanton curl while I run my fingers through my hair. It doesn't matter that it's a greasy rat's nest. He makes me feel sexy and wanted just the same.

"Dessert's on me," he murmurs.

The way he says it. The raw quality in his voice. The lust on his beautiful face. I know that *downstairs* means the club. I'm not sure how I'll get through dinner knowing there's dessert waiting there.

"Let's eat," I say, without hiding my enthusiasm. "So we can get to dessert. You know how much I like that."

For a second, there's a flicker of uncertainty in Gray's eyes, but I don't dwell on it. Instead, I take my plate out to the balcony, confident that he's right behind me.

25

GRAY

"Do we have time to clean the kitchen before dessert?" Delilah asks when we finish eating. "Lally said not to let that grease hang around for too long. Otherwise it could be days before the smell goes away."

Days? "You called Lally?" Just imagining their conversation makes me laugh. "I bet she got a kick out of that."

"She was laughing so hard, she might have wet herself." Delilah throws her head back and laughs. It's a glorious sound.

"I'd have paid good money to be sitting in the same room as Lally while you were telling her that you fried catfish in my apartment."

She leans over and slaps my thigh hard enough to get my full attention. I grab her wrist, and pull her onto my lap, exploring her mouth with my lips and tongue until I've sucked all the air from her lungs.

"Why don't you take a shower and put on something easy to take off. I'll call housekeeping and have them come up to clean the kitchen while we're downstairs."

"That doesn't seem right." Her brow furrows, and I smooth the lines with my thumb. "It's a huge mess."

"They're paid well to clean huge messes. Trust me when I tell you they'd rather clean some greasy counters than some of the other things they regularly clean up downstairs." I slide my fingers lower, until I reach the button on her shorts. After untethering it, I pull down the zipper. "You need to wear clothing that gives me better access to your gorgeous little body—all of it. It would serve us both well." I rub the outside of her shorts where they cover her pussy until she whimpers against my neck. "Go shower, and don't be too long." I slap her ass once before nudging her off my lap.

"Delilah."

She turns, with one hand on the French door.

"Do not—I repeat, *do not*—take care of that little ache between your legs while you're in the shower. You won't like the consequence."

To my great surprise, she doesn't respond before she saunters inside.

Fuck. When I planned tonight, I had no idea she was making me supper. A meal that took a lot of thought and effort.

There's a cruelty to tonight's plan that seems particularly evil after all her trouble—her kindness. But I can't change it now. We leave in four days, and I have no idea how shaken she'll be after what's in store for her. The mind is a funny thing—unpredictable as hell. She might need all that time to recover.

I'm torn. I want to stay here, well-fed and happy, pour a bourbon, watch a movie, and fuck her into oblivion between scenes. I get up and go over to the edge of the balcony. It's a clear night and I can see all the way to the ocean. Tonight can't be about what I want. It has to be about what Delilah needs.

I tighten my grip on the railing as I watch the sailboats bob in the distance. It's my job to set her up for success. If she fails, she'll blame herself. Instead of moving her forward, I'll have dragged her back. That can't happen. *End of story.*

While she's showering, I call housekeeping to come up in forty-five minutes, text Mel to come by at 7:30 tomorrow instead of 5:30—Delilah's going to need the time—and phone my sister-in-law Gabby, who I've known and loved my entire life.

"Hey."

"Gray! How are you? It's been ages since I've seen you. I think a long lunch, just you and me, is in order."

"I'm glad to hear you want to see me, because I was hoping JD, Chase, and I could have supper at your house this time?"

"Why? You expect the smell of catfish will still be stinkin' up your place?"

I laugh. Gabby isn't a busybody, but she's never had *any* problem sticking her nose into my private life, and since Christmas when I showed up at Sweetgrass with Delilah, she's been relentless. "I expect the smell to hang around for a bit, but that's not why I'm asking. Although I guess you've heard that Delilah and I are trying each other on for size."

"News travels fast around these parts. But I'm annoyed I had to hear it from Lally. I wouldn't have expected you to say a peep, but Delilah and I are good friends."

I had some misgivings about this conversation. Specifically about how much to share with Gabby, but this settles it. I don't want her all over Delilah. It's one thing to take the relationship out for a test drive at my brother's, but it's another to have Gabby adding to Delilah's anxiety—even if she means well.

"I was hoping you and Delilah would join us for dinner."

"Really?" Gabby hesitates. "Must be something pretty special if you're letting us crash your boys' night. Have some news you want to share with the family?"

She's fishing, and I ignore it. "Delilah and I are taking a trip. The relationship's new. We haven't tried it out with company yet. The trip is a little out of her comfort zone. I was hoping maybe we could practice on you and my brothers."

"*You* were hoping? What about Delilah?"

Gabby doesn't let anything slide. She's tough. I guess she has to be to handle my brother as artfully as she does. "Delilah knows I want to bring her to a family supper. But she's—I bought her a few things to wear on the trip—she's not comfortable with that idea. It makes her feel cheap." This still bothers me a lot. It just does. "I'm going to encourage her to wear her new clothes to your house, but it would be helpful if you didn't make a big fuss."

"Delilah has a lot of pride. I can see how she'd hate you buying her things. It took me a long time to get comfortable spending JD's money, and I'd been around it forever. I'll think about how I can help make it easier for her." Gabby's fully on board. "I'm so glad Smith's giving her some time off. She needs it. Where you going?"

"Visit the Amadi royal family."

She whistles. "That's out of anyone's comfort zone. I can't believe you're friends with that guy—the Prince of Assholes. I'll never understand it."

When she says it, I cringe. I want to tell her that the prince and I aren't really friends. But of course, I don't. "Some relationships are hard to understand from the outside. Take you and JD, for example."

"Isn't that the truth." She chuckles. "I would love to host supper. It makes me so happy that you guys get together every week. Your mother would be ecstatic."

It's true. Julia Wilder would be beside herself if she knew her sons looked out for one another—always—and broke bread once a week. We usually meet at the club on Monday nights when it's quiet.

Gabby's prattling on about something, but since I wasn't really paying attention, I can't respond. "Can I bring something?"

"Only if you want to insult Lally."

"I'd like to live to see another day."

"I've waited a long time for you two to come to your senses," she says. "You're perfect for each other."

I scoff in response to her happily-ever-after talk. But a lifetime with Delilah doesn't sound anywhere near as bad as I make it out to be.

After we say good-bye, I think about going inside to pour a bourbon, but decide against it. Tonight is going to be tough on Delilah, and I want to have the presence of mind to know when to stop, and how to support her when it's over. Whiskey will only make those things more difficult.

The door opens, and I glance up at the gorgeous woman in the doorway. Delilah has on a white sleeveless dress with a zipper all the way down the front that I'm going to enjoy taking off. I'm sure she knew that when she chose it. She's wearing casual sandals, and not a lick of makeup. Her hair is in a loose braid. She looks like a college kid.

My stomach rebels at the thought of what I have planned.

"You told me to be quick, so I didn't bother getting fancy."

I move slowly toward the doorway. "You don't need to be fancy tonight. And for the record, I like you best when you're dressed just the way you are right now. Although naked is my hands-down favorite."

As her smile lights up the porch, it sends the guilt worming its way back into my conscience. We've come a long way in a short time. In large part because Delilah is open to doing whatever the mission requires.

I bring her hand to my mouth and put a small kiss on her inner palm. "The scene tonight will be challenging—for both of us. Will you follow my lead?"

Her thick lashes flutter on her cheeks, as she averts her eyes. "Yes." She nods. "I'll follow wherever you lead."

The sincerity in her voice is alone remarkable. But when she lowers herself to her knees in a posture that is unequivocally submissive, her trust shakes me to the core. This might be her surrender, but she captured my soul as she quietly offered me her submission.

I know the precious gift is only for now. Delilah will expect me to earn it every day, as she damn well should. But she owns me. I can try to convince myself otherwise, but there's no going back from here—not for me.

26

DELILAH

The elevator ride to the lower level is quiet. Gray stands behind me, his arms wrapped tightly around my torso, his chin resting on my head. He doesn't say a word, but he's preoccupied and tense, and his sullen mood begins to make me wonder if kneeling for him was a mistake.

He's not a man who would take the gesture lightly. He knows what it means, especially coming from me. Maybe it was more than he bargained for tonight. Brooding with dessert on the horizon is not at all like him.

When it comes to sex, whether in a scene or not, Gray's fully present and in charge. *Always.* He doesn't share the power, nor does he apologize for the way he wields it. This elevator ride would normally be a prelude, the beginning of a long, seductive tease. But it's not, and the change in him has me unsettled.

The elevator door pings open, and Gray takes my hand and leads me down the grand hall. We pass rooms with plaques affixed to the doors, each one hinting at the fantasy inside. I remember all of it from Christmas. The only thing missing are the boughs of fragrant pine and spruce draping the doorways, and the gilded pinecones scattered on the elaborate consoles stationed up and down the wide hall.

The room we enter has no plaque. It's a spacious suite, with a bathroom and a place for aftercare beyond, I'm sure. It's done in rich golds and purples that complement the dark wood floor, and lush fabrics that remind me of the Sultan's Palace, where we played on Christmas. There have been many *memories* since, but that night will always hold a special place for me, because it was our first time.

A luminous incense lightly perfumes the room—it's luxurious and exotic, mixed with sweet orange and maybe vanilla. Not elixirs for religious ritual, but oils to anoint the body and awaken the senses.

Gray brushes my arm as he passes. His stride is assured, and the stress I sensed earlier is gone. This is his domain. Whatever was weighing on his mind earlier, he must have left at the door.

I look around the room and begin to relax.

Gray observes quietly from several feet away, letting me soak up the ambiance with all its possibilities. The room is ripe for pleasure. Beckoning and cajoling us to add our bliss to the carnal screams of others, swirled into the plastered walls. It's tantalizing foreplay, and he's enjoying it as much as I am.

I smile shyly at him. His eyes flare, but he keeps his distance, letting me explore the Tantra chair on a raised platform in the center of the room. It doesn't have the fragility of the antique at the beach, or the practical simplicity of the one in the apartment that he fucked me on last night. No, this is larger, sturdier, with rings disguised as an adornment, hanging from the carved edges at the bottom. The possibilities make my mouth water.

I glance from Gray to the purple velvet coverlet that is hiding something on the platform floor. It's plush and decadent, meant for a king's bedding, and I wouldn't be at all surprised to find something similar at the palace. But there's more. Something that I suspect is neither luxurious, nor soft.

"What's your safe word?" Gray asks, approaching me.

"Red. Will you tell me more about the scene?" He always does. Not everything, but he hints at what I might expect from him, or what he expects of me.

"I'll show you," he says, leading me to the platform. We stand silently while he carefully pulls back the velvet topper to expose a long, mirrored tray filled with all sorts of delicious torments that excite me.

"I have jewels for you," he murmurs, pointing to the nipple clamps and then to plugs adorned with purple stones. Nearby is a strand of amethyst glass beads, of varying sizes.

Anal beads. I shiver at the beautiful spheres and the pleasure they hold.

"We're going to do a little rope play." The rope is purple too—it looks to be of soft cotton. "Just some simple ties and knots that won't take forever. Nothing elaborate. That's not the objective tonight."

"What is the objective?"

"Pleasure—ultimately, it's always pleasure."

Not the forthright answer I was hoping for. He's illusive. I don't believe for one second that he doesn't know *exactly* where he's taking me and how. He's just not telling.

There is also a satin blindfold and a pair of headphones on the tray. Elaborate binding might be out, but sensory deprivation is clearly on the table.

I look up and smile coyly. Gray's lips twitch at the corners, and his dark gaze scorches my skin until I look away.

My eye finds something unfamiliar. It looks like a wand with a glass end. Maybe a vibrator of some kind? Whatever the instrument is, there's something about it that raises gooseflesh on my arms.

"What is this?" I ask, my fingertips cautiously grazing the object.

"It's a violet wand."

I stiffen. It might not look familiar, but I've read about it.

"For electric play," he adds. "It's special."

For whom? Surely not for me. "I—"

He places his hand gently on my arm. "Just some light play. You'll be highly aware of the sensations—but it won't be painful. The wand won't hurt you. I won't hurt you."

I love a good lightning storm. But electricity makes me nervous.

I'm not afraid of pain, but I don't want to be electrocuted, especially in a sex club. Wouldn't that be a fitting ending for my life? *Jesus.*

Gray reaches for the zipper on my dress and hooks a finger through the ring before beginning a long, slow, downward tug. His eyes never leave mine. "What's your safe word?" he asks again.

I trust him, but I'm not ready to consent to electric play. "Red," I say clearly, "but it won't help if I'm being electrocuted."

He stops, dropping his finger from the zipper, and takes the wand off the tray. "Let me see your arm."

Like a trusting fool, I place my wrist in his hand. He touches the wand to my forearm, and I jump, not because it hurts—it doesn't—but because the sensation comes as surprise. We both laugh—me out of nerves, and Gray because he knows I'm going to like the wand.

He zaps me again, on my upper arm. The purple sparks and rods that light up inside the glass ball are quite beautiful. The next time, the tingle is stronger but not at all unpleasant.

"I won't turn the current up any more than that," he assures me. "But on your nipples, and your wet pussy, where the skin is more sensitive, the zings will pack a more powerful punch."

The anticipation of the pleasant sparks dancing on my skin

is arousing. I nod, and feel the shift in my mind occur as the scene begins.

Gray turns me around, facing the brocade drapes that span the wall. They hang from a brass rod with polished finials, and pool gracefully on the wood floor. From the corner of my eye, I see him reach for something, and the curtain opens slowly to reveal a glass wall and a room filled with people—*men*—chatting in small groups. They're seated in chairs set on risers, like at the theatre, so everyone can see the stage. There must be fifty or sixty men—maybe more.

My breathing is labored, and I feel lightheaded and weak as panic threatens. For the first time since I've been with Gray, I consider using my safe word.

Before I decide, Gray twirls me around to face him, hooking a thumb under my chin so I'm forced to look into his eyes. My brain is still trying to make sense of the room behind me, but it's slogging, struggling more than it should—maybe it doesn't want to know what he has planned. Maybe it's too much to bear.

"You have an audience tonight," he says calmly. "Dozens and dozens of eyes on your luscious body. Probing and judging, but mostly enjoying you, helplessly bound, a servant to my cock."

I'm beginning to sweat, and I'm sure he notices, but there are no reassurances to make me feel better.

"How long do you think it'll take before they have their dicks in hand? Five minutes? Ten? Or will they wait until you're writhing shamelessly, begging for release?"

He pulls the zipper on my dress lower and lower, until it falls open. I didn't wear anything underneath—for him. But now—

Gray slides his fingers into my hair and kisses me. No, it's not a kiss. It's the demanding mark of ownership, and the unrepentant claim leaves me reeling. As I spiral, his words run through my mind on a continuous reel, not just those from tonight but from the last two weeks. *You have an audience tonight. Dozens and dozens of eyes on your luscious body. Probing and judging... There's surveillance everywhere in the palace. You've never done anything like this before. You'll be on display, like an animal at the zoo. It can be unnerving, even for an experienced operative. I can't protect you from that.*

This is a test. A test to determine if I'm mission ready. If I can weather the storm or if I'll fold when the first gust blows through. *You can do this, Delilah. You can do this.* I draw a breath and release it, and do it again. I will outrun my fear—my shame of being watched.

"Close your eyes," Gray instructs, securing the blindfold. The darkness comes as a relief. But it's a short-lived reprieve.

"These are noise-canceling headphones," he explains matter-of-factly, as he fits them on my head. There's not a smidgeon of judgment or sneer in his voice. "The room next door is mic'd." He runs his tongue along my shoulder, biting when he reaches the tendon where it meets my neck. I tremble as he nips at my skin. "The sound will vary. I'll set it to capture the ruckus of the entire room, and at other times I'll turn on the individual areas, so you can hear the grunts of pleasure coming from your adoring audience. They're going to love watching you, Blue Eyes."

I push the bile down. This isn't going to beat me. I won't let it.

Gray's voice disappears, and I hear murmurs and snickering. Someone laughs. Another comments on my ass, and yet another on my tits. I'm not human to them.

The men are behind a wall, but it feels as though they're here in this room, close enough to reach me—to touch me with their filthy hands. Although I know I'm physically safe, there is something terrifying about this—something bone-chilling.

He won't let them hurt you. I repeat this over and over, but the men's voices are deafening, drowning out any attempt to soothe myself. Being blindfolded only makes the catcalls seem louder, and more dangerous.

Gray's voice cuts in as I feel something cool on my lips. "Open your mouth. They want to see you warm the plug, before I slide it in your ass. Good girl," he murmurs, when I part my lips for him. The plug will feel more comfortable going in if it's been warmed first. Normally it's arousing to prepare, but today, there's nothing but humiliation. The taunts and raucous laughter take away all the pleasure.

Gray's mouth is on my nipple, coaxing it to a pointed peak, while his fingers tweak the other. "*Ahhh.*" He's readying me for the clamps. I know it, but still, I gasp at the first pinch, and brace myself for the second bite.

He brushes some loose hair off my face. "You're beautiful in purple. The color suits you. As do the jewels." His voice is a welcome reprieve. When he speaks, the din from the other room falls silent, and it's just us. "I need you to fold your body forward. Let it rest on the platform. I'll help you."

Unable to see, I move carefully, as he guides me to where he wants me.

"Just relax."

I feel the lube collect in the hollow of my back, and Gray's fingers work it between my cheeks and into the pleated hole. His touch feels good, but there's a part of me that's ashamed I feel pleasure in the middle of the spectacle.

"What a whore. She loves it," a nasty voice jeers, and then others join the taunting. There's more laughter as Gray takes the plug from my mouth and slides it into my most private place. I try to tune the noise out, but it's a struggle.

"Let's get you on the lounge," he says gently, helping me stand. "There are three steps to the top." He wraps his arm around my waist so that I don't fall.

I count the steps in my head, trying to block out the noise

from the other room, and reminding myself over and over that this is a test.

But it's impossible to silence the ugly chatter from the next room or the one happening inside my head. I'm fully on display, like a sex slave being sold at auction. *That's how he wants you to feel.*

Gray secures my wrists and attaches the rope to something above my head. There's enough play so I can move my arms as they rest on the platform, but not enough to escape my fate. *You have a safe word. That's your escape. He will respect it. He will.* But I'm not safing out. I will not let a bunch of faceless, nameless freaks beat me.

With little effort, he has me in a loose frogtie, with my thighs spread open. "Pound the whore," someone calls as Gray's fingers dip into me. My walls embrace him. It's not a conscious act, just a reaction.

"You're wet, Delilah," he murmurs, and then his sensuous purr is gone, replaced by the vulgar taunts and whistles.

Hours seem to pass while I wait with only the mocking from the other room.

My mind eventually wanders to the beach house, where there was so much peace and serenity. I focus on the majestic views, and soon the crash of the waves drowns out the impatient catcalls from the other room and I feel myself relax. Just a bit—until the first jolt of electricity hits my naked flesh. My body jerks from the exquisite tingling, and for a short moment, I relish it. But then the crass shouts come flooding back—a stark reminder that we're not alone.

Gray plays on my skin, rousing the nerves in a way that makes my core clench. It feels amazing, but I try not to move, and just focus on staying quiet. I don't want to add to the pleasure for those bastards in the other room. But when Gray pulls off the clamps, I wince and whimper. And the men cheer.

He soothes each nipple with his tongue, until the sting is

nearly gone. I'm still catching my breath when the glass ball grazes my nipple. "*Ahhh!*" His warm mouth wasn't to ease the ache. It was meant to prepare the nipple for the wand.

I'm in an inky cave. There's nothing but black—not even a shadow to guide me as I wait for the next jolt. Will it be to my thigh? My nipple? My belly? The uncertainty adds a heightened awareness that is unsettling and delectable at the same time.

The wand touches my almost bare mound, and I arch my back and squirm. I can't stay still any longer, and the sounds from the other room dim as the pleasure increases. There's no pain, just thrilling charges that skitter through my body.

Before the bliss subsides, the current licks my clit. The first wave has all the excitement of a sparkler, with its beautiful glow. But there is a reason children are taught to hold the sparkler away from their bodies. The second wave comes with the power of a thunderbolt. I jerk and bounce off the platform. Not in pain, but with a heavenly sensation I've never felt before. It's almost too much. But he does it again. And again.

My body absorbs every bit of the hedonistic indulgence, writhing and pulling at my bindings as I thrash. All I see and hear, all I feel, is my own pleasure. There's nothing else.

I feel Gray's soothing hands pet my prickly skin. "Give me a color," he murmurs through the headphones.

"Green." My voice is hoarse, but the word is clear, and not a second passes before Gray's hot mouth is on my cunt. Licking and lapping, tracing circles with a pointed tongue, finding my clit hiding under the hood. He sucks gently, coaxing it out.

I whimper. "Please."

The voices are loud again. "Slut. Whore. Fuck her in the ass until she screams." They're indistinguishable.

"They want to see you come, Delilah," Gray drawls. "You want that too, don't you?" He doesn't wait for my response before his tongue is back on my pussy, his mouth and hands plucking the screaming orgasm from me, as I twist beneath him.

"Good girl," he soothes in a gentle, reassuring tone.

I can't stop whimpering. It's an incoherent babble, dwarfing all other sounds.

Gray unties my legs and massages them with strong fingers. It feels so good that I don't want him to stop. But he turns me over and hoists my hips, adjusting my body on the chair until I'm on my knees, draped over the highest curve. My ass is exposed. But I don't give a damn who sees me.

"I need this," he says, gently removing the plug. "I have something better for you."

The anal beads. The climax will be earth-shattering. I picture the amethyst beads, the long strand, with the glass globes graduating in size. *How many will he push into me?*

The crowd erupts each time he forces a bead inside. But it's a muffled blur. Nothing more than scratchy background music. I barely hear them.

"I'm going to fuck you, Blue Eyes. And they're going to watch while I own your pussy."

Gray pushes his cock into me. It feels enormous, and I groan at the tight fit. But he doesn't stop. He moves in and out, teasing my clit, unhurried, while I loll in a dreamy state. Higher and higher he drags me, and as I approach the peak he begins to pull out the beads one at a time.

I gasp and shudder as he removes the balls slowly, deliberately, each small pop nudging me higher. I'm lost, struggling for breath.

His cock and my cunt. There's nothing else when he pinches my clit, yanking out the final beads while I clamp down around him, screaming my release.

He doesn't slow, and I tremble while he ruts deeply. He's close. I want the headphones off. I want to hear the roar of his release. I twist my head to dislodge the damn things, but it's too late. I don't hear his pleasure.

But I feel it. I feel him empty himself inside me, and I squeeze my walls, milking each precious drop.

He presses his lips to my spine. Resting his forehead there for a moment.

It's quiet. I must have knocked off the headphones.

Gray eases out of me, and the semen begins to find its way out. He pulls me onto his body, nestling us into the welcoming slope of the chair. "Are you okay?" he asks, caressing me gently.

I nod. "Yes."

He pulls the velvet coverlet from the platform and lays it over us, taking great pains to make sure that every inch of my skin is covered. "Are you warm enough?"

"Yes." I don't have the energy for anything more. I close my eyes, and the voices return. I'm not sure if they're real or if they just live in my head now—*maybe forever*. I clutch him tighter as the anxiety starts to burrow its way in again. "Are they still watching?"

Gray is quiet for a moment, before his lips graze my head. "They were never watching."

I'm not sure I understand what he means. I lift my head off his chest, and slowly turn toward the curtain. It's dark. There's nothing there. I don't understand. I saw them. The show's over. Maybe they left.

"It was a trick," he says cautiously.

"A trick?" No. I saw them with my own eyes.

"I blindfolded you to help with the deception. Once the initial shock wore off, you'd figure out there was no one there. It was basically a high-tech hologram."

"But the voices?"

"A recording."

My body that had been so relaxed is now on edge. The limp muscle is rigid and I'm not sure what to think.

"You'll be watched constantly at the palace. We'll be watched having sex. I didn't want your first experience with exhibitionism to be while you were jet-lagged, in unfamiliar surroundings. I want you to feel prepared when you're there. To be confident, that even if you're experiencing something that feels dreadful, you can get through it."

It's not an apology. But I hear the remorse in the clinical words. Somewhere inside me, buried under layers of exhaustion and confusion, I know this game we're playing is hard for him too. But I can't find any empathy right now.

I'm emotionally overwhelmed, and I need an escape, so I allow myself to be dragged over a jagged path toward sleep. My brain has had enough. "I need to sleep. Just for a few minutes."

"Close your eyes," he says with a tinge of regret in his voice. "Sleep as long as you need to. I won't leave you."

I passed the test. I did it. It doesn't matter that they weren't there. I believed they were, and I pushed through and drowned them out. The realization swamps me, and I cry out softly.

"You're safe with me, Blue Eyes—always." Gray rubs small circles on my back. "I promise."

27

DELILAH

We leave for Amidane the day after tomorrow. It's been almost three weeks since the beach. It feels like a lifetime on a merry-go-round. Days poring over briefing material, picking Mira's brain about tiny details that might help me befriend the princess. How I'll actually pull it off is still a bit of a mystery.

I've also had countless meetings with Trippi and with Baz, Gray's new driver, and Gray himself. Then there's yoga with Mel, hours at the range with Gray, and the white-hot nights we spend sealing the relationship. Neither of us will have trouble convincing anyone that part is real. *It is real.*

Although it doesn't mean that what we've rekindled will last beyond the mission. I try not to kid myself too much, but late at night when I'm falling asleep with his body wrapped around mine, it hurts to imagine that it won't be long before I'll be lying in my own bed, alone.

I glance across the seat at Gray, who's banging away on his laptop. Baz is driving us to Sweetgrass so Gray can work a little longer. I offered to drive, but that earned me a snicker and a *hell no.*

Baz has been on the job since Gray assigned Trippi to my protection. That was a knockout, drag-out fight that I clearly didn't win. Like Trippi, Baz is a former SEAL, and though they're often behind the wheel, that's not their primary skill.

"What's eating you, Blue Eyes?" he asks, reaching over to pinch my thigh.

"Nothing a cocktail can't cure."

He smiles and is back to business without another word.

I stare out the car window as we cross the Battery. The ocean is like glass, but the heat and humidity have kept the early evening walkers and runners away. I ran along these sidewalks every morning less than a month ago. Rain or shine. I miss the early morning run, but I'm beginning to learn that spreading my wings is not a bad thing. Plus, I love Mel. I'll miss him when it's over.

The sun is shining, but a small bolt of heat lightning flashes in the distance. It reminds me of the brilliantly evil violet wand. I squirm, remembering the pleasing jolts. *That was some prep work.*

Much to Gray's surprise, I quickly put that evening behind me. There was no malice on his part—*none*—and that made it easy to compartmentalize. I simply stuffed it in the box marked *training* and closed the lid.

I never shared all my concerns about being watched during sex. But somehow Gray knew it was weighing on me. Thanks to his efforts, I made it through the experience without falling apart, and whatever I encounter in Amadi will be easier because of it.

But tonight is the biggest test. *My* biggest test.

I've been a bundle of nerves since Gray suggested supper at Gabby and JD's house. Gabby is my closest friend, and there are few secrets between us. "It's a good test," he coaxed when I took refuge inside my head. "Gabby will know immediately if something doesn't smell right. And she won't hesitate to mention it to either of us. If we can fool my brothers and Gabby, especially Gabby, we can fool anyone."

He's right, of course. But I don't want to fool Gabby. I might be a killer and a spy, but I hate the idea of lying to someone I love. It was bad enough talking to Smith—although I didn't lie to him. I just stayed clear of the truth.

Before we left the apartment, Gray and I had words about my outfit. I insisted on wearing my own things so Gabby wouldn't think I was being bought. That would be too much for me to bear. Gray, on the other hand, was adamant that I get used to my new clothes—the clothes he paid for, because there's no way the government ponied up for a closet full of designer clothes. Gray can say whatever he wants, but I don't believe for one second that Uncle Sam bought two dozen thongs and matching bras from Agent Provocateur. If that's where our tax dollars are going, we should all be pissed.

Gabby knows my wardrobe, and while she would never judge me, wearing things bought and paid for by a man makes me feel like my mother, with every inch of me aching to rebel. In the end we compromised—although it wasn't much of a compromise.

I have on my own jewelry and undergarments, but the sundress and sandals are things the shopper sent over. The jewelry was a hard *no* for me, and the underwear also made me a bit queasy. Too much like a kept woman. In exchange for those concessions, I gave in to the rest.

Baz lets us off in the horseshoe at the front of the house. I fidget with my dress as we climb the steps to the front door without a word. At the top, Gray pulls me into his arms for a kiss, but I jerk away before his lips get anywhere near mine.

"What if someone's looking out the window?"

Gray chuckles. "That's why we're here. Relax. These are your friends. Gabby loves you. Besides, if I had a nickel for every time I caught her and my brother sucking face, and more, over the years," he shakes his head, "we could pay for college for every child in South Carolina."

"I don't like lying to people I love."

He takes my hand and gives it a reassuring squeeze before ringing the bell. "Anybody home?" His voice booms through the screen door.

In seconds, Gabby appears, with JD behind her carrying Gracie.

I shake JD's hand because my relationship with him doesn't involve hugging.

Gray kisses Gabby on the cheek and steals Gracie out of her father's arms, plopping a big smooch on her head. "I brought you a piece of chocolate from Chef Renaud," he says to the little girl, in a loud stage whisper. "Don't tell your parents. What's that? You prefer cigarettes and whiskey? That can be arranged too. Just come see Uncle Gray."

"Give me my daughter back," JD barks. "She's too young for chocolate. You ever give her cigarettes or liquor, you'll be dealing with me and my shotgun."

Watching Gray with Gracie would make most women's ovaries explode. But not mine. I have no interest in children, and seeing him so charmed by his niece is just a burning reminder that our compatibility begins and ends at the bedroom door.

Gabby rolls her eyes at her husband, and touches my wrist. "Any chance I could impose on you to make a pitcher of margaritas?"

Gabby and I bonded over margaritas, and we haven't stopped drinking them since. "If you want a mean cocktail, I'm your woman."

"A pitcher?" JD teases. Although with him, it's hard to tell for sure if he's teasing. "It's just you two drinking them."

"That's right," Gabby responds, "but we have to put up with

the likes of *you two* all night. And Chase. Although he's nowhere near as annoying."

"Where is Chase?" Gray asks.

"He's going to be a little late." JD catches Gray's eye and holds it steady. "I'm going up to put Gracie to sleep. Why don't you go and read to Zack?"

The color drains from Gray's face. It's no secret that he avoids visiting with Zack. His brothers, especially JD, don't like it. I don't know what it's about. A month ago, I might have said that he didn't have the stomach for it. Not everyone has it in them to spend time with a loved one who has deteriorated beyond recognition. But Gray's not a coward, and given his association with the EAD, he's stared down death. No doubt about it. It's something else.

Gray blows a raspberry on the bottom of Gracie's foot until she's giggling so hard the drool's leaking out of her mouth. "I never have a chance to put this sweet little girl to bed. How about if I read to Gracie and you read to Zack?"

JD's brittle expression speaks volumes. He's determined to force Gray to spend time with Zack, and he's not budging. "If you want to put a baby to bed, get your own. They're easy to make. I can recommend a video, if you don't know how. But it's not a do-it-yourself kind of thing."

Gray doesn't react to JD's mocking. There's anguish in his face. Real anguish. For a few seconds, I'm not sure what he's going to do, but he relents, and lumbers toward the wing of the house were Zack stays. I want to wring JD's neck.

"JD," Gabby hisses. "That was an unfair ambush."

Her husband pinches her arm playfully, as he heads to the stairs. "He's my brother," JD says over his shoulder. "Zack is on borrowed time, and I don't want Gray to have any regrets. He barely lives with the ones he has."

JD is heavy-handed and often misguided, although he means well here, I'm sure. But I have an overwhelming impulse to defend Gray. "He's a successful man, and he lives his life just fine," I say with enough snark to halt JD in his tracks.

He turns and scowls at me, but swallows whatever is on the tip of his tongue, and disappears up the stairs.

"I would tell you to ignore him," Gabby assures me, "but you already know that. You also know I'm dying for a cocktail."

If I were married to JD, I'd be dying for a cocktail all the time too. *Not my business.* I smile. "Then let's go juice some limes."

When we get to the kitchen, I set up on the center island to make the drinks. My entire house could fit into this one room, but all of a sudden it seems too small, like the walls are closing in. It's only a matter of time before Gabby begins the interrogation. I can feel it coming as I juice the limes into a glass measuring cup.

"All right, enough with all the secrecy."

Oh God. Here we go.

"I can't believe I had to hear about you and Gray from Lally."

"There's no big secret. I didn't say anything because I don't know where it's going between us. We're taking it slow."

"He's taking you to visit his friend the crown prince—who, by the way, is a first-class bastard. A trip halfway around the world doesn't sound slow to me."

I'm squeezing the limes so hard they're practically squealing. Matchmaking is her jam, and she's not going to stop until there's a ring on my finger.

"Do you have everything you need for the trip? I'm happy to go shopping with you."

"I'm all set. Gray—bought me some things." I can barely spit out the words.

"Ugly things?" she asks. "Because from the puckered expression on your face when you said *bought me some things*, it seems like he picked out some hideous clothes."

I side-eye Gabby. She's barely keeping it together. I start to laugh, and she bursts out laughing too. "Pull yourself together, and get me the tequila."

"It's right behind you," she says. "I want to hear more about the clothes and accessories. You can't go to Amadi without at least one suitcase full of designer clothes and some bling. It's just the way it is."

I measure the tequila carefully, until Gabby clears her throat, signaling that she expects some type of response. "The clothes are beautiful, and there's enough to fill a dozen suitcases. I'm not comfortable wearing things some man paid for, and I'm not comfortable talking about it, either." My discomfort might dissuade some people, but Gabby will just press on more gently.

She hands me a large wooden spoon and a pitcher filled with ice. "I could tell you that those Wilder boys have more money than they could spend in ten lifetimes. But I'm sure that won't make you feel any better than it made me feel when JD started buying me things. It gets easier. That I can say."

I hold out the spoon to give Gabby a taste of the margarita.

"A little more agave," she says. "Not too much." She leans across the counter, resting her forearms on the marble. "Lilah, I've got eyes." *Lilah.* I got the nickname when little Richie Marshall couldn't say Delilah. Gabby's one of the few people left who uses it.

"Gray isn't just *some* man," she says with great emotion. "*Everything* you have inside, you'll give him. That means so much more than anything money can buy—especially to men like JD and Gray. After their mother died, they grew up with nothing. The money didn't love them, or tuck them in at night, or dole out hugs when they were sick or heartbroken. It certainly didn't stand up tall in the foyer to defend Gray."

A cloud falls over me while I add another ounce of agave to the pitcher and stir until it dissolves. I don't know if it's because

I'm telling lies to my best friend, or because my relationship with Gray is temporary. "Gabby, don't get too invested in my relationship with Gray."

As I collect the used limes for the trash, I feel her watching me the way she does before she calls bullshit. I can't get out of here fast enough.

"What about you?" she probes. "Are you invested?"

It's too damn late for me. I'm a lost cause.

"I'm going to see if Gray needs a little moral support," I say, drying my hands on a dishtowel. As I leave the kitchen, it occurs to me that I didn't avoid her question. I answered it straight on.

28

GRAY

Damn JD. What an asshole. I should have known he'd pull this shit. He's always trying to get me to spend time with Zack. I thought Delilah being here tonight would spare me. It takes me weeks to fully recover after these visits. Time that I can't afford right now.

I push through the set of glass doors that separates Zack's wing from the rest of Sweetgrass. It's not because JD has him banished to the far corners of the house. It's so that they can keep things sanitized, and control the spread of infection in this part of the house. Zack is unlikely to survive a bad flu or pneumonia.

Zack suffered a traumatic brain injury in the accident that killed my mother and sister. He's been unresponsive since then, but JD, and now Gabby, make sure he has everything he needs to be comfortable. It's never been that easy for me.

After washing and drying thoroughly, I work a dollop of sanitizer into my hands before entering Zack's room.

"Hey Gray," the nurse, Maureen, says with a warm smile. She's hovering over the bed, adjusting the quilt.

"If I'm interrupting, I can come back." I don't wait for a response before I turn to leave.

"Don't go. You're not interrupting anything. Zack's ready for bed. Just waiting for his story."

That's a lie. He's not waiting on anything. Not now. Not ever. It doesn't matter how much my brothers and Gabby and the nurse act like he's a normal functioning human being. He's not. And it's my fucking fault. I did this to him.

"Are you reading to him tonight?"

I nod, avoiding Zack's curled limbs and blank stare.

"JD started this last night." Maureen hands me a book.

The Adventures of Robin Hood. My stomach twists into a knot that nearly knocks me over. Zack loved fantasy stories when he was a kid.

"I'll take my break while you're here. But I'm right outside if you need me."

I nod. I still haven't looked at Zack. I can't. It's too painful. After it happened, when I eventually made the connection, I forced myself to look at him for hours. It was punishment, to remind me of what I did to him—and to the others. But I don't need reminders. I live with the guilt day in and day out.

If only I hadn't been so selfish. So self-centered. They might still be alive.

It was a warm June day. School had let out the day before. I wanted to hang out with my buddies, and that's all I could think about. But my mother had other plans. She insisted that JD and I had to attend the cotillion practice later that afternoon. We'd been going to classes all year, and today was a dress rehearsal for the formal.

I couldn't understand why we needed to go to a stupid rehearsal when I could be playing video games in the playroom. JD complained too, but I nagged relentlessly. She wouldn't budge, and by the time we were ready to leave, I was a pissy little brat.

Olson, my father's henchman, stopped me on the way to the car, where the others were already waiting. "Bring your mother this sandwich. She hasn't eaten all day and your father's worried about her." I looked at the tuna sandwich wrapped in wax paper. Tuna salad was her favorite. She ate it for lunch several times a week.

"Don't tell her it's from your father. They had a little spat, and she might not eat it if she knows it's from him. But he wants to make sure she puts something in her stomach." What I didn't know at the time was that the little spat was about my mother catching a young girl with my father in his office. "Tell her Lally sent it if she asks. Okay?"

"Yep," I answered, taking the sandwich from him, and jogging out the back door like a little asshole, thrilled to pull one over on her. To punish her for making me waste the afternoon doing dumb things, when I could be hanging out with my cool friends.

"Lally made this for you," I said, handing her the wrapped sandwich, while holding the glee inside. She didn't even ask where it came from, but I lied to her anyway.

The last thing I said before slamming the car door was *don't forget to eat your tuna fish.*

It was the very last thing I ever said to her.

The mayonnaise in the tuna sandwich was mixed with sodium soltrite, a compound mixed at Sayle Pharmaceuticals. Our family company. *My mother's* family company. It incapacitated her, causing her to drive off the road into a ravine with my siblings in the car.

She died on impact. My siblings weren't as lucky. Chase was in the car for six hours, unable to move, surrounded by death, and Zack screaming in pain. Each time I visit, I hear those screams for days.

"Hey," Delilah says softly from the doorway.

"You can't be in here without washing your hands."

"I know," she replies, walking into the room. "I've hung out here before with Gabby and Zack."

She goes directly to the bed and pats Zack's hand gently.

"Hey Zackie, it's Delilah. Remember me? Gabby's friend. I'm Gray's friend too. How are you?"

I draw a breath as she has a one-sided conversation with my brother—the one I can't bear to look at. "He can't hear you."

"Sure he can. What's Gray reading you? Something good, I hope. He likes soulless writers, like Hemingway. I hope he's not making you listen to that crap."

"Hemingway's not soulless," I mutter.

"The man didn't believe in using adjectives. That's what gives language color."

"He believed they complicated sentences. He used verbs to tell his stories."

"Spare me the literature class, frat boy. The night's slipping away. I'm starving and we don't get to eat until you read, so get a move on. Zack and I are waiting."

She sits on the floor and peers at me until I begrudgingly open the book to the page with a stamped leather bookmark. I focus on the words, on the smell of Delilah's perfume, and on her calming presence, which I feel from several feet away. But none of it dulls the memory of Zack running around the backyard chasing the dog, dragging Chase, the quieter and smaller twin, along for the fun. *He was so full of life.*

As if she senses my anguish, Delilah crawls over, and sits at my feet with her head resting against my leg. There is something so visceral, so pure in her actions. They're a quiet reminder that I'm in control, born of strength—not of weakness. I slide my hand into her hair and let the silky strands comfort me as I read to my little brother.

There's nothing I can do to bring my mother or my sister back, or to make it right for Zack. Or even for JD and Chase, whose lives would have been dramatically different if my mother had lived. I can't change any of it for them, but there's one mistake from the past that I can correct.

I didn't intervene when Kyle bragged about his abusive

behavior. I called him out, told him he was a fucking dirtbag, but I took no action. I didn't contact Delilah and tell her to get the hell away from him. And I didn't kill the sonofabitch on the spot, which is exactly what he deserved—and what he eventually got—although not at my hands.

It might be too late for the others. But it's not too late for the woman at my feet.

When I'm through reading, we say good night to Zack. Actually, Delilah says good night, and I grunt when she urges me to say something.

With that behind us, supper is lighthearted and fun. We laugh more than usual with Gabby and Delilah here.

No one raises an eyebrow at our relationship. They've always believed we were destined to be together. Except JD. He's as much as said that I'd rather be alone and miserable, hanging out in a sex club, where everything is fantasy.

Maybe he's right.

29

DELILAH

We had our last team meeting on American soil this morning. Gray, Trippi, Baz, me—and Foxy. For the life of me, I still can't figure out why she's sitting in on team meetings, and Gray hasn't given me a satisfactory answer. It's not that we discuss anything classified in front of her, but it's unusual.

I always liked Foxy, although I never bought into the idea that she's some sweet mamaw. She might have grandchildren, but she can't be much more than fifty and she's in great shape. The granny act is a carefully crafted persona so she can catch you off guard and go for the jugular if you mess with Gray. She didn't get the name Foxy for nothing.

But in the team meetings, there's something about her, the way she takes notes and winces quietly when she disapproves of things she knows nothing about, and that are, frankly, none of her business. It rubs me the wrong way.

"You almost ready?" Gray asks from the bedroom doorway. He looks young and carefree in a pair of jeans and a casual T-shirt, much like the day we left for the beach. It seems like an eternity has passed since then.

"I think so," I say with some hesitation, peeking into the sack with the small compacts I brought along for gifts. "I'm just double-checking my carry-on to make sure I have everything I need on board."

"This isn't a commercial flight. All our luggage is carry-on."

"Right," I mutter, only half-listening. My focus is elsewhere. Checking and rechecking every tiny detail before a mission is my thing. It centers me, and gives me the opportunity to walk through the entire plan sequentially, scene by scene, reel by reel, one last time. If there's a snag, I often catch it at this stage. It's why I've been valuable to Smith's team.

The twist here is that not everything has been planned. While we know a lot about the crown prince, and even the king, Princess Saher has been sheltered from the public eye for years.

I check the inside pocket of my bag, the one that holds my compact. The case with a false bottom that contains a note for Saher in the event there's no safe place to talk. I can't risk being seen writing the note there. The note I carefully packed is written on stationary ordered from France that can't be traced back to us. The paper was treated to repel fingerprints and identifying fibers.

Until we get to the palace, we won't know for sure how to approach Saher. *I won't know how to approach her.* Certainly we've discussed the possibilities, but possibilities are all we have right now. Gray will keep the crown prince busy, but the final decision about how to approach the princess is mine alone. It's too risky for Gray and me to discuss the particulars once we're there. But maybe a go-between could work if we used some type of code, although that has risks too.

"Do you have a handler?" I ask, sliding my iPad into the zippered side compartment.

"Why do you ask?"

Gray is somewhat aloof, and doesn't bother to glance up from his phone. It's almost as if he's blowing me off.

Although it's not as if I asked some crazy question. Covert agents have handlers. I don't care which agency you're with. "If something doesn't go as planned, it would be important to have a contact." He whips up his head, and I now have Gray Wilder's *complete* attention.

"I have a handler," he replies cautiously. "But my handler is not your concern. You're an asset, not an agent. You don't have a handler." He pauses for a beat. "You have me if there's a problem."

"What if—" I can barely form the words. "Something happens to you? Should I contact Foxy?"

"No," he answers curtly, and much too quickly. "Do *not* call Foxy. Do you understand me?"

I nod, watching him stew from the corner of my eye. His reaction is more than a little strange, especially since she's been sitting in on the damn meetings.

"I left the final details for the plane," he says before I can ask any more about Foxy. "But since you brought it up, call Smith if I'm incapacitated. I don't care whether Trippi or Baz are in perfect health. If I go down, you call Smith."

Smith? What? "Smith's been read in?" I'm surprised, but also annoyed that I'm just hearing about this now. I'm sure there will be some bullshit excuse they expect me to buy. I'd like to bang their hard heads together.

Gray bends over to pick up a stray thread from the wood floor. "Smith's been read in on some parts of the op. But if something happens to me, tell him everything you know so he can help you."

"Gray—"

He stalks over and grabs me by the shoulders as if to shake me. "Look at me." His voice is stern, but not as stern as his gaze. "Do not fight me on this. I don't plan on checking out, but if I go down, do *not* contact Foxy. But you figure out how to get a message to Smith right away, and tell him everything. Every. Fucking. Detail."

Smith's clearance goes a lot higher than mine, that's for damn sure. *But still.* Purposefully divulging classified information is a crime—a treasonous crime. Not to mention a risk to national security. I'm no Girl Scout, but I took an oath not to betray my country, and even though representatives of my country have betrayed me, I'm not a traitor, and neither is Gray. "Surely you can't mean everything?"

He scowls at me. "That's *exactly* what I mean."

His eyes flit over my face, as if searching for assurances. "Am I clear?"

Crystal. *And you're deranged too.* But we'll save that part of the discussion for the plane. "How long has Smith known about the mission?"

Gray pulls away, not just his body, but his eyes too. "He knew before you. He first learned about it during that meeting at the Pentagon sometime early in the summer. I filled in some of the details later."

I lower myself to the bed. *He knew before you. He first learned about it during that meeting at the Pentagon early in the summer. I filled in some of the details later.*

The knife wedged into my back is akin to torture. I take a deep breath and lace my fingers together to control the pain. Otherwise, I'm going to fly around in a blind rage, destroying everything in this room that Gray Wilder holds dear. Then I'll deal with Smith.

Gray places a hand on my shoulder.

I swat it away. "You and Smith conspired behind my back." I don't need a response. I know it's true.

"I went to him first because I wanted to pave the way for your conversation with him. He agreed to let you go because he knew you needed the challenge, and an opportunity to live out your dream, even for a single mission. He wants you happy and fulfilled. He cares a lot about you, Delilah. And just like me, he's on your side."

The risk of cavorting with men who require absolute control is precisely this. Not just Gray, but Smith too. There's never a real partnership with them, because their patriarchal bullshit doesn't allow for partners.

"I'm so happy that you and Smith had a little soiree to decide what was best for me even *before* I had a chance to weigh in." I glower at him, with his chin up and shoulders squared. He doesn't want to upset me, and I'm sure he's sorry about that part, but otherwise, the bastard is entirely unrepentant.

"That will *never* happen again. I won't tolerate that kind of misogyny from either of you." I bounce my fingertip off the small piece of luggage to emphasize my point. "It's disrespectful, and I deserve better from Smith, and certainly from you."

Gray sits down on the bed near me, but far enough away that I don't immediately have the urge to get up. "I had a choice of a few contractors to provide backup for this mission. One of those companies was Smith's. Initially, I rejected the idea because it meant coming clean about my work with the EAD— and all the lies I've told over the years." Gray draws a breath, but instead of calming him, it seems to crush his spirit, making the tiny lines around his eyes more prominent. "Telling Smith was hard enough, but now that he knows, there's a risk my brothers will find out too. And the real possibility that they will never forgive me."

His voice is heavy, tinged with sadness, but I'm still too mad to offer even a word of comfort.

"But even with all the risks," he says frankly, "in the end I chose Smith's company because I'm confident that if something happens to me, he'll never leave you behind. He will use every resource he has to help you."

Gray inches closer, placing his large hand over mine.

I don't push him away this time. I don't have the heart, or the desire to shun him.

"If you contact my handler," he continues, "she won't lift a finger to protect you unless she can do it without compromising the agency. She won't even protect me, if it comes to that. Her job is to protect the integrity of the mission, and that of the agency. It's not to save us if things get too messy." He squeezes my hand, and weaves his fingers through mine. "I dragged you into this, and I need to be absolutely certain you'll be safe no matter what happens. I won't apologize for that."

The man's impossible, but I'm thawing.

Gray cradles the back of my head, pulling me toward him. "If I die, I want to die knowing you'll be okay. I need that peace of mind. Give me that."

My heart clenches. I know the risks. There are always risks in this type of work. Every day. I've lain awake worrying about the safety of my team members plenty of times. But this is different.

If I die. If you die, a big piece of me will die with you. If you die, my heart will take its final breath, withering inside a barren shell.

I reach up and rub his arm, finding solace in the friction. "I won't let anything happen to you," I promise him. "I couldn't bear it, Gray." I've kept my emotions mostly in check—at least outwardly—but my voice is thick and weepy, and if I don't get a grip, I'm going to cry all over his clean shirt. "But if you pull any more crap, I'll kill you myself before we're done."

His shoulders begin to shake as the laughter consumes him, and he draws me tight to his chest. I close my eyes and let the familiar rhythm of his heartbeat lull me into a false sense of security. Because there are no assurances in this life.

"I have something for you," he says after a few minutes, pulling away to reach into the nightstand for a black velvet box. "A little something for your carry-on."

I've learned with Gray that marvelous toys come wrapped in pretty velvet boxes and pouches. "A little something for the plane?" I tease lightly, running my fingers over the luxurious nap before opening the deep, hinged box. Four pairs of earrings. The brilliant jewels wink at me: emeralds, topaz, rubies, and sapphires—each pair a different cut and design.

That prickly haze that yokes every cell when I'm overwhelmed has arrived. It prompts me to respond to his extravagant gift in the only way I know. "I'm sure this isn't costume jewelry from Claire's at the mall." I close the box and hand it back. "I can't accept it."

Gray's expression is unreadable as he takes the velvet box from me. He carefully opens the lid, holding the contents not far from my chin. "We won't be able to do meaningful check-ins while we're there. Wear the green pair to let me know everything is proceeding well. Put the yellow pair on if you hit a speed bump that you can manage. The red pair will signal me to quickly find a place where we can talk safely."

God, he's annoying, with an answer for everything. "And the sapphires?" I ask with more of an edge than the moment requires.

"When it's done, I want to see the sparkle of the gems reflected in your dazzling blue eyes."

I tilt my head up. The haze has lifted, but the prickly feeling lingers. "I suppose these are government issue, like the shoes and gowns?"

Gray has the good grace not to lie through his smug little smirk. "These are on me. I hope when we're finished, you'll accept them as a bonus for a job well done. You'll earn them. But like everything else, it's ultimately your choice."

I have no intention of keeping the earrings, but there's no reason to argue about it now. "And what will the consequences be if I don't want them?" It's an impertinent question to lighten the mood. A flirtation laced with innuendo, nothing more.

But a dark, joyless shadow descends over his face, sweeping across the sun-drenched room.

"The flight plan's been filed." He grabs my carry-on bag from the bed. "We need to get going."

I nod solemnly, following him out, with wisps of melancholy trailing behind, but never close enough to swallow us.

30

DELILAH

The sun is shining, with the light drizzle just a memory by the time we reach the plane. It's not just any plane. It's a jet. A Boeing, with the words *Wilder Enterprises* scrolled in imposing navy script along the side. I've flown on private planes. I've actually flown on the Wilders' smaller Gulfstream, but even that doesn't compare to this monstrosity.

The crew greets us inside. "Mr. Wilder." A man who appears to be the pilot holds out his hand. "It's a perfect day for flying. It should be smooth skies all the way to Amidane."

Gray smiles. "That's what I like to hear. This is Delilah Porter. I know that you, all of you, will make her comfortable. Delilah, meet Lou. He'll be the pilot on this leg of the trip. The co-pilot," Gray gestures to a lovely woman who looks to be a few years older than me, "is Lou's wife, Samantha. I believe she's our pilot on the return trip."

"It's nice to meet you, Miss Porter," she says courteously. "I do indeed have the honor of bringing us home."

I detect a faint British accent, formal, but not as posh as something you'd hear on the BBC.

"And finally," Gray says, "Lori and Dobbins round out the

very capable crew. They'll make sure you have everything you need while you're on board." We smile politely at one another.

"Lori, why don't you give Miss Porter a quick tour and help her settle into the bedroom?" Something passes between Lori and Gray, and I can't help but wonder... "The master bedroom," he adds.

Lori nods and turns to me. "You're going to love it," she gushes.

"Trippi and Baz are in the conference room." Gray places a hand on my arm. "I'm going to catch up with them. They need to review the layout of the palace again. You have it down cold, so make yourself at home and relax. You don't need to be seated until takeoff."

Lori leads me around the massive space, pointing out every feature along the tour. The interior of the plane, including the chairs, sofa, and tables is warm tan leather and glossy dark wood.

"The guest bedroom is on the other side of the plane, near the conference room. We also use it as a dining room, although Gray rarely uses it that way."

"Guest bedroom? The plane has a guest bedroom?" I sound like the country girl who's visiting the big city for the first time, *but who has a guest room on a plane?* It would come as a surprise to almost anyone not named Wilder.

Lori laughs. "The plane is designed for comfortable family travel. When Mr. and Mrs. Wilder are aboard—JD and Gabrielle," she clarifies, "Gracie sleeps there."

Of course. I'm sure her daddy has the room outfitted with monitors so he knows every time she passes a little gas.

"This is the master bedroom. It has all the amenities of home. Maybe a few extras."

My large tote with essentials is already on the bed. Lori shows me how the lights and sound system work. The room has a walk-in closet, and an en suite bathroom with a shower that's bigger than mine at home.

"I hung everything from your garment bags so your clothes wouldn't wrinkle any more than necessary. I can unpack your bag once we're in the air," Lori says, pointing to my tote, "if you'd like."

I wrap my arms around my waist. This is just a small taste of the luxury to come. Some people like to be fussed over, but I'm not accustomed to the doting and it makes me itchy. "That won't be necessary. It's a long flight. I need something to keep busy."

"Would you like a drink or a snack before we take off?"

I shake my head. "I'm fine, thank you."

"We'll need to take our seats soon. But you still have a few minutes," she says, before leaving me alone with my thoughts.

After a short time, I've had enough of the room and the wealth and power it represents. I take out my iPad and go back into the main cabin, making myself comfortable in one of the recliners near a window. While I'm configuring my tablet for Wi-Fi, Gray joins me.

"There's been a change in plans," he announces, taking the seat across from me. The plane is taxiing, so the change must not involve aborting the trip.

Gray's agitated, tapping his fingers on the armrest, looking as though he appreciates last-minute changes less than I do. And I *despise* them.

"What kind of change?"

"We're meeting Prince Ahmad on his boat rather than at the palace."

There was an entire section of a briefing book dedicated to *The Great Escape*, the crown prince's yacht. Gray thought there was a possibility that at some point during the visit, the prince would decide he needed more privacy than the palace allows, and we would all spend a night or two on the floating fuck toy.

"Will Princess Saher be there?" I ask, with some trepidation. If she's not there, everything we've prepared for is out the window.

"I highly doubt it."

My heart drops into my stomach as soon as the words are out of his mouth. "Why—what do you think happened?"

Gray glances at me. "Trippi thinks the prince might want to lay eyes on you before he welcomes us to the palace."

"What do you think?"

"I don't like it. We're more vulnerable out on the Mediterranean. But I think it's the most likely explanation."

"Why the last-minute change of heart? He must have had concerns about me all along." And if he didn't, certainly his security had them.

Gray nods, stretching his legs out in front of him. "Gives us less time to regroup. It's exactly what I would have done." He reaches over and squeezes my knee. "This changes nothing. He'll meet you, spend a little time chatting you up—he's good for that—and we'll be on our way to the palace before you know it."

"What if it's not okay? What if after meeting me, he decides I haven't changed my stripes? What if we're walking into an ambush? Maybe I can board the boat alone, and you and the rest of the team can go on to the palace." All those faces on the cards. This is too important. And I certainly don't want anyone in danger because of me.

He scoffs. "You're not going anywhere alone with that asshole. Not while I'm still breathing."

"Did the crew file a new flight plan?"

"Same plan. We'll be boarding a helicopter at the airport."

I have fifteen hours to regroup. No sweat. *Then why is my stomach hurting like a sonofabitch?*

"I need to work for a few hours, but you should take it easy. *The Great Escape* is luxurious, but you'll be working and it won't be very relaxing. Try to stay awake. We'll sleep later. That way, we can begin to adjust to the time change. I have a sedative if you need it."

I stare at the window. A last-minute change is a bad way to begin a mission.

"Delilah, I have every confidence in you. When I told Ahmad I was bringing you with me, I didn't give him an opportunity to say no."

"Does he normally allow you to bring guests?"

He shrugs. "It's never come up. I always go alone. That's why this relationship," he gestures between us, "has to be convincing. I don't think that's going to be an issue," he says, his eyes darkening. "It's going to be fine."

"I know." *Although I don't know.* "I just need a little time to wrap my head around the change. Let me comb through it a bit."

Gray unbuckles his seat belt. "I'm going up front, because if I stay here any longer, I'm going to initiate you into the mile-high club—unless you're already a member."

"I don't belong to any clubs. Certainly not that one."

He smirks, and his eyes twinkle with mischief. "I brought the Lush vibrator along. It's the perfect size for travel. Can I interest you in a little fun and games?"

I could use a big, fat orgasm right about now. The kind that makes my legs shake. "I'm good. Neither of us will accomplish anything if you pull that thing out."

"You can have your way now, because I have things to do, but when I'm finished…" He leans over, his lips hovering just above my ear. "You. Are. Mine."

I glance up at him, and smile flirtatiously. "Then you best get a move on."

Gray tugs my hair back, and moves in for a kiss. But when his mouth reaches mine, he grabs my bottom lip between his teeth, holding it securely for several seconds before releasing it.

He places a small kiss on the bridge of my nose and strides off, leaving my heart racing.

Once he's gone, I push the seat back a bit and put on my headphones to listen to an audio book. Dobbins brings me a Blanton's, which I savor slowly while listening to the narrator's sexy baritone, until the story is over.

Don't ask me about the book, I'm sure it was fascinating, but I've been ogling Gray from afar for the past two hours, and truly, he's a far more interesting character than any author could conjure.

He's abandoned the laptop and is sitting back, studying the clouds. I suppose he has a lot on his mind too. Everyone prepares differently.

Although I don't pretend to know every detail, he put a lot of time and energy into this mission—including thoroughly preparing me for the trip. Some of it's about his need for control, but the rest—the rest was about making it as easy on me as possible.

There are many things that could go wrong, dreadfully wrong. But if they do, I'll die doing something I dreamed about since I was a teenager. But what about Gray? Is this the end of a decade's worth of work? After this, can he still pretend to be the prince's friend, or is that over? And what if the mission takes him down? That's my worst nightmare. It's been nagging since Gray told me to call Smith if something happens to him.

I tip my head from side to side, to stretch the tight muscles. But I can't stop thinking about one of us dying.

Nothing prepares us for when the door closes suddenly. *Nothing.* All the words left unsaid—the opportunities to make things right. That all evaporates with the last breath.

Gray turns around and catches my eye, giving me one of those lazy half-smiles that makes me melt.

He's stopped asking about Archbishop Darden. But I want to tell him. I want him to know that I'm not a cold-blooded killer—that I wouldn't kill a man without an excellent reason. I'm not some crazy, out-of-control chick. I've wanted to tell him for almost a week, but the time never seemed right.

I remove the headphones, setting them on the table beside me, and fuss with my hair, finger-combing the flat strands. I don't want this to go unsaid for another minute. And I don't want to lose my chance to make it right.

31

DELILAH

When I reach Gray, I take the seat across the table from him, tucking my legs up under me. "You busy?"

"Mostly banging my head against the wall. You need something?"

"Company, I guess."

He watches me like he always does. Not so much to figure out what I'm thinking, although he sometimes does that too, but to give me time to right my emotions, and to square them with my thoughts. I burn hot inside. Everything moves lightning-fast. I often need extra time to shape my reflections into words fit for civilized discussion.

Gray understands this idiosyncrasy—in a way that no one has ever bothered to before.

But it doesn't matter how much time he gives me today, because the words, like the reality they describe, are inelegant, with rough, jagged edges. And time won't change any of it.

"I grew up differently than you," I blurt gracelessly.

"Is that right?" he drawls, one corner of his mouth tipping up. "Tell me about it."

"My mama wasn't like yours."

Clouds descend over his brilliant blue eyes. Not the white puffy cotton ball ones, like those outside the window, but stormy ones, bleak and hopeless. Gray never talks about his mother, and I probably shouldn't have brought her up.

"The Marshalls lived across the street," I continue, hoping that my sad story will make him forget about his—at least for a few minutes. "They had a son, Richard, who was born after they had given up all hope of a baby. Mrs. Marshall stayed home to take care of him, and out of the goodness of her heart, she took care of me too." I glance at him and the clouds are gone, but they're likely to return because this isn't the retelling of a fairy tale. "She patiently combed knots out of my hair and taught me how to bake a flaky biscuit and fry catfish without stinkin' up the house—" I smile sheepishly. "That part didn't work out so well."

"It worked out just fine," he murmurs. It's soft and gentle. He's careful not to spook me, so that I don't stop talking.

But what he doesn't know is that no matter what he says, I won't stop. I can't.

"Mrs. Marshall invited me to supper regularly, Friday movie nights, and to the carnival when it was in town. In exchange, I entertained Richie while she fixed supper or cleaned cupboards, or when she visited with a friend."

This was the best part of my childhood. It might be trite to the listener—but not to me. It's part of my story—and the end can't be fully understood unless you know the beginning.

"As the years went on, I spent more and more time with the Marshalls. They insisted on it. When I was old enough to understand, I realized they were the shield between my developing teenage body and the men Mama brought home."

Gray comes around and takes the seat next to me, twirling the chairs until they face one another, with nothing between us. He runs a gentle hand over my hair. I want to hang onto it, because the saddest part of the story isn't yet told and I'm already feeling shaky inside.

"Did one of those men hurt you?" he asks, the wariness seeping around the edges.

I shake my head. "No. There were a few close calls." *One in particular that still makes my skin crawl.* "But it never came to that." I hear the air leave Gray's lungs.

He brings my hand to his mouth and places a kiss on my knuckles.

"Tell me more." He kisses my hand again, then rubs small circles with his thumb on the inside of my palm. "Tell me about your mother."

My mother. She's both a central figure and inconsequential at the same time.

"She was weak, and I don't doubt for a second she would have traded my innocence for her survival, or perhaps even for a piece of jewelry or a pretty dress."

I hear the words as they emerge, and the events are achingly familiar, but the thin, detached voice isn't mine. It's as though someone else is telling my story.

Gray is outwardly calm—for my sake, I'm sure—but rage flickers in his eyes.

"While they never let on in front of me," I continue, dispassionately, "I'm sure the Marshalls knew it too."

The clouds are back, obscuring his vision. This time they're dark and angry, threatening an eruption that would rival anything Mother Nature might summon.

"Mr. Marshall was a math teacher at the high school. He tutored me in algebra, and helped me fill out college applications. We cobbled together enough financial aid and scholarship money so I could have a fresh start. Like his wife, he stepped in to help whenever he could. But I was a huge burden."

"I sincerely doubt that." In his rush to protect me, he's

dismissive. "You were a little girl. I'm sure they were happy to help."

"You don't understand." I jerk my hand away. "They were black. I was a cute little blonde thing. It was rural Mississippi. They were harassed by the sheriff, social services. Even the principal called me into his office one afternoon to question me about the *untoward* relationship I had with Mr. Marshall. He almost lost his job. No one gave a goddamn that my mother left me alone for days on end without a morsel of food, but they lined up one after another to accuse the black man of diddling the pretty white girl."

I pause to rein in some of the skyrocketing emotion. "But you know what? The Marshalls *never* blinked. They *never* once turned their backs on me, not even when the association threatened their reputations.

It wasn't my mama who saved me from a life of poverty, barefoot and pregnant, with a brood of young ones chasing me through the weeds. It was the Marshalls. I owe them everything. *Everything*."

The clouds are gone again, and there's a sparkle in his eyes. "What's so funny?" I ask.

"Not funny. Sweet, actually. You barefoot, running through the fields with blonde babies trailing behind you."

"More like a nightmare," I grumble.

"Do you still keep in touch with them?"

I squeeze my thighs so hard, Gray takes my hands, gently prying my fingers loose.

"What happened, Blue Eyes?"

This is the wretched part of the story, where my brain requires additional oxygen to churn through the sludge. I draw a large breath, and then another, to sustain me. "When I was in college, there was a scandal at the church in town. The priest was accused of molesting little boys." The passion has crept into my voice, accompanying the dull ache inside my chest.

"Richie was one of them," Gray says with the utmost care, as if helping to unburden me of the especially difficult parts.

I nod, my heart breaking like it happened yesterday. "He was fifteen when it became public. It was humiliating. No matter how many times we explained that he was a little boy when it happened—a victim—it didn't help. He was bullied at school, called all sorts of names that were too hard for a teenage boy to bear." I shield my face, because I don't want him to see the anguish twisting through me. "He shot himself with his daddy's gun." I let out a small, strangled sigh.

"*Delilah.*"

Gray pulls me onto his lap, and I let him. Because I still need to finish, and I can't stop to argue or it'll never all come out. And because I feel safe there—safer than anywhere I've ever been.

"I'm sorry," he whispers, softly. "So sorry."

I have no doubt he's sorry—no doubt he would carry my pain if he could.

"The Marshalls never got over Richie's death. Two years after he was gone, they were gone too. Mrs. Marshall developed a brain tumor. It was only a matter of weeks. Mr. Marshall died of a heart attack five days after we buried her." My chest is so tight, I can barely breathe.

Gray holds me closer, and strokes my back with strong, nimble fingers, lightly kneading the stiff muscle.

"Archbishop Darden put that priest—that child molester—in the parish." The rage is building inside me. "He had a history of molesting little boys. But it was a poor parish and our children weren't worth saving."

I nestle into Gray's chest, letting the angry energy tell the rest of the story.

"I'm not Catholic, and I never thought about an archbishop, or how priests are assigned to churches. But while Kate was being questioned, I was there, listening to every detail. Something told me it was the same sonofabitch who kept moving bad priests around, hiding them, to avoid scandal in the church. Sure enough, it took about ten minutes of research to put the pieces together. When I discovered it was the same bastard—I had to do it."

I sound vindictive and hateful, but I refuse to sugarcoat any of it. "There was some element of revenge involved, I'm not going to lie. But what drove me more than anything—I was not going to let that man ruin any more innocent children—or women, or families. He was done."

The emotion—grief, anger, sorrow—it's welled up, and beginning to seep out. I wipe a lone tear from my cheek.

I don't want him to watch me fall apart, so I reach for the anger that's right on the surface, and turn my face to Gray's. "At the time, you accused me of going off half-cocked, but it wasn't like that. I planned his execution to a T." I feel no remorse as I say the words. None.

"I'm sorry about..." He pauses. "I was going to say your friends, but they're your family, really."

I swallow the lump in my throat. "They were."

We sit quietly for a long time.

"I'm honored—beyond honored, Delilah. Humbled," he tucks my head under his chin, "that you shared this with me. But why today?"

I'm wrecked, and it's hard to think. But I quietly play with the words and the feelings. They're looped together in complex knots. But the answer to his question doesn't require pulling too many threads.

"If something happens to either of us—I don't want it to go left unsaid. It bothers me to have you think I'm a crazy woman who runs around murdering clergy."

"Hey." He tilts my head up, until he's peering into my eyes. "Nothing's going to happen to us. There are too many monsters left in this world that need a reckoning. Do you feel bad about it?" he asks, without judgment.

"Killing the archbishop?"

"Yeah," he says softly, his lips grazing my forehead.

"Only that he didn't suffer," I admit, with neither real joy nor remorse. "Otherwise, not in the least. I suppose that makes me a vile human being."

"Ever read Hemingway?"

"Only the SparkNotes. I prefer books with adjectives."

Gray laughs softly. "Hemingway believed, 'What is moral is what you feel good after, and what is immoral is what you feel bad after.' It's my favorite quote."

"It sounds like a justification for bad behavior."

"Maybe for some. But not for those who take stock of their humanity."

I appreciate the effort to soothe my conscience. Although a few choice words from Papa Hemingway will never convince me that I'm not a sinner who deserves to burn in hell. I'm not at all repentant, and therefore don't deserve forgiveness. God will do what he must, but I hope Gray is able to see past my moral failings.

I let my fingertips explore the taut ripples below his rib cage. "Did you notice there wasn't a single adjective in that quote?"

Without warning, Gray stands, tosses me over his shoulder, and slaps my ass. It lifts the mood. Something I desperately need right now.

"Put me down!" I squeal.

"Not a chance."

"Where are we going?"

"Where we can have a little more privacy. There's no way I'm fucking you out here where everyone can hear you scream."

32

DELILAH

Gray deposits me on the edge of the bed, and lowers himself until we're nearly eye level. He weaves his hands through my hair, devouring my mouth until we're both gasping for air.

His warm skin awakens the notes in his spicy cologne—bergamot and leather swirled together, wafting gently, enveloping us in his achingly familiar scent. I'm home.

Gray brushes the tendrils gingerly off my face. "Thank you for sharing that part of you with me. For letting me in *everywhere*."

Everywhere requires no further explanation. I know exactly what he means. Before today, I welcomed him into my body, and even into my head—but that takes little courage. The harrowing places are the dark corners. The shadowy spaces that leave you naked and ashamed.

I reach for him, clinging to his chest with both hands. "I need you." With every cell in my body. "I need the pain—please." There is no shame in my plea. It comes from somewhere dire, but pure.

"*Shhh*," he murmurs. "I'll take care of you. Give you everything you need. Do you trust me to do that?"

I nod.

"Good girl." He places a small kiss on my nose. "Take off your clothes for me—everything but your shoes and jewelry." His voice has made the subtle shift it always does before he takes command—when the moment calls for more than the normal bossy Gray, when it demands the power and control of a man who takes no prisoners. "Leave your panties for me."

I undress, *for him*, laying each item neatly on the bed, until I'm left in a piece of lace, sandals that crisscross around my ankles, and the noisy bangles on my wrist.

"You are spectacular." He's seen me naked more times than I can count, but his voice is almost reverent, filled with awe as if he's seeing me anew. "I don't know what I'm going to do after the mission—I'm not prepared to let you go, Blue Eyes."

I'm not prepared to let you go, Blue Eyes. I don't have time to sift through the tsunami pulling me under before he demands my attention.

"Get back on the bed." When I'm seated, he spreads my knees apart until my cunt is fully exposed to him. "Touch your breasts. Explore the smooth skin." My hands move without embarrassment—all I can think about is pleasing him—pleasing myself. "Silky, aren't they?"

I nod, because I can't speak.

"Squeeze your nipples. Harder."

"*Ahhh*." Every cell in my being welcomes the bite.

"Can you feel the throb in your pussy?"

My eyelids are heavy, and I let them flutter shut, as my head falls back, following the curve of my spine.

"Open your eyes, Delilah. Don't hide from me."

I force the lids open, gazing at him.

Gray lowers his hand to his thickening cock.

I see the outline through the denim.

"See what you've done to me. How are you going to fix it?"

I don't respond because the words have vanished with all thoughts.

He rips the delicate thong off my body and casts it aside. "I think you need to rub your pussy, make it swollen and uncomfortable like you've made me. Go ahead," he drawls. "Rub your pretty cunt, until it aches for me."

My fingers find their way to the wet, slippery folds. I slide the tips of my fingers over my clit, while the other hand digs into the bed linen. My body is on fire. I'm slipping away, but I don't close my eyes. Not even when the urge to hump my hand consumes me. Not even then.

I let Gray see me—all of me—until the impulse to end the torment has my thighs inching together.

"Don't you dare close your legs. I want to see your fingers strum that tight little pussy."

I'm close, and squirming with abandon, when he gets down on his haunches and shoves my hand away. *No!* I push my fingers back between my legs, but Gray isn't having it.

He lifts my legs up and apart, holding them behind the knees. With the first long sweep of his tongue, I gasp and whimper.

He raises his head, and meets my eyes with a wicked gleam. "Pinch your nipples while I lick you. Don't let go until you're coming all over my mouth."

I gasp as my fingers wrap around the sensitive furls. But I don't shy away. I lean into the throb, letting each pulse carry me higher.

Gray licks me with abandon, pushing his long tongue inside my slick core, swirling, before withdrawing. He sucks my clit, gently nudging me closer to the precipice, but releases the swollen bead as my body begins the dance to release. "*No!*" He's going to play at the edge—oh my God. *No.* "Please. Gray. Please."

"*Shhh,*" he admonishes. "The more you beg, the longer you'll wait."

I squeeze my nipples harder.

"You're a dirty, dirty girl, Blue Eyes, and I'm going to give you the release you crave."

My words are a reflection of the cluttered nonsense running through my head. *Please. Yes. More. Don't stop.*

His tongue sweeps across my slick flesh. I buck and moan—and his hands are on mine, prying my fingers from my nipples. When I let go, the blood floods the sensitive peaks, sending currents to my throbbing pussy. I tremble, begging him to end it.

And he does. Spectacularly. Nipping, and sucking, lapping my pussy until the tremors weaken, and I'm wrung out.

When he climbs onto the bed with me, he's naked.

"You don't need pain. You might choose it, but you don't need it. Pain is just a lazy way to ramp up the intensity. But there are other ways to find that high during sex, where your mind empties and peace rushes in to fill the space. Sometimes nothing but pain will do, but there are so many ways to get there. It doesn't always have to hurt."

I'm sobbing. I don't know why. But I'm overwhelmed by *everything*. All of it. The powerful orgasm. Telling him about the Marshalls. And for letting him in—fully inside. Because that's what I did.

"It's okay to cry, darlin'. Sometimes it's the quickest way to get it all out."

"I'm a mess. We have a mission—I need to be ready."

"Think of it as all part of getting ready."

He flips me onto my belly and straddles me, a knee on either side of my hips. His hard cock brushes against my ass, and I wiggle toward it. "Keep still." He holds me steady between his muscular thighs, his hands massaging my back with long, sensuous strokes, lulling me into a dreamlike trance.

"I killed my mother."

My body lurches out of the sex-induced stupor. His confession comes out of nowhere. In a voice that's eerily calm. I wait, with my heart pounding, for him to say something more. Julia Wilder was killed in an automobile accident. She drove off the road after being drugged by her husband. There seems little dispute about that among those in the know.

"You were a child," I say with as much compassion and empathy as he showed me earlier.

His hands freeze, and he stiffens over me.

I reach behind and clutch his hips, digging my fingers into his backside.

"She didn't simply lose control of the car," he says flatly. "She was poisoned. I gave her the sandwich that contained the poison."

Oh Gray. My heart breaks for the little boy forced to carry this burden, and for the man tormented by guilt. I want to turn around and wrap my arms around him, soothe his pain. But when I try to move, he holds me in place. I don't like it, but I'll respect his wishes. He doesn't want to look at me—or maybe he doesn't want me to look at him.

"You were eleven years old. You didn't put the poison in the sandwich. How could you have known?"

"I was angry at her. I lied about where the sandwich came from. She might not have eaten it if she had known it was from my father." He lowers his forehead to the hollow of my back. "I was happy to help trick her into eating it. They would all still be alive if I hadn't been such a little asshole."

"*Gray*. You don't actually believe that, do you?"

"Our lives would have all been different. Even JD's and Chase's, who didn't die, but who live with the consequences of what I did."

"Surely your brothers don't blame you?" I'm ready to wage all-out war on those Wilder boys.

"They don't know. I've never told anyone besides you, and a therapist I was forced to see in college."

"The one who recruited you to the FBI."

"*Mmhm.*"

I've never told anyone besides you... It's a gift—the gift of trust.

"Let me see you," I whisper into the mattress.

After a few minutes, he moves his legs enough for me to flip onto my back. I reach up and cup his jaw, easing my fingers over the stubble. His jaw is clenched. His skin sallow. But it's the suffering in his eyes that reaches in and twists my soul. I don't say anything. I'm just here—fully present, for whatever he needs.

"I trust you, Delilah," he says, the words coming directly from his heart, "with the mission—with everything. You need to trust yourself." He hoists my legs up, pushing my knees into my chest, and slides his cock into me. It's not an easy slide—for either of us.

His thrusts are ruthless. His face contorts in agony, with droplets of sweat forming in clusters.

I reach up to smooth the sorrow, caressing his lips with my fingertips. He nips the tender pads, and jerks his head away, lowering his mouth to mine.

Gray devours me—taking and taking. And I let him, delivering the pieces he misses in benevolent offering. I want to *give* him everything. In this moment, I know nothing else.

Every kiss, every breath, every heartbeat brings us closer—not just to the edge, but to each other.

When I'm almost there *again*, he reaches between us, circling my clit until I come apart, clutching his shoulders as the turbulent waves crest and break, wrecking me.

But Gray doesn't stop to let me catch my breath. He doesn't

stop for anything as he rolls his hips, driving blindly toward release.

With my legs quivering from the final savage thrusts, he follows me into his own anguished surrender. The control has evaporated and his grief escapes in a deafening primal roar, spilling into the cabin, and echoing in my soul long after he's emptied himself inside me.

33

GRAY

We climb aboard *The Great Escape*, Prince Ahmad's luxury yacht. The Great Escape—*pfft. It's more pretentious than Lone Wolf, even.*

Something changed between Delilah and me yesterday. Not a seismic shift, but an intimacy that develops not from carnal pursuits, but from sharing secrets that others don't know.

I can't explain why I confided in her about my mother—not exactly. I've been telling myself it was her reward for opening up to me. Something big and important to entice her into continuing to share more about her past. I've also told myself that it was to demonstrate my unwavering confidence in her. All these things are in part true, but they are eclipsed by a greater truth: I wanted to tell her. Five simple words, filled with complexities.

It's not that I can't explain why I confided in Delilah. It's that the emotions are too thorny to parse through right now. My focus needs to be on the mission and on the safety of my team.

The crown prince is waiting to greet us, dressed casually in linen shorts and a button-down shirt rolled at the elbows. It's similar to what I'm wearing. Unlike the palace, the atmosphere on the boat is always relaxed.

"Your Highness," I say, polishing the exaggerated reverence with a mocking smirk that Ahmad has come to expect from me. "You look well-rested for someone with a new baby in the house."

His eyes light up and his grin widens before he erupts in laughter. My relationship with the crown prince is complicated. It started, in earnest, as an easy friendship. We both come from powerful families with vast wealth, where cultivating genuine friends isn't simple. Despite his selfish ways, which I originally attributed to cultural differences and royal lineage, I once enjoyed his company.

The prince doesn't take my hand, but embraces me, instead. "It's good to see that you're still a sarcastic bastard. I need a bit of levity in my life." He pats me on the back. "I'm so happy you're here."

When he pulls away, he turns to Delilah, who is dressed conservatively with a scarf covering her hair. But even with a modest neckline and her arms and legs hidden by billowy cream-colored fabric, she exudes an effortless sexiness. It's impossible to hide, certainly from men like Ahmad, who are always on the prowl.

"What tender morsel have you brought with you?" The question is directed at me, but his eyes are all over Delilah.

The way he's leering, I'd like to grab him by the neck and toss him overboard. But I can't afford to be a jealous bastard right now, so I force a smile. "Crown Prince Ahmad bin Khalid, please meet Delilah Mae Porter."

Delilah smiles, but doesn't make eye contact with Ahmad. Instead, she places her hand over her heart with her head bowed slightly. "It's an honor to meet you, Your Highness."

Pride washes over me—not because of anything I've done, but because she threw herself into the study, soaking up every detail she could get her hands on, or pry from Mira and me—all for this very moment. She's perfect. I catch a whiff of the brackish water and feel myself relax.

"The pleasure is mine, Miss Porter. I appreciate the show of respect, but on the boat, we dispense with all modesty and most formality. May I call you Delilah?"

"Of course." She's poised, but a bit nervous, which is good. It makes it more realistic.

"It's not necessary for you to lower your eyes in my presence," Ahmad continues, "as it makes it difficult for me to see their beauty. Yes?"

She looks up with a demure smile.

"Much better," he says, with the cunning assurance of an animal with no natural predator. "At the palace it will be different, but while we're on the sea, you needn't cover yourself. After all, this is *The Great Escape*."

Even after a century of secular rule, Amidane women are still required to wear the abaya and behave modestly, rules that Ahmad dispenses with any time it suits him. The laws are stricter for women, but men have onerous restrictions too. No one is permitted to practice religion of any kind inside the country. The king is the supreme ruler—not a demigod, but a god. In his absence, the crown prince has the last word on everything.

A man dressed in a pressed white uniform appears, and nods at the prince.

"Malik, please show Miss Porter to her suite."

Malik is the crown prince's eyes and ears on and off the boat.

"Once you're settled, perhaps you'd like to catch some sun on the top deck," Ahmad suggests before Delilah goes. "You'll find the sunbathers there without swimsuits. You might choose to do the same. I understand it prevents tan lines."

Delilah defers to me for guidance on her outfit, as though it's the most natural thing in the world. It's almost comical. "Wear a bathing suit." I speak to her, but my message is for the prince. "I'm not adverse to tan lines."

Ahmad watches the interaction carefully. Delilah is looking directly at my face, unlike how she behaved with him.

"If there's anything you need, please tell Malik," he says, dismissing her.

Delilah is not his to dismiss, but I hold my tongue. For now.

When she's out of view, I follow Ahmad up the stairs to a private seating area on the middle deck.

He motions for me to sit. "What would you like to drink?"

"Whatever you're having." I roll up my sleeves while he turns to say something I can't hear to a crew member, before taking a seat across from me.

"So you brought along a little plaything." He's not wasting any time, but this tells me everything I need to know about why the plans to go directly to the palace changed. He has concerns about Delilah.

"She's lovely, isn't she?"

"Is there something wrong with the women I normally provide? All you had to do was ask for something special."

When I don't bite, he keeps talking. "Unless she's a plaything for me? A gift for your host, perhaps?"

Fuck you. The crewman brings us each a beer, pouring the contents of the bottles into tall glasses while we watch silently.

"I sent a gift. Did it arrive?"

"It did. Thank you. The port's magnificent. I finished one of the bottles, but I saved the other for us to enjoy while you're here. Tell me, is it as delicious as your blonde toy?" He raises his glass, touching mine in midair, but not offering a good cheer. "You still eat pussy, I'm sure."

"And you still don't, I'm sure."

Ahmad leans in closer, while I sip my beer. "What were you thinking, bringing a CIA agent to the palace?" He's visibly agitated.

I would be too.

"*Former* CIA agent," I explain carefully. Although, by now, his goons have told him everything there is to know about Delilah. "She spent virtually no time doing covert work before she was ousted. You were provided with all the appropriate documentation and paperwork. Don't act like I'm trying to pull a fast one on you."

"What's your relationship with her?" he asks. His stare is icy, but his tone is less hostile, maybe even a bit curious.

I never let my guard down around Ahmad, not for a nanosecond, and this visit won't be any different.

"I'm not sure." It's mostly honest, not that he deserves honesty. "I've known her for a few years. She worked security at Wildflower—undercover." I don't tell him that she was Smith's plant. "We got involved. In the US, fucking your employees is still a big no-no. We've been sneaking around—I'm tired of it. I told her she needed to leave her job with Sinclair Industries if we were going to make it work."

He sits back in the chair, crossing his legs. I've known Ahmad a long time. He's not buying it yet. "Make it work?"

"I want to keep her—at least I think I do. But first I need to see how she fits into my life. In the meantime, she's off-limits. Even to you."

Ahmad begins to laugh. "Tradition requires that I take a wife. But I can't believe you're willing to settle down." He shakes his head.

"*Whoa!*" I raise my hands. "I never said anything about getting married. Let's not get carried away. There's a world of difference between *let's see where this goes* and a ring choking my finger."

Ahmad's aware that I don't do relationships—even agreements with the submissives I train are for set, *and limited*, amounts of time. And they're *never* exclusive agreements—that's not what it's about for me. Submissives are part of my job at the club, an enjoyable part, but that's it. And other kinds of relationships don't comport well with either of my jobs.

"She's worked hard to understand the nuances of the Amadi culture, and I don't see any problem with her at the palace. Otherwise I would have left her behind. But ultimately, it's your decision." *Although I'm pretty much screwed if you send us packing.*

I didn't bring my cards with me, but it doesn't matter. I've memorized every face and their names. I take another drink, eyeing him carefully over the glass.

He nods. "She seems meek for a covert operative."

My lips twitch, because, describing Delilah as meek is—funny as hell. "Meek, *no*. She's a hellion. But she wants to please me. I've decided I like a woman with a little life in her. They're more fun to train."

A thin smile spreads across his face, and his eyes grow dangerously dark. "I love a woman who fights back. *In bed*. It gives me every excuse to subdue her as I please."

Fucker. The bastard needs no excuse to act brutally. It's not that I'm opposed to rough play. I'm not a stranger to the crack of a whip, or the scrape of a sharp knife if the situation warrants, but for me to indulge, it has to be consensual.

"How about if you share her with your host? We can make a trade."

I'd like to break him in half for even suggesting it.

"A trade? That's mighty generous of you. I didn't realize Noura was on the boat."

He gulps his beer, emptying half the glass. When he glares at me, the venom in his eyes is something to see. "*Princess*

Noura, my wife, is not on the boat. Nor is she available for trade." His chest is heaving. "I've ordered men killed for less."

"As have I. I'm not sharing Delilah. When I'm finished with her, *if* I'm finished, you can have first dibs. But until then, she's off-limits, just like *Princess* Noura."

He lifts his chin, but he's decidedly calmer. "Gray, one of the things I've always liked about you is that underneath your playboy exterior, you're a smart, tough sonofabitch. We're cut from the same cloth."

Not a chance, you prick. "Why did you want me to make this trip now?"

"We're friends, aren't we?"

"Cut the bullshit."

Ahmad snickers. "Before your father died, he and your brother, JD, visited the palace to discuss the wholesale purchase of a vaccine and some other pharmaceuticals. My father would like to pursue the negotiation, and he asked me to reach out to you because of our friendship."

So this is how the king planted the idea of the visit with Ahmad. *Clever.* "I could have saved you the trouble. I have nothing to do with Sayle Pharmaceuticals. JD is in charge. But I can put you in touch with him."

Ahmad shakes his head. "I met with him during the visit. It's hard to tell that the two of you are related. He was such a dreary bore."

I chuckle. "That's what he said about you too." Actually, JD said he was an entitled, pampered prick, and he doubted the prince wiped his own ass.

Ahmad laughs, and shrugs. "I suppose your brother and I have different interests." He contemplates me, soberly, for a long minute. "I also needed some cheering up."

"The women sunbathing naked on the starboard deck don't provide sufficient cheer?"

He scoffs. "If only it were as simple as a tight cunt." He

sighs, and pauses for a beat before continuing. "Noura is on the Riviera, recuperating from childbirth and ruminating, I'm sure, over whether I'll divorce her before she has another chance to produce a male heir."

"I hate to be a drag by involving science, but it's the father's sperm that determines the sex of a child."

"Fuck you, Gray. I took biology, too. But it doesn't work like that in my world."

"I take it you don't want to divorce her?"

Ahmad waves me off. "She's easy. Does all that's required of her—aside from providing me sons." He scratches his head. "Noura has the right pedigree. She'll make a perfect queen. Those kinds of women aren't a plentiful resource, especially as Amidane becomes more modern."

"I understand the importance of a male heir to succession. But by the time your daughters are of age, maybe things will have changed enough to allow the crown to pass through women."

He looks me directly in the eye. "That's never happening."

"What if you don't divorce her? Aren't you permitted to have more than one wife at a time? Maybe you can find someone who can produce a male heir." I can't believe I'm actually having this conversation with a straight face. Aside from the archaic custom, this bastard is weeks away from being removed from the line of succession—although he doesn't know his father plans on bypassing him and giving the title to his younger brother. That's why Saher needs to leave the country. She's her father's favorite child, his only daughter, and that makes her a perfect pawn in a succession battle. Ahmad will barter with his sister's life and her son's, to persuade his father to keep him in the line of succession. He won't hesitate to kill them to get his way.

"I've promised reform for women. That's how I've been getting the West to warm up to me. I need their support in order for the kingdom to continue to thrive. I can't take another wife—now is not the right time."

I'm so done with this conversation.

"I don't know what to tell you, buddy. But I'm happy to engage in a little fun and games to cheer you up."

"I plan on taking full advantage of your generosity. But there is one last thing I can use your help with."

"*Jesus,* you packed my schedule pretty full. I thought this was a vacation." I press my shoulders into the back of the chair. "What do you need?"

"In that same vein of making the kingdom more modern, I want to install a sex club in the lower level of the palace. Not a place for big parties, but a place with some fantasy rooms, where the younger princes can work off a little energy. Something along the lines of Wildflower."

"Isn't that why you send them abroad?"

He nods. "Except when the pandemic was out of control, and they couldn't travel and started playing with the local girls. It was a fucking nightmare. I'm hoping you'll spend a little time with me and a designer. What you have at Wildflower would be ideal here."

It's the perfect way to keep him occupied without having to dirty my hands too much. With Delilah here, I'd like to keep Ahmad's *girls* as far away from me as possible. "Filthy fantasies are my specialty."

"I've missed you, Gray," he says sincerely. "I'm glad you're here."

"Me too."

"Enough about my problems. Why don't you change, and take a swim? I instructed Malik to put you in the same part of the boat as Miss Porter, but I also reserved you a room downstairs in the event you see something you'd like to sample." He raises his brow. "I assume she demands discretion, at the least."

I'm not exactly sure what Delilah expects. This is a mission and she knows it could get messy. But I have no interest in sampling any of the local wares.

"I think she'd be pretty pissed if I dragged her halfway around the world and left her alone for long periods of time—to fuck someone else. But I suppose a small, discreet taste wouldn't hurt."

34

DELILAH

I glance at the clock on the nightstand. It's after two in the morning, and I'm in bed reading. Despite our efforts to make the time adjustment easier, I can't sleep, and I don't want to take a sleeping pill. Not in the middle of the ocean with these shady fuckers.

Gray is with Prince Ahmad, who is charming in the same way the devil is charming. He stashed away his little harem during dinner for my benefit, I'm sure. But I'm just as sure they're all decked out and ready to play now.

If all goes well and we're allowed to continue to the palace, this little side trip will have been worth it. It's allowed me to get accustomed to the eyes and ears that are *everywhere*. They mostly fade into the background, and it's easy to develop a false sense of security if you let your guard down, but my antenna is up and fully attune.

The lock snicks, and I automatically reach for my gun, which of course is in Charleston, locked in a safe at Wildflower. But when the door opens, it's Gray.

"I came to check on you," he says, lying near me on the bed, on his side. "Maybe you can put this down, and give me your full attention." He takes the Kindle out of my hand and tosses it on the nightstand behind him.

He smells of whiskey and cigars and white blossoms—jasmine, to be specific. I loathe jasmine, even on a good day. It smells like rotting flowers—and my mother...only she wore a cheap version.

I know entertaining the prince is part of the plan, and I shouldn't be mad. But my emotions have taken me back to the plane, to the cabin where we shared not just our bodies, but our secrets, less than twenty-four hours ago. I'll pull it together, but I'm not a robot that can be turned on and off easily.

My stomach churns as Gray's lips meet mine. The floral perfume is overwhelming. He's drenched in it, and I shove him away before I gag.

He grabs my wrists, holding them firmly above my head. "You want to fight me? Go ahead. But I warn you, I'm in the mood for a little demon."

Oh, you're going to get a little demon. But it might not be the kind you're in the mood for, asshole. "You're coming to me smelling like the woman you just laid, and you expect me to spread my legs for you? You didn't even have the decency to take a shower and wash away the stench of sex before you came to my bed."

When I pause, a sudden panic swarms, nearly crippling me —I'm not in role. I search Gray's face. There's no alarm anywhere. My response is legitimate and natural. It *is* in role. It's exactly the reaction I should have to his indiscretion.

"Is that what you smell, Delilah? You smell sex? Another woman's juices mixed with mine? Maybe there was more than one."

He pulls my hair back, and I see something in his eyes—a glimmer that wouldn't be there if he was being cruel.

No, I don't smell sex. I smell god-awful perfume. Even though he's practically on top of me and my nose is working overtime, I don't smell anything resembling sex. *Maybe you don't want to smell it.*

"I was planning to show you the respect of a shower, but since you haven't shown me any respect, I'm just going to fuck you here and now. Have you suck my dick and taste another woman's cunt on me. Would you like that?" he drawls.

My heart is pounding. I know we're being watched. Now that I almost forgot my role, I can't seem to forget about the hidden cameras.

"Take this off," he says, tugging at my nightgown. "Don't dally."

I hesitate, before my fingers find the buttons on my nightgown. My anxiety grows, along with my anger at Gray, coiling tighter together with each button I untether. He undresses too, which makes me feel slightly more comfortable. But it does nothing to assuage the anger.

"Look how hard you make my cock when you fight me off. Look," he demands, more roughly.

I glance quickly at the flare of the dusky crown, and then into his eyes. There's a flicker of compassion in them, a modicum of empathy, even as he drags me to him.

"On your knees, Delilah, and suck it good, or you'll spend all night on your knees practicing until you get it right."

I reach for the compassion I saw in his eyes, clenching it to me while he weaves his hands into my hair.

His fingers have a firm hold on my scalp, but he doesn't shove his cock down my throat. He lets me set the pace. My tongue laps at the taut skin, and I smell a faint muskiness—that's him. I taste nothing on his cock but the salty bead forming at the tip.

He didn't have sex. That's what he was trying to tell me. *Do you smell another woman's juices mixed with mine?* No. No, I don't.

My pulse slows, and the cameras are a distant memory.

I gaze at him for a few seconds, before pulling his cock into my mouth, the way he likes. I'm rewarded with a loud hiss of air. *He didn't shower.* Because if he did, he wouldn't reek of that putrid perfume. Even if he cleaned himself with a washcloth, there would be a lingering telltale scent. I bury my nose into the well-groomed hair. *Nothing*—it smells only of Gray. My throat relaxes with little effort, and I swallow him deep, again and again, until he wrenches away from me.

"Are you wet?" he pants.

I sit back on my heels, softly gasping for breath, and nod.

He reaches down, his fingers exploring my needy pussy. "You are wet. You enjoyed swallowing my cock, didn't you?"

"Yes."

He brings his fingers to my mouth, and I suckle until the ache between my legs is my most pressing concern.

"You know what I enjoy?" He pauses, as if waiting for a response. "Fingering you, Delilah, until you come hard. Until you're shaking and pushing my hand away, and I have to tighten my grip on your throat to let you know that *I decide* when you're done."

I shiver at his words and harsh tone. It's not the shudder of repulsion, but the tremble of desire.

He takes his cock in hand, pulling and jerking on the swollen shaft. My gaze flits between his busy hand and his eyes. There's no warning, at least none that registers, when he erupts. I squeeze my eyes shut, while he sprays his cum all over me—in my hair, on my cheeks and arms, and across my breasts.

The signal is clear to anyone watching. He's marked me. I'm his.

"Next time," Gray warns in a scathing tone, "don't question me about where I've been or who I've been with." He pulls me to my feet. "Let's go take that shower you were so concerned with, because I have no desire to sleep beside someone who smells like a filthy whore."

35

GRAY

Last night was a good test—for us both. Delilah was challenged, and she stayed in control, with her anger pushing at the edges, which made it all the more believable.

I was cruder with her than necessary, but I wanted Ahmad to love the show so much that he would crave more. That even if his good sense was telling him to turn us away, he wouldn't listen.

We're engaged in a dance. Letting our real emotions creep in just enough to create a realistic scenario, but not enough to shatter us and blow our cover to smithereens. I'm acutely aware of how difficult it is for Delilah, and I do what I can to help her. But that's a dance too.

She needs me to respect her as an operative—as a deserving partner in this mission. If I coddle too much, it has the opposite effect. It implies, with all the subtlety of a blaring siren, that I don't have confidence in her abilities.

None of this is easy on me, either. It weighs on my mind, and in my heart, more than it should. Certainly more than I can afford, right now. That's for damn sure.

Ahmad and I are having breakfast on the upper deck with

a trio of nearly naked women. Not one from Amidane, or from the United States, for that matter. One woman is Eastern European and the other two, Burmese. They appear to be just above the age of consent. *Maybe.* Are they here of their own accord? It appears that way, but appearances are deceiving. Although it doesn't matter, because that's not why I'm here.

My purpose is sealed with official orders, and I'm not allowed to veer off to save anyone. It doesn't matter whether the scourge of the sex trade lurks nearby, or something equally as evil. I have to look the other way. It's one of the most infuriating aspects of this life I chose. But like it or not, that's how this business works. When the government climbs into the mud with pigs, they never come out smelling good.

One of the young women is sitting on Ahmad's lap while he feeds her orange sections and grapes. The other two are flanking me. I have absolutely no interest in slipping *anything* into their mouths, so they've taken to bringing bites of food to mine.

That's when Delilah appears. Despite what Ahmad told her, she's dressed modestly in a summery outfit that covers her arms and falls below her knees. Her conservative clothing sets her apart, and above, the women at the table. In the crudest terms, she's a queen and they're whores.

She approaches us with her head high and shoulders back. Delilah's a hair below five feet five, but her presence is unmistakable, especially today.

Her sunglasses hide any disapproval in her eyes, but I see her body stiffen when one of the young women brushes a piece of croissant across my bottom lip, urging me to eat from her hand. I'm sure Ahmad saw Delilah's reaction too, because he whispers something to the girl on his lap and when she gets up, he shoos the others away too.

"Good morning. I hope you slept well," he says, standing to

greet Delilah. The sign of respect, especially coming from him, is a bit of a surprise.

I stand too, because she certainly deserves my respect, and because this is her show, and she's killing it.

"Come sit by me," he says without a glance in my direction. "Leave that dog you brought along to his own devices."

I scowl at him, hoping to send a silent message, but he ignores it.

"Coffee or tea?" he asks.

"Coffee would be wonderful," Delilah replies. "Thank you."

The waiter brings her coffee, along with some yogurt topped with drizzled honey and crushed pistachios. "Would you prefer something else?"

"This is perfect."

Ahmad peels a fresh orange, carefully removing the bitter pith, and feeds her a section.

She laughs softly, before taking a bite.

I'm two seconds from tossing the table over, and grinding my heel into his neck. I clear my throat, and he smirks.

"As much as I would enjoy indulging you, I will stop. I think we've made your friend Gray jealous." He glances at me, and then whispers to Delilah, "I suspect he prefers to indulge you himself."

"Where did you say Noura was? The Riviera?" I grin at him, waiting for a response.

Ahmad narrows his eyes, and chuckles. It's not a happy sound, more of a threat, or perhaps a promise. I don't give a shit. But he doesn't need to worry, I wouldn't fuck Noura if he paid me to do it.

During breakfast, we chat about art, Brexit, and movies. Delilah holds her own. She doesn't give herself enough credit, but despite her humble beginnings she's well-educated and well read.

"I'm needed at home this evening," Ahmad says soberly.

"We'll enjoy the last rays of sunshine and freedom before leaving the boat. We'll disembark late afternoon, and travel the last leg by helicopter." He turns to Delilah. "This suits you?"

She smiles shyly at him. "I spent the last few weeks reading about the palace and your customs. It would be an honor—and a delight—to visit there, if it suits you."

Oh, baby. Delilah's polish and deference is familiar to him. She's not as sophisticated as Noura, who grew up in a palace herself, but that would be too studied anyway. Ahmad would be suspicious. Delilah's a little nervous at the seams, like anyone meeting a prince for the first time, but she has the luster of the women he met in the Ivy League.

Either he has seen enough of Delilah to be swayed, or he's decided being in her company is worth a small risk. Maybe both. I need to remind Trippi to stay close to her. Ahmad will have no qualms about helping himself if the urge becomes strong enough. We didn't need Trippi and Baz to be as vigilant on the boat, but the palace is enormous and Ahmad knows all the hiding places.

Delilah finishes her coffee, and excuses herself to change and pack.

"I didn't expect to leave for the palace so soon. If at all." I want to know what he's thinking.

"She was thoroughly vetted," he says. "As you can imagine. I just wanted to see for myself that she wasn't a threat."

"And?"

"And I think she's far too lovely for your ugly ass, but I have no concerns. Although, she'll be observed closely, because a beautiful face hides a multitude of sins."

I stare out over the ocean, while the waiter brushes the crumbs from the table. It's inviting today—perfect for a swim off the boat. Although on the open sea, the calm surface can be deceiving. I glance at Ahmad when the waiter steps away.

"Close observation doesn't involve your hands—or your dick for that matter, Your Highness."

"Be careful, Gray. Your weakness is showing."

"Don't be fooled. Every time I mention Noura, your eyes send poison darts in my direction. And I'm quite sure she's not your weakness."

He nods. "It's a matter of respect, not just toward her, but toward me too. Noura is my queen, not to be sullied by another man."

"Then we do understand each other."

He nods curtly, and drinks some water. "It appears that way."

The fucker can say whatever the hell he wants, but I don't trust him for a single second. Especially with Delilah.

But there's no turning back now.

36

DELILAH

Italian marble floors, intricately carved ceilings, and gold embellishments adorning every piece of real estate, the sprawling palace is grand, dwarfing even the excess of Versailles. It's an audacious display of vast wealth and power, especially callous in a country where people are starving. The Amadi royal family is estimated to be worth upward of twenty-one billion dollars.

This is *real* oil money.

When we arrive at the palace, Gray disappears with the crown prince, and I'm ferreted off to a winding tour that ends in the wing where honored guests stay. Baz remains with Gray, and like on the boat, Trippi shadows me. Our security seems primarily for show. We aren't allowed to have weapons anywhere in the palace, and even if we were, the four of us would be no match for the small army of soldiers both inside and out.

As we tour, I keep an eye out for Princess Saher, but we don't go anywhere near the private residences, and she's nowhere to been found in the common areas. It's disappointing, but not a surprise.

My room and Gray's are connected by a sitting room, Fatima, the knowledgeable tour guide, explains. Trippi and Baz have rooms across the hall.

By the time we get into the suite, my belongings have been unpacked and stashed in drawers, cupboards, and a walk-in closet. It feels like a gross invasion of privacy, but because I haven't brought an entourage of maids and assistants with me, not entirely unexpected.

"This," Fatima explains, holding up an envelope with a raised seal, "is an invitation from King Khalid. He would like you to join him for light refreshments this evening in his private quarters."

She doesn't ask if I can attend, so I assume this is more of a summons than an invitation. Not that I had any intention of begging off. This mission was set in motion by the king. I suspect that he'll make an effort to help us connect with Saher.

"Will Mr. Wilder also be attending?"

She tilts her head to the side, looking at me curiously. "Of course," she says in perfect English.

For a moment, I wish Mira was here to answer the myriad questions I have about tonight's protocol. I hadn't anticipated *refreshments* with the king.

There's a knock from the sitting room, and Fatima answers the door. She speaks to a woman in hushed tones, before shutting and locking the door.

"We have some tea and snacks in the sitting room, if you'd like to relax there."

"Thank you." I want to ask if Saher will be joining us this evening, but that wouldn't be at all prudent.

Fatima hands me a card. "My office is in this wing. I will check with you regularly, but you can also reach me at this number, anytime, day or night. I'm available to answer any questions or concerns you might have while you are with us."

Fatima is not just a tour guide—she's our attaché for the

trip. I'm sure she can answer questions, but unlike Mira, I have no idea who she reports to, and I can't trust her.

When I'm alone, I open the envelope and carefully take out the card. But before I'm finished reading, there's another knock on the sitting room door. I assume it's a maid, but when I open the door, Gray, in all his gorgeousness, is standing there.

I'm so relieved to see him that in the space of two seconds, I've launched myself into his arms and I'm holding on tight. I'm not sure which of us is more surprised by the uncharacteristic impulse, me or him.

But he recovers quickly, holding me tight against him for a few minutes while his lips graze my head tenderly.

When I finally pull away, he eyes me carefully. "I came to tell you that dinner will be brought to our room," he says. "It's already been a full day and the king would like to spend some time with us this evening."

I hold up the invitation. "Fatima, our attaché, mentioned tonight. I was just opening the invitation and trying to decide what to wear. Although, to meet with the king, maybe an abaya and one of the chiffon headscarves I packed would be appropriate."

Gray nods, still studying my mood. I'm sure he's thinking about my leap into his arms. I still don't know what got into me. Gray and all the comfort and safety he provides—that's what's gotten into me.

"You're an American. The abaya isn't required, but King Khalid will appreciate it. How about jewels? Did you pack some?"

Gray's checking in with me, and his concern warms my heart. I smile. "Yes. I brought several pieces to choose from. I have a pair of emerald earrings that I think I'll wear tonight."

"Choose whatever feels right," he says quietly, smoothing my hair with his hand. The ends slide between his fingers, while he gauges my reaction. "Why don't you come sit with me, and we can relax a bit before we shower. Unless you'd like a nap."

"A nap? Is that a euphemism for something more lively?"

A lecherous smile follows a small snicker. "Shower is a euphemism for something more lively. But I thought you might like to rest first."

I know we'll be watched. My most vulnerable moments will be fully on display—perhaps even recorded. Strangers will be aroused by what they see. Perhaps even the crown prince. But I don't care. Right now, I need Gray and everything he gives me. "You underestimate my stamina."

Gray reaches behind him, and the lock snicks. "I underestimate nothing," he says, his eyes burning. "Let's get you good and dirty, so we can get you clean."

AFTER WE'VE GOTTEN DIRTY, then clean, we nap for an hour, which doesn't leave much time to get ready. It also doesn't leave too much time to stew about whether the princess will be there tonight.

Fatima comes by at the appointed time to shepherd us to King Khalid's private residence at the opposite end of the palace. Trippi and Baz don't accompany us, because as the king's visitors, he'll personally vouch for our safety. Considering he can't trust a soul in the place to get a message to his daughter, I'm skeptical about his ability to protect anyone. It's a farce, like so much else here.

We're ushered into a room with several people. Ahmad, I've met, but I recognize the others from the photographs I studied. The older man is King Khalid. He's seventy-eight, but the Parkinson's tremor makes him seem older and feeble. The crown prince's half-brother Prince Faud bin Khalid is here, as well as Princess Saher. My heart hammers so hard, I'm grateful for the extra layer the abaya provides. I hold my gaze steady in the direction of the king, but as custom requires, I never look directly into his eyes.

King Khalid greets us through a translator, first Gray and then me. But it's clear he understands the gist, if not everything, we say. I understand everything he says too. "If there is anything you require while you are in Amidane, it must be brought immediately to my attention." He nods at Fatima.

The king motions for us to sit, and offers me the seat closest to him. "You have met the crown prince, but have you met Prince Faud and Princess Saher?"

"I haven't had the pleasure."

"It's my pleasure, Miss Porter," the prince says kindly. "I'm scheduled to be in Aman tomorrow, and I won't be back before you leave. So we'll just have this evening to get acquainted."

Prince Faud is younger than Ahmad, and doesn't have that smug look his brother wears all the time.

After the introductions, Gray and the princes chat animatedly in the corner, and the princess, the king, and I are left mostly alone at the table. Mostly, because staff hovers nearby. Ahmad glances over at us periodically, the way a mother does when she wants to be sure her children are behaving.

"Saher is a lovely name." It's trite, but anything to engage her in conversation.

"Thank you," she replies. "Traditionally, it is a boy's name. My parents were hoping for a boy and had considered only boys' names."

"That is not true," the king interjects. "You were the light of our lives from the moment you were born. Pure poetry." He reaches for her hand, and turns to me. "The name we had originally chosen, before she was born, did not do her justice. We wanted something unique. The songs and poetry of Kazem Saher were favorites of ours, and we decided that our beautiful daughter should be named Saher."

"It might be nothing more than a fairy tale concocted to amuse a young girl, but I never tire of that story." She brings her father's shaking hand to her lips and places a small, tender kiss there.

Saher speaks English fluently, although not as flawlessly as her brothers, who studied in the United States and London. She's charming, but reserved, almost standoffish with me, which could pose a huge problem. Fortunately, tonight, the king bridges the gap with lots of questions for us both.

When the food is served, *the boys* rejoin us. Gray takes a seat beside me, and Saher watches us carefully, not missing a single interaction. She also eyes Ahmad occasionally. Her gaze flits from Gray, to me, to Ahmad, and back. It's as though she's sizing us up, and our relationship to one another. It's a little off-putting, but it gives me an opportunity to study her unnoticed.

"What will you do while Gray is occupied?" she asks.

It's an interesting way to phrase the question, but I'm not complaining. I'll take any and all engagement she offers.

"I'm hoping to visit the World Heritage sites, maybe do a little shopping." The last thing I need is more things, but according to the briefing book, Saher is a big shopper—it's one of the few reasons she's allowed to leave the palace, albeit with guards. "Otherwise, I'll probably read and do a little yoga."

"What kind of yoga practice do you have?" she asks, with a sparkle in her voice. She is so much friendlier now that we've eaten.

"Right now, my practice is limited to Ashtanga."

"Hot?"

"I've never tried it, but it looks challenging."

She beams. "It is challenging, but rewarding. If you would like to join me in the morning, I can have someone escort you to the studio. I usually begin my practice at ten, once my son has had breakfast and is with his tutor."

Oh. My. God. I don't dare steal even a tiny glimpse at Gray. "That would be wonderful," I gush. "Thank you."

The next hour passes quickly. All I can think about is yoga with Saher. An opportunity to have her alone. At least as alone as we will ever be.

When Gray excuses himself, Saher comes around the table and takes his seat. "The studio is just women. We have complete privacy, so wear whatever you would at home. Just cover yourself while on the way to the studio. A mat and everything else you need will be provided."

"Thank you. I can't tell you how much I'm looking forward to stretching my muscles. It was a long trip."

She smiles brightly and nods. If I didn't know better, I would say that she's almost as excited as I am. "I will send my maid at ten, to escort you."

"I can ask Fatima, our attaché, to take me there if it's easier for you."

"Fatima?" She raises an eyebrow and her expression is wary. "That's not necessary. Fatima is a very busy woman." Clearly there's bad blood between those two. Saher pauses for a beat and her smile returns. "After, we can enjoy lunch on the terrace, and I will help you decide the best places to shop. Yes?"

Ahmad is watching us closely. I've felt his eyes on us since Saher took Gray's seat. He doesn't like us chatting. I need to appear less eager so that he doesn't stop us from getting together.

"Perhaps Miss Porter would prefer to have lunch in the dining room or in the garden," Ahmad says. "She's not here to satisfy your insatiable thirst for the West."

Saher is flushed, but holds her head high. "There are few places for me to visit where I can practice my English—the crown prince is correct, though. I love to hear about Western culture." She turns to her brother. "About all cultures. Forgive me, Miss Porter."

I don't want to get involved in a pissing match between the crown prince and his sister, who he clearly controls, but I want to signal some solidarity with her, and show some small kindness. Not just because I need her friendship, but because her brother is a total asswipe.

"I'll tell you everything you want to know about American culture, if, in exchange, you'll share the beautiful Amidane culture with me. I read several books to prepare for the trip, but it's not the same as hearing stories from someone who loves their country."

She flashes me a grateful smile.

"Saher," Ahmad says, like the condescending bastard he is, "you should sleep if you plan on having a full day tomorrow. I heard the little one was up several times last night."

There is a flash of fear in her eyes when Ahmad mentions her son. "His stomach was upset, but he's better now."

"Weak stomach. Must be his father's genes."

Saher doesn't respond to her brother, but she doesn't cower, either.

Ahmad is lucky we're on his turf, because otherwise I'd grab him by the neck and kick him so hard in the balls, having a male heir would no longer be a concern for him.

The princess stands and crouches beside her father to say good night. She kisses his forehead, and he murmurs something that sounds like a blessing. When she stands, her hands smooth the wrinkles from her abaya. "Good evening," she says politely, meeting only my eyes, before making her way out of the room.

Not long after, the king excuses himself, and that's our cue to say good night too.

37

DELILAH

"Wow," I say, leaving the studio. "My muscles are going to be screaming later. That was a great workout." And the fact that Saher and I were in the same room sharing an experience adds to the exhilaration. "Heat makes it a completely different experience."

"Screaming?" She looks perplexed.

"In pain," I explain.

"*Ahh*, yes. It is exhausting and energizing at the same time."

Saher leads me into an area where there are showers, changing rooms, and a lap pool behind a glass wall. I study the area, looking for cameras and opportunities. I see neither, but they're here—at least the cameras. "Do you practice every day?"

"Hot yoga, two or three times a week," she replies. "The other days I do Pilates or a gentler yoga practice."

"Would you mind if I join you while we're here?" As soon as it's out of my mouth, I realize I might have been so forward as to be impolite. "Forgive me. I don't mean to intrude on your routine."

"I would enjoy the company. Normally the class is larger, but everyone is on holiday. It is quite lonely the month they are away." Saher hands me a bottle of water and a fresh towel. "I should have mentioned to bring a change of clothes to shower. I always go back to my room after class and I did not think.

"There is a spa through that door," she adds. "You can book a massage, or a manicure, or any beauty treatment you would like."

We mop up some of the perspiration and cool down a bit, mostly in silence. I'm not sure she remembers inviting me to lunch last night. The little stint on the boat means that we'll have less time here, but I don't want to be too pushy. It could backfire.

I take my abaya off a coat hook just inside the entrance to the studio, pausing for a second, to be sure that the one I take is mine. Unlike the ones we wore last night that had some embroidery, these are plain, and identical.

Saher watches me with a bit of mischief in her eyes. "They all look the same." She laughs.

They all look the same. Yes. This might be useful in delivering a message. But I can't put all my eggs in one basket. I need to be open to other possibilities.

"But mine," Saher explains, "usually has a small drawing or a note from my son, now that he has started to write." She pulls out a piece of paper from the deep pocket, with three stick figures: one large figure, a medium-sized one, and a smaller one that appears to be a child. It's a family. They're smiling and holding hands. A little boy's dream that has no connection to reality. "He always leaves me a little surprise."

"It's adorable. He's talented." I'm not taken with children's drawings or their other antics, but I've learned that making a fuss over a beloved child is expected, and I need to make friends with this woman.

"I will send Raksha back to your room with you. She will wait while you shower and rest. At one thirty, we will have lunch."

My brain is scattered in a dozen different directions, sifting through scenarios that might allow me to pass a message to her, and I almost miss the part about lunch.

"I would love to have lunch with you, but if you need Raksha—I don't want to impose. Would you prefer if Fatima escorted me to your suite at one thirty?" I gauge her reaction carefully. Like last night, she stiffens at the mention of Fatima.

"I would not prefer. I will send Raksha. You can trust her."

But apparently not Fatima.

We part at the end of the hall. Trippi, Raksha, and I go in one direction, and the princess in another.

———

GRAY IS NOWHERE to be found when we get back to the rooms. When he left this morning, he said he'd be gone until late afternoon, but I'm a little disappointed anyway. All the sneaking around like teenagers and pretending we're not sharing a bed has made my hormones explode. Either that, or I'm an exhibitionist at heart. *I don't think so.*

Raksha tidies up the sitting area while waiting for me. She's quiet, and I don't ask her any of the millions of questions I have about the princess and the royal family, because that would be sure to make her uncomfortable, and maybe alienate Saher.

She says a few words to staff we pass along the way, but the palace staff are mostly migrants, and they speak to one another in a dialect I'm struggling to understand. We also pass numerous soldiers along the way to Princess Saher's quarters. Some are more circumspect about ogling than others. I miss my weapon.

When we arrive, Raksha pulls a key out of her pocket, and unlocks the door.

I follow her inside.

"Welcome," Saher says, coming into a main room to greet me. A little boy is on her heels, hiding behind her legs.

My heart clenches as soon as I see him. This is the child we're trying to save. This small, harmless boy and his mother are prisoners. *They deserve to have their story heard.*

She steps aside, taking his hand. "Prince Amir bin Jalaal, please meet Miss Delilah Mae Porter. She is our guest."

He has a head of dark hair and a shy smile. The formality is stiff, but as soon as the introduction is over, she crouches and plants a kiss on the crown of his head. "Just a few more minutes with your tutor," she assures her son. "Then you may play. There is a surprise if you behave while I visit with our guest."

Raksha raises her brow and grins at him. It's genuine and affectionate, and I'm certain they adore each other. Although it's too early to trust her. The petite maid scoots the boy back through the doorway he entered while he asks about the surprise. Listening to him ask about the surprise makes me smile. It's exactly what I would do.

"Are your muscles screaming?" Saher asks impishly.

"Soon."

"We are all women," she says, helping me remove my abaya. "Soon Amir's tutor will be a man," she sighs, "but until then, we are free to dress as we like here."

She hands the black robe to another young woman, who appears out of nowhere. "It's not necessary for you to wear the abaya in the palace, provided you dress modestly, but still you choose to wear it."

She's probing, but I suspect it's more out of curiosity than anything else. "It's a privilege to be a guest of the king, and I want to respect your customs." *And the more respectful I am, the better my chances of success.*

"When in Rome," she quips.

I'm taken aback for a second, and don't respond immediately.

"Did I confuse the proverb? My English is not always on point. Or my Italian." She chuckles.

"No, it's absolutely correct. Look at you," I tease, "a woman of the world."

We share a laugh, and she glows.

"Let's sit on the terrace. It's peaceful there."

Like everything else in the palace, the terrace and courtyard are lush and manicured, with a fountain rivaling the Trevi itself. It's difficult to believe we're in the desert.

Raksha brings juice and dates, and coffee so rich and potent, I might never sleep again.

"I have something for you." I pull a wrapped package from my purse. It's one of the gifts I brought along to be used as a small thank-you. "It's a compact made by silversmiths in Charleston, where I live," I explain while she unwraps the package. "It's designed to look like the famous gates made by Philip Simmons." I tell her about the gates, with their heart shapes that grace buildings all over the city.

She smiles wistfully. "Such a romantic notion, gates of hearts."

"They're quite beautiful. You'll have to come visit and see for yourself."

Saher blinks a few times, and takes a sip of coffee. "You are soon to be betrothed," she shakes her head, "*engaged* to Gray?"

For some reason, this embarrasses me. It's almost as though she sees how much I want him—but *engaged*? *I don't think so*. "No." I shake my head. "Gray and I are still getting to know one another. He's special, but it's too early to discuss the future."

She cradles the glass of coffee between her hands, smiling wistfully. "He loves you."

My immediate reaction is to push back on that ridiculous remark, but I'm more measured, and shrug instead. This is what we want people to believe, after all.

"My mother and father loved each other in a romantic way. It is uncommon in my world."

According to the briefing book, Saher's mother died unexpectedly, although the US government believes the crown prince is responsible for his stepmother's death. She had a lot of influence over her husband, which didn't sit well with the prince.

"Yesterday, when we were with the king, I saw how Gray gazed at you, and how your eyes were soft when you looked at him. It was like a movie."

I feel my cheeks warm, but I don't let myself get sidetracked by her fantasy.

"I was not intruding—it is just—you are very beautiful, and I was uncertain if you were here for the crown prince's enjoyment. But you have no interest in Ahmad. I saw that too."

She's right about that. My only interest in Ahmad is watching him burn. "You're protective of Princess Noura."

"Have you met Noura?"

I shake my head.

"She and I are friends. We were once good friends." Her brow is knit tight. "But I am, how do you say, like poison."

"Toxic."

"Yes. Toxic. Princess Noura keeps her distance. I do not blame her. She has herself and her daughters to think about. She will need all the goodwill she can garner to deal with the prince when it comes time. Amadi women do not have the same freedoms that men enjoy, but we make up for it by forming strong bonds with each other."

Like the one I'm trying to forge with you—although ours won't be real. At least I don't think so.

"In the United States, women have many freedoms, but we still form strong bonds with other women. Sisterhoods, we sometimes call them."

Raksha collects the glasses, and tells Saher that Amir is playing happily with his new action figure.

"It must be lonely for Amir at the palace with the other children on holiday."

According to the information I was given, Amir is a prisoner in the palace, as is Saher. Unlike her son, who cannot leave the grounds, she is permitted to come and go, but her outings are brief and local because she doesn't trust her brother. I'd like to hear Saher's take on her circumstances. Not that the specifics are important to the mission, but personal conversation builds friendship.

A cloud descends, marring her young, flawless features. Her life has been so tragic, it's easy to forget she's twenty-four. "Amir does not have much opportunity to play with the other children."

Her pain has a pulse that I feel from across the table. My nurturing instincts leave a lot to be desired, but she looks so forlorn that I sit on my hands so that I don't get up and wrap her in a hug.

"Amir's father, my husband Jalaal, was killed for disloyalty to the king." She gazes at me, and I can't tell if it's grief or terror I see. "Inside the walls of the palace. Our home. Ahmad had me dragged to the back courtyard and forced me to watch as they murdered the father of my three-week-old child. It was a message, for me, that my son could meet the same fate if I do not behave as they desire."

I want to know more, but I'm concerned she's already said too much, and that the punishment will be to keep us apart. I know she's under surveillance—she must know that too. *Why is she telling me this?* "Perhaps we shouldn't discuss this."

She studies me for a moment. "You are worried that there are ears listening. That it is not safe to talk openly."

YES! But I don't reply.

"Do not worry. What I tell you is not a secret. Jalaal's

murder was a warning, not just for me, but for everyone. It was open and celebrated. The traitor was dead."

She's bitter, but resigned. I doubt she celebrated. "Did you love him?"

"Like you love Gray? *No.* I grew to have great affection for him. But I am a princess, and my duty is to marry someone my family chooses for me. A man who brings honor, or something else they want. Jalaal was chosen for me."

Although the briefing book contained everything she just confided, hearing the story from her, in the flesh, is staggering.

"Jalaal's family believe that they are the rightful heirs to the kingdom. My father wanted to appease them by making the marriage. But it was always doomed. I do not know what Jalaal did to anger the king, or more likely, the crown prince." She peers into my eyes, and I know instantly she believes her brother was behind the murder. "But this is why Amir cannot play with other children. He is not allowed to cultivate friendships that might become alliances as he grows to be a man."

These people are freaking nuts. I mean, *insane*. Saher is in an impossible position—as is her child. Amir will not survive to adulthood. In her heart, she knows it too. I want nothing more than to get them the fuck out of this hellhole. Maybe the boy can have a real life, and maybe Saher won't have to watch her son murdered in the name of a crown. The responsibility to complete the mission has never felt heavier than now.

"I'm also a widow," I say quietly.

Saher puts down her glass to give me her full attention.

"I'm not sure if I loved my husband either." I've never admitted that to anyone. Not even to Gabby. But somehow it seems right to share with her. "I was alone and confused, and he offered me—I don't know exactly what it was, but it made me feel less broken." I smile at her. "Life is complicated."

Raksha brings out a tray with our lunch, and the sober mood lifts. We spend the rest of the afternoon discussing the

Kardashians and American movies. Saher is a binge watcher. And she also wants to know whether I keep the door between my bedroom and the sitting room locked.

"Unlocked," I confess, with a hint of embarrassment.

She grins broadly. "Maybe one day we will know each other well enough that you will tell me if he makes your toes curl."

As she says it, I feel a small tug low in my belly, thinking about all the ways Gray makes my toes curl.

When it's time to say good-bye, she insists that Raksha stay with me through the visit. "You should have a woman with you who is trustworthy. She will take the room next door to yours. It is empty. She is discreet. Raksha knows the palace well, and she can help you with anything.

"Do not trust Fatima," she whispers, embracing me. "She is loyal only to Ahmad and herself."

38

DELILAH

Gray has been keeping the crown prince plenty busy for the last forty-eight hours, and I've seen so little of him. Last night, he crawled into my bed smelling like he'd been rolling in a musky flowerbed. But the late hour and the roiling stench didn't stop him from curling his body around mine, like it was his God-given right.

"I've been thinking about fucking you all day," he murmured, rucking my nightgown up around my hips and slipping his hand into my panties. "How are you, Blue Eyes?"

"Tired," I muttered through sleep, but not too sleepy to shove his hand away. "And not interested."

I was interested earlier, plenty interested, but as I waited alone for hours while he caroused with the prince, my petals dried up. It doesn't matter that Gray's only job while we're here is to distract Ahmad. My head knows that, but my emotions, no matter how much I try to convince them otherwise, aren't having any of it. I'm a professional and I'm working to get through the morass with all its tangles to complete the mission, but it irks me when I'm alone at night.

When I woke up this morning, my bed was empty and the

pillow next to me was cool to the touch. Before I left for yoga, I tried Gray's bedroom door, but it was locked. By the time I got back to the suite, he was gone.

Saher and I spent the afternoon sightseeing, and there was no time to dwell on Gray. I was focused entirely on finding an opportunity to get her the message—but there was none. I'm beginning to feel a little desperate. The clock is ticking loudly. This is when mistakes happen. I need to stay focused.

I slide my hand into the pocket of the abaya, feeling the outline of the small compact that contains the note. I've been carrying it around with me all day, and brought it to dinner, just in case.

Gray is sitting at one end of a banquet table, panty-melting in a custom tux, and I'm at the other end beside Ahmad. I expected to see Saher, but she's not here. I'm not sure what it means, but I hate when plans change.

The banquet is in honor of our visit, and I chat amicably with the other guests seated near me, speaking to Ahmad as little as possible without being outright rude.

At the end of the meal, guests begin to stand and stretch, many saying their good-byes. Out of the corner of my eye, I see Gray approaching. I haven't seen him all day. There's so much I want to discuss with him, but of course we can't talk about any of it. Although, being with him, just the two of us, would help quiet my mind. I glance around the room. *I wonder how much longer before we can escape to the suite?*

"Hey," he says softly. "Your earrings were on the dresser in the room. I put them in the top drawer." I left the emeralds out to let him know that everything was on track. "You didn't want to wear them?"

"I really did, but I wore them yesterday."

He laughs. Our interaction is chaste, but the flare in his eyes tells a different story.

He wants what I want, to get lost in the intensity he creates, letting it spiral and spiral, the pressure building and building until the coils are wound impossibly tight, and then, only then, does he release the spring, sending me into a free fall.

I can almost smell the arousal, the pheromones seeping through his sun-kissed skin. The tension escalates as we stand inches apart, unable to touch each other in public.

"Even covered from head to toe, you look gorgeous," he murmurs. "Good enough to eat." The predator has come to play, and for a small time, the din fades into the background and there's no one beside us in the room.

"We have just a few more days in paradise before we head home." His reminder falls hard, jolting me into the here and now.

But I don't need his prodding. I have a plan. I just need an opening. A tiny window where everything falls into place. "It's incredible here, but I'm almost ready to leave. You know what a homebody I am."

He gazes at me, running his straight pearly whites over his bottom lip. "I need to go. I just wanted to tell you that I miss you."

What? It's like a punch to the gut, stealing the air from my lungs. "Aren't you coming to the room with me?"

He shakes his head. "I have a meeting."

"A meeting? At this hour? In a tux?" I sound like a nagging, jealous girlfriend, but honestly, I don't give a shit. "Does this meeting involve—"

"Don't start, Delilah." His voice is well-modulated and hushed, as is mine. I'm not sure how much of this is real, and how much is for show. All I know is my heart sags with disappointment—just a drop.

"I'm tired," I snap. "I've had a big day, and another tomorrow. I need some uninterrupted sleep. Don't bother coming to my bed."

Gray's eyes flit briefly to something behind me. "I wasn't

planning on it," he sneers, in a cruel twist. "You ready?" he asks, glancing over my shoulder, dismissing me.

"Just waiting for you," Ahmad says, the levity in his voice is unmistakable, adding to my embarrassment. "Miss Porter, shall I have something sent up to help you sleep?"

The fucker. I am so angry, I'm afraid to open my mouth, but I turn my head slowly, reminding myself of the reason I'm here. "That won't be necessary, Your Highness. I know just the prescription for sleep."

The prince might not pick up on the innuendo, but Gray most certainly will. I gaze up at him and smile sweetly. Let him spend some time thinking about me rubbing my pussy. "Good night, gentlemen." I saunter away with my head high, pausing to say a few words to everyone I pass on the way out of the room.

Just a few more days in paradise before we head home. Hopefully tomorrow will hold more opportunity than today.

39

DELILAH

It's done.
Just like that. No fanfare. No exploding fireworks. Nothing but my pounding heart when I handed Saher my abaya, and slipped my arms through hers, making a quick getaway before she caught on to the switch.

"I wonder what surprise Amir left you today?" I said cheerily, as the door closed behind me. Then I disappeared down the hall before Saher noticed that she had the wrong robe. Even Trippi had trouble keeping up with me.

It's done. The sense of relief is exhilarating. I've never felt anything like it.

I turn off the shower and reach for a fluffy towel, patting my skin dry. I can't wait to parade in front of Gray with those sapphires in my ears. I can't wait to see the expression on his face.

It's done.

Although, in many ways, the real risk comes now.

We took precautions so the note couldn't be traced to us. So there would at least be plausible deniability if Saher panics and takes it to her brother. But I push the thoughts away, because for just a few minutes, I want to revel in *mission accomplished*.

I belt the robe around my waist and go out into the bedroom. Raksha is there, waiting, hands clenched by her side. *Trouble already?* "What is it?"

"Fatima is here for you. She says it is important to speak with you immediately."

My heart falls into my stomach. I need to contact Gray. *And say what? You don't even know why she's here.*

I gesture toward the sitting room, and Raksha nods. "Shall I get dressed first?"

She nods. "I will tell her you are preparing yourself, and you will be available then."

What could she possibly want? My gut is churning. What if Saher went to her about the note? *No.* There's no way she would have gone to Fatima. With little thought to my outfit, I finish dressing, add a bit of makeup, and go to the sitting room where Fatima is waiting.

"Hello."

"Hello, Miss Porter. The king wishes to see you."

I'm not sure what I expected, but *the king wishes to see you* wasn't on my list of possibilities. I don't like this. "The king?"

She nods, smiling.

"Will Mr. Wilder be joining us?" I need to buy some time to think.

"I don't know," she says with a small smile. "I'm simply carrying the message."

Carrying the message. Fuck. "Give me a moment to get an abaya, please."

"A moment, but we must hurry. The king has a very full schedule, and he does not like to be kept waiting."

"I understand."

From the bedroom, I try to reach Gray, but the call doesn't

go through. It was a long shot. The reception here is spotty at best. I consider sending a text or an email, but decide against it.

"Do I go?" I ask Raksha.

"You must," she says resolutely.

Yes, I must. But I'm shaking inside.

I open the door to the hall, and thankfully Trippi is there, right where I left him. "The king wants to see me. I can't reach Gray. Please let him know."

There's a flicker of alarm in his face. "I'll escort you."

I shake my head. "Not to the king. We need to observe protocol. I'll be fine."

"I'm up for bucking protocol," he says. "Pretty sure I've done it once or twice in the past."

"Shall we go?" Fatima asks from behind me.

"I'm in good hands," I assure Trippi. His jaw is tight, and he doesn't appear at all convinced. "But do let Gray know where I am so he doesn't worry."

While Fatima and I wind our way through the palace, she makes polite chitchat. "Are you enjoying your visit?"

"It's been wonderful. Everyone has been so kind and accommodating." *Hopefully that will continue where I'm going.*

We cross over into the official working area of the palace. This is not what I expected. "The king is in his office?"

"He is," she says simply, leading me down a long, wide hall lined with soldiers, and through a set of security doors. The gold plaque on the door reads *Crown Prince Ahmad bin Khalid.*

As we pass staff working in tight cubicles and offices, I squelch the rising panic. "I thought it was the king who summoned me?"

"He will be king one day. Soon," she says brazenly, outside the crown prince's personal office.

40

DELILAH

"Your Highness," Fatima says with the utmost reverence. "Miss Porter is here, as you requested."

The crown prince ignores her, walking around his gargantuan desk to greet me. "Come in, Miss Porter. Have a seat." He motions to a chair in front of the desk. "I'm so pleased you decided to meet with me."

Really? Did I have a fucking choice?

He nods at Fatima. "You need not wait. Close the door when you leave."

Fatima looks almost as twisted up inside as I feel.

I raise a finger to stop her. "Your Highness, if I may."

He nods, sitting on the edge of his desk, towering above me.

"I don't want to cause a scandal and ruin either of our reputations."

He lifts his chin toward the door, in a gesture for Fatima to go. "Ruin our reputations?" He snickers when the door clicks shut. "I'd say it's a bit late for that, Delilah, don't you agree?"

While I try to make some sense of what this all means, he goes to the wall behind the desk and draws the drapes. "But don't be alarmed," he assures me, as the drape opens to a line of soldiers carrying serious artillery. They stand at attention, facing away from the office. "You will be well-chaperoned." His tone is light, but the signals he's sending are deadly serious.

"Is Gray joining us?" I ask, my voice steady and strong.

He sneers. "While you're with me, I assure you, you won't need Gray."

He has the look of a jackal as he approaches me. I need to keep him at arm's length.

"Let's take a seat on the sofa, where we'll be more comfortable."

Maybe this isn't about the note.

I sit at the far corner of the tufted sofa, hoping to put some distance between us, but he pivots and takes the chair closest to me. "You've come a long way from your modest beginnings in Mississippi."

"Have you visited Mississippi?"

He shakes his head. "I have never had the opportunity. But had I known about you, I would have moved mountains to get there." He teases with a smile, but it feels more mocking. "Gray is quite a prize, isn't he?"

"We're very different, that's for sure." I smile patiently, but my patience is wearing thin.

"Different is good. It kindles the fire like nothing else. You and I are different too, Delilah."

While I'm not a stranger to cutting off assholes at the knees, I take great care to be respectful. "We are, Your Highness."

"When we are alone, even in the palace, you may call me Ahmad. Your Highness makes me feel old and out of touch. I assure you, I am neither."

I could kill this jackass with one hand tied behind my back. Although that would create a nasty mess for Gray to clean up, and I wouldn't be around to help because those motherfuckers outside the window would gun me down in a heartbeat.

"It seems Gray does not pay enough attention to his beautiful kitten."

Kitten? I glance briefly in the direction of the soldiers, and it reminds me to play nice. "He's been looking forward to spending time with you, and I support that. You've kept him busy."

"You didn't sound *supportive* or pleased last night."

"I don't share well, sir."

His smile turns into a chuckle. "Neither do I." Ahmad leans back in the chair, crossing one leg over the other. "Whatever Gray has offered you, I can offer you more. You have only to look around to see that it's true."

I need a shower.

His pick-up game is weak, but that doesn't make him any less dangerous. "Gray has only offered me his company, and that's all I'm interested in."

"His company?" He laughs out loud. "What do you offer him in return, kitten?"

This is over. "Your Highness, I mean no disrespect, but this conversation is going in a direction that's making me exceedingly uncomfortable. I'm sure you don't want that."

"You're charming, Delilah. If we had met at another time, perhaps things might have been different."

I don't say a word, because there is no way I could ever convince him that I would be willing to allow his filthy, murderous hands on me.

"You've won my father's affection, and Saher's. Even Gray's, which is impressive," he adds. "But I'm not entirely sold. Beautiful women have been the downfall of many great men—especially women named Delilah."

Really? I've never heard that before. "I'm a visitor in your country, your home. I have no interest in making trouble for anyone—men or women."

He glares at me for some time, his face darkening as the

seconds tick by. "Saher married a traitor. She carried the traitor's baby in her womb. Like his father, he will grow up to believe that Amidane is rightfully his, and he will die a traitor, like his father."

Jesus Christ.

"Saher is a prisoner of her own making. Don't fill her head with fantasies that will never be hers. It will make her captivity more painful than it is already."

"It's not my place to tell others how to live their lives."

"Of course it is. You're an American—and a woman at that. You can't help yourself. It's in your genes."

I fold my hands in my lap. This conversation isn't going well. It's not that it's veered off track. It was never on a good path. "I'm not sure what it is you expect of me."

He studies me for a long time, before placing a call from a phone on the end table beside him. It's on speaker.

"Tell Gray where you are," he instructs as the phone rings.

"Hello."

My heart skips a beat when I hear his voice.

"Gray, it's me."

"Delilah? Where are you?"

"I'm with the crown prince. In his office."

"Is anyone else with you?" His voice is controlled and brittle, with rage buttressing every word.

I glance at Ahmad, who is sitting there like he owns the world. "Just the two of us. We're on speakerphone."

Gray is deathly quiet. The prince is grinning. The combination raises gooseflesh on my arms. "Are you okay?" he asks cautiously.

"I am."

"Is she okay, Ahmad?" Gray demands, with a fury I've never heard from him.

"She seems very well."

"Delilah, go back to the room," Gray says. "Right now."

I get up, but the prince remains seated. "Miss Porter, ask my secretary to call Fatima. She'll escort you back to your suite. Or perhaps you prefer Raksha."

He wants me to know that nothing happens here without him knowing. Even something as simple as a maid being reassigned. Ahmad gauges my reaction, but I don't flinch.

"Either would be fine," I reply with a small, polite smile. "Thank you."

"I expect an explanation, Ahmad. And it fucking better be a good one." That's the last thing I hear as the office door closes behind me.

I pause for a moment to collect myself, as the stress melts off me. I dodged a major one, but I might not be so lucky next time.

The prince's secretary doesn't bother with either Fatima or Raksha. He sends a young woman in the office to escort me back to the room. I'm so preoccupied with the thoughts racing in my head, I don't really remember anything about the walk.

Raksha is dusting when I arrive. The compact that was in the abaya that I handed to Saher this morning is on the nightstand, with a note canceling the shopping we had planned for the afternoon. It's on Saher's stationary, but not signed.

I don't know if Saher canceled the outing, or if it was canceled by the prince, or someone else. Raksha doesn't know, either—although that seems unlikely.

The prince's threats, and now this. My gut's sending warning flares, but without any clear direction. I'm in limbo, and I hate the feeling.

What seemed like a great coup two hours ago is suddenly blowing up in my face.

41

GRAY

I've had enough.
 Enough bullshit. Enough tits shaking in my face every night. Enough of Ahmad. And certainly enough of fucking with Delilah's head—sitting on the scales just right, so they don't tip too far in one direction or the other—the relationship and the mission, teetering precariously while I hold my goddamn breath. Maybe it's my head that's been fucked with enough.

It's time to go home. Let these stupid bastards with their fucked-up family dynamics clean up their own damn messes.

If only it was that simple.

I nod to Raksha, who's become a fixture in the sitting room with her embroidery, and knock on the door to Delilah's room, before entering.

"Hey." Her face is washed out, and her shoulders slumped. I've never been more pissed at Ahmad. "How are you doing?"

"I'm fine."

If she thinks she's going to brush me off, she's nuts. I put her in this position, and I'm going to take care of her. Her pain, her fears, and her anxiety are mine.

I place my hand on her upper arm, gripping gently. "What happened? I want the details. All of them."

She shrugs, but's not enough to free herself from my tightening grip. "I think the prince was testing me. Sending me a message not to fill Saher with Western ideas. He wasn't hiding anything. It was his idea to call you."

Only because he knew you would tell me about meeting with him. "How did you end up there?"

"It's a long story. Fatima told me *the king* wanted to see me." She glances up at me warily. She was tricked, and I'm sure she's plenty pissed. "I asked Trippi to get a message to you."

"By the time he reached me, I was already on the phone with you." The bile rises in my throat every time I replay that call in my head. Her voice was controlled in the way it gets when she's anxious. Ahmad was fucking with both of us.

"What are you doing here?" She pulls out of my grasp. "I thought you were busy on a project today."

"Fuck that. I was doing Ahmad a favor. He can shove it up his ass." I wrap my arms around her from behind, pulling her flush against me. After a few minutes, her body still hasn't relaxed one iota.

My eyes fall on the dresser, where a topaz, a ruby, and a sapphire sit side by side, as though she couldn't make up her mind, or she didn't have enough holes in her ears to wear all three.

I've run into a snag but I can handle it, I'm in trouble and need to talk, and it's done. That's what they signify, but what it means—at least how I read it—is that she's in trouble...emotional trouble.

Fuck.

Jet lag, not enough time to fully prepare for something this big, that bastard Ahmad toying with her... I don't give a shit what he said to me on the phone. He would have fucked her in a heartbeat if he thought he could get away with it.

I swivel her around, so I can reach her mouth, and ravage it with a long, rough kiss. Someone else might caress her gently as a way of saying I'm sorry. But that's not us. And it's not what *she needs* right now.

My blood runs cold, when I force my mouth away. "I know what you need." My heart aches, as she gazes at me with more trust than I've earned. "Will you allow me to give it to you?"

"Here?"

"I'm afraid so, Blue Eyes. I don't think it can wait."

"I'll follow you, wherever it takes me." These words, from her, never fail to humble me.

I don't deserve Delilah's submission right now, but I'm going to accept it. I kiss the bridge of her nose, before sticking my head into the sitting room. "Please allow us some privacy. Perhaps you can take a walk." Raksha nods, and I open the door to the hall where Trippi is stationed. "Take Baz and hang out at the end of the hall. I'll let you know when I need you back."

"She okay?" he asks.

"Okay? She'd have your balls in half a second if she knew you asked."

He shakes his head and chuckles.

I shut the door and turn to her. "Take off your clothes. For me."

She tilts her head to the side, and I see the hesitation. Something that I will not allow. "Now, Delilah, unless you want my help. I'm in the right mood to rip the clothes off your body to tatters."

She lifts her chin, and my cock twitches. With every piece of clothing she removes, it lengthens and thickens. The curve of her breasts, how her hip meets her thigh, the dip of her navel— it all calls to me at once.

I step closer to her and place my hand on her throat, fingering the very places that would rob her of breath. She gasps, and shudders. "Drape yourself over the footboard. Face and hands on the mattress."

Her mouth opens slightly, and I see her begin to relax. It kills me. All that we accomplished in the last few weeks, I'm about to eviscerate. The very minute my belt lands on her ass, it'll all be gone.

I don't warm her up. I don't warn her. I don't have to. She knows what's coming, and she's relishing the assault.

Crack.

Crack.

Crack.

Over and over, leaving my handprint on her flesh.

When her skin is well-flushed, I slide my fingers to her pussy. She's wet. But not wet enough.

I step back and pull off my belt, folding it in half so that the first strike will have the snap of a whip. *This is for her*, I remind myself. *Not for me*. It's not what I want for her, but what she needs from me at this moment.

I let the belt fly, and she screams—the harrowing sound muffled by the linen. I let it fly, again, and again, until the stripes on her ass, where it meets her thigh, are raised and angry—until I can't stand it anymore.

I toss the belt aside and reach between her legs, rubbing her clit with the fingers of one hand and sliding three fingers from the other into her swollen cunt. "Keep your face buried in the mattress."

No one, not one fucking person gets to see her face when she comes. That privilege belongs only to me. In seconds, she's choking my fingers, bucking off the bed, and I finish her off, yanking her into the abyss without mercy.

While she's still whimpering, I take off my clothes and crawl into bed, pulling her on top of me and stroking her back while she cries. Delilah is not a crier, and it's heartbreaking to hear her sobs, but she needs to release the bottled emotion. It doesn't matter that I feel like a monster. All that matters is what she needs.

When she's finished, when all the pent-up stress and anxiety is gone, I grab my shirt and wipe the remnants of a good cry and the smeared mascara off her gorgeous face. "You okay?"

She nods, smiling at me through hazy eyes. Content and unburdened, I want this feeling for her—always. *But not like this.*

"You up for a shower?" She nods, again, the languid smile lingering like a punchy drunk. "Then let's go. I'm not done with you."

In the shower, I turn the water on full blast, both fans, and some music. I'm careful to shield her ass away from the sting of the hot water. "Why is there a ruby, a topaz, and a sapphire out?" I murmur softly into her neck, while the spray rains on us from all sides.

She turns and twines her arms around my neck. "It's done," she whispers, licking my ear, and even though this is partly business, my cock hardens at her touch. "But I'm terrified for her."

"You can't save her." She stiffens as I mutter the words into her skin. There is absolutely no doubt she heard me.

I slide my hand into the hair at the back of her neck, with a firm hold, and walk her deeper into the shower, until she's in the corner, facing the stone. "This is going to be quick and rough. I suggest you hold on." With one hand fisting her hair, I nudge her legs apart with my knee and sink into her pussy, balls deep with one thrust.

"Oh, Blue Eyes. You're so hot and tight. My cock can't get enough of your sweet pussy." *This is not going to last long.*

She gasps and moans, egging me on. My fingers find her belly, creeping lower and lower, until she's sandwiched between my throbbing cock and my hand, both working her until she can't stand of her own accord.

My balls are heavy, and the telltale prickle is gathering at the base of my spine.

I can't stop.

I can't stop.

I can't stop.

"Hold on." It's the last thing I remember before sinking my teeth into the cord at the back of her neck, and riding out the wave.

After we've soaped up and rinsed off and fucked again, I hold a terrycloth robe for her to step into, and belt it around her waist. "We're leaving in the morning, or as soon as we can get clearance to fly."

She licks her lips, and nods. There's reluctance in that nod. "After I eat something, I'll pack."

"Let Raksha help you. It'll go quicker, and you'll have more time to relax."

Delilah leaves the bathroom without replying. I'm sure the idea of someone helping her pack gives her heartburn. Although not as much heartburn as I'm planning to give her on the trip home.

When I go into the bedroom, Delilah is in her robe, holding an envelope. "It's from Saher," she says, handing me the card. There's a sparkle in her eyes.

Please join me for shopping in the morning. We leave promptly at eleven.

"I'm going," she announces, with a fire in her eyes that dares me to say otherwise.

"We're leaving as soon as we're cleared to go."

"I haven't bought one souvenir to take back with me. At the very least, I need something for Gabby. Please." She begs not only with her words but with her eyes. "I need to do this one thing."

Souvenirs. What a crock of shit. But brilliant, at the same time. I understand why she wants to see Saher one more time—to silently plead her case. But her job is done and we need to get out of here. Delilah was to pass the message, not to ensure that the princess followed the instructions.

"Wheels up the very second we have clearance to fly. If time allows you to go shopping, fine. But there are no promises."

42

DELILAH

"After the stunt Ahmad pulled yesterday, I'm not excited about this."

I wince, and the glossy stain I'm applying smears past my lip line. But when I glance at Gray in the mirror, I realize he didn't misspeak. He's still pissed, and doesn't care if Ahmad is privy to our conversation. I sometimes forget that not only does Gray have the kind of power that all multi-billionaires have, but that he is also the son of a former president. That kind of power can stand up to kings and queens, and the shield it provides is incomparable.

"I'll be fine. You might be slightly poorer, but otherwise, there's nothing to worry about." I stay in role, reminding him to, also. "Besides, because of the weather we can't leave until late this afternoon, anyway."

He mumbles something about me being up all night praying to the weather gods. I might have been chanting and pleading all night, but it had nothing to do with weather.

"Take this," he says, placing a credit card that he knows full well I won't use, near my purse. "And take some more Advil, before you go."

He flashes me that wolfish grin I'm so fond of, which sparks an idea for the long trip home.

"What will you do while we're gone?"

"Have a word or two with Ahmad. We spoke by phone yesterday, but he deserves to hear it from me in person. Take Trippi and Baz with you. I'm sure they'll love a shopping trip."

I don't like the idea of leaving Gray at the palace without an ally. This place is fraught with peril, most of it shrouded in secrecy. We're vulnerable here—even Gray, who can take care of himself. "Trippi *and* Baz?"

"It's the only way I'm allowing your little shopping trip to happen."

I open my mouth to argue, but I'm silenced before a single word emerges.

"This isn't a negotiation. Save your breath."

Raksha escorts me, flanked by Trippi and Baz, to the limousine where Saher is waiting. "Good morning." My voice is cheery and upbeat as I climb into the seat next to her.

"Hello," she says softly. Her eyes are ringed with dark circles, and she has lines on her face that I don't remember seeing before. "Thank you for joining me."

I do something next that pushes the boundaries of protocol, and is completely out of character for me. It's something Gabby would do, or Lally, or Mrs. Marshall. But not me. I reach down and place my hand over Saher's, squeezing gently. "I wouldn't have missed it."

Saher nods, staring out the side window. After a few uncomfortable minutes, she turns toward me. "Saks is not too far," she says brightly. "The store in Amidane carries brands from all over the world."

We chat for a few minutes about high-end shopping, which

I know very little about, so mostly I listen and try to ask questions that don't sound too unsophisticated.

About twenty minutes into the trip, Saher presses a button to speak to the driver. "We've changed our minds. Pull right into there." She points out the window. "To Harvey Nichols."

Wait. We've changed our minds? What? I can't get a good look at Trippi and Baz from where I'm sitting, but I'm sure they're alarmed too.

"I'm sorry, Princess," the man seated next to the driver says. "We were told you were going to Saks. We cannot deviate from this instruction."

"You can and you will."

Whoa.

"I am King Khalid bin Abdullah's daughter. You pray every day to remain in the good graces of my father."

She's a fighter, God love her.

"The crown prince instructed—"

"The crown prince has my respect," she interrupts tersely, "but the king, while he has even a single breath in him, has not only my respect, but my loyalty. As he should have yours. Shall I call his secretary and have him wake my father from his nap so that he can tell you what he told me, that I may shop in any store that captures my fancy?"

Without another word, the driver crosses the median and pulls into the front of Harvey Nichols. This gives "bitches get things done" a whole new meaning. Still, I'm wary of the change in plans, and I'm sure my two sidekicks are none too happy either.

She turns to me. "You will love the merchandise. It is of high quality. Saks is in the US—you can go there any time. This will be special."

She has a plan. I see it in her eyes. Hopefully it's not some half-cocked scheme, or a trick *on me*.

We leave the bodyguards, mine and hers, behind, because

men are not allowed in the store. "We will be one-and-one half, to two hours, at the most," Saher instructs the driver. "Let us go," she says to me.

Once inside, two saleswomen fawn all over us. It's not me, but the princess who is not only the king's daughter, but no stranger here.

Saher whips around the room, handing hanger after hanger to the saleswomen, with clothing in both our sizes. I say very little, but nod and gush in all the right places.

In thirty minutes, she's amassed quite a haul. "We should start to try on the clothes so we have enough time."

The dressing area consists of a few smaller changing rooms off one large room, with a few chairs, a triad mirror, and refreshments. When we're settled, she dismisses the saleswomen. "We would like privacy, please. I will call you if we need help. In the interim, would you please find us some accessories to wear with our new clothes?"

"Yes, Princess Saher, of course." They fawn one more time before leaving us alone.

As soon as they're gone, Saher pulls me into one of the small changing rooms. "Try this," she says, handing me a designer gown with a floppy bow at the shoulder. It's not something I would ever be caught dead in, but she didn't ask my opinion, and I'm not here to shop anyway.

I assume she's going to find her own changing room, not because I'm modest, but because this one is tight. But she doesn't. She strips down to her birthday suit, and grabs another gown off the hanger. She holds a finger to her lips, and motions for me to take off my panties and bra. This is getting weird, but I'll give her a little more rope.

After we're dressed to the nines in ballgowns without a shred underneath, she takes our belongings, all of them, and arranges them on the floor in a heap, like she's going to start a bonfire. Then she covers the pile with the stacks of clothing we brought into the dressing room. *Oh my God.* She's a savvy little thing. She thinks our clothes are bugged.

I begin to help her, until everything we brought into the room is piled on the floor.

She hands me another dress, and motions for me to follow her into a changing room on the far end of the larger room.

"We only have a few minutes before they come back," she whispers. "I don't understand. Who asked you to pass me the note?" she demands. "Is it a trick by the Americans?"

"No. It's not a trick." I want to tell her it's a message from her father, but I can't. "Please trust me. It's for your safety and Amir's. When your father receives a cable about his sister's declining health, you must act immediately."

"The last time I begged to take Amir abroad, I was punished." Her tone is dire. "They would not let me see my son for one month. Ahmad promised that the next time the punishment would be far more severe."

"I can't force you to act, but I hope you will. We haven't been friends long enough for you to trust my motivation, but I would never do anything to put you in danger."

Her features contort as she struggles to process all of it. We're going to run out of time. I need to say something that will convince her it's safe.

"Your father will smooth the way for you."

She eyes me suspiciously. "And once we are in London?" she asks with some skepticism.

"You'll be protected by the British government. That's all I know. This wasn't engineered by the Americans. I promise you."

"But we will be prisoners there, like here." Her shoulders slump under the weight.

She's right. But the Brits won't have her and Amir murdered. "It's your decision. But I'm not sure it will continue to be safe here."

The saleswoman calls from outside the dressing room.

"We are not yet in need of assistance," Saher replies quickly.

"I want to trust you, but Amir is my life. He is my reason for being." The emotion in her voice is so tangible, so real, I could hold it in my palm.

The image of the Marshalls at Richie's funeral pops into my mind. They were broken. Devastated beyond repair. I can't push the grisly image away.

"Amir is a prisoner, but he is alive," she adds, the gravity of her circumstances gripping us both.

I don't make any more assurances, or encourage her to take the risk. Because honestly, I am one small cog in a big wheel, and I don't know what's in store for her—for either of them.

The saleswoman calls again, from outside the dressing area. She has shoes for us to try on.

Saher sighs as we leave the cramped room. It's a deep, mournful sigh, of a mother whose child's life hangs precariously in the balance. Her decision can save him, or doom him. Or as Saher knows too well, perhaps there's no winning hand to be played.

43

DELILAH

Boarding the plane is an adventure. Every bag, every electronic device, every article of clothing is swept for explosives and recording devices. Trippi and Gray are like men possessed, combing through every inch of our belongings. Baz and I repack bags as items are cleared.

It drives home the danger lurking in Amidane. I shudder, thinking about the implications for Saher.

When we got back to the limousine after shopping, the guard in the passenger seat informed Saher that the crown prince wanted to speak to her the moment she returned to the palace.

She didn't seem surprised. While we hugged good-bye, I begged her to let me have Gray intervene on her behalf.

But she shook her head. "You cannot save me. No one can." It's the same thing Gray said, but it wasn't any easier to hear it from Saher, and I can't stop thinking about it.

"Delilah." I finish zipping a small suitcase and glance up. Gray looks worn and edgy. We're not out of the woods yet, and many a mission has gone sour at this stage, especially when people begin to let their guard down.

"We're done here," he says briskly. "Take a seat so we can get out of this shithole as soon as humanly possible."

NINETY MINUTES LATER, the pilot announces in her very proper British voice that we've left Amidane airspace.

Gray visibly relaxes, and reaches for my hand. "You did great, Blue Eyes. You're the hero."

"Do I get the game ball?" I tease, trying to deflect the praise. Or maybe I'm trying to shield my heart from the reality that the mission being over means Gray and I are over too. I haven't allowed myself to dwell on it much. I've been too worried about passing messages, and until a few minutes ago, our plane being shot out of the sky. But it hits me now with a profound sadness that makes my soul ache. *Put it away for now, Delilah. You can wallow in your misery at home.*

"Not the game ball, but I do have something for you." His weaselly expression spells trouble.

"What?"

Gray starts toward the front of the plane, ignoring my question. It better not be some wildly expensive jewelry like those earrings he supposes I'm keeping. I don't know where he thinks I go to wear jewels.

Although I do have to admit, it was fun pretending to be some glamorous high-society chick for a little while. More fun than I expected. I loved the intrigue, and the covert nature of the mission. I loved everything about it, even when it was hard, or in the end, when I felt lost.

Covert operatives are expected to experience a wide range of emotions. It goes with the territory. But that's done too. The mission, with its clandestine opportunity, was one and done. I knew it when I agreed. But that doesn't stop me from wishing there were more opportunities for covert work—*with Gray.*

He proved himself to be a worthy leader. I'd follow him into battle. That's for sure. In truth, I'd follow him anywhere.

Before I get too carried away with my thoughts, Gray is sauntering down the aisle, carrying a tray. His boyish grin makes his eyes twinkle like a rascal. He sets the tray down in front of me and lifts the silver dome.

"Pop-Tarts!" I squeal like a child. The pale-pink icing is smoothed to a shiny glaze, with a sprinkling of pastel sugar crystals. They're smaller and far more delicate than the toaster pastries from the box on a supermarket shelf. But they look amazing.

"Yep."

"Where did you get them?"

"Take a bite, and I'll tell you."

I take a small bite of the strawberry-filled pastry. It tastes nothing like what I'm used to—it's sweet and buttery and wonderful. "It's delicious. Really delicious," I add, taking another bite.

"They're from a small bakery in Paris I love. The pastry chef is a bit of a snob, but when I explained that I was trying to win over a beautiful woman, he was all over it."

The emotion winds its way into my chest, and it takes up so much space, I have trouble swallowing even another small bite. "Paris. Not exactly around the corner. Thank you. I can't believe you went to all this trouble—for me."

"You earned it. Besides, I would do anything for you, Blue Eyes. But those Pop-Tarts just took a phone call." He reaches for his briefcase and pulls out a manila envelope. "This is a bonus for a job well done."

"The government is handing out bonuses now?" I ask, opening the tiny clasp.

"That's from me."

His face gives nothing away, but God knows what he's scheming. *At least it isn't jewelry.*

I pull out the paperwork, and read until my brain stops firing. I glance at Gray. "Please tell me you didn't sign over the deed to your beach house to me. *Please*," I plead.

"I can't tell you that." The response is resolute. He's dug in—I sense it.

Well, you're going to be disappointed.

With trembling hands, I put back the paperwork, and shove the envelope at him. "I'm just going to pretend this didn't happen."

He places his hand on mine, lacing his long, strong fingers through my smaller ones. "It's a gift." His hand tightens around mine. "It comes with no strings."

I'm having trouble breathing, and my first inclination is to fight, but I don't. He doesn't deserve the churlish response of a little girl who is embarrassed and overwhelmed, and doesn't know what to do with her feelings. I can't accept this outrageous *gift*, but he deserves a civil response from me.

"A gift is a bottle of bourbon or a nice pair of gloves. Maybe concert tickets. Not waterfront property worth millions of dollars." My voice is starting to get prickly and I pause for a beat to recalibrate. "You love that place. It's your escape."

"I do love it. But not as much as you love it. I've never seen you happier than you were gazing out over the ocean."

There's nothing worse than trying to reason with a man who's decided that his idea is the best thing he's ever heard, and has his mind set on it.

"I can replicate the house anywhere," he continues. "But you won't."

Because I can't. "Gray—I can't afford the property taxes on the beach house, let alone the upkeep."

He rifles through the envelope and pulls out a single sheet of paper. "It's been taken care of for the duration of your lifetime."

I don't even glance at the paper. "It's too much."

"I don't have anyone special to spend money on. My brothers have more than their great-grandchildren can ever spend. I set up a trust for Gracie, so she'll always have her own money—money her father doesn't control." The mischief in his eyes tells me JD doesn't know about this little gift. Even in the middle of a testy discussion, it makes me smile.

"But other than that," Gray says softly, "there's no one. Let me do this."

No! "I don't know. I'm not sure I can."

We sit quietly for a long while. Each alone with our separate thoughts. I don't know what his are like, but mine are so jumbled they don't resemble anything coherent. The only thing I recognize in the morass is my mother. *"Don't be a little fool," she says, primping her hair, with the smell of cheap jasmine practically gagging me. "Let him take care of you."*

That would be a big *no*.

"I promised myself when the mission was over," Gray says, his brow crinkled tightly, "I'd help you make it right with Smith or find some work that suits you better. I convinced myself that I'd introduce you to a few guys, stand-up men and experienced Doms, who would be good to you." His voice is heavy with sorrow, the grief twisted into every strangled word.

He might not be thrilled about it, but he's willing to *introduce* me to experienced Doms. *What did you expect, Delila? You are a fool.* I swipe a lone tear from the corner of my eye before he notices.

"But I can't do it," he concedes with the rawness that accompanies unfettered emotion. "I'm not prepared to let you go, Delilah. I love you."

The tears are falling too fast to swipe them away unnoticed. Gray gets up and lifts me off the seat, carrying me into the bedroom while I sob into his chest.

He kicks the door shut behind us, and lays me on the bed. My eyes are closed, but I feel the mattress dip beside me.

"I want us to be partners, in everything." He brushes some hair off my face, his fingertips so gentle it makes me melt. "The club, the work I do with EAD, and in every other aspect of my life—I want you by my side. We make a great team."

I feel as though I need to say something to acknowledge his unguarded confession, but I can't find the right words to convey what I'm feeling. I don't even know what I'm feeling. "This comes as a surprise. A shock, really." I gaze at him, grazing my fingers over his scruff. "I need some time to sort through it all."

Gray kisses my nose. "Take as much as you need." His eyes glaze over, and his Adam's apple bobs not once, but twice. "There are two other things to throw into the mix for you to consider as you're deciding." He rolls onto his back, staring at the ceiling. "I knew Kyle from the Bureau."

44

DELILAH

I draw a slow, jumbo-size breath, and brace myself, because the other shoe is about to drop. I feel it in my bones.

"He was an abuser," Gray says flatly. The same way he might say grass is green or cotton balls are soft—simple, incontrovertible facts. "The worst kind of sadist. He bragged about how he preyed on you, reeled you in, and groomed you for pain."

The sear in my chest is pure agony. Gray's words are a rusty blade piercing the skin and snaking into the muscle until it's wedged deep.

It's one thing to know I followed the scraps into the trap like a fool—manipulated and gaslighted for years. A *victim* of my own stupidity. But it's quite another to have others know the extent of my idiocy. To have Gray know.

My relationship with Kyle was tortured and conflicted, especially as I got older and wiser. I've worked hard to create the perfect façade around it, not just for the benefit of others, but it's a lie I tell myself too. Not to protect Kyle. He doesn't deserve my loyalty. I keep the truth hidden to protect *me*.

Gray knows I was weak and stupid—an operative who

couldn't even save herself from an asshole. He knows everything. *He's always known.*

I cover my face with my arm. *Jesus Christ*. It's so humiliating.

"I've never forgiven myself for not reaching out to warn you the fuck away from him."

I want to shake Gray. To grab him by the throat and scream *shut up!*

"I should have killed the sonofabitch when I had the chance. I'm sorry, Delilah. I let you down."

"I didn't need a protector then, and I still don't," I spit out, with as much dignity as I can muster. "It was a lesson that needed learning."

My head is throbbing, the loose fragments racing through my mind in damning circles. Then it smacks me in the face. *Oh God. No, please. No.*

Smith's father, General Sinclair, was the head of the Joint Chiefs during all that mess with the congressman. He was there when I testified, and at the end of the hearing, he approached me in the hall: *"A life well-lived is the best revenge,"* he said, handing me Smith's card. *"Tell my son I sent you."*

Was it all a con?

"Did you arrange my job with Smith?"

He turns his head toward me, meeting my eyes. "Nope. I had nothing to do with that."

I feel myself relax a little. "There's no need for you to harbor any guilt for what happened between Kyle and me. I take full responsibility for my part in it."

Gray rolls on top of me, pinning my hands near my head. "Oh no, you fucking don't," he growls. "That was not your fault. None of it."

"I had a brain and two good working feet. I could have walked away. I wasn't a prisoner."

He glowers at me, and I turn my cheek to the mattress so I

don't have to look at him. I don't need him trying to make excuses for me. It only makes me feel worse. "Get off me."

He doesn't budge.

"You were an anxious kid who had never been out of her small Mississippi town. You had stars in your eyes about joining the CIA. He was a grown man, trained in high-stakes mind games. He had a federal badge. It wasn't a fair fight."

I've never allowed myself to make excuses for my choices. That's a coward's game. I take responsibility for every decision, especially for the ones involving Kyle. I am not a helpless victim, and I will not allow Gray to make me one.

He eases off me, onto the mattress, and turns on his side, stroking my arm with his fingertips.

"Don't touch me."

He takes a ragged breath, and moves his hand.

"We knew each other three years," I say with the sharp bite of a woman whose feelings are bruised. "We were friends. We had sex. We were teammates on a mission where trust was everything. But you never thought to tell me that you knew my husband. Not even when I asked."

"I couldn't say anything when you worked at Wildflower. It would have blown my cover. After you quit, we didn't say a civil word to each other."

"And whose fault was that?" I snap. "There was no reason you had to carry a ruse that far."

"It wasn't just subterfuge. I was pissed you went to Smith instead of coming to me after we spent so much time together —after what happened at Christmas. It felt like a betrayal. And then not talking just became what we did."

I roll onto my side with my back to him. It's bad enough I have to listen to this, but I don't need to look at him.

"I didn't tell you while we were getting ready for the op— there was too damn much going on already, and so little time. And," he pauses, "I hoped *you* would tell me about your marriage one day. That you'd trust me enough to show me that part of you." He sighs. "But I'm tired of waiting. I want us to start—not over...what came before is worth keeping. But I don't want secrets between us."

I let my eyelids flutter closed, focusing on the familiar rhythm of his breathing. But it provides no comfort today.

Gray curls behind me so we're almost touching. He doesn't lay his hands on my body, and I don't push him away.

Two things for you to consider. That's what he said when we started this *discussion*. I don't know if I have the energy to deal with any more, but I can't stand the thought of a landmine still out there waiting to detonate. "You said there were two things."

He's so quiet and his breathing is so shallow, for a few moments I think he's asleep. But he's not.

"I delivered my father to his death," he says dispassionately, his tone devoid of *any* emotion.

I gasp softly. *His father was the president.*

"I lured him to within easy range of the bullet. I wanted to take the shot myself, but couldn't get anybody to buy that plan."

His lack of emotion is chilling.

We're discussing a presidential assassination like we'd talk about hunting turkey. Even the conversation we had about the archbishop's death had more verve. "Was it sanctioned?" I ask cautiously. "Because that's the vibe I'm getting."

He lays his hand on my hip. "Please don't ask me to share the details."

It was sanctioned. Jesus. "Why are you telling me any of it?"

"Because going forward, there are no secrets. Nothing separating us." I feel his knees dip into the back of mine. "I don't want there to be any doubt about how much I trust you. I'm going to take a lot from you, Delilah. The little girl inside you—the one who drops her Gs hard, and is proud and resilient—her anxiety will increase and her innocence will disappear in my world. It's bound to happen."

"She's not innocent. That's the whole point. She's simple, scrappy and tough, and she knows the streets are dangerous."

"She's also forgiving and loyal and much too hard on herself. Whatever you think you've done, I've done worse." He wraps his arms around me, enveloping me in his body. "I told you about my father because I want you to have serious power —in case you ever need it. My world is dangerous, and the danger often lurks in unexpected places. Think of it as the ultimate safe word, to use if you ever need to save yourself."

I allow myself to slip into sleep, dragged by the emotional tsunami. I don't fight it, because I need the escape that even restless sleep provides.

I WAKE up a couple of hours before we're scheduled to touch down. Gray isn't in the room, and I'm relieved to have a few minutes alone to think.

Last night comes flooding back. He lured his father, *the president*, to his death. Suddenly, *I knew Kyle from the Bureau* doesn't seem like such a big revelation.

Damien Wilder was the monster of all monsters. Molested little girls, and had his wife and daughter killed. There were so many other evil deeds, but selling dangerous compounds to the enemy, compounds that could be lethal to our soldiers on the battlefield—simply to line his pockets—that was a bridge too far even for his most ardent supporters.

There were hushed whispers that the assassination was an inside job, but no evidence ever surfaced. Shortly after the funeral, Americans moved on to other things. All but the most fanatical kooks tire of conspiracy theories eventually. In truth, President Wilder needed to die. Even more than Archbishop Darden.

I shower and compose myself before going out into the

cabin. Gray's there. His dark hair above the leather seat is what I see first. I square my shoulders as I approach. There's no telling what fresh hell our next conversation might hold. But I'm well-rested and clear-headed. And more than anything, I don't want to fight with him.

"Good morning, or afternoon," I say, sitting across from him. "I haven't slept that long in forever. Did you sleep?"

"Here and there. How are you?" he asks cautiously.

"A good night's sleep always makes things clearer."

"Have you decided?" He's hopeful, and confident that we can make it work—but I'm not sure. I haven't had as much time to rifle through the layers.

"If I want to be your partner in crime?"

He laughs, and I hope the sparkle in his eyes is a good barometer of his mood.

"No. I haven't decided."

"Would it be easier to make a decision if I slipped a ring on your finger?"

What? "No." I put my hands up to stop any further discussion along those lines. "I need to go back home. To Mississippi."

"Are there answers there?"

"I'm not sure, but something's telling me that I need to go and see for myself if the little girl inside—and the woman she's become—is strong enough to survive in your world without losing herself. Her values. Her very essence."

He nods, resigned to the necessity of the trip. "Give me a day or two to put out fires at Wildflower, and then we can leave."

I shake my head. "I need to find those answers alone. If you're with me, the setting will be different, but it'll all still be murky."

Gray leans back and stretches his legs out, tapping his foot against mine. "Take Trippi with you."

"I need to go alone."

He gets up and takes the seat near me, arranging the chairs until our knees are practically touching. "We have no idea what we just left behind, or what the next few weeks hold. None. Take Trippi, or don't go."

Inky flickers have replaced the sparkle in his eyes. It's about to storm, and it's going to be a belly-washer.

"I will not be your prisoner."

"You damn sure will be, if that's what's necessary. Your safety, *your life*, isn't up for negotiation." His jaw is so tight, it's twitching.

"Look," he adds, with far less harshness. "I fully respect your need to get away from me, but there's no reason for you to avoid Trippi. He doesn't talk much. It'll be like you're alone."

He's cajoling. But it's true. Trippi's not a chatterbox. "I'll think about it," I mutter, but we both know Trippi's coming with me.

Neither of us say another word until the wheels hit the tarmac.

Gray's not happy, but he doesn't fight me when I insist on going back to my house for the night. I'm sure there will be security all over the place, but I appreciate him not making a big fuss about it.

When it's time to say good-bye, he cups my face and presses his lips to mine. The kiss is at once a slow burn, filled with pleas and promises, and a mournful dirge.

Before I pull away, I cradle his jaw, enjoying the prick of the stubble on my palm. "Do you know what my favorite quote is?" He tilts his head to the side, waiting for me to tell him. "*Some men just need killin'*."

A lazy smile spreads slowly across his face, and embers of hope catch fire in his eyes. He pulls me into his chest. "I love you, Blue Eyes. Pack that away, and keep it with you."

45

DELILAH

I haven't been home in a while, and there are chores to tend to that can't wait until I return from the trip. At least that's what I tell myself. The truth is, I haven't been to Mississippi since we buried Mr. Marshall, and I'm not looking forward to revisiting ghosts from the past.

By the time I work up the courage to go, nearly a week has passed.

I'm in my driveway when Trippi pulls up in a black Mercedes sedan, wearing a somber suit. The poor guy doesn't have a chance to get out of the car before I start flappin' my jaw. "We are *not* taking that thing."

"Good morning, ma'am. It's a comfortable ride. What exactly is the problem?"

"We'll take my car."

He glances at my soft-sided Jeep. "That would be a resounding *no*. I'm not driving that thing for fifteen hours through the back roads and across state lines."

"Who said anything about you driving? You can ride shotgun."

Poor guy looks like he ate something that didn't agree with

him. He's right. I love my little Jeep, but it's not built for a long trip. The bouncing gets old after a while.

"Okay. Here's what we're going to do," I tell him. "You go back to Wildflower, and choose a vehicle from the fleet that doesn't look so *Driving-Miss-Daisy*-ish. And while you're at it, put on a pair of jeans or some shorts, anything that looks less like you're a pallbearer at my funeral. Makes me nervous."

Trippi, God love him, is watching me like I've lost my mind.

"You can take the first shift behind the wheel," I offer, as an olive branch.

He turns around and gets into the car, slamming the door so hard it rattles. But he doesn't say a word, returning an hour later in a shiny black Grand Cherokee with a sunroof, and wearing a pair of faded jeans.

"Good choice." I toss my bag in the backseat and take the passenger seat up front. I'm sure he'd prefer me in the back with the bag.

"Where we going?" he asks, backing out of the driveway.

"Gray didn't tell you?"

"All he said was that I'm to escort you to Mississippi, and to pack casually. You'd give me the details."

"Ever hear of Digger's Hollow?"

"Can't say that I have."

"It's near Vicksburg, in a corner of the state nobody visits." That doesn't seem to ring much of a bell for him, either. "It's fifteen hours to the Mississippi border from here, but Digger's Hollow is clear across the state. A few hours from Baton Rouge."

He rubs a thumb along his jaw. "Enter it into the navigation."

I play with the nav, but I can't enter a location. "Something's wrong. It's not working. I'll plug the address into my phone."

Trippi is quiet. I am too, but only on the outside. Inside, my mind is hard at work, combing through every word Gray said on the plane. I've spent hours and hours this past week examining every side, weighing the evidence for and against. Do I want to be his partner, *for life*? Ring or no ring, that's really what he's asking.

I click through the four distinct parts that I keep coming back to. The part about him knowing Kyle is where I always end up first. I'm still embarrassed, but less so now, and I do understand about protecting one's cover. I've all but forgiven him on that account.

Then there's the beach house. *Sweet Jesus*. What else is there to say?

The Parisian Pop-Tart? *I'm keeping him forever*.

The president? While it does give me pause that *the president* he conspired to murder was also his father, *some men just need killin'*. I haven't changed my mind about that.

Trippi's phone rings forty-five minutes into the drive. "Yeah. Fine as a fiddle," he says sarcastically. "She's sitting right here, waiting for an opportunity to drive." He scoffs. "Like that's ever happening."

I give him the stink-eye as he hands me the phone. "Hello."

"Hey," Gray says. "I know I'm supposed to give you some time, but I thought you'd like to know Saher's plane landed in London overnight. She's under the protection of the British government."

"She went." *She went*. I can barely form the words. "She got on the plane." *Oh, God*. "I can't believe it. I wasn't sure she'd take the risk." If I were in my kitchen right now, I'd be dancing and cheering loudly for her and her sweet little boy.

"She's not out of the woods."

The thought is sobering. He's right. The celebration should wait.

"Neither are you," he adds, emphatically. "This might be the most dangerous time. Watch yourself."

"Thanks for letting me know about Saher. I feel like she and

Amir have a fighting chance now." There's nothing more I want to say, but it pains me to hang up. "I'll call you when we get back."

I hand Trippi the phone, and he grunts a few times before ending the call.

WE STOP at a small convenience store for drinks, but I stay in the Jeep. When Trippi comes back, I'm in the driver's seat. He shakes his head, but doesn't complain.

"Let's go," he says. "Try not to kill me."

"Just think. You could be with Baz right now on vacation, lying on the beach with someone warm and pretty."

He doesn't reply.

Trippi is a big, scary-looking dude, who gives off a Southern California vibe unless he's trying to intimidate you. But he's from the center of the country, if I remember correctly.

"You're from Missouri?" I ask. I'm not into idle chitchat, but it's better if I talk while I'm driving. It'll keep me from disappearing inside my head. It's dusk, and we've been on the road for more than twelve hours. I need to concentrate. Besides, I've already spent too much time in my head this trip.

"Yep. The heartland. Where mom, apple pie, football, and ribs rule."

"Ribs are Southern food."

"*Pfft.*"

"So no girlfriend, huh?"

"I'm gay, Delilah."

Oh.

"You surprised?"

"With all that mom and apple pie shit, I figured you hooked up with the girl next door. But to be honest, I never gave your love life any thought until now."

"Once someone knows I'm a SEAL, their mind never goes there. You ever met a gay SEAL?"

"Maybe." I shrug. "I don't know."

"You should check out some gay SEAL porn. It's an eye-opener." His laugh booms through the Jeep.

"I'll pass. But thanks for the tip."

"Your loss." He reclines the seat a bit, and settles in. "What the fuck are we doing?"

"Going to Mississippi."

"I get that part. But why?"

"That's where I'm from. I need some answers."

"You got family there?"

"No."

"Friends?"

"*No*. What got you so chatty all of a sudden?" I'm churlish, which he doesn't deserve.

"I'm a chatty guy. Not at work. I have a role to play there—serious driver and bodyguard to a mouthy blonde who handles herself pretty well without anyone's help." He opens a bag of kettle corn and offers me some. I shake my head. "But we're on a road trip," he continues. "To find some answers in bumfuck Mississippi."

I grab the bag of popcorn out of his hand. "I changed my mind."

"If you don't have family or friends there, where are those answers going to come from? Are we going to stake a flag and wait for a sign from God? Maybe a burning bush or a flood?" He snatches the popcorn from my lap.

"I don't know," I admit after stewing a bit. "Something's been pulling me to Digger's Hollow. Can't explain it. I think the answers are there—although as we get closer, I'm not as sure anymore."

Trippi gazes out the window. "I'm no expert. But I suspect the answers you're lookin' for are in Charleston, with Gray."

"What are you, Dear Abby? I talked to Gray. There were no answers. Only more questions."

"Oh, I get it. You were looking for something easy. I never pegged you for a lazy-ass woman."

"I'm not," I snarl.

"Finding answers takes a lot of work and a lifetime of discovery. They unfold one day at a time, one problem at a time. The good times, they don't provide answers. Only the turbulent times."

This conversation has me agitated. *Of course, there are no answers in Digger's Hollow.* Well, we've come this far, and I'm not turning back now.

"Hey," Trippi shouts. "Lift your foot up off the gas. I want to live to see the Chiefs accept the Lombardi trophy. It's their year."

I ease up on the pedal, but I'm still twitchy.

We're alone on the road, cloaked in darkness, with the streetlights few and far between. It's a lonely part of the drive. Fits my sullen mood perfectly.

"Home must have been a real sucky place," Trippi says, needling me.

I liked him better when he didn't talk.

"That's the only reason anyone would go there looking for answers. People who have happy childhoods never go looking for anything."

"My mother wasn't as batshit crazy as the crown prince, but she had her own special charm. If that's what you're askin'."

"She pass?"

"No. But I haven't seen her in years. She hasn't had any influence over my life since I was a teenager. Maybe before."

"Sure she has. She's got a stranglehold on you. Pulling your strings from afar. Why else would we be going to Digger's Hollow?"

Fuck you.

We ride in silence for another hour, but it's not quiet inside my head. There's nothing in Digger's Hollow. I'll ride by the old trailer, if it's still there. Park across the street and let the memories of my mother chasin' rich men convince me that after all is said and done, I'm just like her.

Only I didn't chase Gray, looking for a payday. *I didn't chase him at all.*

Without warning, I pull into a path on the highway, where police officers set up speed traps, and change direction.

"What the hell?" Trippi hollers. "What are you doing?"

"I need answers. Apparently, they're in Charleston. Plug it into the navigation."

46
GRAY

There's a faint scratching sound outside my office door. Almost like a small animal. I continue to listen, but I don't hear it anymore.

Jesus, I need some sleep. But I'm not ready to go up and lie in my bed *alone*, with nothing to do but jerk off while I think about Delilah and wait for her to make a decision. *Fuck that*. It doesn't matter what she decides. I'm not going to walk away that easily. I'll fight to my death to convince her to give us a chance.

I get up and pour a bourbon. The club closed two hours ago, and other than me, the only person still here is the security guard.

There's that noise again. I take my gun from the desk drawer and go to the door, opening it cautiously, but there's nothing.

When I step out into Foxy's area, nothing seems out of place there either. I slide my gun into my back waistband, and rifle through a stack of folders on Foxy's desk, until I find the one I need.

As I turn to go back into my office, I notice a shadow on the floor that shouldn't be there. It's too big for an animal.

I reach for my weapon, but a gun's wedged into the back of my head before I can grab it.

"Hands out in front of you," the man emerging from the shadows barks. He's of medium build, dark hair, dark clothing, and English is not his primary language.

I've never seen him before.

He trains a gun on my chest as he approaches.

When the assailant behind me moves for my weapon, I twist free and dive to the ground, pulling him with me as a shield. Just as I grab my gun, a bullet from behind shatters my shoulder, but before I'm restrained, I get a shot off that kills the bastard from the shadow. Three intruders. One down. Two to go.

"We will kill you if you do not cooperate." The smaller of the two glowers at me with nothing but hate in his eyes.

Another man skulks from somewhere in the shadows. He's wearing a Yankees baseball cap, and carrying a large duffel. *Four intruders, not three. One down. Three to go.* I repeat this to myself, so I don't lose track of the moving pieces. Unlike the others, the Yankee's fan is hesitant. He seems to be here of his own volition, but he's not brandishing a weapon.

No one bothers to check to see if their friend is still breathing. They don't even glance in his direction. *They're trained killers.*

"What do you want?" I demand, as they cuff me. My voice is louder and sterner than my position warrants. The response is a swift smack in the head with the butt of a gun. Not hard enough to take me down, but hard enough to make me see stars.

I resist as they bind my legs together and drag me into the office. The taller of the men squeezes my injured shoulder to subdue me. *Fuck!* It hurts like a sonofabitch, but I continue to struggle, because once I'm in that room, there's nowhere for me to go, and my chances only get worse.

One shuts the door, and the other two shove me onto the conference table. I wriggle to free myself, as they secure me with straps to the table. But they're quick and well-trained and I'm screwed. These are not run-of-the-mill burglars. *Mercenaries or soldiers is my best guess.*

They grunt and mutter a few words to each other in English, nothing that gives their purpose away. They're Amadis, I suspect, but it's a mistake to jump to conclusions too quickly.

I don't shout for help. It's a sure sign of weakness. Besides, they wouldn't have reached my office unless they took down the security guard first. There's no one to help.

I've been trained for this moment. I'm not sure it makes it any easier, but at least I'm not shitting myself—yet.

They make no effort to conceal their faces, and they don't blindfold me—because they don't plan on me being alive to identify them.

"Where is your whore?"

They have to be Amadis. They're talking about Delilah. No one else would ask for her in that way.

"I don't understand." I respond in a colloquial dialect often used by the Amadi people, to see if I'm correct. The recognition on their faces is my answer, but one of them is stupid enough to respond.

"Delilah Porter. Where is she?"

A boost of adrenaline floods in, and my heart races at her name. But I need to stay in control. "She's a bitch," I say with some distaste. "We had a fight on the way back from Amidane. She took off and I haven't seen her. Maybe she's at home."

With any luck, she and Trippi are tucked away in rural Mississippi.

"She is not at home."

The gun comes down hard on my face, and within seconds my left eye is so swollen I can't see out of it. I need to get word to her. To Trippi.

"Where is she?" the shorter of the three screams into my face.

The pain in my shoulder is lessening. I'm coasting on adrenaline. "If you release me, I'll help you find her."

The gun comes down on my right cheek in response, and the pain is excruciating.

"Where is the whore?"

"Let me call her." I know that neither Delilah or Trippi can be tracked by their cell phones. It's a safety precaution. There is no immediate response from my captors, but I see their eyes dart about in an unspoken language.

While I wait, I hear baseball guy tussling with the zippers on a bag behind me, but I can't see what he's doing. "You'll never find her without my help," I say calmly, even though I'm holding back panic.

"If you do not tell us where she is, we will kill you."

You're going to kill me anyway. They haven't entirely shut down my offer to call her. But I'm not hopeful.

While I try to think of some way to warn Delilah, my brothers' faces appear inside my head. We're playing pool, not far from where I am right now.

I'm so sorry. I didn't mean for you to find out about my covert life like this. I hate that you have to plan another funeral.

We're still playing pool when Delilah's beautiful face comes into focus. *You'll be okay,* I assure her. Good thing I re-deeded the beach house when I did. *She'll be okay.*

I say my good-byes to them, because there's no way out for me. But I can save Delilah. The best option to get her a message is my death. When Foxy discovers my body tomorrow, or when she finds me missing, she'll suspect the Amadis, and she'll contact the rest of the team immediately to warn them.

It's the only option. I watch the attackers carefully. At least I'll die knowing that I protected her with my last breath. Unlike so many others, I didn't fail her. As I lie here, I find great solace in that thought.

I feel the internal shift the instructors described during EAD training. The moment when you stop fighting the inevitable, and make peace with something bigger than you.

I don't believe in God. But like other sinners at the hour of death, I pray for a quick end. If it doesn't come that way, I'll dig deep for the mental toughness to resist, like I've been trained to do. I might not have lived a virtuous life, but I will go out with honor.

"Doctor," the lanky man calls in his native language. "It's time."

The quieter of the trio approaches. He stands back from the table in his baseball cap, holding a mallet and chisel.

Sweat is spilling out of every pore. I'm drenched. The human stench is humbling.

The shorter of the three waves a pair of needle nose pliers in front of my face. "You will tell us."

I reach into my cavernous soul for courage, but it's empty. Instead, I find it in the memories of Delilah, flashing before my eyes.

"I'm not telling you a fucking thing," I growl.

47

DELILAH

I lean over and slap Trippi's arm playfully. "You were right. We needed to stop to sleep."

"I'm always right," he says, pulling up to Wildflower. I gaze out the window at my future. In the moonlight, it doesn't seem so scary, anymore.

I'm eager to see Gray. To talk to him. To negotiate. To compromise. I love him, and I'm through denying myself. I'm not my mother.

I glance at Trippi. "Do you want to take my phone, since yours is dead?"

"Whose fault is it that my charger is in the town car?"

I snicker, and hold out my phone.

"Nah." He shakes his head. "I'm all set. I'm going straight home."

"Suit yourself." I grab my bag from the backseat. "Thanks for making the trip with me."

"Thanks for not making me hang out in Digger's Hollow, waiting for a sign."

After shutting the car door, I slap my hand against the chassis, gesturing for him to go, but he waits for me to get to the door. Gray never asked for my key back when I left Wildflower. I'm sure he assumed I turned it in to Smith. I didn't. And I hope it still works, because I'd love to surprise him.

The grin on my face explodes when the key turns. *Voila!* I push open the door, and wave Trippi off. He pulls a quick U-turn and he's gone.

When I reach down for my bag, I notice that no one is in the guard house at the far side of the building. *That's really strange.*

I walk over to the edge of the portico, and my eye lands on a puddle at the perimeter of the parking lot. Something is dripping off the curb near the arborvitae. It hasn't rained for weeks.

The prickle of awareness creeps in slowly, as I draw my weapon and go around to the gate, hugging the tall bushes as I move. When I snake back around through the brush, TJ, the security guard who mans the parking lot gate, is on the ground between the fence and the bushes. He has a hole in his head, but I touch his neck, searching for even a faint pulse.

He's still warm, but he's dead. *Fuck.*

Gray. Gray! The panic rises, but I squelch it as I place the call. Gray doesn't pick up. My hands are trembling as I call Smith. I scan the area, looking for threats while waiting for him to answer.

"Sinclair," he barks.

"Bring a team to Wildflower. The security guard at the gate took a bullet. He's dead and I can't reach Gray."

"On my way," Smith says. "Is this related to the op?"

"Can't say for sure." I glance up. There's light peeking through the shutters in his office. "I think Gray's inside."

"Do not go in until we get there. I repeat. Do not go inside without backup."

"Hurry." I hang up without making any promises.

Other than the light in the office, the building is dimly lit, with some areas in total darkness.

Gray never turns on the alarm until he goes upstairs for the night. Security wasn't near the door when I unlocked it, but that's not unusual, although I would have expected the guard to notice the door ajar by now.

This is bad. Worse than TJ being dead, bad. I can feel it.

I scan for danger one more time before abandoning my position. It's clear out here. At least it appears to be.

Without lowering my guard, I approach the front of the building low to the ground, and squeeze through the door, making as little noise as possible. Once inside, I creep along the wall so as not to cast a shadow. It's dark in the inner hall and I almost trip over something. *An arm. Fuck, fuck, fuck, fuck.*

It's not Gray. There's no real relief, just building fear. *What if I didn't get here in time for Gray?*

The guard appears to have bled out—there's no pulse. It's Ainsley. *Shit.* I take his weapon and proceed cautiously, every move deliberate. I dread what's waiting for me ahead. Gray can't be dead. He just can't be. *Get it together, Delilah. There might still be assailants in the building. This is no time for a meltdown.*

"*Fuckkkk!!*" Gray's harrowing scream cuts into the deathly silence.

I want to run toward the voice, but I know better. My heart pounds wildly as I inch along.

"Where is she?" a man's voice shouts. "Where is your whore?"

They want me. Gray groans. It's tortured, sending chills up my spine. From outside Foxy's office, I see Gray's door is closed. But that's where the voices—

There's a body on the floor. I inch closer. He's not moving.

Maybe I can make a deal. My life for Gray's. They're asking for me. *It won't work.* It'll just get us both killed.

"Where is Delilah Porter?"

The sound of my name strikes terror in my soul. I need to get him out of there. *How?*

A distraction. That might work. I could go in through the back door of his office. Surprise them.

I slip into the dining room and crouch under a banquet table at the far end, out of sight. Risk be damned, I have to make the contact.

Delilah: Gray is being tortured. What's the code to the back way into his office?

Foxy: How many?

Delilah: Unclear. Two voices besides Gray's.

Foxy: You can't get into the office unnoticed. In the storage room, there's a false wall that contains a vault with gear. Can you get there?

Delilah: Yes.

Gray screams as I make my way to the storage room. Foxy texts instructions to open the safe and I follow them explicitly, grabbing a pair of night vision goggles and a silencer from inside.

I'm going to create a distraction. *What kind of distraction, Delilah?*

Gray's warning blasts in my head. *If you contact my handler, she won't lift a finger to protect you unless she can do it without compromising the agency. She won't even protect me if it comes to that. Her job is to protect the integrity of the mission, and that of the agency. It's not to save us if things get too messy.*

Screw it. I'm not entirely certain, but to be safe, I send one last text.

Delilah: If you do anything to clean this mess up before I get him to safety, I'll claw my way out of hell and find those grandchildren you love so much, and I'll torture their parents while they watch, slit mommy and daddy's throats, and let the kiddies live out the rest of their lives with the horror.

Foxy: You're on borrowed time.

"AHHH!"

My heart jolts at the sound of his voice. It's tormented, and growing weaker.

Think, Delilah. Think.

Okay. I have it. Create the distraction, wait, kill, and then take the other one. I repeat this like a mantra as I go into the kitchen, and set off the smoke alarm. There's no mistaking the sound. It's the internal alarm that's used for testing. It's not hooked up to the central system. But it's loud.

I'm on pins and needles waiting for the door to open, praying to a God I've never known. As soon as the figure turns the corner, I take the shot using a silencer, and he's down. My breathing is ragged as I take his gun, and slink toward the office.

The door is ajar. It will be a few minutes before his friend comes looking for him, and I need to decide whether to enter the office or wait.

"Where is your bitch?" a man yells from inside.

He's going to punish Gray now. That's been the pattern: Question. A brief silence. Gray's tortured voice. Over and over.

I position myself outside the doorway. I can't see much, only the back of the attacker, hovering over someone on a table —*that must be Gray*. The strangled cry comes, and I lean into the doorway and take the shot while the bastard is distracted by the scream.

Two down.

Without thinking, I enter the room. The presence of a third man surprises me. He freezes, eyes wide, and I shoot him in the forehead without hesitating.

My gaze goes to the table. To Gray's bloody, swollen face. It's agony. His shirt has been cut away and his chest looks like it's been sliced in several places. I need to get him out of here. *Now.*

"How many are there?" I ask, lightly brushing my hand over his hair.

"Four," he mutters. My knees wobble, and I blow out the breath I'm holding.

"It's going to be okay," I promise him. "They're all dead. But we still need to get out of here in case there are others on the way. Can you sit up?"

He shakes his head. "Ribs. You. Go."

I nod. My soul weeps. It's a brutal technique used by the Amadis and others to torture captives. They break one rib at a time, until eventually, both lungs are pierced and the victim dies. Gray can't go anywhere. And I'm not going anywhere without him.

I call Smith while I lock the office door, and pin a chair under the knob. It's not much protection, but it's something.

"We're about to enter," Smith barks. "Where the fuck are you?"

"Gray's office. I think it's over. But use caution. He needs an ambulance." I toss the chair and unlock the office door for Smith before returning to Gray.

"Right outside," Smith replies.

Gray's breathing is shallow, and he slips in and out while I unstrap him from the table. I use the utmost care, but he grimaces as each strap loosens. "An ambulance is right outside. I know it hurts like a sonofabitch. They'll give you medicine for the pain as soon as they get here. You're going to be okay." I murmur it over and over, as much for me as for him.

"You—shouldn't—be—here. Consequences," he chokes out each word in a lucid moment. I smile softly at his threat.

"I came to tell you I love you." I rub the top of his hand. "And of course, I'm here. Where else would I be? The queen's the most powerful player on the board—always in service to her king."

His hand tightens around mine, and he chokes up blood. He's barely breathing, and I pray that both lungs aren't damaged. If they are, he won't be alive when they get here. "Stay with me, Gray."

Somehow I manage to keep the worst of the alarm out of my voice. "Don't you dare go anywhere. Not before I get that ring you promised." I hear Smith's team in the building. "And the damn thing better be big enough to choke a chicken—screw that, a horse."

Smith barges in with the EMTs right behind him. A sob escapes that I can't stop.

Reluctantly, I let go of Gray's hand and back away slowly from the table so they can work. I make a call, my eyes never leaving Gray's face. "It's done. Sinclair Industries is cleaning up."

"Gray?" Foxy asks.

"Bad shape. But he's fighting. The EMTs are working on him."

"I've known him since he was wet behind the ears," she says with considerable distress. "I would have never done what you suggested."

"We don't always get to choose our orders."

"No. But we always get to choose whether we follow them."

She's loyal to Gray—to the bone. No one likes their loyalty questioned, and I feel a pang of regret. "I'll keep you in the loop."

"One more thing," Foxy says in a stern tone. "Those grandchildren are real and entirely off-limits."

"Understood," I agree mindlessly, my entire focus on Gray.

I end the call with Smith beside me. "I told you not to go in," he scolds. "That was a stupid, stupid thing to do."

"As stupid as handing a delirious woman your weapon?" That's exactly what he did when Kate was in trouble. "I don't think so," I toss over my shoulder, blowing past him to get closer to Gray.

They're positioning him onto a stability board to get him on the stretcher. "Can we get a hand here?" one of the EMTs hollers.

Smith and I are there before all the words are out of his mouth.

The transfer is difficult. Gray isn't conscious, but I feel every bump, every bounce, every anguished move, as a stab of pain I'm experiencing myself.

"Is he going to survive?" I whisper to the medic once Gray is on the stretcher safely.

"He's young," the dark-haired emergency technician says briskly. "That's in his favor."

"Caucasian male, thirty-four, unconscious. Blood type unknown." The younger EMT lists Gray's vital signs and other pertinent information into a walkie-talkie on our way to the ambulance. "Multiple contusions, several broken ribs. A gunshot to the shoulder. High suspicion of internal bleeding, and a pneumothorax on the left side. We bagged him."

"We'll prep the surgical trauma room," a woman says calmly from the other end.

"We're on our way."

I clasp Gray's cool hand until he's lifted into the ambulance. A reel plays in my head. *Motorcycle rides. Sitting in his lap with my eyes closed and a breeze blowing lightly. Gray teasing about the smell of catfish. The distress consuming him when he told me about his mother's death. Supper at the beach house under millions of stars. I love you, Blue Eyes. Pack it away and take it with you.*

My brain is sluggish and my emotions are tangled, but my eyes are sharp, trained entirely on Gray. They don't stray until the ambulance door closes, and it speeds away.

I hug myself tight as the lights cut through the darkness and disappear. But it's not until the wails of the siren grow faint that I give myself grace and let the tears fall freely.

It can't end this way. *It just can't.*

48

GRAY
TWELVE WEEKS LATER

A punctured lung, a shattered shoulder, a dozen broken ribs, an orbital fracture, a concussion, and countless contusions. It was ugly. But I survived.

Early on, there were days when I longed for the peace death surely provides. But through the surgeries, the intubation, and the initial rehab, the bossy blonde—emphasis on bossy—was having none of it. And every time I opened my eyes and she was by my side, like an angel, I wanted none of it either. I needed to live—if not for me, for her.

The initial four weeks were particularly rough. I couldn't do a thing for myself. *Nothing*. When I was finally discharged from the hospital, we hired a live-in nurse. Delilah squawked a bit. She wanted to take care of me herself. But there was no fucking way I was letting that happen. My body might be broken, but my mind was sharp. Our relationship was too new, too fragile to take away all the mystery. And I had too much pride to subject either of us to the most unpleasant matters.

There were two major breakthroughs during my recovery that propelled me forward.

At the end of the first month, Delilah rushed into the

bedroom where I was resting after a particularly rough rehab session. She was pale, and shaken. "You're never going to believe this," she said, placing my laptop where I could see the screen.

Crown Prince Ahmad bin Khalid Dead in a Fiery Helicopter Crash in big bold letters splashed across the screen.

Ahmad's death didn't shock me as much as it shocked Delilah. Political coups are messy, and I was still numb from a near-death experience. "I guess the crown prince didn't want to go away quietly."

"What does this mean?" she asked, her face ashen and her voice laden with concern. "I'm glad he's dead. But what does it mean for us?"

I shake my head. "Nothing. The king was going to remove him as heir to the throne. Ahmad would have had no qualms about killing his brother if it was necessary to consolidate his power. I doubt the king was willing to risk it. It has nothing to do with you or me."

The worry eased from her face, and I was happy to provide some small measure of comfort, because I'd been a worthless fuck since the attack.

After Delilah left the room, I stared at the screen that day, and the next. I consumed every word of every news article about his death. Devoured every broadcast. I ordered a half dozen newspapers with the headline of his demise.

I kept the newspaper clippings tucked into various places so I could look at them anytime it was hard to breathe or when the pain was particularly excruciating. It saw me through some of the rougher patches, driving me forward when I wanted to throw in the towel.

I won't apologize for reveling in his death.

In a twisted way, it fueled my recovery. But while it buoyed me, it didn't fully restore my spirit. That took a force of nature, beautifully packaged.

As the weeks drag on, I've become such a miserable wretch that even my brothers and Gabby stop visiting.

Mel still comes by three times a week. Not for me, but for Delilah. "Some people are worth the extra effort," he told me one day. "You might want to take that to heart, son."

I'm making physical progress, albeit slower than I would like, but my mind is one big clusterfuck of emotion. Anger, resentment, pity, shame—it's a huge party, and I'm the guest of honor with nothing to do but lick my wounds. And although I don't care who watches, Delilah has had a front row seat to the misery. She nudges and nags, but she never complains. In some ways, that makes it easier for me to descend into the darkness.

Despite my apathy, Wildflower is running smoothly. Delilah and Foxy fill me in daily, and try to enlist me in decision-making, but I have little interest in anything besides brooding.

Although Delilah is never far from my most pressing thoughts.

My brooding and moping are mostly about her. I toy with the idea of sending her away. Her mere presence makes me feel small, like I've lost my purpose in life.

She saved me. And she risked her life to do it. That's not how it's supposed to work. I should have been protecting her. *I should be taking care of her now.*

It's not misogyny or an outdated notion. It was my role in the relationship that we forged. *I lead. She follows.* But some days, I can't walk from one end of the apartment to the other without getting winded. I'm of little use to anyone. Especially Delilah.

But I can't do it. I'm too selfish. I love her too much to send her away, like a decent man might do. I'm taking the coward's way out instead. Acting so obnoxious that eventually she's going to tell me to go fuck myself, and slam the door behind her. It wasn't a conscious decision. Not at first. But when it became obvious, even to me, I didn't stop the destructive behavior. I still haven't stopped.

There are footsteps approaching, and I glance up from my tablet to Delilah sashaying into the bedroom. Her beauty and resilience still slay me. She has a bounce in her step, even after working all day and evening. Even knowing that she's coming home to a cranky bastard.

"Everything's closed up downstairs," she says, handing me the remote to the bullet vibrator I'd made her wear in public that first night we had supper at Wildflower.

"What's this about?"

"It's the remote to that evil little vibrator," she says, with the throaty voice of a vixen. "I know the app's on your phone, but I didn't want to mess with it. I thought we'd use the remote instead."

"I know what it is," I sneer. Sex had been an important part of our relationship. It had been a safe harbor for Delilah's submission. The one time where she always let me lead, without argument. But we haven't had sex since the plane on the way home from Amidane. I glare at the vibrator with disdain. "What exactly do you expect me to do with it?"

She steps closer to where I'm resting, and straddles my legs with her feet on the floor and her hands on the arms of the chair. She's in my face. "What I expect," she declares in a clear, exacting voice, "is for you to show some interest in meeting my needs. That is, if you can stop feeling sorry for yourself for the ten minutes it'll take to give me an orgasm."

Shame washes over me, and I feel smaller and less like a man than I had already been feeling. I lash out without bothering to sugarcoat a single word. "Meet your own needs. Or have you gotten so spoiled you've forgotten how to take care of yourself?" I toss the remote across the room, but it doesn't go far, because I'm still a weak sonofabitch.

Without blinking, Delilah picks the damn thing up off the floor. "Fine," she replies, in a voice that means things are far from fine.

But I don't give a shit.

She doesn't spare me even a small glance before she reaches under her skirt, pushes aside the lacy thong, and dips her fingers into that pussy I once worshiped. With great aplomb, she pulls out the small toy—all while I watch, captivated by her self-assurance.

"Stand up, turn around, and bend over. Ass in the air," she demands, grabbing a tube of lube from the nightstand.

She's never spoken to me in this way. *No one has. They wouldn't dare.* Sure, she's been insolent and argumentative, putting me in my place when the occasion called for it, but this is different. This is a direct challenge, aimed at the very heart of who I am. "What the hell are you talking about?" The bitterness curls around each syllable.

"Since you don't want to control the remote, I figure you must want me to shove this special Lush prototype up your ass, so I can control the remote. Works for me."

I gape at her. The vibrations inside are the equivalent to an earth-shattering seismic event, catapulting me from the bowels of hell, and unleashing a basic, primal drive that shakes me to the core.

"It works for you, does it?"

Her face tilts up, in a huffy little pout—a rebellion.

You are not staging this kind of a rebellion against me, Blue Eyes. Not while I'm still breathing.

"I'm the team leader. That kind of insolence won't be tolerated." My tone is firm, and unyielding. It invites no backtalk. "There will be consequences. Not just today, but ongoing."

Her brow is raised, as she continues to test me. It's a silent, but unmistakable prodding.

"Take off your clothes, Delilah, *for me.*"

A ghost of a smile forms as she undresses slowly, shaking her gorgeous ass at me more than necessary. It awakens my cock from a slumber that's lasted too damn long.

When fully naked, she drops the vibrator and the remote into my lap, and stands waiting for instructions, with her hands behind her and her eyes lowered.

"I won't be needing these." I place the toys on the table next to me. "Get the leather case from the bottom shelf of my closet." I stand, and the pain claws at me with every movement, but I don't wince. "But first, come here."

Delilah steps closer, so close I feel the heat emanating from her body.

With the resolve of a dying man wanting to save himself, *wanting to save us*, I slide my fingers through her silky hair and press my mouth to hers, feeding off her lips, her tongue, exploring every crevice of her body with eager hands and probing fingers. I've missed this so damn much. Missed *her* so much.

All I hear are the sounds of arousal. Pounding hearts, blood coursing, and Delilah's sultry moans and purrs filling my soul until the need for more pulls us apart. "Go," I murmur, but neither of us wants her to go. I sure as hell don't.

Eventually she turns toward the closet, rolling back a satchel of toys that she lays at my feet. I can't bend to rifle through the bag. The realization rattles me, and the anxiety starts to build. Aside from a few unsatisfying attempts at jacking off in the shower, my dick has been largely dormant. *What if—*

"Sir," she whispers, jolting me from my fears.

Dominance isn't about sex. For some people, it doesn't involve sex at all. I've repeated this countless times to Dominants and submissives just entering the lifestyle. For most of us, it's who we are at our center. The roles are a state of mind, not a sexual missive.

I gaze at the remarkable woman who threw me a lifeline tonight. "Take out the Hitachi."

Her eyes shimmer at the word. The flush creeps across her chest in a web pattern, making my dick throb.

"Do you need to be bound?" It's a challenge, because I know before I ask that she's too damn proud to say yes.

She lifts her chin, and shakes her head. "No, Sir."

I motion to the Tantra chair, steadying her while she drapes her prone body over the highest arch, where I can have easy access to everything that will give us both pleasure.

"I want to see *my* pussy," I demand.

She spreads her legs for me, hooking her feet around the chair.

My cock jumps at her glistening pink flesh, and I lower my mouth. It's impulsive, and not what I had planned. But it's what I need. It doesn't matter that my chest aches to bend. I need to taste her more than I've ever needed anything.

"I take care of you. It doesn't matter if it's with my mouth, my fingers, my cock, or a toy. I do the fucking. Do you understand?"

"Yes," she gasps. The word tumbles off her tongue with a breath.

I lower my mouth, and lick, and suck, and nip, sliding my tongue into her wet little hole until she tightens and thrashes, with my name on her lips, and the tremors of her release on mine. Her orgasm, her needy little moans, her trembling body—it's like a shot of energy that spurs me on.

I want more. More of her. More of everything.

"What's your safe word?" I ask, plugging the wand into an outlet.

"Red." She's panting, but she doesn't hesitate.

I slap her exposed pussy twice before I hold the wand to her quivering flesh. Her back arches as she white-knuckles the sides of the chair. "Is this what you wanted?" I taunt, while I yank the first orgasm from her.

"Yes," she screams, as my cock grows thicker and harder. "*Yes.*"

I ask the question over and over as I wrench one orgasm out after another. She stops answering after the third time I ask. But I'm a man possessed, and her trembling body is the only response I need.

"*Please*. I can't. No more," she pleads. But she never uses her safe word.

I run my hand over her inner thighs, enjoying the satiny skin against my fingers. "I decide when you're done. And I don't think you are." I lower the wand and turn it higher.

With her legs shaking as she writhes through the next climax, I let the toy drop and unbuckle my belt, tugging at the button and zipper, until my angry, fat cock is in my hand.

I hover over her, pulling and jerking the swelling shaft while it weeps.

My eyes never leave Delilah's, but I don't really see her. I don't think of her softness, her sweet musky scent, or even how much I love her. I'm blinded by a desperate need for release—from my demons, my pain, and the fortress I built around my soul after the attack. I don't want to live like this anymore.

I'm so close. All I know is the force driving me over the edge in a gallop to bliss. I hear the roar of release detonating every cell. Every nerve. I shudder as it claws its way out of the pain.

"This is what I wanted," she cries, finally answering the question I repeatedly posed to her. Her voice is joyous, like a prayer for the rain that falls after a punishing drought. As I spray thick ropes of cum over her skin, I see the blurred edges of a jubilant smile.

Now we're done.

Not just her, but me too. Done with the pity parties, and the sullenness that's become a way of life. It's done. *Done.*

When I look back on tonight, I won't remember anything about sex or consequences. It was so much more.

Delilah gave me back my honor tonight. My purpose. I was rudderless, headed into the darkest depths of the ocean, and she threw an anchor.

The feisty little blonde gave me my life back. *Again.* She forced me to take it.

Beginning tomorrow morning, and every one after that, I vow to wake up early, rehab, shower, put on a suit and go downstairs to work. I'll set lofty goals, because I have big plans for us, and I promise myself that I won't act on them until I'm back to normal.

It's all the incentive I need.

EPILOGUE
EIGHT MONTHS LATER

This morning, I received an engraved invitation to join the king for dessert. *My king.* I was instructed to take the elevator to the lower level at exactly eight o'clock. I have no idea what Gray's planning, but I do know that Jolie and Gil, the fantasy creators, have been here a lot recently, reimagining some of the rooms.

As I descend into the playground of the rich and powerful, I think of nothing but Gray's heart-stopping smile and his bright-blue eyes that twinkle playfully again.

While I'm sometimes overwhelmed by the excesses of the life we lead, I no longer worry about earning my keep, or that I'm not enough. I do, and I am. It's that simple. And when it's not, the man who owns my heart, sets me right.

Gray and I have forged a true partnership. At work, at home, and at play.

Most portrayals of Dominants and submissives are crafted to fit a stereotype. We found our own unique identity, as every couple should.

The rules are negotiated frequently, and compromises are made. Except in the bedroom. I choose to follow there. It frees me in a way that's impossible to explain to anyone who doesn't appreciate the dynamic.

Although Gray looks healthy and gorgeous, and he's regained all the muscle he lost, I'll go to my death with the image of him strapped to the table in his office, bloodied and barely breathing. The space has been entirely redone, the table is gone, but I still see the horror every time I enter the room.

His body *and* his mind have healed. The former took courage, perseverance, and heart. More than most humans have inside them for a lifetime. The latter took the threat of a vibrator shoved up his ass. If I had known it was going to have such a big impact, I would have made the threat sooner.

The elevator stops with a tiny bounce that makes the butterflies in my belly swirl faster. When the doors open, my man awaits.

"I hope you have something special for dessert. I put on my favorite dress." It's actually Gray's favorite, with a lace-up bodice that he loves to unfasten with skilled, unhurried hands that never fail to bring me pleasure.

He pulls me to him, kissing me slowly, until I sway into his body, brushing against his cock. "You're a tease," he murmurs. "Let's go find your treat."

Gray leads me to a room at the very end of the hall. The plaque outside the door is covered. "Go on," he encourages. "Peel off the wrapping."

I glance between him and the plastic covering. "Is this my kind of dessert, or your kind?" I tease.

"We have similar appetites. But you'll have to see if it suits you."

I pull the sticky covering off. *Queen's Quarters* is etched into the brass plate.

He hands me a shiny key and nods.

My hands are a little shaky as I slip the key into the lock and turn it. Not because I'm afraid, but because I'm eager and aroused. And Gray has the hungry look of a predator. I know everything that comes with that sexy look.

I pull open the door, and Gray flips the switch that illuminates a crystal chandelier hanging in the center of the room. It's similar to the one at the beach that I love. The one that makes shadows dance on the ceiling.

The room is decorated opulently, in every shade of blue, the palest creams, and warm gold tones.

"Jolie wanted to make the room silver and blue," he explains, "but the silver felt icy and aloof. I wanted something more inviting. Something that would envelop you in warmth, especially after we play. You get so cold."

I turn to him and take his hand, squeezing his fingers. "It's beautiful." My heart is full, but the words don't come easy.

"This is your room," he says, the edges of his mouth curling ever so slightly. "Dedicated to your needs and desires. You're the queen. No one else plays in this room besides you."

I blink away the moisture building. "Who will I play with, if it's only me?" I ask coyly.

Gray laughs, and his eyes glitter with the best kind of mischief. "Mostly the king, although you might need a knight to save you on occasion, or maybe even a rogue. Although the king is a bit of a rogue."

His expression turns dark and sultry, but I'm a tad overwhelmed and I don't respond in kind. I don't respond at all.

"Why don't you explore a little?" Gray is in tune to my moods, my fears, and anxieties. He must sense that I need space to untangle the welling emotion.

I ignore the throne in the room, the stocks, the hooks on the ceiling, and those protruding from the walls, cleverly disguised as embellishments. I walk past the bank of drawers filled with the queen's toys, or maybe they belong to the king. I glance up at the goodies for impact play that are part of every room on this floor. But what captures my attention is the wall of portraits, each positioned in an ornate gold frame.

Some are sexy images that I realize are actually priceless paintings. Interspersed between the precious art are renderings and photographs, framed exquisitely, making them appear priceless too. There are pictures of Digger's Hollow, of me as homecoming queen, and another as a Magnolia Princess—the pictures had appeared in the newspaper, years ago. They've all been enhanced and fit in perfectly alongside the more valuable pieces. There's also an array of photos Gray took over the last several months—candids of me, and a picture Gabby took of us at Christmas.

"This is where the past and the present meet to build the future," he says quietly.

"I still worry that my life will swallow you and turn you into something that neither of us recognize." He combs his fingers through my hair, gently brushing the loose strands off my face. "This is where we come to recalibrate when we can't find the little girl from Digger's Hollow, or when my own demons are rumbling, or when the world is making so much noise that it threatens our love."

The lump in my throat is far too big to swallow. Gray wraps his arm around my shoulder, and kisses my head.

I'm lost. Lost, because although the bones of this fantasy were designed by Jolie and Gil, Gray's hand is all over it. There is not one object in this room, big or small, that doesn't have some significance. There is *nothing* in this space that doesn't have a reason for being here, one Gray can explain to me if I ask. I'm sure of it.

But I'm mostly lost, because his love is so much more than I ever dared to imagine for myself.

"Come with me," he says, leading me toward the door where we entered.

"This is where the queen disrobes." He points to a small

alcove with an elaborate coat rack and a tufted bench. "No clothes are worn in the Queen's Quarters. While she's far, far more important than the politicians, the media moguls, and the titans of industry who play on this floor, like them, she must fully submit to the fantasy when she enters, handing over her worries, her fears, and her burdens. They remain at the door."

I'm not overwhelmed by the riches in this room, or even by the comparison to the rich and powerful. No, I'm overcome by this man—his regard for me, his seemingly endless love. A man who would pour himself into creating a jewel box just *for me*.

"The only thing you're permitted to wear once you enter is this," he says, pulling out a velvet pouch from his pocket.

I assume it's a bullet vibrator or some other small devilish toy, and I grin at him.

Gray no longer has the hungry look of a predator. His characteristic smirk has become a small, humble smile, and his eyes have a vulnerability that he would be loath to admit.

As soon as he places the pouch in my hands, I know it's something weightier than a toy.

I stare at it for several seconds, using my index finger to circle the circumference of the object through the luxurious nap.

"Do you need some help?"

I shake my head, and pull open the strings, gently removing the ring from the pouch.

It's silver—maybe white gold or platinum—with a brilliantly cut stone. A sapphire, I think. But I'm not sure of any of it. It's not the sort of thing a girl from Digger's Hollow comes across every day. The one thing I do know is it's big enough to choke a chicken—maybe even a pony.

Gray tips my chin up. "It's a blue diamond," he explains, without making me feel inadequate. "This one is pure, without any secondary colors to muddy it. It's the color of your eyes when you're happy, and when you're aroused," he adds, tracing the contours of my face. "It's rare, like you."

He takes the ring out of my hand, and slips it on my finger. "You don't need to tell me now. Wear it and see how it feels."

I reach for him, and he wraps me tight against his chest. I can't talk, because I'll start to cry and I still hate that. But I don't need to wait. It feels right. Not the ring, but his arms. His heartbeat. His rock-steady presence.

We hold each other for a long time, while the last year melts away, reshaping itself into foundational bricks sturdy enough to build a life on.

I peek around him to the words inscribed in gold leaf on the wall:

YOU CAN HAVE STRUCTURE WITHOUT SUFFOCATING.

YOU CAN GUIDE AND LEAD WITHOUT BEING OVERBEARING.

YOU CAN FOLLOW WITHOUT RELINQUISHING ALL POWER AND CONTROL.

YOU CAN HOLD EACH OTHER UP WITHOUT HOLDING EACH OTHER BACK.

Without a drop of hesitancy, I gaze into his eyes, letting my fingertips caress his strong jaw. "I will follow, wherever you lead, for all my days on this earth."

There is no gentleness as he claims my mouth. No apologies. I wouldn't want it any other way.

"The queen kneels, you know," he murmurs near my ear. It's playful, but the gravel in his voice suggests a game not meant for children.

"She sucks cock, too," I whisper. "I watched *The Crown*."

He throws his head back, his chest heaving with a rich laughter that will warm me on the coldest days, for the rest of our lives.

When he unlaces my dress, his fingers engage in a long, slow tease. He doesn't seem at all surprised to find I'm not wearing a single thing underneath.

"You're a dirty little queen." He grins wolfishly. "The best kind."

―――

Thank you for reading Decadent! If you enjoyed The Devil's Due series, you're going to LOVE **A Sinful Empire**! You can start it **FREE HERE**!

FOR SNEAK PEEKS and treats sign-up for my newsletter **HERE**

JOIN me in my group, JD'S CLOSET, for all sorts of shenanigans **HERE**

If you enjoyed Decadent, please consider leaving a short review so others can find it too!

AFTERTHOUGHTS

Thank you so much for reading my dirty little fairy tale!

Delilah and Gray are a tribute to the notion that people are complicated. Most of us are neither all bad nor all good. We're some twisted combination of the two.

Their story was so much fun to write. Because it's the fourth book in the series, the characters' personalities were already baked-in—*for the most part*. What's that? Gray surprised you? Surely you didn't expect that I had already shown my entire hand. What fun would that have been!

Decadent is a work of fiction. But as I've said many times, while I write to entertain, I can't seem to help myself from sneaking an actual fact or two into the story, or flashing a light, however brief, into a dark corner. I hope you walked away with the impression that BDSM isn't a cookie cutter lifestyle on the fringes of society.

Dominants and submissives come from all walks of life. They create their own unique dynamic, and there is much more to the lifestyle than pain and kink. As in every aspect of life, there are also abusers in the community who take advantage of every opportunity to meet their own sadistic needs, or simply to get laid. Delilah's husband, Kyle, was exactly the kind of poser that can cause irreparable harm to an inexperienced submissive. But it's a lesson we can all learn from. It doesn't matter what type of relationship we are involved in, we must be mindful of the red flags, and insist that we have a voice. Don't let anyone take that voice away from you.

Above all, I hope that Decadent brought you great pleasure, a small escape, and some bedroom inspiration.

What's next for me? I'm writing a book in Vi Keeland and Penelope Ward's Cocky Heroes series, and then I'm back to the dark corners of the world. A port wine empire and a broody, sexy bastard named Antonio. Wait until you meet him!

In the meantime, stay well, and try to surround yourself with people who love you.

xoxo

Eva

ACKNOWLEDGMENTS

While I suspect there will be at least one novella in the future, the Charleston series is essentially complete. I have loved each of these characters, (although not equally) and for me, the good-bye is bittersweet.

Little in life is accomplished without the help and generosity of kind souls. Decadent is no exception.

Veronica, I write these words, again, because they remain true. The Devil's Due series would not exist without you. Neither would Eva Charles, the author. The debt of gratitude I owe you, not just for your professionalism, but for your friendship, is ever growing, and you continue to be a beacon in my little corner of the literary world.

Dawn Alexander, unlike Gray Wilder, I'm happy to repeat myself: There is not enough space in the back of any book for the thanks I owe you. Your patience and ability to cut through incomplete thoughts and barely formed ideas is unparalleled—as is your patience. You are a brilliant gem! Sexy Sinner is next, and then we head to the dark corners of a port empire. I heard that there might be an arranged marriage involved, but who knows?

A heartfelt thank you to Nasrine and Saleema for reading the manuscript with a special eye on areas of sensitivity. I am forever grateful for your ability to get straight to the crux of the matter, and for all your input. I hope that one day we live in a world where our first and last names can be used freely, without fear of reprisal. You are AMAZING, and I so appreciate your good counsel.

Nancy Smay, I'm not sure what I would do without your guidance. You are a font of knowledge—nothing, including the tiniest details regarding government clearance, escapes you. Thank you for your vast expertise on all matters, and for your unending patience with my love of commas. I'm sending you a big virtual smirk—LOL.

Faith Williams, I'm convinced you have magical powers! Your thoroughness is incomparable. Truly. I will always be indebted to Cali MacKay for recommending your services. I so appreciate your flexibility, and good nature. There is no question, Decadent is better because of you.

Virginia Tesi Carey, you are a bright light in what can sometimes be a challenging world! The thought of releasing without your eagle eye on the manuscript right before I press send, horrifies me. Thank you for your ongoing support, friendship, and your generous spirit.

Candi Kane, I am fortunate to have had the opportunity to not only work with you on Decadent's release, but to get to know you some too. I have met very few people in my life who could not only run a small country, but could do it while making boatloads of guacamole—LOL. I hope you continue to have time for me in your busy schedule.

Catherine Anderson, thank you for being a blessing! You are truly a lovely human being, and a consummate professional, with mad skills. Your gracious demeanor aside, you know how to get stuff done.

Thank you to the lovely and talented Letitia Hasser of RBA Designs who made the original covers. There aren't enough positive adjectives in any language to bestow on you. Thank you for another gorgeous cover!

A HUGE thank you to the mega-talented Murphy Rae for the stunning series covers! With such paltry guidance from me, you somehow created four gorgeous covers that are exactly what the series needed. I am forever grateful to you!

Thank you to L. Woods PR, Candi Kane PR, Enticing Journey, and Give Me Books. You make everything look effortless! You are all wonderful to work with, and just plain amazing.

To the bloggers, bookstagrammers, and bookTubers, there is no way to fully thank you for all that you do to promote my books. There are few professions where people spend hours of their time for the benefit of others, out of kindness, and not for the monetary rewards. Thank you for your tireless energy and generosity in promoting Decadent, and the entire Devil's Due series. It would not have flourished without you.

To the readers, thank you for embracing this series, and for your ongoing love and support! Your generosity, kind words, and willingness to share the stories with others gave the Wilders and their friends tremendous life. I am repeatedly humbled by all the love you've shown the characters, and me.

To the members of JD's Closet, I can't say this enough: I love, love, love you all so hard! Your support, encouragement, naughty sense of humor, and friendship mean the world to me. I hope you find as much love, fun, and support in the group as I do. I also hope Gray is hot enough for all my dirty girls! #teamgray, #teamsmith or #teamjd—what's your pleasure?

Andy, there really are no words to describe how much I love you, or how much love I feel from you. When Delilah says, *I'm overcome by this man—his regard for me, his seemingly endless love. A man who would pour himself into creating a jewel box just for me,* it could be me talking about you. There have been so many jewel boxes in our life together—big and small, and I hope many more. And yes, I'm up for an adventure. Don't ask me again.

ABOUT EVA

After being a confirmed city-girl for most of her life, Eva moved to beautiful Western Massachusetts in 2014. There, she found herself living in the woods with no job, no friends (unless you count the turkey, deer, and coyote roaming the backyard), and no children underfoot, wondering what on earth she'd been thinking. But as it turned out, it was the perfect setting to take all those yarns spinning in her head and weave them into sexy stories.

When she's not writing, trying to squeeze information out of her tight-lipped sons, or playing with the two cutest dogs you've ever seen, Eva's creating chapters in her own love story.

Let's keep in touch!!

Sign-up for my monthly newsletter for special treats and all the Eva news! **VIP Reader Newsletter**

I'd love to hear from you!

Check out my website!
evacharles.com

MORE STEAMY ROMANTIC SUSPENSE BY EVA CHARLES

THE DEVIL'S DUE SERIES

Depraved

Delivered

Bound

Decadent

A SINFUL EMPIRE TRILOGY

A Sinful Empire (A Prologue Novella)

Greed

Lust

Envy

CONTEMPORARY ROMANCE
THE NEW AMERICAN ROYALS

Sheltered Heart

Noble Pursuit

Double Play

Unforgettable

Loyal Subjects

Sexy Sinner

Printed in Great Britain
by Amazon